For Paul

1

'Just do it.' Fourteen-year-old Harry Fletcher stuck his chin in the air. 'C'mon, just do it,' he urged his younger brother.

With his eyes downcast, twelve-year-old Spencer shook his head.

From the corner of his eye, Fletch, as Harry was more commonly known, watched as their uncle began to unbuckle his worn leather belt, and he stuck his chin out even farther, his eyes silently warning his brother to do as he said. 'Stop being a baby and just punch me,' he hissed. He was a handsome lad with a shock of dark brown hair that tended to stand up on end like a brush, and across his nose was a splattering of freckles.

When Spencer made no attempt to move, Fletch pulled back his clenched fist and punched his brother square on the jaw. The younger boy dropped to the linoleum floor with a heavy thud.

Frank Smith threw his head back and roared with laughter. One of his favourite pastimes was making his two nephews, actually step nephews, fight for his pleasure. 'I'll make a man of you yet.' His tone became serious, and he began pulling the belt through the loopholes of his denim jeans.

Spencer's bottom lip trembled. He knew what was to come; it was a daily occurrence in their house. He curled himself into a foetal position and placed his hands protectively over his head, whimpering.

'Don't do that.' Fletch stepped in front of his brother and reached out his arm, in an attempt to stop his uncle. 'I've already belted him one, ain't I?'

Frank glanced up at the clock on the kitchen wall and noted that he was missing out on valuable drinking time. 'Yeah,' he grunted. He was a large man, rough around the edges, who made his living ducking and diving. He had a reputation for being a bully.

Frank fished around in his pockets and pulled out a handful of loose change. Stuffing the coins back into his denim pocket, he strode across the kitchen to where his stepsister kept the housekeeping tin, and took out a handful of notes.

The fact that he had just taken the rent money and last few measly quid that was expected to feed his family for the week meant nothing to him, and why should it? After all, they weren't even his kids. As long as he was all right, then sod everyone else – that was his motto. With the money clenched in his fist, he gave his two nephews one last menacing look, and then slammed out of the house.

'You should have just hit me,' Fletch scolded, as he stretched out his hand and heaved his brother up from the floor.

'I didn't want to.' Spencer spoke in a slow drawl, his voice trembling.

'You need to toughen up a bit,. You know what he's like when he's had a drink,' he said. 'One of these days, you'll end up getting the belt, and next time, I might not be able to stop him.' He inspected the angry red mark his fist had left across his younger brother's jaw. 'You'll live.' He grinned. 'Are you hungry?'

At this, Spencer nodded.

Set on the kitchen counter was a wooden bread board, and amongst the scattered crumbs, the knobby end of an uncut bloomer loaf had been left. They hadn't had any breakfast yet and Fletch could feel his tummy begin to rumble. He tore the bread in half and passed a chunk across to his brother. 'Come on.' Stuffing a piece of hard crust into his mouth, he chewed on it, then swallowed. 'Let's get out of here, in case he comes back,' he said, slinging his arm around his younger brother's shoulders. 'We'll go and knock for Stevie.'

* * *

'See, I told you. Look.' Stevie Williams pointed his finger towards a ground-level broken window that had been covered over with a piece of thick cardboard.

They were around the back of the local shopping precinct at the Heathway, in Dagenham. The shop in question that had caught Stevie's attention was the off-licence.

'If we get in there, we could pinch some booze and fags.'

Fletch nodded. The goods would sell for a fair few quid and Fletch knew their mum would be desperate for the money. As it was, she worked two cleaning jobs, whilst her stepbrother lazed around the house, day in and day out, waiting for the pub to open.

'We're in,' he said. He didn't bother to ask for his younger brother's opinion. He knew for a fact that Spencer would copy whatever he did; he always did.

Checking that the coast was clear, as quietly and as carefully as he could, Fletch pulled away the piece of cardboard and peered through the gaping hole.

'What can you see?' Stevie asked, crouching down beside him.

Fletch turned his head to the side and gave a wide grin. 'Boxes and boxes full of booze.' He straightened up and turned to look at Spencer. 'You're the smallest. Wriggle through the gap, Spence, and pass a couple of bottles out.'

Spencer did as he was told. He laid down on his tummy, wriggled his feet and legs through the tiny gap, and, holding on to his brother's and Stevie's hands, he lowered himself down.

The cellar was damp, dark and musty, not that Spencer appeared to notice. 'Which ones?' he asked, peering into the darkness.

'Get those ones.' Crouching down in front of the window, Fletch pointed his finger towards the nearest box. 'And be quiet... don't make any bloody noise,' he whispered.

One by one, Spencer passed the bottles through the open window.

'Whisky.' Stevie's eyes were as wide as saucers. 'We'll get loads of dosh for this lot.' He grinned.

'And if we keep schtum about it,' Fletch answered, 'we can come back for more another day.'

Careful not to make any noise, they heaved Spencer back through the window, and set about replacing the cardboard cover.

'This is our secret,' Fletch warned. 'We don't breathe a word about this, to anyone, right?' He looked at his brother, and then to his best friend. They both nodded in agreement.

They collected up two bottles each, and with their haul safely concealed under their jackets, they made their way back around to the front of the shopping arcade.

'Get a load of that car.' Stevie whistled through his teeth. 'Gotta have some dosh to own a car like that.'

Fletch was thoughtful. He looked across to the car in question. It was a silver-coloured Jaguar, and without missing a beat, he strode towards it.

'What are you doing?' As he chased after his friend, Stevie turned his head from side to side, his eyes darting nervously around him. 'You're gonna get us caught. If someone calls the cops, my mum will go apeshit and I'll end up being grounded, for life, probably,' he groaned.

Fletch came to an abrupt halt. 'We need to sell this stuff, don't we?'

His eyes wide, Stevie nodded.

'Well then?' Fletch continued marching ahead of his brother and best friend and, reaching the car, he tapped his knuckles on the driver's window.

* * *

Billy King was a man to be reckoned with. With thick, dark hair and piercing blue eyes, he was undisputedly a player amongst the criminal fraternity. Protection racketeering was his game, a game in which he thrived, and only a fool would refuse or try to worm his way out of paying him what was owed. After all, he wasn't known as Billy 'One Punch' King for nothing.

He was sitting inside his car, waiting for one of his henchmen, when he spotted the three boys. He watched them walk towards him and he allowed himself to smile. His car was his pride and joy, and he knew for a fact that many a man and boy gave it a second glance. The Jag screamed power and wealth.

'Nice car, mister.'

Billy wound down the driver's window. 'Gets me about.' He grinned.

The boy looked around him, then opened up his jacket. 'Do you wanna buy some booze?'

Narrowing his eyes, Billy looked to the boy then to the whisky bottles. 'Where did you get those from?'

'We pinched them from the offie, back there.' It was the smallest boy who answered.

Snapping his head towards his brother, Fletch gave him a sharp dig in the ribs. 'Shut up,' he hissed. 'You're not supposed to tell anyone where we got them from.'

Billy laughed out loud. They reminded him of himself when he'd been a young lad. 'What are your names?'

'I'm Harry, but me mates all call me Fletch, cos me surname's Fletcher, see. This is my little brother, Spencer, Spence,' he corrected. 'And this is my best mate, Stevie.'

Billy looked, sizing them up. He had an upcoming job planned out and needed someone small. 'Fletch', he said, narrowing his eyes, 'are you Frank Smith's boy?'

At the mere mention of his uncle's name, Fletch's shoulders slumped downwards, and he shook his head. The last thing he needed was for Frank to catch wind of what they'd been getting up to. No doubt he would take the cash for himself and spend it on booze down the pub. 'He's our uncle.'

Billy's smile grew even wider. 'I know him; in fact, I did some business with him a few years back.' He tilted his head to one side, thinking it through. 'I've got a job on and need a young boy, or boys,' he added as an afterthought. 'What d'ya reckon, are you interested?'

Turning to look at each other, the three boys began to whisper amongst themselves.

'Will we be paid for it?' Fletch asked, cocking his head to one side.

Billy nodded. The boys continued to whisper amongst themselves and he scratched at his jaw as he studied them. 'You'll have to smarten yourselves up a bit though,' he warned. 'I can't have any boys who work for me walking around looking like street urchins.' He looked down at his own crisp white shirt and tailor-made suit. 'It's bad for business, if you get my drift.'

Fletch looked down at his outfit. It was fair to say that his jeans and T-shirt had seen better days, not to mention his jacket had a ripped pocket that flapped around with every step he took. 'Okay,' he said, shrugging his shoulders. 'We're in.'

'Jump in then, boys.' He unlocked the rear door. 'I'll speak to your uncle and clear it with him first. In the boozer, is he?'

'Yeah.' Scrambling across the cream-coloured leather back seat, Fletch replied. He'd never seen such splendour before, and his mouth dropped open in awe at the feel of the cool leather against his skin. It must be their lucky day, he decided, and he nudged Stevie beside him, his eyes wide with excitement.

* * *

Narrowing his eyes, Frank slipped off the bar stool when he saw Billy 'One Punch' King and his number two, Joseph Hatton, striding towards him. He took note of his two nephews and their friend trailing behind them, with their heads hanging down low, and groaned in both annoyance and fear. The last thing he needed was to have King on his back. What the fuck had the boys done now? Whatever it was, it must be something bad to bring the man himself into the packed boozer looking for him personally.

A shiver of fear ran down his spine and he held up his hands. 'What the fuck have the little bastards done this time?' he growled, giving his nephews the evil eye.

Billy smiled brightly, hiding the fact that he thought Frank Smith was not only beneath him, but a scumbag to boot. 'It's not about what they've done, Frank. It's about what they're going to do,' he said, placing his arm around the man's shoulders.

* * *

Later that evening, Frank staggered home from the pub and let himself into the house. His cheeks were ruddy, and he stank of booze. All thanks to Billy King, he was on to a nice little earner and in his back pocket was a bundle of cash, courtesy of the man in question.

'What the fuck is this?' he asked, eyeing a plate of egg and chips on the kitchen table.

All eyes turned towards him.

'Well?' he demanded. He lifted the edge of the plate and then let it drop back down on to the table with a loud clatter. 'I asked you a question; what is this?'

The two boys looked fearfully from their uncle to their mother, their eyes wide open, praying she wouldn't try and backchat him. After all, they lived in his house, and another of his favourite pastimes was to threaten to throw them out on the street.

'It's all I could afford, Frank.' Jenny Fletcher looked down at the Formica-covered tabletop. There had barely been enough food to go around, and even after going without a meal herself, she still felt guilty at the paltry fried egg and handful of chips she had served each of her two sons. They were growing lads and it just wasn't enough to fill their tummies.

'And you expect me to graft my arse off all day for this tripe?' It was more of a statement than a question, not that Frank lifted his finger to do a day's work. In fact, the most he'd done all day was to slip off the bar stool and visit the gent's toilets.

'I...' Too afraid to answer, Jenny wrung her hands together.

She had been a beautiful, vivacious woman once, a brunette with long, glossy locks that fell down her back like a thick blanket. Now, she was nothing but a former shadow of herself, with dark rings beneath her sunken eyes and a hacking cough that ravaged through her thin frame, leaving her gasping for breath.

'Well?' Frank roared, his face turning red with anger. When she didn't answer him quickly enough, he overturned the table in one swift movement. The plates crashed to the floor.

Tears welled up in Jenny's eyes as she looked at her sons' faces. Now they would have to go to bed feeling even hungrier than usual. 'I'm sorry, Frank,' she wept, rushing forward to clean up the mess.

'It's all right, Mum; I'll help you.' Glaring at his uncle, Fletch crouched down beside her and began to pick up the pieces of broken crockery.

The expression of contempt spread across his eldest nephew's face was enough to send Frank into a fit of fury, and he bounded across the kitchen, hauling the boy to his feet and pushing him out of the way. 'Think you can backchat me, d'ya?' He reached out and grabbed a handful of his stepsister's hair in his fist, pulling her towards him. She slipped on the grease from the egg and chips and crashed heavily to the floor.

'Leave her alone.' Fletch thumped at his uncle's back.

'Or what?' Spinning around, Frank's eyes were virtually popping out of his head, he was that angry.

'I'll...'

'You'll what?' Frank sneered.

'I'll tell Billy King.' It was no idle threat, and they both knew it.

Frank swallowed deeply. 'Yeah, well.' He took a step away from Jenny and unclenched his heavy fists. The last thing he wanted was for Billy to take away his cash supply. 'Get this place cleaned up.'

He turned to look at his youngest nephew and pulled out a ten pound note from his pocket. 'Go down the chippy and get a couple of bags of chips and a few saveloys. Oh, and get a bottle of pop while you're at it,' he added as an afterthought, doing his best to keep his elder nephew sweet. 'Here, and you'd best take this.' He handed his stepsister a roll of cash. 'You need to buy the boys some new clobber, smarten 'em up a bit.'

Her hands still trembling, Jenny took the money and gave her eldest son a warm smile. Just maybe her stepbrother wasn't so bad after all.

* * *

'So, this is what I want done...' Billy King glanced across to the gated lock-up.

Situated at Tilbury Docks, the area was in darkness. Two large Alsatian dogs jumped up at the gates, snarling and growling, protecting their territory. 'I want you to squeeze through those gates and go across to the office. Jemmy open that window.' He pointed towards the farthest window of the Portakabin. 'Climb through and look around for a blue ledger.'

The three boys looked up at him with a blank expression. They had no idea of what a ledger was.

'It's a blue book, about so big.' He placed his hands ten inches apart.

They nodded.

'All you have to do is bring me that book. It belongs to me and I want it back.'

'What about the dogs?' Fletch looked to the dogs fearfully and ran his hand through his short hair, making it stand up on end. He'd been bitten by a stray once and, ever since, had been afraid of them.

'Don't worry about them.' He turned towards Joseph and waited for the man to pass him a carrier bag, filled to the brim with cheap offcuts of meat, from the boot of the car.

'And what about me? What do I do?' Frank hopped from one foot to the other, barely able to contain his excitement.

'You, Frank' – Billy took the carrier bag and passed it across – 'your job is to feed the dogs. If you want your nephews to come back in one piece, then you'd best make sure you keep those mutts happy.'

Frank snatched the carrier bag and groaned. He'd imagined himself having a more active role, rather than just feeding the dogs to keep them quiet.

'So, are you all clear on what you have to do?'

They all nodded.

'Right then, Frank, start feeding those dogs.'

Complaining bitterly as he did so, Frank delved his hand into the carrier bag and grasped a chunk of bloody meat. He looked down to see his hand stained red and groaned even louder. 'This meat fucking stinks.'

'Just throw it over the gate.' Billy rolled his eyes. Just how much of a dim-witted fool was Frank Smith? He sidled up to the man, not sure that he fully understood the seriousness of his role. 'Unless you want the dogs to tear those boys apart, limb from fucking limb, then you'd best start chucking that meat over. Do you understand what I'm telling you, Frank?'

Not liking this turn of events, Frank nodded submissively. Jenny may have taken a lot of flak from him over the years but touch one of her precious boys and it was a different story altogether. Eyeing his nephews, he began chucking the meat over the cast iron gate, with a lot more enthusiasm than he'd had previously.

'Right then, come on, boys.' Billy led them towards a small gap in the gate. 'Squeeze through there and make a run for it to the cabin.'

Fletch looked towards the gap, the cabin, and then to the dogs. His heart began to pound inside his chest and his palms were clammy. He could hardly lose face and tell Billy that he was scared.

'Come on, Frank, start feeding those fucking mutts.'

At a steady pace, Frank threw the chunks of meat up and over the fence.

'Go on,' Billy urged the boys.

One by one, they wriggled through the gap and pressed themselves up against the metal gate. Fletch was the last to squeeze himself through, and, not taking his eyes away from the dogs, he moved closer to Stevie and his brother. 'Run,' he hissed, his voice merely a whisper.

The dogs turned their heads, sniffing the air. They barely gave the boys a second glance as they ran across the forecourt.

'Here you are. Nice dogs.' Frank spoke in a sing-song tone as he threw the meat over the gate.

Too engrossed in the meat that Frank was feeding them, they gobbled up the chunks and whined for more, their tails wagging.

Using a crowbar, the boys struggled to prise open the Portakabin window. Finally, and with a loud pop, the glass came away from the seals holding it in place. Carefully, they placed the pane of glass on the floor and leant it up against the cabin wall, then set about pushing Spencer up and through the open window.

'Keep that meat coming,' Billy barked, not taking his eyes away from the boys.

Frank chucked the meat over even faster. The dogs on the

other side of the iron gate jumped up in the air, snatching the meat between their powerful jaws, before it had even had the chance to land on the floor.

Looking nervously back at the dogs, Fletch stood on tiptoes to look through the window. 'Remember, it's a blue book,' he called out to his brother.

Spencer searched around the office and pulled open a series of drawers. 'Is this it?' he asked, holding a hardback blue book up in the air.

'I dunno.' Fletch shrugged his shoulders. 'Give me it.' He took the book from his brother and held it aloft for Billy to see. In the distance, Billy gave a thumbs up.

Down to his last handful of meat, Frank glanced across to the Portakabin. What was taking the boys so long? 'I'm getting low on meat,' he stated.

'Just keep it coming,' Billy answered through gritted teeth.

Fletch and Stevie began to haul Spencer back through the window. He landed on the floor with a soft thud. They picked him up and brushed him down. 'We have to go.' Fletch looked once more to the dogs and shuddered. 'Come on.'

'I'm out.' There was more than a hint of alarm in Frank's voice. 'I'm out of meat.' He looked to where his nephews were still standing beside the cabin, then to where the dogs were. 'I'm out, Billy,' he said, his voice rising.

Billy turned his head. 'I told you to pace yourself, not give it to them all in one go.' He looked to where the boys were. He took a step closer to the gate and wrapped his fingers around the iron bars. 'Move,' he shouted.

Hearing the alarm in Billy's voice, the three boys looked up. Their ears pricked; the dogs also looked up.

In a blind panic, Stevie and Spencer ran. Frozen to the spot,

Fletch could only watch in fear as the dogs ran across the forecourt, growling and snarling.

'Run,' Billy roared.

The two boys slipped through the gap in the gate.

'Run,' Frank urged. He stepped closer to the gate and, like Billy before him, he grasped hold of the metal bars, his eyes darting from the dogs, then to his eldest nephew. 'Fucking run.'

The dogs were almost upon him. With just a spilt second to spare, Fletch came to his senses, made a dash for it, and darted across the gravelled forecourt. The dogs changed direction and chased after him, snapping at the air.

'Run, Fletch,' Spencer and Stevie screamed.

With his chest heaving, Fletch ran as if his life depended on it, which just so happened to be the case. He could hear the dogs gaining on him, could hear their powerful jaws snapping, and he cried out in fear as he launched himself at the gate. Scrambling to the top of it, his throat constricted, and the pain in his chest intensified as his small frame shook. Behind him, the dogs jumped up in a frenzy, barking and growling as he slid down the other side.

With a loud thump, he landed on the floor in a heap. He could barely breathe, so acute was his fear.

It was Billy who dragged him to his feet and, taking one look at the boy's deathly white face, he began to laugh. 'Fuck me, I thought you were a goner there for a minute.'

Amidst backslapping, Fletch wiped himself down. His heart was beginning to slow down to its normal, steady pace, as he turned to look, with wide eyes, at the dogs on the other side of the gate. 'That was a close one,' he gasped.

'Close?' Billy laughed even harder. 'Any closer, and those fucking dogs would have taken a chunk out of your arse.' He pointed angrily towards Frank. 'You can blame your uncle for that. I told him to pace himself, not throw the whole lot over in one go.'

'I didn't.' Frank looked down at the floor, his cheeks turning scarlet.

With the precious ledger containing every debt owed to him tucked safely underneath his arm, Billy grinned widely. 'Come on,' he said, slinging his free arm around Fletch's shoulder. 'You all did a good job. Well done, boys. But right now, I need a drink. What d'ya reckon, Frank?'

Frank agreed. After what he'd just witnessed, Billy King could say that again.

2

TEN YEARS LATER

The Two Puddings, in Stratford, East London, was where Billy King was hosting his wife's fortieth birthday party.

Birthday banners and streamers had been placed strategically around the bar area. Along the far wall, tables had been placed side by side and covered over with starched white linen cloths. A finger buffet consisting of sausage rolls, sandwiches, quiches, cockles and whelks had been laid out and, with no expense spared, sitting proudly in the centre of the wooden tables was a two-tiered iced fruit cake. The atmosphere was jolly, exactly how Billy had planned for the occasion to be. Nothing but the absolute best would do for his wife.

* * *

In the kitchen, Jenny Fletcher had set out the ironing board, and with her son's shirt spread over the board, she began ironing out the creases.

'Has Frank already gone?' Freshly showered and shaved, Fletch walked into the kitchen, bare-chested.

'You know what your uncle is like.' Jenny rolled her eyes. 'He couldn't wait to get out of the bleeding door.' She placed the iron on the metal holder, passed the shirt across, and watched as her eldest son slipped it on.

Casting her eyes over her two sons, she felt a familiar sense of pride. They were not only handsome, but also big strapping lads, which was a miracle in itself, considering the little amount of food there had been to go around when they were growing up.

'Will you be okay on your own?' Buttoning up his shirt, Fletch glanced across to his mother.

'Of course I will.' Jenny nodded towards the living room. 'That new game show is on the box at eight. It's meant to be good... everyone is raving about it.'

'And you'll remember to lock the back door, won't you?'

'Already done.' She grinned. 'Oh.' She walked across the kitchen to where the housekeeping tin was kept, took it down from the shelf, prised open the metal lid, and took out two ten pound notes. 'Here, take this and have a good time tonight.'

'Mum,' Fletch scolded. 'We don't need your money.' Not only did they work for Billy, but they also had a nice little sideline selling used cars, the majority of them cut and shut. 'We earn enough working for Billy.'

'No, come on, take it.' Of course she knew they earned good money. Across her fingers were several large diamond and sapphire gold rings. And the fact that they had bought her a real mink fur coat for her birthday was more than enough to tell her that they were doing well for themselves. Gone were the days when she struggled to put a meal on the table. The feasts she was able to put on for her sons and their friends were legendary. 'I want you both to have a good time tonight.' She pressed the crumpled notes into her son's hand.

'Thanks, Mum.' Fletch took the money and kissed his mother

on the cheek. When he returned home from the party, he would slip the money back into the housekeeping tin.

She looked over at her youngest son. 'And you, you behave yourself tonight. No fighting and no getting too drunk. You'll look after him, won't you, Fletch?'

'I don't need looking after. I'm twenty-two, not a baby,' Spencer complained in his usual slow drawl.

'I know you're not, sweetheart.' She wrapped her arms around his waist and gave him a hug. Standing at least three inches taller than his brother, Spencer was a big lad and towered above her. 'Watch him,' she mouthed.

Fletch nodded. It went without saying that he would watch out for his younger brother. 'Right then,' he said, clapping his hands together, 'are we ready?'

'Yeah.' Spencer grinned from ear to ear. He couldn't wait to get to the party.

'Come on then.' Fletch pulled on his jacket and pushed Spencer out of the kitchen. 'Bye, Mum,' he called out.

'Bye, my darlings.' As the front door slammed shut after her sons, the house became eerily quiet. She quickly tidied away the ironing board and iron, then walked through to the lounge. Taking a seat in her favourite armchair, she sighed and picked up her knitting bag. The boys were growing fast, and before she knew it, they would fly the nest, leaving just her and Frank alone. The very thought of only having him for company was enough to make her shudder.

* * *

An hour later, Fletch strode across the floor of the Two Puddings, with Spencer and Stevie following closely behind him. He shook Billy's hand, then turned his attention to Susan, Billy's wife.

'Happy birthday.' As he leant forward to kiss her cheek, the scent of her sweet perfume hit his nostrils, and the words caught in the back of his throat. He'd heard that Billy's wife was beautiful, and despite catching fleeting glimpses of her at his boss's house, nothing could have prepared him for just how beautiful she was up close.

Wearing a classy, fitted, knee-length powder-blue dress, with a string of pearls around her neck, Susan's blonde hair was tied up in an elegant chignon. 'Thank you,' she breathed, tilting her head to one side to look up at him, her blue eyes sparkling.

Fletch returned her smile, feeling suddenly shy. He was thankful for the interruption when Stevie nudged him in the ribs. 'Beer?' he asked.

Tearing his eyes away from her, Fletch accepted the offer.

'It's a free bar, lads, so knock yourselves out.' With his hand clasped tightly around his wife's waist, Billy grinned at them.

As they walked towards the bar area, Fletch was unable to stop himself from looking over his shoulder. If the rumours were true, then it was no wonder Billy treated his wife like a queen and wrapped her up in cotton wool.

'Bit of all right, her, ain't she?' Stevie whispered in his ear.

Fletch shrugged his shoulders, hiding his true thoughts. Stevie could say that again. In all his life, he'd never seen such a beautiful woman.

They ordered their beers, courtesy of Billy, and swallowed down large mouthfuls of the amber liquid, quenching their thirst.

'Looks like your uncle is enjoying himself.' Stevie winked.

Turning his head, Fletch raised his eyebrows and looked across the pub floor. Frank would chase after anything with a pulse. He watched as he danced his way around a group of women, young enough to be his daughters, and inwardly groaned. 'He's a fucking embarrassment, that's what he is.'

Spencer grinned widely. 'Give him a break, Fletch. He's having a good time, that's all.'

Fletch rolled his eyes. What about their poor mum, sitting at home all by herself? Even though Billy had extended his invitation to Jenny, Frank had flatly refused to bring her. 'He'll chase after anything in a skirt,' he stated, turning up his nose.

Stevie nudged him once more, his body suddenly tense, as he pulled himself up to his full height. 'Look lively.'

Fletch looked up and groaned. 'What now?' He looked over at his uncle for a second time.

'The Bannerman brothers have just walked in.'

'Oh shit,' Fletch muttered. He hastily glanced towards his brother, before turning his body around to watch a group of men entering through the pub doors. 'That's all we fucking need.'

The Bannerman brothers were a rival firm, hailing from across the water, in Bermondsey. It was no secret that there was no love lost between the two firms. In fact, to put it mildly, they despised one another, and were locked in a bitter turf war. Placing his beer down on the wooden bar top, Fletch made his way across the busy room. He came to stand beside his boss, leant in close, and whispered in his ear.

Billy's face was a mask of hatred as he turned to look across the bar. The Bannerman brothers had been a thorn in his side for as long as he could remember, and to add insult to injury, not only had they turned up uninvited on his wife's birthday, of all days, but they had humiliated him in the process.

'There is some business I need to take care of.' He released his arm from around his wife's waist and smiled down at her apologetically as he did so; the smile didn't quite reach his eyes. 'Fletch, look after her,' he instructed, and clicking his fingers towards Joseph Hatton and his remaining henchmen, he tore across the packed boozer, seething with anger.

Standing protectively beside Billy's wife, Fletch could feel her body heat, he was that close. He had to physically stop himself from taking sly glances at her. There and then, he wanted to berate himself. Now wasn't the time to be having fanciful thoughts about Billy King's missus. Unless he was very much mistaken, World War Three was about to kick off.

'What is all that about?' Feeling confused by her husband's sudden departure, Susan stood on her toes to look across the crowded room.

Her voice broke his thoughts. How was he supposed to answer? He could hardly tell her the truth, could he? 'I dunno.' He shrugged.

She gave him a warm smile. 'So, you're the famous Fletch I hear so much about?'

Fletch was even more alarmed, and he shifted his weight from one foot to the other. 'Yeah,' he finally answered, wanting to kick himself for sounding so dumb. The truth was, he had never had much experience with women, at least not actually talking to them, anyway. Usually, his relationships only lasted a few weeks before he became bored with them and got rid.

She patted his arm, sending a shiver down his spine. 'Billy talks highly of you.'

He thanked her and then tore his eyes away to look across at her husband, his boss. The atmosphere in the pub had turned decidedly frosty.

* * *

Billy King could barely keep the snarl from his face as he marched across the pub floor. Who the fuck had allowed the Bannermans in? He'd specifically told the doormen that they were barred, and not to give them access should they turn up. His eyes flickered across to the men on the door. They would feel the full force of his wrath before the night was out.

'What the fuck are you doing here?' he growled, approaching the group of men.

The elder of the two brothers, George Bannerman, spread open his arms. 'Free country, ain't it?' As always, he was impeccably dressed. Despite being a tall, slender man, he was also strong and could hold his own. He looked around the packed boozer, and his eyes fell upon the sparkly birthday banners. 'I didn't realise it was a private party,' he said with mock surprise. Beside him, his brother and other firm members sniggered.

'Yeah well, it is, so now you can fuck off.' Billy's temper was beginning to rise.

George began to laugh. 'A little dicky bird told me it was your wife's birthday.' He nodded his dark blond head across the bar to where Susan was standing. 'You don't mind if we stick around, do you? Offer our congratulations, maybe even buy the lady a celebratory drink?'

Billy lunged forward. It took two of his men to hold him back. 'Get out,' he roared. His face had turned bright red, and he clenched his fists, ready to attack.

George laughed once more. 'I'm coming for you, King,' he said, stabbing his finger forward before giving a slight inclination of his head, indicating for his firm to leave the party. 'Oh.' He paused, slowly turned around, and glanced once more in Susan's direction. 'Give our regards to the birthday girl.' He winked.

'I'm gonna kill him.' Billy was so incensed; he could feel the anger seeping through his pores. He watched as the Bannermans left the pub and breathed heavily through his flared nostrils. 'I'm gonna fucking kill him,' he spat. 'If it's the last thing I ever do.'

'You okay, Boss?'

Billy waved his number two away from him and gave the

doormen a menacing glare. 'I told you to keep that lot out,' he screamed at them.

The head doorman, Barry Whitlow, gave a shrug of his shoulders. Who was he to tell the Bannermans that they weren't welcome? After all, he wasn't stupid, and certainly didn't have a death wish.

Throwing back his fist, Billy swung it towards the big man, hitting him square on the chin. The man fell to the floor in a crumpled heap. 'Next time,' he spat, 'do as I say.'

* * *

Spencer sidled up beside his brother. 'What's going on?' he asked.

'The Bannermans have turned up,' Fletch answered, keeping his voice low.

Clenching his fists into tight balls, Spencer made to move forward, eager to get stuck in.

'Leave it,' Fletch warned, pulling back on his brother's arm. 'Billy will sort it out.'

'Yeah, but it's the Bannermans.'

'No buts.' Fletch tightened his grip. 'I told you to leave it, Spence.' His voice had a steely tone to it, and with one hand still curled around his brother's forearm, he used his free hand to beckon Stevie forward. 'Get him out of here, will you?' he shouted above the music. 'I don't care where you take him, just get him away from that lot.' He flicked his head towards the Bannerman firm.

Stevie narrowed his eyes. He glanced across the pub floor, and then back to his best friend.

'Please, mate, just do as I ask.'

'Come on,' Stevie sighed. He threw his arm around Spencer's shoulders and led him back to the bar area.

Fletch couldn't help but sigh with relief as he watched his younger brother being led out of harm's way. The last thing he needed was for Spencer to be on the Bannermans' radar.

* * *

Sitting inside his car, George Bannerman chuckled out loud. 'Did you see his face?' He grinned. 'I thought he was gonna have a heart attack. The bastard was practically foaming at the mouth at one point.'

Albie Bannerman nodded. Like his brother, he was impeccably dressed. 'Jumped-up ponce. That prick needs a good hiding,' he said, clenching his fist.

George laughed once more; nothing would give him greater pleasure than to see Billy King brought down.

With his hand on the door handle, Albie was ready to jump back out of the car. 'We should have finished him,' he growled. He pulled a firearm out from the waistband of his trousers and looked to his brother. 'We should have topped him while we had the chance.'

'Too many witnesses.' Not that it mattered in the grand scheme of things, because witnesses could easily be bought off or scared into keeping schtum. 'He'll get what's coming to him.' He glanced once more towards the pub doors and turned the ignition. 'We've shown our faces, rattled a few cages, so to speak. Come on, time to get out of this shithole.'

'Yeah,' Albie agreed, screwing up his face. 'It fucking stinks this side of the water.'

* * *

The next morning, Fletch and Spencer were up and out of bed early. Billy had called a meeting at his home in Ongar, Essex, and would have their guts for garters if they turned up late.

Jenny was already pottering around in the kitchen, buttering a plateful of toast, when her sons came down the stairs. 'Tea?' she offered, her hand hovering over the teapot.

Fletch glanced at his watch. 'No thanks, Mum.' He grabbed a slice of toast, took a bite, and chewed on it before swallowing. 'We can't stop.' He took a second bite whilst shrugging on his jacket.

'This is fucking bollocks.' Standing beside the kitchen doorway, Frank yawned loudly. He had a raging hangover, all thanks to the free bar. 'It's only just gone eight. What's he calling a meeting this fucking early for?'

Turning to look at his uncle, Fletch groaned. Still wearing his underpants and an off-white singlet vest that had seen better days, Frank wasn't even dressed. 'Come on, Frank, get a move on; you're gonna make us late.'

'Fuck him.' Entering the kitchen, Frank took a seat at the table and swallowed down a large gulp of tea. Grimacing at the bitter taste, he spooned in three tablespoons of sugar.

'Frank,' Fletch urged, as he tapped at his wristwatch, 'we have to go.'

'All right, fucking hell.' Frank clutched at his aching head. 'At least let me have a cuppa first, will ya?'

'Are you still half cut?' Gritting his teeth, Fletch pushed his brother out of the kitchen and stabbed his finger forward. 'Where's your loyalty, eh?'

'Loyalty?' Frank threw his stepsister a sly glance. 'I'm all ears, boy.' He lit a cigarette and leant back in the chair. 'Let's talk about loyalty.'

'Frank,' Jenny warned.

'You...' Ignoring her, Frank stabbed the cigarette in his

eldest nephew's direction. 'You would know all about loyalty, wouldn't you?' He flicked a layer of ash on to the linoleum floor and sucked his teeth. 'You've got a short memory. You forget where you come from, boy. You forget the hell I plucked you from.'

Taking a nervous glance at his brother, Fletch swallowed deeply. Of course he hadn't forgotten, how could he? The memory of his childhood was forever ingrained into his brain.

'And now you, of all people, want to talk about fucking loyalty?' Frank cocked his head to one side, his voice a low growl. 'You've got the front to stand there and judge me, to accuse me of shit?' He narrowed his eyes. 'Maybe if you took your head out of King's arse once in a while, you'd actually learn the meaning of the word.'

'Frank.' Thumping her palms down on the table, Jenny breathed heavily through her flared nostrils. 'Enough.' Her eyes darted nervously towards her youngest son who was standing in the doorway of the kitchen, hoping and praying that he didn't understand the hidden meaning behind her stepbrother's words. 'Please, enough of this now.'

'What?' Frank spread out his arms, his expression the picture of innocence. 'I'm only speaking as I find, but don't worry.' He winked. 'The family secret is safe with me.'

Taking a step forward, Fletch's chest muscles strained against the thin fabric of his shirt. 'Watch your mouth, Frank.'

'I gave you a home,' Frank roared. 'If it weren't for me, you'd be living on a scrap heap. It was me.' He poked himself in the chest. 'I was the one who took you all in when no one else wanted you.'

Glancing around the outdated kitchen, Fletch gave a bitter laugh. 'We would have been better off on the scrap heap. At least then we wouldn't have had to put up with you and your shit. At least then Spencer wouldn't have been so scared as a kid that he would piss the bed every night.'

'That was nothing to do with me and you know it.' Frank had the grace to look down at the floor.

'Nah, maybe it wasn't all your fault, but you didn't help the situation, did you?'

'Fletch.' Jenny put her hand on her son's arm. 'That's enough now, son. Your uncle is right, he did take us in. He gave us a roof over our heads, a home.'

Shrugging his mother away from him, Fletch stared at her open mouthed. 'Took us in? We're not talking about a stray dog here, Mum.' He narrowed his eyes. 'Whether we like it or not, we're family.'

Frank leant back in the chair. He loved nothing better than to goad his nephew, and to know that his words had got the younger man's back up. It made his day a whole lot sweeter. With a smirk spread across his face, he lifted the cigarette to his lips, inhaled a lungful of smoke, and opening his mouth to form the shape of a perfect O, he puffed out a series of smoke rings.

'Fletch, what's going on?' Spencer asked.

'Nothing.' Turning his head to look over his shoulder, Fletch gave his brother a reassuring smile. 'It's him, he's still pissed; you know what he's like when he's had a skinful.'

'Why are you arguing?'

'We're not.' He grinned. Turning back towards his uncle, the smile slid from his face. He knew exactly what it was Frank was referring to, not that he would ever tell Spencer. As far as he was concerned, his brother must never know the truth. He must never know where they had come from. 'We'll be waiting in the car. You've got ten minutes, so move your fucking self.'

Watching his nephews leave the house, Frank winced as the front door slammed shut behind them. 'He's getting too big for his boots, that boy,' he stated to his stepsister. 'Ordering me around... who the fuck does he think he is?'

Jenny remained silent. She watched as he slurped at his tea and then she turned her back on him. A smile creased her face. Ever since her sons had begun working for Billy King, she had noticed a shift in power. No longer did Frank rule the house with an iron fist. She delved her hands into a sink of hot soapy water and set about washing up the breakfast things, all the while basking in his discomfort.

'You know what his problem is, don't you?' Frank spat. 'He's got too much of his father in him.'

The smile slid from her face, and, drying her hands on a tea towel, her back stiffened. 'He's nothing like him,' she bristled.

Billy King owned an impressive house. Situated at the end of a long driveway, the grounds surrounding it were both vast and secluded. The house itself had six bedrooms, two large sitting rooms filled with oil paintings and Chinese silk rugs, and a dining room with a solid oak table that could comfortably seat ten people. It was in this room that Billy conducted his business.

Despite the earliness of the hour, he was pleased with the turnout. 'How did they know we would be there?' It was more of a statement than a question, and, placing a cigarette between his lips, Billy cupped his hand around the flame from his solid gold lighter. Not for the first time did he wonder if there was a spy in his camp. 'Well?' he demanded as he exhaled a lungful of cigarette smoke. 'How the fuck did the Bannermans know it was my wife's birthday party? Or that we would be in that particular boozer?'

The men turned to look at each other. For all intents and purposes, they were as equally confused as Billy was.

Billy thumped his fist down on the dining table. 'Someone in this room,' he said, stabbing his cigarette forward, 'must be giving them information.'

Once again, the men looked towards each other.

'Nah, I can't see that happening.' It was Keith Lewis who finally spoke. He plucked a cigarette from his own packet and paused before placing it between his lips. 'I mean, come on, if someone was running their mouth off to the Bannermans, we would know about it, wouldn't we?'

'Well, they didn't just grasp the information out of thin air, did they?' Billy sneered.

Fletch looked between the two men. It was no secret that they despised one another, all thanks to Billy and his philandering ways – that, and the fact that Keith had returned home early from work one day and caught Billy in his bedroom, with his wife bent over the bed they shared, her red lacy knickers around her ankles, legs spread wide apart.

'I dunno.' Fletch shrugged. 'I think Keith's got a point.' He delved his hand into his pocket and pulled out his lighter. He flicked the ignition, sucked on the cigarette and exhaled a stream of blue smoke lazily through his nostrils.

'Nah.' Billy tore his eyes away from his adversary. 'They know too much. I know for a fact that there is a snake in this room.'

'Yeah, and you'd know all about that,' Keith muttered under his breath.

Billy raised an eyebrow, his tone goading. 'Yeah, and so would your missus.' He gave a cocky wink. 'Tell her I said hello.'

Knocking over the dining chair in his haste to jump up from his seat, Keith's face turned red, and he balled his fists ready for action. 'Fuck you,' he bellowed.

'Nah, you're all right,' Billy chuckled, 'I'd rather—'

'Seriously, Bill,' Fletch interrupted. Just like Keith before him, he jumped up from his seat and held out his arms, in a bid to keep the peace. 'This really ain't helping matters, is it?'

Billy sucked on his cigarette and gave a nonchalant shrug of his shoulders.

With the situation once again relatively calm, Fletch resumed his position at the table.

'Can we just get back down to business now?'

Billy looked around the room. 'As I was saying...' A nerve twitched at the side of his jaw and his eyes fell upon Keith for a second time, silently daring him to retaliate. Even though it was he who was in the wrong, there was nothing he would like better than to have an excuse to smash his fist into the man's face. 'There's a snake in this room.'

Fletch thought this through. Billy was right. It was more than a little bit strange how the Bannermans were able to stay one step ahead of them. Could there really be a spy in their camp? 'Maybe it was the guv'nor of the Two Puddings who told them?' he asked.

Billy shook his head.

'So, what are you thinking then, Bill?'

Stubbing out his cigarette in a heavy crystal ashtray, Billy lounged back in his chair and massaged his temples. He didn't know what to think; that was the truth of the matter. He looked around the dining table. The only thing he knew for certain was that amongst his men – men that he had trusted without a second thought – there was a snake in the grass.

His eyes settled on Spencer, and just as quickly, he dismissed the idea. Spencer was a lump, a strong lad, and not to mention physically capable, but he was far too dim-witted to be running his mouth off to the Bannermans. As he continued to stare across at the boy, an idea formed in his mind.

'So?' Fletch repeated. 'What are you thinking, Bill?'

'Nothing.' Abruptly, Billy stood up.

Confused, Fletch narrowed his eyes and looked around him. 'What do you mean, nothing?'

'Exactly what I said, nothing. Just drop it.' He waved his hand, dismissing the conversation.

'Yeah, but if someone...'

'I said, drop it,' Billy growled. He walked across to the dining room door and held it open. The meeting was over.

Reluctantly, the men got to their feet.

Still feeling confused, Fletch hung back slightly and, reaching the door, he looked Billy in the eyes. 'I don't get this,' he said, his voice low. 'You said someone was giving out information.'

Billy clapped him on the back. 'Like I said, forget it.' He watched the men walk from the room, and as they neared the entrance hall, he called Spencer back towards him.

Fletch made to follow his brother and Billy held up his hand. 'Just Spencer,' he said, closing the door to the dining room firmly behind them.

Turning towards Stevie, Fletch raised his eyebrows. A surprised expression was etched across his face. 'What's all that about?'

Equally confused, Stevie shrugged.

* * *

Billy smiled across the room to Spencer and gestured for him to take a seat. He knew the boy wouldn't ask questions. It wouldn't even occur to him to do so, which was exactly what he was counting on.

'I've got a little job for you, Spence.' He smiled.

Without saying a word, Spencer grinned widely and basked in the attention Billy gave him.

* * *

'So, what was all that about?'

Spencer screwed his face up. 'What?'

'You know full well what.' Coming to an abrupt halt, Fletch stood in front of his brother, blocking his path. 'What did Billy want with you?'

'Nothing.'

'Spence,' Fletch warned.

Rolling his eyes, Spencer gave a nonchalant shrug of his shoulders. 'He's got a job for me.'

'A job?' There was a hint of surprise in Fletch's voice. 'What sort of job?'

'Just a job.'

Fletch was thoughtful. Since when had Billy King started delegating lone jobs out to Spencer? He looked across the driveway towards Billy's house. He was in half a mind to have it out with his boss and find out what was going on.

'It's just a job, Fletch.' Spencer broke into his thoughts. 'He wants me to follow someone, that's all.'

'Follow someone... follow who?' Fletch demanded to know.

'I dunno yet.' As Spencer made his way across the paved driveway towards his brother's car, the promise he'd made Billy to not tell anyone about the plan they had made, even his own brother, was still fresh in his mind.

Still deep in thought, Fletch turned to look at his best friend. 'What do you reckon?'

Stevie shrugged. They all knew just how protective Fletch was when it came to his younger brother. Spencer, for his part, struggled to comprehend what was going on around him and even though he didn't realise it he was often the butt of someone's joke. He was easy to manipulate and could be convinced the sky was pink or rainbow-coloured. He barely knew right from wrong, something that Stevie knew for a fact terrified Fletch. In the wrong hands, Spencer was dangerous; he believed everything he was told and if someone told him to jump off a cliff he more than likely would. 'He's only following someone; it's nothing too heavy is it? He'll be all right, he can handle it.'

'Yeah, I suppose so.' Fletch gave the house one final glance before unlocking his car doors. He still didn't like it and he had a feeling there was a lot more to it than just Spencer following someone around. There and then, he made the decision to keep a closer eye on his brother. 'Jump in,' he told them. 'I'll drop you both back home, then I have to shoot off. I've got some business of my own to take care of.'

Susan King climbed out of the silver Mercedes, closed the door gently behind her, and gave her driver, Joseph Hatton, a wide smile. He didn't return her smile. She'd always had an inkling that Joseph didn't like her, that he didn't think she was good enough for Billy. As she crossed over the street, his beady eyes followed her like a hawk, making her inwardly shudder.

She didn't need to buy much, if anything at all. More importantly, the shopping trip was an excuse for her to get out of the house for a while. As beautiful as her home was, she couldn't help but feel suffocated by it. She needed to breathe some fresh air into her lungs, and her shopping trips gave her the perfect excuse to do just that.

She pushed open the shop door, smiled a greeting towards the proprietor, then made her way down the aisles.

* * *

Even though he knew he was playing a dangerous game, Fletch was unable to stop himself. He fancied Susan something rotten, and not only did he think she was classy, but she was in a different league to any other girl he'd ever met before. The fact she was Billy's wife wasn't enough to deter him; if anything, all it did was make him that little bit more cautious. Over the months he'd heard Joseph complaining many a time that he was sick and tired of driving Susan around. He wasn't a gofer, Joseph had whined bitterly to anyone who would listen, and so Fletch had come up with some half-hatched plan to actively seek her out.

Walking the aisles, Fletch pretended to be looking for something. He heard the little bell above the shop door tinkle as it indicated someone was entering the premises, and felt his breath catch in his throat. From the corner of his eye, he spotted her and as she came closer, he straightened up, then turned around with a mock expression of surprise etched across his face.

'Hey.' He smiled. 'Fancy bumping into you here.'

Susan frowned, then broke into a smile. 'Fletcher?' she enquired, tilting her head to one side as she looked up at him.

'Fletch,' he corrected her.

'Of course.' Her smile grew wilder. 'What are you doing here?'

Taking a sneaky glance towards Billy's Mercedes parked outside, Fletch shoved his hands in his pockets. 'Just grabbing a couple of things. How about you?' As he said the words, his cheeks flushed a deep shade of pink, and he wanted to kick himself; why did she always seem to have the ability to make him sound so stupid?

Susan laughed. 'What I meant was, I didn't know that you lived here in the village.'

'I don't.' Fletch shook his head. 'I was passing through.' They both knew it was a lie and as his cheeks flushed even pinker, he averted his eyes. After an age, he cleared his throat and flicked a glance towards the car. 'I see you've got Joseph driving you around.'

Susan followed his gaze. 'Yes,' she answered with a sigh.

'Not much of a conversationalist, is he?'

'No, not really,' she laughed. 'He never really has been one for small talk.'

'You know, maybe,' he said, leaning in closer and breathing in her scent, 'you should ask Billy to let me drive you around instead.'

Her eyes twinkled as she laughed. She couldn't deny that she found him attractive, and the very thought made her bite down on her bottom lip. Billy would kill her stone dead if she so much as looked at another man, let alone if he were to find out she was attracted to him. 'Perhaps I will.' She held out her hand. 'It was nice to see you again, Fletch, take care of yourself.'

Fletch took her hand in his, noting how tiny it was compared to his own. 'Yeah, you too.'

He watched as she wandered off down the aisle and could barely contain his excitement at being in her company. Checking that the coast was clear first, he managed to slip out of the shop unseen, and make his way down the street in the opposite direction to where Joseph Hatton had parked Billy's car.

There was something about Susan King; she drew him in, in a way no other woman had ever done before, and no matter how hard he tried, he was unable to erase her from his mind.

* * *

That evening, Susan sat perched on the edge of the velvet chaise longue. She was in the main bedroom and her husband was standing across from her, undressing.

'I was thinking...' She cleared her throat before continuing. 'It isn't fair to Joseph to have him driving me around everywhere.'

Billy snapped his head upwards. 'Has he said something to you?'

'No, of course not.' She shook her head vigorously, her cheeks blushing. She could barely believe she was going to do this. 'I was just thinking that maybe you should give him a break.' She watched her husband's reaction closely.

'Yeah, maybe.'

She stood up, walked towards him, and as she placed her hand across his bare back, her fingertips caressed his skin. 'How about that young man you introduced me to at my birthday party?'

'Who, Spencer?' he asked, screwing up his face. 'He ain't the full ticket. I wouldn't trust him to drive you to the end of the driveway.'

'No.' She shook her head. 'What was his name?' She tilted her head to one side as though thinking it over. 'That's it, Fletcher.'

'You mean Fletch?'

'Yes, that's him. He seems nice, polite, trustworthy.'

'Yeah, he is.' Billy nodded. He took a few moments to think it through. As fond as he was of Fletch, he wanted him out of the way for a while, or at least wanted him out of his brother's way. 'Yeah.' He turned and kissed his wife's forehead. 'He can start tomorrow.'

Susan gave her husband a smile. She swallowed down the guilt she felt and promptly turned her head away from him, sure that he would notice her blushes. 'Good. I'd like to go shopping tomorrow. Please tell him not to be late.'

3

Albie Bannerman strutted out of the Red Dice Casino. Situated on Southend seafront, it boasted a sea view. It had just gone 5 a.m. and the area was virtually deserted as he breathed in lungsful of fresh sea air. Above his head, seagulls were already squawking as they circled the early morning sky.

He was on a lucky streak and had come away from the casino happy. In his back pocket was a bundle of cash, and he grinned widely as he strolled towards where he'd parked his car the previous evening.

He was about to cross the street when a white transit van pulled up beside him. He barely gave it a second glance as he stepped off the kerb.

He heard the driver's and passenger's doors open, saw a rush of figures race towards him, and before he could even think the situation through, they had bundled him into the back of the van, kicking and screaming.

The figure who pinned his arms behind his body was a big lump. No matter how much Albie struggled, he was unable to release himself from the tight grip the man had on him.

A second man came into view, and he pulled a makeshift balaclava off his head.

'Hello, Albie.' He grinned, his voice loud. 'Fancy seeing you here.'

Pulling back his head, Albie spat in the man's face. 'You no-good prick,' he roared as he struggled to release himself once more. 'I'll fucking knock you out.'

'Knock me out? You wouldn't be able to throw a sausage across the street, let alone throw a punch, you stupid cunt.'

The fist that landed in Albie's stomach caused him to double over in pain. Winded by the blow, he struggled to catch his breath.

'You won't get away with this,' he growled.

Billy King laughed out loud. He looked across to Spencer and gave him a conspiratorial wide grin.

'I think you'll find I just have.'

Without even breaking a sweat, he proceeded to beat the living daylights out of him. In fact, to put it mildly, he hadn't even started on the man yet.

Susan shrugged on her coat. From the corner of her eye, she watched Fletch as he shifted his weight from one foot to the other. Not for the first time did she regret asking her husband to switch drivers.

'So, where to, milady?' It was said tongue in cheek, and a wide grin spread across Fletch's face.

Susan turned up her nose at his choice of address. 'Please, don't call me that.' It was bad enough that Billy put her on a pedestal; she didn't want his employees doing the same.

'Sorry,' he said, shamefaced. 'Where would you like to go

then, Mrs King, or should I call you Susan?' He tilted his head to look at her. 'Or how about Suzy?'

Susan lifted her head to look at him. Suzy was a nickname given to her as a child by her grandfather; she could barely remember the last time someone had addressed her by the name he had affectionately called her. She brushed past him, more than aware of the ripple of electricity that simmered between them. 'I don't think Suzy is appropriate, do you? Billy wouldn't like it,' she told him. 'And I'd like to go the village shops, please.'

'Okay.' He shrugged his shoulders and grinned. 'Mrs King it is then.' He bowed his head and held open the front door for her.

They walked across the paved driveway, her high-heeled shoes clip-clopping with every step she took. She stopped beside the car and Fletch ran around to the front passenger door, unlocking it. She made no attempt to move forward, and he raised his eyebrows slightly.

'Oh,' he muttered, once it became clear that she intended to sit in the back of the car. He shoved the passenger door closed and made his way around to the rear of the vehicle.

He watched her climb inside, closed the door behind her, and wanted to kick himself. Only five minutes into the job and he was already making rookie mistakes. Opening the driver's door, he got in, started the ignition and drove the car forward. As much as he hated himself for it, he couldn't resist taking sly glances at her in the rear-view mirror.

Staring out of the window, Susan turned to look at the back of his head. 'It's quicker if you turn left here,' she stated, as they neared the end of the driveway.

'Okay.' Fletch nodded and flicked the indicator. He glanced up to look in the mirror and caught her eye. Hastily, she looked away and he smiled to himself; she was so beautiful, and didn't even realise it. Billy was one lucky bastard.

* * *

As a bucket of icy cold water was thrown over him, Albie Bannerman gasped. He coughed and spluttered as the water burnt the back of his nose and throat.

'Wakey, wakey.' Billy grinned.

Tied to a chair, Albie struggled against the ropes that confined him. He could feel his left eye was swollen shut, could feel a split gum and a dislodged tooth wobble. He spat out a mouthful of blood. 'You won't get away with this,' he growled.

Billy sighed as though bored and spread out his arms. 'As I've already stated,' he said, his tone mocking, 'I have got away with it.' He crouched down beside the man and looked him in the eye. 'And there ain't fuck all you can do about it, is there?'

As he struggled against the ropes once more, Billy's laughter rang loudly in his ears. Through hooded eyes, he watched as the man straightened up, and he took this as his cue to look around him. There were just two of them present, King and the lump who had confined him.

He turned his attention to the small room. The floor and walls had been covered over in sheets of thick plastic. With a stone staircase along one wall, he took a wild guess that he was being held in a cellar. There were no visible windows. It was difficult for him to take a guess at the location, or to even know what time of day it was. For how long had they held him captive? How long had he been unconscious for? It could have been days, for all he knew.

'So,' Billy said as he turned around, 'who the fuck is it that is giving you information?'

Albie snarled.

'I asked you a fucking question.'

Albie remained silent. He was no fool and knew for a fact that the moment he divulged who the snake in the grass was, they would kill him.

Clenching his fists once more, Billy lunged towards him. 'Who the fuck is it?' he roared.

Still, Albie didn't speak. Despite the situation he found himself to be in, he took a moment of satisfaction to see King so rattled. He smirked to himself. He was already a dead man, so he may as well have some fun while he still could.

* * *

George Bannerman drummed his fingers across the desk. He was sitting in his study, or his office, as he liked to call the wood panelled room and stared at the man standing opposite him.

'I can't give you any more information. I'm done,' he whined.

George raised his eyebrows.

'He's already suspicious. And if he finds out it was me, then he's gonna kill me stone dead.'

'And how exactly is that my problem?' George spread out his arms.

Panic slithered through Joseph Hatton's veins. 'Please,' he begged. 'You have to help me out here, if he finds out...'

'Nah.' George flicked his hand dismissively. If there was one thing he loathed more than Billy King, then it was this man standing in front of him. There was nothing worse than a snitch.

'Please, Mr Bannerman.' Joseph was close to tears, so deep was the fear inside of him, as he clasped his hands together in front of his body, to get his point across. 'Like I said, he is already suspicious and it's only a matter of time before he looks to me. He's bound to; he ain't fucking stupid.'

Lounging back in his chair, George studied him. After what

seemed an age, he spoke. 'The problem is,' he said, 'I need you to stay inside. I need to be able to stay one step ahead of him.'

It was jealousy that had caused Joseph to run to the Bannermans, and a sneer creased his face. It was becoming harder and harder to gain information from Billy.

On more than one occasion, he'd found him closeted away with his protégé, Fletch, discussing matters in private. Ever since the kid had turned up, all he ever heard was Fletch this, Fletch fucking that. Well, fuck Fletch. What about him?

He was supposed to be Billy's number two, and for the past six months he'd been demoted to driving Susan King around. And now, even Fletch had got that job.

'Give me protection,' he implored George, 'and I'll find out everything you want to know.'

George smiled; this was more like it. 'Deal.' He stood up from behind the desk. 'Should King get wind of our arrangement, then in due course we will offer protection.'

Joseph stuck out his hand, ready to shake on the deal.

Ignoring the outstretched hand, George walked towards the office door and pulled it open. 'Don't let me down.' He gave a chilling smile and put out his hand, signalling the end of the meeting. 'You can see yourself out.'

Joseph swallowed deeply. He couldn't help but feel as though he'd made a pact with the devil himself.

* * *

Fletch watched as Susan crossed over the street and made her way back to the car. He jumped out and held open the door for her. She squeezed past him, their bodies close. It took all his restraint to stop himself from pulling her into his arms and kissing her there and then.

'Thank you.'

He gave her a smile, closed the door behind her, and climbed into the car.

Sitting behind the wheel, he caught her eye in the rear-view mirror. 'Wouldn't you like to learn to drive yourself?' Even his mum had a little runaround. She loved the independence her car gave her.

Susan shook her head. 'Billy wouldn't like that.'

Fletch narrowed his eyes. He continued to hold her gaze. 'I could teach you if you'd like. I taught my mum and there's no stopping her now.'

'I've already told you, Billy wouldn't like it.' She turned her head away, breaking his gaze.

Fletch shrugged and started the ignition. 'Seems like Billy doesn't like a lot of things,' he muttered under his breath.

As much as she would love to learn to drive, Susan knew it was something her husband would never allow. From the very first moment she had laid her eyes upon Billy King, he had controlled her, in some form or another. She glanced down at her wedding band. The twenty-two-carat gold ring was a constant reminder that she belonged to him, and him alone.

'Just take me home, please.' There was a sudden sadness to her voice.

Fletch began to drive the car forward. After just a few hours in her company, it was clear to see that there was so much more to Billy King's marriage than what he led people to believe.

* * *

Albie Bannerman's breathing had become laboured. His head hung low. His face was battered, bruised, and had swollen to twice its usual size. He could barely breathe, so acute was the pain in his chest.

Kicking out his heavy boot once more, Billy was incensed. Not a single piece of information had Bannerman given them – not one single word. A part of him admired Albie's reluctance to spill the beans. Any other man would have sung like a canary hours ago – just to put an end to the beating.

He began to pace the cellar, contemplating his next move. They couldn't let him go. He knew that much, not that that had ever been his intention. He crouched down, wiped his hand across his jaw, and stared across to the man. Finally, he stood up and turned to look at Spencer.

'Kill him,' he said, with a wave of his hand.

Spencer rolled up his sleeves, took the blade Billy handed to him, and then set to work.

* * *

The next morning, Fletch was in the kitchen, happily munching on a bacon sandwich. Nothing could dampen his mood, and, sitting at the Formica table, he sank his teeth into slices of thick buttered bread. He took a large bite, chewed, then swallowed. He was about to take a second bite, when Spencer walked in. His face was flushed, and his eyes were wide with excitement.

'What's up with you?' Fletch studied his brother.

'I need you to come and see something.' Spencer hopped from one foot to the other.

Between mouthfuls of his sandwich, Fletch quickly swallowed. 'See what?' he asked, taking another bite.

'Just something.'

Fletch raised his eyebrows. It wasn't like his brother to be so cagey. 'Can I finish eating first?'

'Yeah.' Spencer continued to hop from one foot to the other.

Rolling his eyes, Fletch shoved the last corner of his sandwich into his mouth and chewed. 'Come on then but make it quick; I have to collect Suzy in a couple of hours.'

'Who's Suzy?'

The mistake almost made Fletch choke on the breadcrumbs. 'I mean Mrs King,' he said with a wave of his hand. He picked up his car keys and followed Spencer out of the kitchen.

'You're gonna like this.' Spencer looked over his shoulder.

Fletch rolled his eyes for a second time and glanced down at his wristwatch. His brother had better not make him late.

Fletch brought the car to a halt outside one of the derelict houses that Billy owned. 'What are we doing here?' He stared out of the window and turned to look at his brother. 'What's going on, Spence?'

'You'll see.' Spencer began to climb out of the car. As he walked down the pathway, he could barely contain his excitement. 'You're gonna really like this.'

'So you keep telling me,' Fletch groaned.

Taking a brass key from his pocket, Spencer slipped it into the lock.

'Does Billy know that you've got the keys to one of his houses?' Fletch put out his hand.

'Yeah, of course he does.' He opened the front door with a flourish. 'Come on.' He grinned. 'This way.'

Spencer led the way down a set of concrete steps towards the cellar. As he turned his head to look back at his brother, a lopsided grin was spread across his face.

'What's this?' As he approached the bottom step, Fletch

recoiled backwards. He took in the plastic sheeting, the blood spattered across the floor and far walls, and the overturned wooden chair. He sucked in his breath and looked across to his younger brother. 'What the fuck is this, Spence?'

'Good, ain't it?' Spencer's eyes lit up and he shifted his weight from one foot to the other, barely able to keep still.

Looking around him, Fletch brought his hands up to his head. 'What have you done?' He stared at his brother, then crouched down and inspected the blood. 'What the fuck have you done?'

'What?' Spencer grinned.

'What? What do you mean by "what"?' There was an underlying hint of hysteria in Fletch's voice. He straightened up, bounded across the plastic-covered floor, and slammed his brother up against the crumbling concrete wall, his forearm plastered across his chest, restraining him. 'What have you done?'

Spencer continued to grin.

'Do you understand, Spence?' The hairs on the back of Fletch's neck stood up on end and he closed his eyes tight for a moment. 'Do you understand what you've fucking done?' He raised his fist in the air, ready to strike out.

'Yeah, of course I do.' Spencer cowered backwards, blinking rapidly as he waited for his brother's heavy fists to rain blows down upon him. The full enormity of the crime he and Billy King had committed didn't even register in his brain. 'Bannerman was asking for it.'

Throwing his brother away from him, Fletch turned to look at the crime scene once more. 'Bannerman?' he gasped. His eyes widened and he felt the colour drain from his face. 'You mean to tell me you've killed one of the Bannermans?'

'Yeah, the youngest one, Albie.'

With his hand placed on the concrete wall to steady himself,

Fletch's heart began to beat faster. He couldn't get his head around this. One minute, he'd been happily eating his breakfast, contemplating the day ahead of him. The next, he was standing in what could only be described as a slaughterhouse. At least that was what it looked like if the blood splatter was anything to go by. 'Please, tell me you haven't? Not Albie Bannerman.'

'Yeah,' Spencer repeated. He narrowed his eyes, unsure of why his confession had caused such a reaction in his brother. 'Don't you like it?'

'Like it? What exactly am I supposed to like? I can't believe it; I can't believe what I'm seeing and hearing.' Fletch turned his head, a snarl creased his face. 'You idiot, Spence. Do you even realise what this is gonna cause? Do you realise the trouble all of this is gonna bring us?'

Spencer's heart plummeted. He'd fully expected his brother to see what a good thing he and Billy had done. Between them, they had disposed of one of their rivals. 'But it's a Bannerman,' he stammered.

'Yes, a fucking Bannerman,' Fletch growled.

'Yeah, but he was a right ponce.'

'Ponce?' Fletch gritted his teeth. 'Do you even know what that word means, Spence?'

Spencer shrugged. He didn't have a clue what the word meant and was only repeating back one of words Billy often used.

Shaking his head, Fletch looked once more to the blood-splattered sheeting. 'This has got to go.' He tore across the room and began pulling the flimsy sheets of plastic away from the walls. 'We need to get rid of this.' He stabbed his finger towards his brother.

'Why?'

'Because it's evidence, that's why.' Clenching his fist, Fletch was in half a mind to batter his brother, to knock some sense into his skull. 'Move,' he hissed. 'You start that end.' He nodded across to the far end of the cellar. It was on the tip of his tongue to ask what had happened to the body. How had they disposed of Albie Bannerman? He continued tearing down the plastic. He had to know, he decided, and coming to an abrupt halt, he turned his head. 'What did you do with him? What did you do with the body?'

Spencer remained silent. He didn't want to anger Fletch any further than was necessary.

'What did you do with him, Spence?'

'We put him in a car and Billy said I should throw the blade into the Thames.'

'And?' Losing patience, Fletch glared. 'What did you do next?'

Spencer gave his brother a sidelong glance. His voice was low as he spoke. 'I did what he asked. I threw the blade into the Thames.'

'No, Spence.' He gritted his teeth, his voice a mere growl. 'I meant, what did you do with Bannerman?'

'I'm not allowed to say.'

'Spence,' Fletch warned. 'What the fuck did you do with him?'

His eyes downcast, Spencer shrugged his shoulders. 'I don't know; I don't remember.'

Fletch bounded across the cellar for a second time and slammed his brother up against the wall. 'I'm gonna ask you one more time, and if you don't tell me, I swear before God, I'm going to batter your fucking brains out. What did you do with him?'

Spencer blinked rapidly and cowered backwards again from the oncoming assault. Instinctively, he knew that Fletch meant every word he spoke. 'All right... all right, I'll tell you. We chucked him in the boot of a car, and had it crushed.'

'Crushed?' There was shock in Fletch's voice, and he brought his hands up to his head once more. The full severity of the situation was brought home, and he breathed heavily, wishing that he was anywhere else, other than this cellar, listening to the gory details of Albie Bannerman's premature demise.

'Yeah, Billy said it was the best way to get rid of him, so we took the car to a breaker's yard down Crow Lane.'

Crow Lane, situated in Romford, housed several breaker's yards and scrap metal merchants. He knew exactly where his brother meant. 'And it's gone? The car has been destroyed?' he asked, taking a step backwards.

'Yeah.' Spencer looked to the floor. 'We even waited there until it had been done,' he said, glancing up at his brother through hooded lids.

Fletch nodded, satisfied. At least that was something to be thankful for. He walked back across the cellar and resumed pulling away the plastic sheeting that had been crudely tacked to the walls, all the while silently cursing Billy King.

He should have known. He should have known something wasn't right when he'd singled out Spencer to do a job for him. There and then, he blamed himself. Why hadn't he questioned Billy at the time? He could have put a stop to it. He would have even taken Spencer's place. It was too much of a secret for his brother to keep. *Why?* he repeated to himself. It was a question that would go on to haunt him for the rest of his days.

* * *

George Bannerman pulled up opposite his brother's house. Albie's car wasn't on the drive. He opened the car door, stepped out, and looked up and down the deserted street. Where the fuck was his brother?

As he walked down the pathway of the semi-detached house,

he could already hear his sister-in-law screaming at the kids to behave themselves. He had never been a big fan of his brother's wife, June. She had too much to say for herself, that was half the problem, and if there was one thing he despised, it was people who had the audacity to try and answer him back.

He rapped his knuckles on the front door. Within moments, it was flung open.

'Where is he?' she questioned, with her platinum blonde hair pulled up in curlers, and a cigarette dangling from the corner of her scarlet-painted lips. 'Where the fuck is Albie?' she screeched. 'It's been five days since I last saw him. Where the fuck is he?'

George recoiled. Her high-pitched voice went right through his head. 'I was hoping you could tell me that.' He stepped across the threshold into his brother's house. As usual, it looked like a pigsty. The kids' toys littered the floor, and a mound of washing had been left to pile up on the staircase.

'How would I know,' June sneered at her brother-in-law. 'I'm only his wife. He never tells me anything.' She stormed through to the kitchen, kicking a plastic toy car out of her path. 'If I find out he's got another tart on the go, I'll fucking scalp him,' she hissed.

George put out his hand to placate her. He'd already been to the flat where his brother's bit on the side lived, and she had seen neither hide nor hair of him.

George took in the untidy kitchen and sighed. The sink was full of dirty crockery and the work tops were heavily stained. No wonder his brother never seemed to want to spend any time here. He looked out of the kitchen window towards the overgrown garden, where his young nephews were racing up and down the pathway on bicycles. His brother may play around with other women, but he loved his three sons, and would never willingly up and leave them.

'Well, where is he then?' June exhaled a plume of cigarette smoke above her head. The truth was, she was worried. Her Albie may not be perfect, but she loved the bones of him. 'I just want him to come home.' Tears welled up in her eyes and she glanced towards the back garden. 'Me and the boys, we miss him. It's not like him to not come home at all. How am I meant to manage without him? I've got no money. How am I meant to feed the kids?'

George sucked his teeth. 'Yeah, I get the picture,' he growled. He took a roll of cash from his trousers pocket and handed it over. 'That'll see you through until he comes home.'

June snatched the money and tucked it safely inside her bra strap. 'Thanks,' she mumbled.

He chewed on the inside of his cheek as he thought the situation through. Something was amiss. He knew that much. 'Let me make some calls.' He gave her a small reassuring smile that didn't quite reach his eyes. 'I'll find him, don't worry. Before you know it, he'll be back home.'

Puffing on her cigarette, June absentmindedly nodded her head.

Leaving the house, George took his mobile phone from his jacket pocket and crossed over the street. He was worried all right. There was something about his brother's little disappearing act that wasn't sitting right with him. He opened the car door, climbed inside, and began making a series of calls.

'I'm calling a meeting,' he growled into the phone. 'Round everyone up and meet at my house within the hour.' He looked across to his brother's house once more, and with a heavy heart, threw the phone down beside him and started the ignition. He would scalp Albie himself if he found out he had been on a bender and was just lying low some place.

* * *

Fletch had never felt more furious. He brought the car to a screeching halt on Billy King's driveway, threw open the door, and jumped out. Without hesitating, he stormed towards the house and thumped his fist on the front door.

'Fuck me, you've got a knock like a copper.' Billy was all smiles as he flung open the door.

Barging his way into the house, Fletch took deep breaths in a desperate measure to calm himself down. 'Why?' he demanded to know. 'Why Spence?'

'Why Spence, what?' Billy opened his arms as though genuinely puzzled.

'You know what,' Fletch hissed. 'Why did you get him to do it?'

'What's the problem?' Billy ushered his protégé into the dining room and closed the door firmly behind them. He took a seat at the oak table, placed a cigarette between his lips and lounged backwards, as though he didn't have a care in the world.

'You bastard, I'll...' Fletch held on to the back of the dining chair and glared at his boss. 'I'll...'

'You'll what?' Lighting his cigarette, Billy slammed the solid gold lighter down on the dining table with a loud clatter. He exhaled a lungful of smoke, then clenched his jaw. 'I picked him because he's a fucking lump, all right?' He gave a carefree shrug of his shoulders. 'I knew he would be able to handle the situation.'

'You were bang out of order,' Fletch growled. He could feel the anger building inside of himself and balled his fists. More than anything, he'd like to wipe the smug smirk from the older man's face. Nothing would give him greater pleasure.

'He works for me. It's what I pay him to do,' Billy interrupted, sitting forward. There was a steely tone to his voice. 'I had a job that needed doing and it was Spencer I chose. What's the big deal? You wouldn't be complaining if it were Stevie or Joseph, or one of the others, would you?'

Fletch bowed his head as he thought this through. There was some truth to Billy's words. It was true that he wouldn't have complained if it were one of the others. Only it wasn't one of them; it was his brother. He wiped his hand across his jaw. 'He can't handle something like this,' he warned, tapping the side of his head. 'It'll fuck him up.'

'You're too protective, that's your trouble.' Billy stabbed his finger forward. 'He's a big boy now. Let him spread his wings a bit.'

Fletch gave a bitter laugh. 'Killing someone... is that your idea of him spreading his wings? And not just anyone, Albie fucking Bannerman, of all people.' He took a deep breath. The realisation of what Spencer had done, of what he'd become involved in, hit him full on, and a new startling terror filled him. 'If they find out he was involved, they'll come after him; you know they will. They'll kill him.'

Billy stood up and walked around the table. He would need to have serious words with young Spencer. He'd specifically told him not to tell anyone about the murder they had committed. 'They won't find out.' He kept his voice low and leant in closer. 'And if they do, it's because that brother of yours couldn't keep his fucking mouth shut.' He returned to his seat and spread out his arms. 'I needed someone I could trust, and let's face it, he's far too stupid to be the one who is going behind my back and running his mouth off to Bannerman.'

'What?' Fletch's face contorted angrily. 'What did you just say?'

'You heard,' Billy answered with a sigh. 'He's too dense to be the one going behind my back.'

'He's not stupid or dense,' Fletch stated defensively.

Billy raised his eyebrows. That was a matter of opinion. 'Whatever,' he said with a shake of his head. 'Someone is talking, and I need to know who it is.'

'And you used my brother to do that?' He clenched his fists tightly once more. His temper was beginning to get the better of him, and he took a step forward, ready to attack.

Noting the younger man's stance, Billy stretched out on the chair. For all intents and purposes, he appeared unconcerned by Fletch's outburst. The only signs he gave that he was about to kick off big time were the fact that his eyes flashed dangerously and that a vein pulsated at the side of his temple.

'Slow yourself down,' he warned, stabbing his finger forward.

'Slow myself down? Seriously? Did you just fucking say that?' Fletch roared. 'I'm telling you now,' he growled. 'I swear before God, if they touch one hair on my brother's head, I will kill them, all of them. I'll hunt them down and tear them apart, limb from fucking limb.'

Billy gave a smug grin; it was exactly what he'd expected the younger man to say, and was all part of his plan.

'I mean it, Billy.'

With a short temper, blinding right hook, and a protective streak over his younger brother that bordered on obsessive, Billy didn't, for a single second, doubt Fletch's words. 'As I've already stated, it won't come to that.'

'It had better not,' Fletch warned. He gave his boss one last look of contempt, then stormed across the dining room, and yanked open the door so hard that it almost came off its hinges.

Billy jumped up from his seat and roared at him, 'Someone is talking, and one way or another, I will sniff the grassing cunt out, if it's the last thing I fucking do!'

As Fletch stepped out into the hallway, he locked eyes with Susan; the look across her face made his heart hammer inside his chest. Instinctively, he knew she'd heard everything that had been said and a wave of shame flushed over him. Without saying a single word to her, he walked out of the house and, striding across the driveway, he jumped back into his car. He started the ignition and sped away from the house. *Fuck Billy King, fuck the Bannermans, fuck all of them.*

4

George Bannerman drummed his fingers on his desk. Standing across from him was Joseph Hatton. He could sense the man's unease, could feel his fear. It radiated from him like a beacon.

'I've not heard anything,' Joseph repeated, his voice stammering. 'Not a dicky bird.'

He thought this through. So, if King wasn't involved in Albie's disappearance, then where the fuck was his brother? He glanced down at his mobile phone, hoping, praying that he would hear something from him.

'Nah,' he growled. 'This has got King's name written all over it.'

Joseph's heart plummeted at the precarious situation he found himself to be in. 'I honestly don't know anything, Mr. Bannerman, honest I don't. Billy hasn't said a word. If he'd have said something, you know I would have told you straight away. We made a deal, didn't we?'

George sneered as he studied the man in front of him. He knew Joseph Hatton's type. He would do and say anything to save his own skin.

'Well then, you'd best get out there and find out exactly what I want to know, or...' He left the threat to hang heavy in the air.

'I will do.' Joseph practically ran towards the door in his eagerness to get away from him.

Frustration flowed through George and he fought the urge to smash up his office. Picking up his mobile phone, he took a deep breath to steady himself. He dialled his brother's telephone number for the fifth time that morning alone. When he reached the answering machine, he switched off the call and toyed with the device in his hands. Tapping in a series of digits, he made a second call.

'Hello, Mum,' he said into the mouthpiece. 'Have you heard from our Albie today?'

His heart sank as he listened to her reply. Where the fuck was he? It was the one and only question at the forefront of his mind. If nothing else, Albie loved the bones of their old mum, and would never go days, let alone more than a week, without checking up on her. George said his goodbyes and switched off the call. The mystery of his brother's disappearance gnawed at him.

Finally, he made one last call and tapped in the telephone number for Mickey Shank, a distant cousin. Shank wasn't his real surname. It had derived from Mickey's love of slicing people up, just for the sheer fun of it. He was known to carry big fuck-off blades around with him. In fact, his sole purpose in life was to cause as much damage as was humanly possible with his knives.

'Mickey.' He smiled into the phone, instantly hiding his mistrust of the man. 'Got a little job for you.'

* * *

'Come on, Fletch.' Swallowing his pride, Billy was standing in the middle of Frank's kitchen. It had been just over a week since Fletch had thrown his little hissy fit, and the fact that he had made a personal visit to the younger man was the closest he would ever come to apologising for using Spencer in the murder of Albie Bannerman.

Fletch remained silent. Sitting at the kitchen table, he lit a cigarette and pretended to leaf through a newspaper.

'Come on, lad.' Frank shot a sly glance in Billy's direction. He was worried all right – worried that Billy would take away his cash supply. He looked up at the clock on the kitchen wall. The pub would be opening soon and seeing as he wasn't the kind of man to put money away for a rainy day, he was running short of cash. In fact, if the situation didn't improve in double-quick time, he would have no other choice but to raid the housekeeping tin. 'Listen to what Billy's got to say. Hear him out.'

At this, Fletch snapped his head upwards. 'Fuck off, Frank,' he growled. 'You don't even know the half of it.'

Frank threw his arms up in the air. It was true. He didn't know what had gone on between Billy and his nephew. The only thing he did know was that King could easily replace them if he so wished.

'You try and talk some sense into him.' He none-too-gently pushed his youngest nephew forward.

'Come on, Fletch.' Standing just inches away from the table, Spencer gave his brother a lopsided grin. 'No real harm was done.'

'No real harm was done?' Bumping back his chair, Fletch jumped up in a fit of rage. 'Are you stupid or something?' Immediately, he regretted his choice of words. 'I'm sorry, Spence, I didn't mean that.' He stabbed his finger towards his boss. 'You were bang out of order.'

'For which I'm apologising.' Billy gave his protégé a wide smile. 'Enough now, eh? You've made your point. Come back to work.'

Fletch gave a hollow laugh. He looked at the faces staring back at him, sighed, and rubbed his hand across his forehead. 'I need to speak to Billy, alone.'

'You heard the man, both of you get out.' Billy's voice was loud.

Frank swallowed down a retort. Is this what life had come to? Being thrown out of his own kitchen? 'Come on,' he grumbled to his nephew. 'Leave them to it.'

Billy waited for the two men to leave the room, then took a seat at the Formica-covered table. He reached into his pocket and took out his packet of cigarettes, lit up, and exhaled a plume of smoke above his head. 'Okay, I admit it: I was out of order.' He spread his arms open and gave a cheeky grin. 'In hindsight, I should have run the situation past you first.' There was more than a hint of sarcasm in his voice.

Fletch opened his mouth to speak, and Billy held up his hand, cutting him off.

'I know that you don't like it, but I need to know what's going on. I need to know who the grass is. And there is someone; I can feel it in here.' He poked himself in the chest. 'There's only one way the Bannermans can be getting their information, and that is from one of you lot, because it sure as hell isn't fucking coming from me.'

'I get that.' Fletch sighed and lowered his voice. 'But you should never have used Spencer, you know he isn't...' He closed his eyes for a moment, not wanting to say the words out loud. 'You know that he... isn't right, not up here.' He tapped his temple to emphasise his point. 'If the Old Bill comes knocking, he won't be able to handle it. He'll crumple, and that's if Bannerman doesn't get his hands on him first.'

'That won't happen—'

'You don't know that,' Fletch interrupted.

'Yes, I do.' Billy leant closer. 'Bannerman won't go to the Old Bill. We both know that, and if we all keep our traps shut, he will never find out who it was that killed that ponce Albie.'

Fletch thought this through. He could see Billy's point. It wouldn't be in George Bannerman's best interests to go to the police.

Billy lifted his chin and gave a coy smile. 'Is all forgiven?'

'Yeah, I suppose so.' Against his better judgement, Fletch nodded. The way he saw it, he didn't really have much of a choice on the matter; it was far safer to have Billy on side than to go against him.

'Good.' He leant back in the chair, a wistful expression upon his face. 'From all accounts, Albie Bannerman's missus is a bit of a goer.'

'What?' Fletch narrowed his eyes.

Billy chuckled. 'I've heard she's up for a good time, and what with her old man out of the picture' – he winked – 'she's fair game—'

'You wouldn't,' Fletch butted in.

Billy laughed even harder. 'Yeah, I fucking would.'

Fletch's mouth fell open. 'But what about—'

'Listen, what my Susan doesn't know, doesn't hurt her, does it?' He gave a wide grin. 'In fact, I think I need to take a wander south of the river... would be rude not to in the circumstances.'

Fletch screwed up his face, causing Billy to laugh even louder.

'Anyway...' Billy stood up and stretched out his back muscles. 'You can collect my missus tomorrow morning; fuck knows why, but for some reason, she likes you.' He chuckled loudly. 'And remember' – he stabbed his finger forward – 'keep schtum about Bannerman's old lady. If my Suze gets wind of it, I'll know where it's come from,' he warned.

Fletch could feel his cheeks redden and he nodded. It was no secret that Billy played around. He had done so throughout his marriage apparently, but to target Albie's wife, that was low, even for Billy's standards.

'Right, that's that then.' Billy walked towards the kitchen door, but, placing his hand on the door handle, paused and turned back round. 'Oh, and one more thing, Fletch.'

Fletch looked up.

'Don't ever threaten me again.' He stabbed his finger forward. 'That's your first and only warning, do you understand me?'

Shamefaced, Fletch took the warning on board. For all intents and purposes, he knew that he'd had a lucky escape. There weren't many people who spoke to Billy the way he had and lived to tell the tale.

* * *

Susan's heart skipped a beat when she saw Fletch hovering beside the front door. It had been just over a week since she'd watched him storm out of the house and out of her life. She busied herself, collecting her handbag and shrugging on her coat to hide the thrill of excitement that shuddered through her.

She could hear her husband's gruff voice coming from the dining room, and, taking a deep breath, she moved across the marble floored hallway, her high-heeled shoes clip-clopping as she walked.

'Where to, Mrs King?' Fletch stuck his chin in the air as he waited for her to answer him. He knew how to play the game, and even though he wanted to smile down at her he kept his manner both cool and professional, exactly what Billy expected from him.

She opened her mouth to speak but was distracted by her husband's large frame standing in the doorway. 'Take her wherever she wants to go,' he instructed Fletch.

'Just the village shops, please.' Susan glanced across to Billy. 'And then maybe to lunch at that new little bistro that recently opened on the High Street; the reviews are exceptional.'

Fletch nodded.

'Here, take this.' Billy delved his hand inside his trousers pocket and pulled out a roll of cash. He passed the money across and planted a kiss on her forehead.

It took all of Susan's strength not to stiffen and she threw a glance in the direction of her husband's employee. She noted that he turned his face away and her heart quickened. Placing the money inside her handbag, she was eager to get out of the house and away from her husband. 'Thank you.' She smiled. She made to make her way forward and Billy put out his hand to stop her.

'Fletch, I want a word first.' Billy cocked his head towards the dining room.

* * *

'What's up?' Following his boss into the room, Fletch closed his eyes as he gently shut the door behind him. At the back of his neck the tiny hairs stood up on end; had he inadvertently alerted Billy to the fact he was attracted to his wife? Had Susan herself told Billy that she thought his behaviour was inappropriate?

Billy stood casually beside the dining table. 'What do you know about pills?'

'Pills?' A flicker of relief washed over Fletch, and he narrowed his eyes. 'What pills?'

'Those pills that the kids are all raving about.'

'Not a lot.' He took a wild guess that Billy was talking about a new wave of drug doing the rounds, Ecstasy, or Es as they were more commonly known on the street. 'Why? Do you want some?'

'Like fuck I do. Give me a drink any day of the week over any of that shit.' He was thoughtful for a moment. 'I've heard that there's a lot of profit to be made from them.' He shrugged. 'By all accounts, kids are turning up in their thousands to get their hands on them.'

'Yeah, you mean raves.'

'Raves?' Billy's eyebrows shot up.

'Yeah, they're sort of like organised parties that are put on in a warehouse or empty field. The promoters just turn up and take over. Me and the boys were gonna go to one a few weeks back.'

Billy pursed his lips, thinking it over. 'Can I leave it with you to find out more about this rave lark, then? If there's money to be made, I want a slice of the action.'

'Yeah, of course.'

Satisfied, Billy gave him a wide smile. 'Go on, take my missus wherever she wants to go, but look after her,' he warned.

'Yeah, I will do.' Fletch gave a half smile and backed out of the room, sure that Billy would notice his blushes.

* * *

Leaving the house, Susan breathed in a lungful of fresh air before making her way towards the silver Mercedes parked on the driveway. Dutifully, Fletch opened the car door and she climbed inside. She waited until he had driven the car to the end of the sweeping driveway, then, taking a look over her shoulder at the house, she turned back in her seat.

'Where have you been?'

He looked up into the rear-view mirror and locked eyes with her. 'Nowhere.'

'I heard you and Billy arguing.'

Fletch shrugged his shoulders. 'It was nothing.' It was a lie and they both knew it. He flicked the indicator and turned on to the lane. He could feel her eyes boring into the back of his head and resisted the urge to squirm in his seat.

'It didn't sound like nothing.'

'It's all sorted out now.' He looked up and locked eyes with her in the rear-view mirror for a second time. A cheeky grin spread across his face. 'Anyone would think you missed me, Mrs King.'

Averting her eyes, Susan swallowed down her embarrassment. She could hardly tell him that he'd just hit the proverbial nail on the head, that she'd longed to see him and every day had hoped that he would appear.

'Don't be ridiculous,' she groaned.

She heard him chuckle and turned her head to look out of the car window, her skin flushed pink.

'I'm right, ain't I?'

'No.' She looked up at the rear-view mirror, with a half-smile. 'You've got some—'

'Front,' he interrupted her, laughing. 'Yeah, it's not the first time someone has said that.'

'I was about to say nerve, actually.' She grinned. 'But yes, I can see their point.'

'All part of the charm.' He winked, pulling the car over to the kerb. 'You know,' he said as he turned in his seat and gave her a cheeky grin, making her tummy flutter, 'it's nice to see you smiling for once; you should do it more often.'

She nodded. 'Actually, you're right, I should, and it does feel nice to smile.'

'Maybe it's the company you're keeping.' He gestured towards himself and grinned.

'You're right, you do have a lot of front.' Shaking her head, she threw him a wide smile and opened the car door.

As she crossed over the street, she could feel him watching her and breathed deeply, resisting the urge to look over her shoulder. She couldn't deny that he had a certain something about him, and she chuckled to herself. He'd barged his way into her otherwise mundane life like a blast of fresh air.

* * *

Dripping in gold, Mickey Shank was grinning from ear to ear. He pulled open his camel-hair trench coat to reveal a samurai sword.

George Bannerman blew out his cheeks. 'That's impressive, Mickey.' He gave the man a cautious smile and glanced around him. They were in the middle of Greenwich Market, surrounded by market stall traders selling their wares and unsuspecting law-abiding citizens out doing their weekly shopping.

'It's the only one in the country,' Mickey boasted, leaning in closer.

George smiled once more. How Mickey hadn't been locked up in a secure unit, such as Broadmoor, he had no idea. There was more than an underlying hint of madness about him that you could see in his eyes.

A troubled childhood was the root of Mickey's problems. With an absent father and an alcoholic, drug-fuelled mother who was oblivious to her son's screams whenever her latest bit on the side would punch and kick the living daylights out of him, he didn't stand a chance growing up. Pushed from pillar to post, foster care placements had been his only salvation – his only chance of a normal life – until his foster carers decided that they, too, couldn't handle him and wanted rid.

It was the madness that usually got to them in the end, that and the stash of knives they would find hidden underneath his mattress. Even from a young age, Mickey had been obsessed with blades. They made him feel safe. To a certain degree, George supposed that they still did, and after the childhood Mickey had had, he understood his need to keep himself tooled up.

Still, Mickey and his madness had come in useful over the years, even if that meant he and Albie had needed to put the hard word on him from time to time to make sure that he did their bidding. In fact, as far as George was concerned, Mickey owed them – he owed them big time. He'd lost count of the number of times they had needed to bail him out of a tricky situation or give him an alibi over the years.

'Let's grab a cup of tea and a bite to eat,' he said, guiding Mickey towards a café across the street, hoping more than anything that he would do his coat up. The last thing he needed was for the Old Bill to turn up and cart them both off to the nearest nick. After all, Mental Mickey, as he and Albie had often referred to their second cousin, was hardly inconspicuous.

Settled at a table towards the back of the premises with mugs of tea in front of them, George spoke. 'It's Albie; he's on the missing list.'

Mickey shook his head. 'Sorry to hear that. What do you want me to do?' he asked, eyes lighting up as his gold-encrusted fingers delved underneath his coat to touch the sword hilt. 'Slice up the bastard who done him in?'

'No, not yet.' Putting out his hand to quieten the man down, George looked around him once more. Mickey could be a liability at the best of times. 'I don't even know if he has been done in. No, what I want you to do is to put the feelers out, ask around, see if anyone knows anything.' He watched Mickey's reaction over the rim of the mug. 'You're good at that, getting information from people,' he added, with a smirk.

'Yeah, I can do that.' He took his hand away from the sword and picked up his steaming mug.

'If you locate Albie, I'll pay you some hefty wedge.'

Mickey wrinkled his nose. He was more interested in cutting people up than having some cash in his back pocket.

'And I mean some serious wedge an' all.'

'Yeah, all right.' He swallowed a mouthful of tea. 'On one condition. When I find the cunt responsible, I get to play with him.' He toyed with the hilt of the sword once more with a beaming smile spread across his face. 'This girl needs to earn her stripes.'

'Knock yourself out,' George answered. Silently, he sipped at his tea. He'd set the wheels in motion. All he had to do now was wait for Mickey to work his magic and give him the information he so desperately needed.

* * *

An empty field in the Essex countryside was where the latest rave was taking place. Much to the chagrin of the police, the illegal parties were organised with military precision and the promoters were able to convey thousands of people to the venue with the minimum of fuss.

Parking his car against a grass verge, Fletch turned to look at the throng of partygoers making their way across the vast, open space. From the confines of the car, a vibrating hum of music could be heard in the distance.

'Remember, this is work.' He turned to look at his brother as he sat in the back of the car. 'That means we're not here to get out of our nuts, right? We're here to scope the place out and that's it.'

'But we can still have a good time while we're at it, can't we?' Stevie pulled out from his jacket pocket a small polythene bag containing several white pills. He dangled the bag in front of Fletch's face. 'You know you want to.' He grinned.

'Yeah,' Fletch chuckled. 'Just keep your eyes peeled. We need to know who is selling what. What security they have, etcetera.' He looked across the field, opened the car door, and stepped out.

There was an excitement in the air as they traipsed across the mud-splattered grass. As they got closer, the sound of music intensified, and a vibration could be felt under their feet. They paid their ten pound admittance fee and made their way around the perimeter of the rave, watching everything that went on.

Taking the tiny white pill that Stevie handed him, he placed it on the back of his tongue and washed it down with a mouthful of bottled water. With virtually zero security, as far as Fletch could see, it was going to be a piece of cake for Billy to take a slice of the action.

'What d'ya mean there ain't no security? There has to be.'

It was the next morning, and, lounging back on the dining room chair, Fletch shook his head. 'I'm telling you, Billy, there's none, well, no one worth bothering about anyway. Just a couple of suits walking around, and a couple of kids on the gate, giving it large, and believe me, they are raking it in... and that's without the money they're taking from the pills.'

'No.' Billy laughed out loud. 'You've made a mistake. You must have been too out of your nut to see what was going on.' He stabbed his finger forward. 'I keep telling you to lay off them pills. I sent you there to work, not get wasted.'

'I'm not mistaken, and I wasn't wasted.' He lowered his eyes. 'Besides, I only had a couple of pills, and that wasn't enough to stop me from seeing everything that went on, as clear as day.' Lounging back even farther, Fletch grinned. 'Trust me, there is hardly any security, Billy, at least not enough for us to have to worry about.'

'Fuck me! What kind of amateurs are these pricks?' He was thoughtful for a moment. 'I can't fucking believe it.' He shook his head. 'You know what this means, don't ya?'

'What?'

'It means we can take the fucking lot, more or less, hassle free. It'll be the easiest night's graft we've had in a long time.' He lit a cigarette and shook his head once more.

'Two bob fucking amateurs. The soppy cunts won't know what's hit them.'

'That's not the best of it.'

'What d'ya mean?' Sitting forward in the chair, Billy frowned.

'The pills. Someone is supplying them.'

'Yeah, well, that's obvious. Even an imbecile would be able to tell me that.' He rolled his eyes, waiting for Fletch to get to the point.

'I asked around, and it seems that the Es are being supplied by a firm.'

'And?'

'A firm from across the water.'

'From across the water?' Billy slumped backwards and his voice took on an incredulous tone. 'Don't tell me it's the fucking Bannermans.'

'Yep, the very same.'

'And on my fucking patch an' all, the no-good cunts,' he growled. 'I bet they're having a right laugh at my expense.'

As he watched a flurry of emotions spread across his boss's face, Fletch gave a stilted smile. 'So,' he asked, spreading out his hands, 'do you still wanna go ahead with it, then?'

Recovering from his initial shock, Billy grinned back. 'Does a brown bear shit in the woods?'

Fletch lifted his eyebrows. He would take that as a very firm yes.

* * *

Eric Porter leant back in his leather recliner, puffed on his cigar, and eyed the man in front of him warily. 'So, what is it I can do for you, Mickey?' His eyes flickered towards his girls, or his brasses, as he commonly referred to the women who worked for him.

As soon as they'd spotted Mickey Shank through the glass partition leading to his office, they had scurried out of harm's way. The last time Mickey had entered his premises, one of the girls had ended up with a six-inch slit across her left bum cheek. According to Mickey's irate protests, she had looked at him the wrong way. Poor girl couldn't sit down for a week.

'If it's one of the girls you're after, then I'm sorry, but they are all booked up for the day.'

Mickey Shank grinned. He liked Eric, liked his astute business mind. The man in question not only owned a string of the best porn shops and brass houses across London, but also owned a series of one-armed bandit arcades. In other words, he had a lot of fingers in a lot of pies.

He turned his head and noted that the sitting room where the girls usually lounged around, waiting for their punters to arrive, had emptied out in double quick time.

'Was it something I said?' He laughed out loud.

Eric gave a nervous laugh. 'Like I said, Mickey, the girls are all booked up.'

They weren't, but Mickey wasn't to know that. His antics during the last visit had near enough caused a riot, and the girls had threatened to walk out and never come back. They were a funny lot, his brasses. They'd scratch another girl's eyes out if she so much as looked at one of their punters, but the minute one of them was injured, they stuck together like a pride of lionesses.

As a way of smoothing things over with them, he'd given the girls his word that he wouldn't allow Mickey anywhere near them again, and as he often stated to anyone who would listen, his word was his bond, unless there was some serious wedge at stake.

'Good job. It's a bit busy today then, ain't it?' He turned back to look at the man, his tone becoming serious. 'You ever seen a samurai sword?'

'Yeah, once or twice.' Eric narrowed his eyes, not sure where Mickey was going with the conversation.

'Bet you ain't ever seen one like this though.' He pulled the ornate sword out from underneath his coat and held it outwards. Sunlight streamed through the windows and bounced off the single-edged, jewel steel sword, causing reflections to dance around the room. 'This beauty can slice through bone like a hot knife through butter.'

'I don't doubt that for a second.' Eric gave him a wide smile, showing crooked nicotine-stained teeth. He puffed again on his cigar. 'So, what is it I can do for you, Mickey? I take it you didn't come all this way just to show me your new toy?'

'Toy?' Mickey's eyes flashed dangerously. 'Fucking toy?'

'I meant your new blade.' Eric put out his hand to placate the man.

'It's a sword.'

'That's what I meant.' He nodded across to the weapon. 'Sword, blade, they're all the same to me, and let's face it, no matter what fancy name you wanna give it, they can still cause a person some serious damage.'

'Suppose so.' Waving his hand in the air to clear the cigar smoke, Mickey sat forward. 'I'm looking for me cousin.'

Eric screwed his face up. 'Cousin? What fucking cousin?'

Unpredictable and paranoid at the best of times, Mickey jumped up from his seat and slammed the point of the sword towards Eric's stomach. 'My fucking cousin.'

Beads of cold sweat spread across Eric's forehead. 'All right, fucking hell. I was only asking which cousin you meant. I mean, you come from a big family, don't you, Mickey? It could be any one of your cousins on the missing list.'

'I'm talking about me cousin Albie, Albie Bannerman.' He eased the sword away from Eric's stomach and hovered over the man. The weapon remained poised in his fist, ready and waiting to strike out.

'How would I know where he is?' Eric stammered. 'That ain't my scene, Mickey, you know that.'

'Because you know everything that goes on in the Smoke.'

'Nah, Mickey. I'm small-time, you know that. I spend my days holed up here with the brasses, keeping me nose clean.'

Mickey laughed out loud. There was nothing small-time about Eric Porter. 'Get on the blower and make some calls. Find out where he is.'

Eric looked up helplessly. Who exactly was he meant to call?

'I said, get on the blower,' Mickey roared.

'All right, fucking hell, all right.' Picking up the telephone receiver, he tapped in a series of digits. Sweat poured out of him, and, using his other hand, with the cigar still clasped between his fingers, he dragged a handkerchief across his forehead. 'I tell you what, Mickey, why don't I give you a bell later on this afternoon, once I've got something concrete for you, at the very least a name.'

Thinking it over, Mickey nodded. In a round about way, it made sense. He couldn't do much holed up in Eric's brass house. 'It's a good job I like you, Eric.' He smiled.

In return, Eric gave a cautious smile and watched with bated breath as the man walked out of the office, whistling loudly as he did so. The very thought of being on the receiving end of Mickey Shank's temper, if he didn't like you, was enough to make him shudder.

5

All thanks to Eric Porter, George had the start of a blinding headache and he rubbed wearily at his temples. For the past twenty minutes, he'd listened to Eric screaming blue murder down the phone, demanding to know why he had sent a nutcase like Mickey Shank to see him. And even more importantly, how was he supposed to magic up information out of thin air, single-handed? He wasn't a miracle worker, he bitterly complained.

'Just phone around your contacts and find out what you can,' George growled down the phone. 'Between you and your cousin, you're bound to find out something.'

He ended the call and sat back in his seat. He wasn't a big fan of Eric, or his cousin, Dirty John, come to that. Still, if they managed to find out what he wanted to know, then he would give them both a very generous drink on Albie's safe return.

Even now, he couldn't rid himself of the niggling thought that Billy King was somehow involved. His hatred of the man was enough to make his blood boil; to send him into a frenzy of anger. He caught sight of his reflection in the glass windowpane of the drinks' cabinet. His bulging wide eyes made him look manic, crazy even. His thoughts turned to Mickey. Perhaps the apple hadn't fallen far from the tree after all.

* * *

On returning home from one of her shopping trips, Susan smiled. 'Thank you, Fletch.'

'No problem.' He returned her smile, jumped out of the car, and opened the rear passenger door for her.

Left standing on the driveway, he twirled the car key around his forefinger, watching as Susan sashayed her way towards the front door; it was a sight he could never tire of. Other than the Mercedes and his own car, the driveway was empty. Billy was obviously out.

'Fuck it,' he muttered to himself. Billy didn't care about her, not really, not as he should. All she was to him was a trophy wife, someone he could parade around when the mood took him, another object he viewed as belonging to him, his property. Without missing a beat, he chased after her.

Hearing footsteps behind her, a startled Susan spun around.

His cheeks were flushed pink as he strode across the marble hallway and looked his boss's wife in the eyes. 'What was the real reason you asked Billy to change drivers?'

'I...' Susan shook her head. 'There was no reason behind it,' she lied.

'Yes, there was.' He took a step closer. 'We both know Billy would never have pulled me out unless you asked him to, so why did you do that?'

'Like you said, I thought it would be a nice change from Joseph.' She placed her handbag on the hallway table, averting her eyes as she did so. 'I don't like him.' She gave a little shudder.

'There's something about the way he always watches me. He gives me the creeps.'

'You're lying.'

She made to walk away from him, and he grasped her wrist, pulling her back. She looked down at his hand still clasping her wrist and tried to pull it free. 'You've got some—'

'Front,' he interrupted. 'Yeah, we've already established that.'

Her heart began to beat faster, and, swallowing deeply, she glanced towards the front door; fear was etched across her face. 'Billy will be home soon.'

'No, he won't.' Fletch's gaze flicked towards the door. She was right. Billy could walk in at any moment.

'I think you should leave.'

'Is that what you want?' He jerked his head towards the door. 'You really want me to leave?'

She tugged at her arm and he reluctantly released her wrist. She had never looked more beautiful to him than she did right now. 'Answer the question: would you be happy if I left, and you never saw me again?' There was an urgency to his voice and his breath caught in the back of his throat as he willed her to answer.

Susan closed her eyes, brought her hand up to her face, and lifted her head. 'Please,' she begged of him, 'don't ask me to answer something like that.'

'Why not?' He took a step closer and searched her face; he needed to hear her say the words out loud, needed her to tell him that she wanted him as much as he wanted her. 'Just tell me the truth: would you be happy?'

She hesitated and gave a shake of her head; it was so slight that if he'd have blinked, he would have missed it.

He glanced again to the closed front door and inched closer to Susan. He was more than aware that he was skating on very thin ice, and that every fibre in his body told him to run away from this woman as fast as his size ten feet would allow him to, yet he was unable to stop himself; he wanted her more than he'd ever wanted anyone or anything else in his life. It wasn't only lust he felt – as time had gone on, he'd come to care for her. He'd never met anyone like her before; she had a gentle quality about her and reminded him of a tiny bird in a cage, albeit a golden cage. From what he'd gathered, hers was a loveless marriage. It wasn't love that kept her and Billy together but control; she belonged to him and he regarded her as he did his house or car. Even in her own home, he had his soldiers watching her every movement; he wouldn't even allow her the freedom to come and go as she pleased. Billy didn't respect her, and a part of him doubted that he ever had. Time and time again he'd watched his boss slip off to spend the night with a random woman. It broke his heart knowing that his Suzy, as he privately thought of her, was at home waiting for Billy, alone and too scared to go out or move without his specific say-so.

Susan had managed to crawl her way underneath his skin, and no matter how much he tried, and he really had tried, he just couldn't erase her from his mind. She made him want to look after her, made him want to take them both away from the life they were living and have a fresh start; a life where drugs and violence didn't belong, a place where they could live and be happy, a place where Billy didn't exist. The fact Billy would kill him if he ever found out how he felt wasn't enough to deter him; he couldn't stop, he couldn't bear the thought of not having her in his life and if that meant going up against his boss then he was prepared to do just that, even though deep down he knew he had no chance of winning. Billy was not only a lot stronger but also well connected; at the snap of his fingers, he could arrange a hit on Fletch, and his notoriety was enough to ensure it was carried out with no questions asked.

'Even with all this...' He glanced around him. 'Even with everything you have, I don't think you're happy.' He poked himself in the chest. 'In here, you're not happy, are you?'

She shook her head and looked down at her feet. 'It means nothing to me; the house, the cars, the money, none of it matters.'

'I know you better than you think I do.' He stepped forward, backing her up against the wall and forcing her to look up at him. His face was poised just inches away from hers. 'I know you even better than Billy does. I've watched you, studied you, and I know that he makes you feel nervous; you can't be yourself around him, you don't even smile when he's in the same room.' His thumb reached out to touch her throat, and he gently stroked the delicate skin there. 'Did you know that whenever you're nervous, your vein' – he moved his thumb to the side of her neck – 'it pulsates each time you swallow.'

Despite herself, Susan swallowed deeply, and the blood vessel at the side of her neck bobbed up and down, proving him right. The action caused him to lift his eyebrows and softly chuckle, as if to say, *See, I told you so.*

'I think you told Billy to switch drivers because you wanted me to do this.' He placed one hand on the wall above her head, lowered his face to meet hers, and brushed his lips across her cheek.

She didn't push him away or slap his face for being so forward, and right there and then, his heart skipped a beat and elation coursed through his body. He'd been right all along; she wanted this to happen, just as much as he did. Maintaining eye contact, his breathing became noticeably heavier, and he licked his tongue across his bottom lip.

'Tell me it's what you want,' he said, his voice deep and husky.

Susan gave a slight nod of her head.

'Tell me,' he urged her. 'I need to hear you say it.'

'Yes.' Her voice came out as a whisper. 'It's what I want.'

He swooped in for a kiss, relishing the taste of her. The scent of her perfume filled his nostrils, and, clutching his hands in her hair, he pulled her body even closer.

Coming to her senses, a flush of heat spread across Susan's skin. She pulled herself free and shook her head. 'We can't, Billy will—'

He placed his finger against her plump lips, silencing her. 'Don't worry about Billy; he's never going to find out.'

* * *

From the corner of her eye, Jenny Fletcher studied her eldest son. She noted the big grin on his face and smiled; it was good to see him looking so happy.

'Mum, could you iron this for me, please?'

He handed across his favourite shirt and she lifted her eyebrows. 'Who are you getting yourself spruced up for?'

'No one.' He gave her a coy look and slung his arm around her shoulders, kissing the top of her head.

'You can't fool me,' she laughed, opening out the ironing board. 'I could smell you coming down the stairs, you've splashed on that much aftershave. Have you met someone?'

'No, of course I haven't.' His cheeks blushed a deep shade of pink, and he looked away. The blatant lie caused Jenny to laugh even harder.

'She must be special.' She indicated the shirt she had spread over the board and gave him a little wink. 'Well, whoever she is, I hope that she makes you happy. That's all I want for you, darling.'

'Mum, I'm going to work, that's it.'

'In your favourite shirt?'

'It's just a shirt, nothing special.' He rolled his eyes and turned to walk out of the room. No matter how hard he tried to hide the truth from her, he knew his old mum would be able to suss him out. She had a knack for doing just that. 'I'm just going to work,' he muttered.

Pursing her lips, Jenny nodded and set to ironing out the creases. As her son left the kitchen, she gave a little chuckle. 'Just going to work. Pull the other one.' She grinned. 'It's got bells on.'

Susan was already waiting on the doorstep when Fletch pulled on to the driveway. Her cheeks were flushed, and she gave him a broad smile.

'I'm not late, am I?' he asked, jumping out of the car.

'No, of course you're not.' She watched as he moved towards her and her heart skipped a beat. She loved his smile; it lit up his entire face and had been one of the first things she had noticed about him.

'Where's Billy?' He looked around for Billy's Jag.

'Out, all day apparently.' She gave him a coy grin and reached out for his hand; his touch made her body tingle, and she ran her finger over the small scar on his thumb. 'He said that he won't be back for hours.'

Lifting his eyebrows, Fletch matched her smile. 'So, we've got the place to ourselves then?'

She could hear the longing in his voice and, nodding, she couldn't help but giggle.

'I take it you don't want to go shopping today?'

'No, not today.' She shook her head and pulled him into the house. After today, everything would change between them; they could never go back to how they were before, not that she ever wanted to. She'd never felt more alive than she did when she was with him; she adored the way he laughed, his scent, even his cheeky banter. He was the whole package and every inch of her craved him like a drug; she had done so ever since Billy had introduced her to him at her birthday party.

He kicked the front door closed behind them and, glancing over her shoulder at the driveway, she eagerly led the way up the solid oak staircase. The fact they were playing an extremely dangerous game and that if her husband found out, he would kill them, was pushed to the back of her mind.

* * *

Hurtling down the A13 at breakneck speed, George Bannerman and his firm were on their way to Southend, in Essex. Out of thin air, Eric Porter had managed to magic up some information. An associate of his had been moonlighting as a doorman at a casino in the seaside town and could positively remember seeing Albie.

'This girl is gonna be earning her stripes tonight.' Mickey Shank could barely contain his excitement, and as he sat on the backseat, he hugged his sword towards him, with a maniacal grin. 'It can take a man's head clean off his shoulders. Glides through muscle and bone like a hot knife through butter.'

'Give it a fucking rest, Mickey,' George snapped. For the past twenty minutes, Shank had regaled them with stories about the damage he'd committed over the years.

'I was only saying…' The corners of Mickey's lips turned down.

'Yeah well, we get the fucking picture.'

Twenty minutes later, George screeched the car to a halt outside the Red Dice Casino and they all jumped out. Without taking even a moment to pause, he and his boys bounded into the venue and strode across the blue and red swirling carpet towards the reception desk.

'Jed Morris?' George barked at the receptionist.

She pointed her finger past the slot machines to where the poker room was situated at the back of the premises.

* * *

Jed Morris was built like a brick shithouse and had long, swinging dreadlocks that he kept tied off his face. Despite his fierce reputation on the street, he had a heart of gold.

He spotted the group of men striding across the casino and made his way towards them.

'Mr Bannerman?' He put out his hand. 'Eric told me to expect a visit from you.'

George nodded. He shook the outstretched hand and got straight down to business. 'You saw my brother in here?'

'That's right.' He walked across to where the roulette tables were. 'He spent the night here at this table.'

'Was he alone?'

'From what I could make out. He stayed until about four in the morning. He told me he'd had a good night.' He patted his back pocket. 'He left happy, if you get my meaning.'

'So, he was up on his luck?'

'Yeah.' Jed nodded. 'That was the impression he gave me.'

As he took in his surroundings, George thought this through. Could it simply be that Albie had been robbed of his winnings, and subsequently suffered a misfortune? 'And you're saying he was definitely alone? He didn't speak to anyone? No one was bothering him?'

Lifting his shoulders, Jed shook his head. Ever since his telephone call with Eric, he'd wracked his brain, going over and over that night in his mind, trying to recall if he'd missed something, if anything had seemed amiss. 'I'm pretty certain he was alone, but I can't tell you if he spoke to anyone or not. It was a busy night. We had to throw a rowdy stag party out. You know the type. Jumped-up pricks who've had too much to drink and think they own the gaff.'

'Yeah,' George sighed. It was beginning to look like a wasted journey after all. He rubbed at his temple. 'If you think of anything else, no matter how small or insignificant it might seem, let me know.'

'I will do, Mr Bannerman.' He shook George's hand once more and watched the men leave.

* * *

They walked back out on to the street. As always, the area was busy. Day trippers strolled the promenade, eating ice creams and candy floss. The scent of burgers and onions frying wafted towards them, and in the distance, George could hear children playing on the beach. Their squeals of delight as they paddled in the sea was suddenly loud to his ears, depressing him.

'Well, that was a waste of time,' Mickey sulked. He'd had visions of taking a swipe at anyone who dared look at him the wrong way. 'I reckon we should go back in there and slice that bastard up.'

'For what reason?' George barked. He'd known all along it was a bad move bringing Mickey along for the ride.

'I don't like the look of him. The wanker knows more than he's letting on.'

'Get in the motor, Mickey.' Losing patience, George blew out his cheeks. He took note of the madness in his cousin's eyes and took a step forward, his voice low, dangerous. 'I said, get in the fucking motor.'

Mickey swallowed deeply, and, without saying another word, he did as he was told and climbed into the car. The tone in George's voice instantly transported him back in time, to an occasion when he had been just sixteen years old, and his alcoholic, waste-of-space mother and her deadbeat lover had been brutally murdered.

He licked at his dry lips and squeezed his eyes shut tight in a bid to push the sickening images away from his mind. As he gripped on to the door handle, flashes of George and Albie standing over the mutilated bodies swirled around his head. He swallowed down a mouthful of bile.

'Get in the motor,' George had roared, as between them they had pulled him shaking and crying away from the murder scene. Even then, even at such a young age, he'd known better than to argue back. You didn't argue with the Bannermans, even though, by rights, it should have been him calling the shots. After all, he had been the one wielding the bloodied knife that fateful day.

Slipping on to the driver's seat, George started the engine. With one final glance at the casino, he drove the car forward. Just moments later, he slammed his foot on the brake, causing the occupants to throw their hands out in front of them to save themselves.

'What the fuck?' they complained.

'It's Albie's motor.' He threw open the car door and jumped out, making the car behind swerve across the road to narrowly avoid hitting him. 'It's Albie's motor,' he repeated.

Following suit, George's firm climbed out. 'Are you sure?'

'Of course I'm fucking sure.' He looked the car over with a critical eye. There was no physical damage, no tell-tale signs that anything untoward had taken place. He was getting closer to finding his brother, he knew he was.

* * *

By the time Billy returned home, Fletch was sitting inside his car, exactly where Billy expected to find him. He rolled down the driver's window and gave his boss a wide smile, hiding the fact that he had just spent the entire morning in bed with his wife, doing the unthinkable.

'You all right?' Billy strolled across the driveway and leant his hand on the roof of the car.

'Yeah, I'm good.' Shame rippled through Fletch and he rubbed his hand across his face, hoping that Billy wouldn't notice his flushed cheeks or rumpled hair that he'd spent over ten minutes trying to flatten down.

'Any dates yet for the next rave?'

'Nah.' Fletch shook his head. 'It's gotta be soon, though. We're gonna need to be ready to rock and roll as soon as I hear anything.'

'Yeah.' Billy was thoughtful. 'Organise a meeting pronto. Everything needs to be put in place.' He began to move towards the house, then, stopping abruptly, he turned around and stormed back to Fletch's car.

It was so sudden that prickles of fear ran down the length of Fletch's spine, and he braced himself for Billy to drag him through the open window and pummel his fist into his face. He flicked a glance up at the rear-view mirror; guilt was written all over his face. Billy knew, he had to. The violation of trust he'd committed radiated off him in waves and if he knew one thing, it was the fact that Billy wasn't stupid; he had a nose like a bloodhound – it was what had kept him at the top of his game for so long.

'What about Spencer?'

'What about him?' Even as his body relaxed, the unexpected question was enough to make Fletch's forehead furrow.

'Does he know to keep his mouth shut about Bannerman?'

'Yeah, of course he does.'

'You've put the hard word on him?'

'Yeah.' Swallowing deeply, Fletch nodded. He'd mentioned it in passing; that had been the extent of him putting the hard word on his brother. As of late his mind had been elsewhere, namely on Billy's wife. Suzy was like an obsession to him, and in a short space of time she'd become his everything; he thought about her day and night and lived for the moments they could spend together.

'Good.' There was a steely glint in Billy's eyes and his tone became threatening. Spencer Fletcher was the weakest link, as far as he was concerned. 'Make sure he knows to keep schtum.'

'I will do.' Reminded that Billy was an extremely dangerous individual, Fletch bowed his head. He would need to have a serious word with his brother and remind him to keep his trap shut, for both of their sakes.

* * *

'I know. You keep on telling me.' Sitting at the kitchen table, Spencer rolled his eyes.

'It ain't a game, Spence. You killed a man, and not just any man, it was Albie fucking Bannerman.'

'I know,' Spencer shouted back. 'I know all of this, Fletch. Why do you keep having a go at me and banging on and on about it?'

Fletch averted his eyes. He could hardly tell his brother the truth... that his life was at risk if he opened his mouth and let slip what he and Billy had done to the youngest of the Bannerman brothers.

'I'm just worried, that's all, and I'm not having a go at you, Spence.' He lowered his voice and sat forward in his seat, watching from the corner of his eye as his mum entered the kitchen. 'I just want to make sure that you're clear on the situation, and that you remember to keep schtum.'

'What are you having a go at him for?' Jenny eyed her two sons suspiciously.

'I'm not,' Fletch groaned.

'Well then, leave him alone.' She gave her youngest son a wide smile and patted his arm. 'Where's your uncle anyway?'

'Where he always is,' Fletch snapped. 'Down the fucking pub.' He scraped back his chair, stood up, and took in his mother's startled expression. 'I'm sorry, Mum. I didn't mean for it to come out like that,' he said, giving her a half smile.

The truth was, as much as he'd needed to put the hard word on his brother, it was himself he was also worried for. Billy would kill him if he ever found out about him and Susan. There must be something wrong with him, he decided, he must have a death wish. He pondered this over. The problem was, if everything did go tits up, if Billy did find out about what he'd done, then there would be no one to back him up, no one to help fight his corner. Of course, he knew he could count on Stevie – even Spencer to a certain degree, not that he would want him involved – but as for Frank, well, his uncle was about as much use as a glass hammer. Besides, they would have to prise him out of the pub first.

'It's okay, son.' She watched as he walked from the kitchen and turned to look at her youngest boy. 'What's up with him?'

'I dunno.' Spencer shrugged his shoulders. 'Had a right go at me, he did.'

'Did he now?' Jenny was thoughtful. She'd bet her life on it that her eldest son was having girl trouble. 'You leave him to me.' She winked. 'I won't have anyone upset my baby. How about some chocolate cake?' she asked.

Spencer grinned happily. Already, the conversation he'd had with his brother was gone from his mind.

* * *

It was early evening by the time Fletch, Spencer and Stevie made their way back towards Billy's house.

The dining room was standing room only, and as they pushed their backs against the wall, Billy looked up, in acknowledgement of their arrival.

'We're gonna rob a venue, one of them raves,' Billy told his men. 'We're gonna take over the doors and take a cut from every pill that's being sold.' He put his hand out towards Fletch. 'Fill 'em in.'

Taking a step forward, Fletch spoke. 'These raves are raking in the cash. Now, we won't know until the actual day, when or where they will take place. So, we need to be ready to roll as soon as I get the information.'

Joseph leant back in his chair; across his face was a scowl. When the fuck had all of this been planned out? He chewed on the inside of his cheek, glaring at Fletch, the oh-so-fucking-fabulous golden bollocks. Once again, he had been pushed out of the loop, and as a result, he was livid.

'Would have been nice to have been told beforehand,' he growled.

'You're being told now,' Billy snapped back. 'Carry on.' He waved his hand in the air.

'So,' Fletch continued, 'we're gonna need to be tooled up, just to put our point across. These kids are fuck all anyway, but should they start getting lairy, an iron bar to the face should do the trick.'

At this, Billy nodded. 'All you need to do is wait for our instruction as to when and where you go.'

'Yeah,' Fletch added. 'Everything is organised by word of mouth, and directions are usually left in various public telephone boxes. All we have to do is keep following them until we get to the venue. It's simple really.'

'Sounds pointless to me,' Joseph grumbled. He looked around the room and locked eyes with Keith, knowing for a fact that the man would see his point. 'I mean, robbing a kids' party, for fuck's sake. We're hardly gonna come out rolling in dough, are we?' he sniggered.

Fletch laughed out loud. 'It's a bit more than a kids' party. Think of it as a nightclub, only put on illegally.'

'Still,' Joseph protested, 'I can't see us making any profit doing this.' The truth was, he just didn't like the fact that it had been organised behind his back, and more to the point, he didn't like the fact that it had been organised by Fletch.

'That's where you're wrong.' Billy sat forward in the chair. 'They're raking in thousands of pounds each week, and seeing as it's on my manor' – he spread out his arms – 'that means I'm owed a cut of whatever they take.'

Still, Joseph was unsure. He tugged at his brown hair, thinking the situation through. 'And who supplies these pills? Who's putting the money up front for them?'

Lounging back in his chair, Billy flashed him a wide grin. 'I'll give you two guesses.'

There and then, Joseph felt his heart sink and his bowels loosen. 'Bannerman,' he offered.

'You've got it, and from now on, everything will be going through me.' He lifted his eyebrows slightly. 'Bannerman, the lanky streak of piss, can go and take a running jump. Who the fuck does he think he is, having the audacity to peddle on my patch?'

* * *

Darkness had descended as they travelled down the country lanes in a convoy towards the latest rave that was taking place. Just as Fletch had predicted at the meeting the previous evening, directions had been left in public telephone boxes, instructing the ravers where to go.

Leading the way, Fletch drove Billy, Stevie and Spencer in his car. He turned the car on to a private road. Up ahead was an abandoned warehouse. Lit up like Battersea Power Station, the soon-to-be demolished building was a death trap.

The upper levels were no longer accessible, and the leaking roof, previously robbed of all its lead, was in serious need of repair, not that it made much of a difference to the partygoers, who made their way inside the venue amidst a heady strum of music blaring out.

He pulled the car over and switched off the engine. 'See them,' Fletch said as he nodded towards two young men standing at the entrance doors. 'They organise the raves. Now, I've checked them out and they are fuck all for us to worry about. Public school kids with mockney accents, and too much dough to flash around. You know the type, born with silver spoons in their mouths, thinking they can make a quick buck.'

At this, Billy raised his eyebrows. 'Not on my manor, they

fucking can't.' He continued watching them. For all intents and purposes, the situation was turning out to be even easier than he'd imagined. He climbed out of the car; in his hand he held an iron bar. 'And what about the heavies? How many do you reckon are in there?'

Sucking his teeth, Fletch looked around him as he waited for the rest of Billy's firm to get out of their cars. 'Ten, tops. We can easily take them; it'll be a piece of piss.'

Billy didn't doubt that for a second. He waited for his men to regroup, flicked his cigarette butt to the ground, then swaggered forward. He clasped his fingers tightly around the iron bar, eager to get stuck in, and even more eager to take what he was owed.

* * *

Edward Johnson didn't have a care in the world. You name it, he had it – a gleaming, brand new Porsche with private number plates, a penthouse apartment that he was renting in Mayfair, a series of beautiful women draping themselves all over him, and enough cash in his back pocket to ensure that he maintained his lavish lifestyle. He was fast on his way to making his first million, and it was safe to say that life was better than good – life was fantastic.

With dirty blond hair tied back into a low ponytail, he was a good-looking man. Dressed in a pair of denim jeans and a faded acid house T-shirt, he blended into the crowd, masking his public school roots. Standing on the doors to the warehouse, he was mentally calculating how much money he and his business partner, Michael Adams had made that night, when he felt Michael nudge him with his elbow. He turned his head to glance over his shoulder, and for a moment, the hairs on the back of his neck stood up on end.

As a promoter, he had known from day one that putting on the illegal raves would come with a huge risk. The risk being that not only could they be closed down if the Old Bill caught up with them, but even more worryingly, he could end up being carted off for a night in the cells, and then prison, in that order. The very thought was enough to bring him out in a cold sweat. Still, the lure of wealth, flashy cars and stunning women hanging off his arm was too much of an opportunity for him to miss out on.

He studied the group of men as they approached. They didn't look like Old Bill as he'd first thought, and his body relaxed slightly.

'Evening, fellas.' He spoke with a mockney accent, disguising his clipped tones.

The situation escalated so quickly that Edward didn't even have time to think, let alone react. Edward and Michael's arms were pinned to their sides and an iron bar was waved in front of their faces.

'You're on my manor,' a gruff voice growled.

Edward took a step back, blinking rapidly. 'I…' he stammered.

'Don't start stuttering and fucking muttering,' Billy growled. 'You're on my fucking turf, and now you owe me, big time.'

Hoping and praying that backup would promptly arrive to sort these thugs out, Edward turned on the charm and flashed a wide smile, showing perfect white teeth that had cost his parents thousands of pounds in dentistry fees.

'Come on, fellas, there's no need to be like this, is there?' He opened out his hands. 'It's all about the love nowadays, lads.'

'Is this prick for real?' Billy turned his head to look at Fletch. 'You're on my fucking patch,' he roared.

The wrought iron bar that hit Edward full on in the face broke his nose, and as he staggered backwards, blood exploded from his nostrils. He began to scream.

'My nose!' Gone was the mockney accent, and in its place, the clipped tones he spoke with were thick and nasally. 'You've broken my nose.'

As quick as a flash, Billy lifted the iron bar and swung it forward a second time, this time landing against Edward's full, fleshy lips. A loud crack could be heard as the teeth Edward was so proud of snapped and splintered, before crumbling to pieces.

Amidst Edward's screams for help, Billy stepped closer. 'That's just for starters. Pay up before I do you some serious fucking damage, starting with your kneecaps.'

* * *

Fletch glanced inside the venue, fully expecting George Bannerman's heavies to rush outside and intervene. He flicked his head towards his brother and Stevie.

'Take the dough; take the fucking lot.'

Under his watchful eye, they shoved handfuls of cash into several carrier bags.

'Where are the pills?' he asked.

Unable to focus on anything other than the pain coming from his broken nose and shattered teeth, Edward swung his head to the right.

'I don't deal with the pills,' he lisped, his eyes barely focusing, as blood poured from his face.

At this, Fletch laughed. 'Don't give me that old bollocks.' He turned to look at Edward's business partner, so far unscathed by Billy's wrath. 'Where are the pills? And don't even think about trying to mug me off.'

Without hesitating, Michael pointed his finger inside the venue. Unlike his friend Edward, he was rather attached to his face the way it was, thank you very much.

'See, it's not so hard, is it?' He watched Billy slam his fist forward and felt neither pity nor remorse. They had given the man ample opportunity to tell them where the merchandise was, and he, like the stupid fool he was, had chosen not to do so.

'So,' Billy said, 'from now on, we take a percentage of whatever you earn.' He gave a small grin. 'Think of it as a partnership.'

Edward dutifully nodded. Even he could see that he had no other choice but to agree to whatever it was they wanted. His life was depending on it.

Fletch jerked his head to the side, indicating for Billy's firm to follow him inside the venue. 'You three stay there,' he instructed Keith, Stevie and Spencer. 'And if that posh twat starts getting lairy, lamp him one.'

Ever since Albie's disappearance, Pete Wilson had stepped up as George Bannerman's number two, a role that he took very seriously. It was nearing one in the morning, and he swung his car on to the private road. Up ahead was the warehouse, and his intention was to collect the cash they had made from the Ecstasy tablets, and then pass it across to his boss later that morning, after he'd had a few hours kip and a decent cooked breakfast.

He parked the car, climbed out and made his way towards the building. As he neared, he took in Edward's obvious facial injuries and narrowed his eyes.

'What's gone on here?' he asked, his voice raised so he could be heard above the blaring music.

Slumped on a chair, Edward's battered and blood-smeared face was held between his hands, and he gave frightened sobs between each painful breath that he took.

'He needs an ambulance,' Michael exclaimed. He glared

towards the heavies, who had refused to help his friend in any way, shape, or form.

'No ambulances.' The last thing they needed was the Old Bill turning up to investigate what had gone on.

'But he needs medical attention,' Michael protested. He took his mobile phone from his jacket pocket and began to tap.

'I said, no fucking ambulances,' Pete roared.

He snatched the device out of the man's hand, dropped it to the floor, and then proceeded to stamp on it with his heavy boot. With his meaty fists clenched and poised, ready to attack, he took a menacing step closer.

'If you're that bothered about him, then drive him to the nearest hospital yourself, but I'm telling you now, if you even think about calling anyone, then you're gonna end up looking worse than he does. Do you get my drift? Do you understand what I'm saying?'

Michael's hands trembled and he nodded several times. He helped Edward up to his feet, all the while cursing the day he had involved himself with his friend's get-rich-quick scheme. The agreement they had had with George Bannerman had all been well and good whilst the money was rolling in, but now this was the upshot of working with known criminals. Not only was his friend scarred for life, but his own life was in danger to boot.

'I'll take him myself,' he said, his voice quivering. Quietly, he led Edward away. More than anything, he was thankful just to get away from the terrifying situation.

Watching the two men leave, Pete turned his attention back to the heavies. 'Now, will someone tell me what the fuck has gone on here?' He took in their shameful expressions and inwardly groaned. 'Where's the merchandise? Where's the dosh?' Even as he asked the question, he knew what the answer would be, and he felt his heart sink to his boots. 'Don't tell me it's gone?' he asked. Looking through the doors of the warehouse, a wave of panic swept over him.

The heavies mumbled 'yesses' and 'yeps'.

'What? All of it?' Pete roared.

Again, they muttered confirmation. 'It was King and his firm. We didn't stand a chance against them,' they protested. 'They turned up mob-handed. What could we have done to stop them?'

Jabbing his finger forward, fury rippled through him, and he breathed heavily through his flared nostrils. 'Mob-handed?' he spat. 'Are you gonna be the one to tell Bannerman that, eh?'

Their silence told him everything he needed to know. George Bannerman wasn't the type of man to be crossed, and it would be fair to say that he was going to go mental when he found out that not only the cash, but the Es he had stumped up a small fortune to pay for were gone. 'He's gonna go apeshit,' Pete yelled as he stormed back to his car. 'Fucking apeshit.'

* * *

There was at least thirty thousand pounds in used notes spread across Billy's dining table, and several large polythene bags filled to the brim with tiny white pills.

He placed the money into piles and handed them out amongst his firm. 'A good night's work, eh, lads?' He grinned. Turning to look at Fletch, his grin grew wider. 'This is your cut, mate.' He held out a large carrier bag stuffed with used notes. 'Who said that crime doesn't pay, eh?' he chuckled.

Fletch's eyes lit up. Without even counting the money, he knew the final sum would run into the thousands.

'Here, and take these with you when you go. Put them in the safe house for me.' Billy lowered his voice as he passed across the bags containing the Ecstasy tablets. 'Make sure that they're stored safe and that no one can get their hands on them.'

'Yeah, I will do.'

Billy was thoughtful and, slinging his arm around Fletch's shoulders so he could speak privately in the younger man's ear, he lowered his voice. 'I'm gonna take off for a bit, just until the dust settles with Bannerman, and I suggest you do the same, mate.'

'Take off? Take off where?' Fletch raised his eyebrows.

'The villa in Marbella. I've already got a flight booked; I head out early tomorrow morning.'

To say that Fletch was shocked was an understatement. His mouth fell open as he followed Billy out of the dining room. 'Where am I supposed to go?'

'I don't know.' He glanced down at the carrier bag. 'You've got enough dough there to splash out on a five-star hotel for a week or two. Think of it as a little holiday.' He gave a wink. 'A well-earned rest.'

'Holiday? But I don't even have a passport.'

At this, Billy laughed. 'Fuck me, you need to get with the times mate.'

'It ain't funny, Bill, where am I meant to go?'

'I dunno.' Billy made to walk away, unconcerned by his protégé's predicament.

Fletch swallowed deeply. 'And what about Mrs King? Will she be going with you?'

'Nah.' Billy shook his head. 'It's safer that she stays here. In fact, one of you lot can check up on her, make sure that she's okay.'

Fletch's heart leapt. There would be only one person checking up on his boss's wife, and that would be him. 'I'll do it. I'll stay behind and check that she is all right. I can make sure that there've been no comebacks or anything. I mean, it's not as though I can go anywhere else, is it?'

'Good man.' Billy slapped him on the back and grinned. 'I knew I could count on you.'

Returning the smile, Fletch averted his eyes. Even though he felt guilty, it wasn't enough to keep him away from Susan.

Pete Wilson's premonition could not have been more correct. George's fury was not only unnerving, but it was also downright scary. He had screamed, hollered, and roared for what felt like hours.

'I'll fucking kill him,' he spat. 'I'll tear his head clean off his fucking shoulders.'

Warily, Pete watched his boss pace up and down the length of the sitting room. More than once he had needed to duck down, in order to dodge the pieces of furniture that flew past his head. He was almost too afraid to speak. Gathering up the courage, he cleared his throat and tensed his body, waiting in anticipation for George's next outburst.

'So, what do we do now?'

'What do we do?' George spat back, his voice taking on an incredulous tone. 'What we always fucking do: you, you useless cunts fuck-up, and I, as per fucking usual, will try to salvage something from the situation.'

Pete swallowed deeply. 'So,' he asked, taking a step backwards in a bid to create a reasonable distance between them, 'do you have a plan?'

'Do I have a plan?' At this, George leapt forward and swung out his heavy fist, feeling nothing but satisfaction as his knuckles landed upon the side of Pete's jaw. 'A fucking plan?' he roared. 'What, so you useless pricks can fuck that up as well?'

'Sorry, George.' Lying in a crumpled heap on the floor, Pete was seeing stars.

Shaking out the tension in his hand, George desperately tried to think. What he wanted to do was take back his merchandise and then kill King, stone dead. Before he could do that, he needed to know of King's whereabouts, and there was only one man who could tell him that. He pulled Pete to his feet.

'Get out there now and find that no-good rat, Hatton. Drag him in here by his fucking hair if you have to,' he growled. 'If I find out he had a hand in any of this, I'm gonna muller the fucking life out of him.'

6

Reaching out her arm, Susan caressed Fletch's bare back, her fingertips tracing along the length of his spine.

He looked over his shoulder and gave her a warm smile. 'I have to leave soon, Suzy,' he said apologetically.

'Why?' She shuffled along the unmade bed and pressed herself closer to him. 'Billy won't be back from Marbella until early tomorrow morning. We've got hours to go yet.' She cocked her head to one side and seductively twirled a strand of blonde hair around her finger. 'Come back to bed,' she purred.

'I can't. I need to go and look for Spence. I need to check that he's okay.'

The corners of Susan's lips turned down and she lowered her head. It wasn't often that Billy went abroad without her, and if truth were told, she was dreading his return.

'Hey.' Running his thumb underneath her chin, Fletch tipped Susan's head up to meet his. 'I'm sorry, babe,' he sighed, 'it's just Spence, you know.'

'Why do you worry about him so much?'

He turned away, swallowing down the usual sense of guilt he felt.

'I know he's your younger brother, but he isn't a child any more, Fletch. He doesn't need you as much as you think he does—'

'It's more than that.' Fletch interrupted her, his tone a lot harsher than he'd intended. 'I owe him.'

'You owe him?' She pulled the crisp Egyptian cotton sheet around her and frowned. 'I don't understand. How do you owe him?'

'He's...' He paused, trying to find the right words. 'He needs me.' He ran his hand through his dark hair, feeling embarrassed. 'He's not quite right, is he?'

Susan gave him a sad smile. They all knew that Spencer wasn't quite right, or as her husband had not-so-kindly pointed out, Spencer Fletcher wasn't the full ticket. 'Two sandwiches short of a picnic' was his favourite put-down.

'He hasn't always been like this,' he said defensively.

'What do you mean?' Susan narrowed her eyes.

'It was me.' Fletch turned to face her and gave a small shrug of his shoulders. 'It was all my fault.'

'But how? I don't understand.'

He closed his eyes tight and swallowed deeply. 'When we were kids...' He stopped himself just in time, unsure if he was doing the right thing by baring his soul. He'd never told anyone the truth about Spencer before, not even Stevie. It had always remained an unspoken family secret but with Suzy he felt as though he could tell her anything. He didn't want there to be any secrets between them; he trusted her, and he knew she would never judge him. It wasn't in her nature; she looked for the good in people and accepted them as they were, faults and all.

'Go on.' Susan sensed him faltering. 'You wanted to say something,' she gently coaxed.

'When we were kids…' He turned away from her and rested his forearms on his knees, stalling for time. To this day, he still felt ashamed of himself for what he had caused, for what he had done to his brother. 'Our old man…' He paused, cleared the lump from his throat, and began again.

'When we were kids, our old man he used to have a bit of a temper on him, not that he ever really needed much of an excuse to knock us about. My mum would try to calm him down and put a stop to it, but being only five foot nothing, she didn't stand a chance against him. More often than not, we would wake up to find her crying in the kitchen with a blackened eye or a split lip. She'd tell us that she'd walked into the door, but we knew the truth. We'd hear them arguing. We'd hear the slaps and punches. One day, I must have been, I dunno, about seven, Spencer was five. I was being cocky, giving my dad some lip, backchatting him, that type of thing.'

He gave an embarrassed smile. 'He went to whack me one, only I was too fast for him and darted out of the way. He ended up missing me, but…' He looked away, his cheeks flushed, as shame ran through him. 'He caught Spence by mistake…'

He closed his eyes as he recalled the moment. All these years later, he could still hear the sickening thud as Spencer's head smacked against the corner of the kitchen cabinet.

'Spence ended up hitting his head. He dropped to the floor and was out cold for what felt like hours. It was probably only minutes in reality. My mum was screaming, I was screaming, and my dad… my dad, he was shaking Spence, trying to wake him up. There was claret all over the place. I thought he was dead. I really thought he was dead.'

Susan gasped and placed her hand across her mouth. Her

heart went out to him; she'd had no idea his childhood had been so bad.

'Finally, he did wake up, but...' He stared into the distance. 'He was never the same after that.' He shrugged and turned his head away. 'He was different, I suppose.' He shook his head at the memory. 'Even now, he finds it difficult to remember things. It was all my fault.' He turned his body back to face her, his eyes filled with regret. 'Don't you see? I made him the way he is. He has to live like this, all because of me.'

'No.' Susan was aghast. 'You were a child; you can't blame yourself.'

'But I do, though.' His shoulders hunched downwards. 'If I hadn't given my dad lip that day, then it would never have happened. I should have protected Spence better. It should have been me.'

'No.' Susan pulled him into her arms. 'It wasn't your fault,' she soothed.

Fletch shook his head. Despite her words, he would always blame himself. 'I should have taken the beating. If I'd have let my dad catch me, then Spence would have been okay.'

'And... this is the reason you live with Frank?'

'Yeah, good old Uncle Frank.' He gave a half smile and shook his head. 'More like out of the frying pan, and into the fire.' He pushed himself back slightly and studied her. Seeing as he was baring his soul, he may as well tell her everything. 'Fletch isn't even my real name.'

Susan's eyes widened.

'It's Harry,' he laughed. 'Once we'd left Dad, my uncle started calling me Fletch. It started out as a nickname and it's kind of stuck ever since.'

'Harry.' Susan softly repeated back the name. 'I like it.' She smiled. 'And what about your father?'

'What about him?' Fletch screwed his face up, full of hatred for the man.

Susan tilted her head to one side. 'What happened to him? Did he go to prison?'

'Nothing happened.' He shrugged, confused by the question. 'Mum left him, and he's stayed away from us ever since. I doubt he even knows where we are.'

'And you don't have any contact with him?'

He eased himself out of her arms, thankful for the dim lighting. The last thing he wanted to see was her pity. 'I have to go, Suze; I have to go and find Spence.'

'Okay,' she said as she watched him begin to dress. 'You're a good brother to him. He's lucky to have you.'

'Is he?' He turned to look at her and tapped two fingers against his temple. 'What I did, what I caused, it's in here, and it never goes away.' He gave her a weak smile, knelt on the bed, and kissed her on the lips, putting an end to the conversation. 'I have to go.'

'Will I still see you tomorrow night at Billy's homecoming party?'

Pausing at the bedroom door, Fletch nodded. Billy would expect him to be there, and the last thing they both needed was for Billy to start asking questions. 'You know you will.'

Left sitting alone on the bed, Susan sighed. She heard the front door close, heard his car speed away from the house, and slumped back against the plump pillows. No wonder he was so protective over his brother. There and then, her heart not only broke for him but also made her love him that little bit more.

* * *

From the safe distance of the lane, to the right of Billy King's driveway, Joseph Hatton was sitting inside his car. He reached up to touch his face, still swollen and bruised after George Bannerman had half-battered him to death, and felt nothing but anger towards his boss, and even more so, his protégé.

Even though he knew that Billy was supposed to be in Spain, on the off-chance, he had driven over to the house to see for himself if the man was, in fact, abroad. He couldn't help but wonder if it was all just another lie, another situation he had been left out of the loop of. For all he knew, Billy may never have even left England.

He studied the house, noting that it was in darkness and that Billy's car was in fact missing from the drive, an obvious indicator that he wasn't at home. He'd been about to turn the ignition when he saw the front door open. He pushed himself down, hidden out of sight, watching everything that went on through the gap between the two front seats.

A figure stepped over the doorstep. From his vantage point, Joseph narrowed his eyes. 'What the fuck?' he muttered to himself. Even though his car was absent, he'd fully expected to see Billy step outside the house.

He pushed himself down the seat even farther, watching as a car pulled out of the driveway and turned left on to the lane. He waited until he could no longer see the car's tail lights in the rear-view mirror, then shifted his position to look at the house.

Why the fuck was Fletch creeping out of Billy's house at this time of night? An upstairs light snapped on, and he sat contemplating what this could mean.

His mouth dropped open, and, after getting over his initial shock, he almost laughed out loud at this latest development. There could be no other explanation for it.

The wonderful protégé, Fletch, must be having it away with

Billy King's missus. He started the ignition. A wicked grin crept across his face, and he debated within himself whether or not he should inform George Bannerman of these latest developments. If he did, then it was bound to earn him a few extra brownie points, and God only knew how much he needed them.

* * *

The Royal Oak pub, in Barking, was where Fletch found his brother with his best friend. As he strolled into the public bar, just making it in time for last orders, he was smiling contentedly.

'Are you okay, bruv?' He slung his arm around Spencer's shoulders. A pang of guilt rippled through him. Ever since Susan had entered his life, he'd neglected his brother. Spencer usually followed him around like a lost puppy. There and then, he decided to make more time for him. 'I've been looking everywhere for you; why didn't you answer your phone?'

'I didn't hear anything,' Spencer groaned.

'They had a bloody singer on,' Stevie explained further. 'Fuck me, she was bad; my ears are still ringing.'

Fletch turned his head to watch the woman in question as she packed away her speakers and equipment.

'What are you having, Fletch?' Downing the remainder of his lager, Spencer placed the empty pint glass down on the bar top and pulled a twenty pound note from his jacket pocket.

Turning his head back from the singer, Fletch cast his eyes across the pumps. 'I'll have whatever you're having.'

'Where've you been, anyway?' Stevie regarded his friend over the rim of his pint glass. 'I thought you said you were coming out with us tonight?'

'Yeah, where've you been?' Spencer looked over his shoulder

as he waited in line to get served at the bar. Held aloft in his hand was the twenty pound note.

'Nowhere.' Fletch shrugged. He could barely keep the smile from his face.

Taking in the grin across his friend's face, Stevie narrowed his gaze. 'Come on, out with it,' he laughed. 'Where have you been?'

'I told you, nowhere.' He took the filled pint glass from his brother and swallowed a mouthful of the amber liquid down.

'Were you with that bird?' Stevie nudged his friend in the ribs.

'What bird?' As Fletch put on a puzzled look, panic filled him. Had he found out about him and Susan? 'What d'ya mean by that?' he demanded to know.

'You know, that one from the Two Puddings. The one who gave you her phone number last week? You know.' He brought his cupped hands up towards his chest. 'The one with the big tits.'

Relieved, Fletch shook his head. He was barely able to recall the girl's name and had promptly thrown away the scrap of paper with her telephone number scrawled across it. 'Nah. I've already told you, I'm not interested. I only went along with it so you could pull her mate.'

'So, where've you really been then?' Spencer asked.

He tapped the side of his nose and winked. 'Never you mind.' He downed his beer and turned his back on his brother and best friend.

'You're turning into a right touchy bastard,' Stevie complained. 'It ain't like you to be so cagey.'

'Leave it out,' Fletch groaned. 'I don't have to tell you two everything. I am entitled to have some privacy, you know.'

'Privacy, hark at him.'

'I reckon he's got some bird on the go.' Spencer gave a lopsided grin. 'What's her name again?' He tilted his head to one side as he tried to think. 'You're always talking about her.'

Stevie burst out laughing. 'Yeah, he's definitely got a bird. He was like this when he fancied Lisa Munford, back in school. He actually reckoned he was in with a chance with her.'

'I was in with a chance.'

'Yeah, you and everyone else.' Stevie winked.

Fletch couldn't help but laugh along with them, but his thoughts turned to Susan. The way he felt about her was no schoolboy crush, and there was certainly no denying the fact that he had fallen for her, hard. The smile slipped from his face and a looming image of Billy entered his mind. If Billy ever found out about it, he was a dead man walking.

'That's it, I remember now.' Spencer flashed them a wide grin, proud of himself for being able to recall the name. 'Her name's Suzy.'

As he choked on his drink, Fletch's blood ran cold. 'Nah,' he was quick to answer, 'I don't know anyone called Suzy.'

* * *

Stevie playfully punched his best friend on the arm. 'Fucking hell, Fletch,' he laughed. 'You have got it bad. Must be serious then, between you and this bird of yours?'

Fletch shrugged. It was the next morning, and they were standing outside a jeweller's in the Dagenham Heathway shopping centre.

'What do you reckon?' He jerked his head towards a heart-shaped golden locket with a matching gold chain displayed in the shop window.

'Yeah, it's nice.'

'Yeah, it is.' Fletch nodded. He wanted to buy Susan an early Christmas present and planned to give it to her on the quiet, at the joint Christmas and homecoming gathering Billy was putting on later that evening.

'Are you gonna buy it then or not?'

'Yeah.' Still standing outside the shop, Fletch continued to admire the necklace.

'Well, go on then.' Stevie rolled his eyes and pushed his friend forward. 'We ain't got all day...'

'All right.' Fletch made to enter the jeweller's. 'Wait here for me.'

Stevie rolled his eyes for a second time. He glanced down at his wristwatch and tapped it impatiently. 'Come on then, mate, get a move on, eh? I wanna go and get me barnet cut before we go out tonight.' He pointed to his dark hair. 'I'm starting to look like I've got a fucking busby stuck on me head.'

Despite only arriving back in England earlier that morning, Billy was on a mission. He was sitting in his car with Joseph beside him in the passenger seat. Lighting a cigarette, he leant forward over the steering wheel, not taking his eyes away from the breaker's yard in Crow Lane, Romford.

'What are we doing here, then?' Joseph glanced across to the yard, where scrapped cars were piled high on top of one another.

'Just some business I've got to take care of.' Remaining tight-lipped, Billy placed his hand on the door handle, ready and waiting to jump out.

'Surprised you ain't got Fletch with ya.' A sly expression creased Joseph's face.

'We're not joined at the fucking hip,' Billy snapped.

'I did wonder,' Joseph mumbled.

'What's that you said?'

'Nothing.' Joseph shook his head and shifted his weight in the confines of the cramped car.

'No, come on, out with it. If you've got something to say, then fucking say it.' He gave his one-time number two a sidelong glance. 'Well, come on, it ain't like you to be backwards in coming forwards.'

Joseph shifted uneasily again. What was the point in even saying anything? All thanks to Fletch, he'd been well and truly pushed out of the loop. He hadn't even been involved in the planning of the rave robberies. If he'd known, he could've at least given Bannerman the heads up on the situation.

'He's driving my Susan around anyway,' Billy stated. Not that he would have brought Fletch to the breaker's yard. He was a touchy little so-and-so at the best of times and seeing as this was the final resting place of Albie Bannerman, he had a feeling it wouldn't have gone down too well.

'Bet he's loving that.' The sly facial expression became a grin.

'What's that supposed to mean?' Flicking his cigarette butt out of the window, a vein at Billy's temple twitched. 'What the fuck do you mean by that?'

'Just that they seem to get on well.' Joseph shrugged.

'He treats her with respect.' Billy stabbed his finger forward. 'If he didn't, I'd break his fucking neck.'

Joseph raised his eyebrows. Respect, is that what they called it nowadays? Fletch was definitely slipping King's missus one. Where was the respect in that? He was about to voice his opinion when he snapped his mouth closed. He'd already said too much, and planted a seed of suspicion in Billy's mind, not to mention he still hadn't, yet, decided whether or not he should inform George Bannerman of these latest developments. The car engine purred to life and he glanced across to his boss.

'Thought you were going in to the yard?'

'Nah, it can wait,' Billy growled. He flicked the indicator and pulled out into the road. Joseph's words were ringing in his ears. A sense of jealousy rippled through him. There and then, he decided to keep a closer eye on his wife and protégé.

* * *

Resembling a Santa's grotto, Billy King's mansion was decked out with a seven-foot Christmas tree, expensive garlands and glass baubles. Fletch had never seen anything quite like it before; it put his uncle's lounge, with paper chains strung up on the ceiling with peeling Sellotape, the three-foot artificial Christmas tree, multi-coloured lights, plastic baubles and tattered tinsel, to shame.

In the kitchen, he gave Susan a wide smile. As he watched her pouring out drinks into crystal glasses, he could hear his uncle's booming voice cracking jokes in the lounge.

'I've got something for you,' he said quietly.

Susan placed the brandy bottle down on the kitchen counter and turned around.

'What is it?' She smiled.

'This.' Stealing a glance towards the kitchen door, Fletch delved his hand inside the pocket of his jeans and pulled out the gold locket.

'For me?' Susan gasped.

'Yes, for you. Who else would I buy it for, eh?' He gave her a little wink and indicated for her to turn around. Checking that the coast was clear, first he pushed her hair to one side and brushed his fingertips across her skin as he secured the safety clasp in place at the nape of her neck.

'It's beautiful.' Susan looked down at the locket. 'Thank you.'

She stood on tiptoes to kiss his cheek, and he caught hold of her hand.

'When can I see you again?'

'You're seeing me now.' There was a twinkle in Susan's eyes, and she cocked her head to one side to look up at him. 'And you'll see me tomorrow when you come to collect me so I can go Christmas shopping.'

'You know what I mean, Suze. I hate all this creeping around; I want to be with you all the time, I want you to be mine.' He swooped in for a kiss and held her to him. 'When can I see you?' he whispered in her ear.

'Soon.' She smiled, breathing him in and savouring the familiar scent of his cologne. 'I promise.'

Taking a sip from his bottled beer, Stevie kept a surreptitious eye on the lounge door. What was taking Fletch and Susan so long? He turned to look at Billy. He was engrossed in a conversation, oblivious to where they both were, and tore his eyes back to the door. It didn't take this long to pour a few drinks, surely? He was in half a mind to take a wander into the kitchen and see for himself what the hold-up was, when Billy called out, 'What's keeping those drinks?'

'Yeah, come on, we're dying from thirst in here,' Frank shouted.

Stevie hastily averted his eyes and looked to the floor, wishing more than anything that Frank would shut up. He had a horrible feeling he just couldn't shrug off, and the last thing he wanted was for Billy to take it upon himself to see what was taking his wife so long.

He looked up as the lounge door opened, saw their flushed

faces as they entered the room, saw the gold chain hanging from around Susan's neck – the very same gold chain Fletch had bought just that morning – and inwardly groaned. What the fuck was his best mate playing at?

'What kept you two so long?' Holding out his hand for the glass, Billy eyed his wife suspiciously. Still, Joseph's words rattled around inside his mind, and he swallowed down ripples of mistrust and jealousy.

'Nothing.' Susan gave her husband a wide smile. As he lowered his eyes to take a sip of his drink, she quickly slipped the locket inside the neckline of her dress, hidden out of sight.

'We were just chatting about Christmas, that's all.' Fletch glanced towards Susan.

'Yeah, well, next time, less of the fucking chat.'

'Whatever you say, Boss.' He gave Billy a smile, then moved across the lounge to sit on the sofa. 'You okay, mate?' He slapped Stevie on the shoulder, and without waiting for a reply, he turned his head to watch Susan as she moved around the room handing out drinks. Unable to tear his gaze away from her; a lustful glint in his eyes.

'Yeah.' Looking at his mate, Stevie swallowed down his anger. He couldn't believe that Fletch would be so stupid, so careless. After all, this wasn't just any woman. It was Billy King's missus. He continued to seethe as Fletch sat beside him. His best mate couldn't be more blatant even if he tried.

* * *

At the end of the night, Susan and Billy stood on the doorstep, watching Fletch, Stevie and Spencer leave.

'Are you sure you don't wanna call a taxi from here?'

'Nah.' Spinning round, Fletch grinned. 'We'll order one from the village. Need to walk off all of those mince pies.'

'They're good lads.' Billy chuckled, leaning against the door frame.

Silently, Susan nodded. Automatically, her fingers reached up to touch the gold locket Fletch had given her. It may not have cost the earth, but it was the most precious piece of jewellery that she had ever received.

Straightening up, he slung his arm around his wife's shoulders and pulled her forcefully towards him. 'Yeah, they're good lads,' he repeated, his tone becoming serious. 'But if I ever catch one of them sniffing around you, I'll cut their fucking bollocks off. You belong to me, remember that. I own you... lock, stock, and fucking barrel.' He gave her a chilling smile, kissed the top of her head, then returned to the lounge.

Left standing on the doorstep, Susan turned to look at her husband's retreating form. Was he suspicious of them? she wondered. The hairs on the back of her neck stood up on end and, glancing once more towards the driveway, her body shuddered.

Billy would never let her go; she knew that as well as she knew her own name. He would rather see her dead than see her happy with another man. There and then, she knew what she had to do.

As much as it was going to break her heart, she needed to end the affair. Tears filled her eyes and she swiped them away with her fingertips. She would have to tell Fletch it was over between them. She had no other choice on the matter. It was either that, or a certain death for them both.

* * *

'What the fuck are you playing at?' The three men had reached the halfway point of the lane, and, stopping abruptly, Stevie hissed out the words.

'What?'

'You know what. You and King's missus. I saw it. I saw the fucking necklace.'

Fletch's breath caught in the back of his throat. He bounded across the pavement, slammed his best friend up against a hedgerow, and clasped the front of his shirt in his fist. His breath streamed out in front of him. 'You don't know fucking anything.'

'I saw it.' With ease, Stevie pushed Fletch away from him and breathed heavily through his nostrils. 'Are you on a death wish or something?' He tapped the side of his head. 'Have you got a screw loose, eh?'

'What's going on?' Spencer looked from his brother to Stevie.

'Keep out of it, Spence,' Fletch growled, looking over his shoulder.

'What was it you said?' He jerked his head in Spencer's direction. 'You don't know anyone called Suzy. You're a fucking liar!'

Shame flooded through Fletch and, dragging his hands through his hair, he looked away.

'If I've sussed it out, then how long before Billy does the same, eh?' Stevie spat.

'Sussed what out?' Spencer asked, his eyes wide.

'I told you to keep out of it, Spence,' Fletch roared, pushing his brother across the pavement and away from him.

'Look at you, like a rabbit caught in headlights. No wonder you didn't want to tell us who she is. You're too scared your dirty little secret is gonna come out.'

'Billy doesn't deserve her, he ain't good enough, he can't give her what she needs. In here' – he laid his palm against his chest – 'he doesn't love her, he never has.'

Stevie gave a bitter laugh. 'And what, you do, I suppose? He's gonna find out, you know that, don't you? And then what, eh? I'll tell you what: you're gonna end up with a bullet in the back of your nut.'

Beads of cold sweat broke out across Fletch's forehead. 'Don't say anything, please, mate, don't say a word.' He held up his hands. 'If he finds out, Billy will kill us; you know he will.'

'Why will Billy kill us?' Narrowing his eyes, Spencer looked from his brother to Stevie once more. He tilted his head to one side as he thought it over. 'Why would he kill us? What have we done wrong?'

'Not you,' Fletch snapped, looking over his shoulder. 'Me.' He lowered his voice. 'He's gonna kill me.'

'But why? What have you done, Fletch?'

'Nothing. It doesn't matter, just forget I even said anything.' He turned back towards Stevie; his eyes beseeched him. 'Please, mate, don't say anything. I'm begging you not to... please.'

Stevie gave a long, dejected sigh. 'I'm not gonna say anything. You're my best mate. Do you really think I would do that?'

Visibly relaxing, Fletch's shoulders sagged with relief and he shook his head. Of course Stevie wouldn't say anything. He should have already known that; they were more like brothers than mates and had always had each other's backs in the past.

'You're playing a dangerous game, though, Fletch. It's gotta stop, you know that, don't you? You and her... it's gotta stop.'

'I can't.' Fletch spread open his arms and gave a half smile. 'I love her, I don't want anyone else, I can't let her go, she's my world, my whole life.' He shoved his hands into the pockets of his jacket and resumed the long walk down the lane.

'You ain't gonna have a life,' Stevie called after him. 'You're gonna get yourself killed. You're gonna get all three of us killed, and for what? Because you couldn't keep your dick in your trousers?'

Fletch spun around. 'It's not like that. Suzy's not like that; she would never have done this if she didn't love me.'

Stevie took Fletch by the shoulders. 'Get rid of her, Fletch, for our sakes as well as yours.'

'I've already told you, I can't, I love her too much to give her up.' He gave a half smile and turned his back on his best friend. The truth was, he was in too deep, far too deep. No woman had ever been able to keep his interest like Susan King had. For the first time in his life, he was in love.

7

After a long, sleepless night, a deep-rooted fear resonated through Susan. She had spent the morning crying, and, as a result, her eyes were red-rimmed and puffy, and her cheeks were blotchy. She couldn't bear to let Fletch go, but even she could see there was no other alternative, not unless she wanted to see him seriously maimed at Billy's hands, or even worse, dead. The very thought of what Billy would do to them if he ever found out about the affair made her feel physically sick, and her body shake with fright.

She heard his car pull on to the drive, and, walking out to the hallway, she paused in front of the ornate gilded mirror that hung there. Wiping away smudges of mascara from underneath her eyes, she hastily smoothed down her hair and made her way wearily towards the front door, thankful at least that her husband was out for the morning, and that he was unable to see her looking and feeling so heartbroken.

With a half-smile, she pulled open the door, took one look at her lover's face and promptly burst into tears.

'Hey, what's all this?' Fletch pushed his way into the house and kicked the front door forcibly closed behind him. 'What's happened?'

He braced himself for her reply. If someone had hurt her, he would kill them, stone dead. Without even giving the matter a second thought, he would smash his fists repeatedly into the bastard's face and happily go to prison for the remainder of his life.

Susan shook her head, the lump in her throat restricting her from speaking.

'What's wrong?' Fear was beginning to get the better of him, and as he pulled her into his arms, his voice rose. 'What's happened? Has someone upset you? Has someone hurt you?'

She wrestled herself free from his embrace. 'It's us,' she choked out.

'Us?' Her answer surprised him, and as his forehead furrowed, a new shiver of fear ran down his spine. 'What do you mean by that?'

She saw his face pale and wanted to cry even harder. 'Us,' she repeated.

'I don't understand, what about us?'

She brought her finger up to his lips, silencing him. 'It's over, Fletch.' Even though her heart screamed at her not to say the words out loud, she'd already made her mind up. She was doing the right thing, she decided. She had to keep telling herself that she was keeping him safe. 'It's over between us.'

'No.' Fletch pushed himself away from her, and as he brought his hands up to his head, he tugged at his dark hair. He felt sick, like he'd been punched in the gut. 'You don't mean that.'

'Yes, I do.' She had to be strong; his life was in her hands. 'It's over between us.'

'Over... but I don't understand,' he repeated. 'Everything was okay yesterday.' He looked down at her; his heart was in his mouth. 'You don't mean this, Suze. It can't be over, not now, not just like that. What did I do wrong?' he begged of her.

Susan choked on her reply. He looked so helpless, so hurt, that she wanted to pull him into her arms and soothe away his upset, to tell him she didn't mean it and that everything would be okay, that she loved him and always would. She knew she couldn't, though; for his sake she couldn't.

'You didn't do anything wrong, Fletch, in fact, the complete opposite.'

'Then why? I'm begging you, Suze, don't do this to me, I...' He snapped his mouth shut before he could say the words, before he could utter out loud that he loved her. 'Don't do this to me.' He narrowed his eyes and took a step away from her. 'It was the necklace, wasn't it? It wasn't good enough for you?'

'No, of course not.' She gasped at the accusation; regardless of how much it had cost, she loved the necklace – she would treasure it for the rest of her days. She reached out to touch his arm, but he snatched it away.

He glanced around the grand hallway. 'You know that I can't give you all of this, that I'll never be able to give you what Billy can.'

'No, that's not true.' She stood open-mouthed, shocked by his words. The house, the wealth that Billy had, meant nothing to her; it never had, and he knew that, she'd told him enough times. 'Don't you see that I have to do this, for both of our sakes. I have to.' She clutched at his hand. 'To keep you safe, I have to let you go.'

'All I see is you wanting to keep a hold on all of this.' His eyes flashed dangerously as he stabbed his finger around the hallway.

'Billy—' she began.

'Fuck Billy,' he spat back. 'You used me. You got what you

wanted from me, and now you're fucking me off out of it. Thanks a fucking lot for that.'

'No.' As he headed for the front door, she chased him across the marble hallway. 'It isn't like that, honestly, it isn't.'

He shrugged her away from him. He could feel the start of tears welling up in his eyes and he shook them away, swallowing down the hard lump in his throat. He wouldn't cry, not in front of her. No matter how much he might want to, he wouldn't shed a single tear in front of her. He was determined of that.

'You got what you wanted, and now you want to finish it. You want to just fuck me off out of it, like I'm nothing, like what we have is fuck all.' He flung open the front door, stormed across the driveway, and climbed into his car. 'Thanks for nothing. See you around... maybe.'

With those parting words, he slammed the car door shut, started the ignition and sped away from the house, leaving a plume of exhaust fumes in his wake. Pushing his foot down on the gas, he hurtled down the lane at an alarming speed. Finally, he eased off the accelerator, brought the car to a halt beside a grass verge, and leant his head against the cool steering wheel.

Tears rolled down his cheeks. He couldn't believe it. He couldn't believe she would do this to him. He'd bared his soul to her. He'd even told her things that no one else knew. He could barely breathe, so intense was the pain that shuddered through his body, engulfing him. He thumped his fist down on the dashboard, all the while his heart was breaking in two for the only woman he had ever loved.

* * *

'Don't look now, but your uncle is up to his old tricks again.'

That evening, as he gulped down his fifth pint of beer, Fletch didn't even bother to turn his head. He had zero interest in Frank, or anyone else around him, for that matter.

'I don't give a fuck,' he growled. Misery engulfed every fibre of his being. He'd never despised Billy as much as he did right now. Just the mere thought of him and his Suzy together brought him out in a cold sweat.

Raising his eyebrows, Stevie continued watching Frank from across the bar. They were in Chains nightclub, in Barking. Music pumped out of the sound system, whilst men, mainly jumped-up city blokes wearing cheap polyester suits, strutted around as though they owned the gaff.

'You have to sort him out, Fletch. He's making a proper nuisance of himself. Look at him, he's had that much chisel, his jaw is still at the fucking bar.'

Turning his head, Fletch watched as a young woman tried to keep Frank at arm's length. Slamming his beer bottle down on the bar, he pushed himself off the bar stool and marched across the dancefloor.

Noting his arrival, Frank slung his arm around Fletch's shoulders. 'Here he is, my nephew,' he slurred. 'I might not show it as often as I should but I fucking love you,' he said, kissing the top of his head.

'Fuck off, Frank, you're pissed.' Fletch shoved his uncle away from him. 'And stay away from her she ain't interested.'

Frank shrugged and, without even hesitating, he moved on to his next unsuspecting victim – a right sort this time, who looked as though she would be up for a good time. Wearing a boob tube and a tight miniskirt that left little to the imagination, she looked like mutton dressed up as lamb and wouldn't have looked out of place at a grab-a-granny night – just his type.

'I'm sorry about that,' Fletch shouted above the music. 'He's had too much to drink but doesn't mean any harm.'

Tina Fellowes smiled. 'It's okay, and you're right, no real harm was done. Tina,' she said, holding out her hand as a way of introduction.

Ignoring the outstretched hand, he gave her a forced smile, then made his way back to the bar.

'Are you happy now?' he spat.

'Yeah.' Stevie narrowed his eyes and turned to look at Spencer. It wasn't like Fletch to be in such a bad mood. 'Get happy bollocks another beer,' he instructed his best friend's younger brother.

Thirty minutes later, Stevie nudged his friend once more. 'Don't look now, but that bird you rescued ain't took her eyes off you.'

Fletch groaned. All he wanted to do was get out of his nut, without being interrupted every five seconds. He gulped at his beer and turned his head to look across the club. She was all right, he supposed, not really his type though.

His thoughts went to Susan and he felt his heart involuntarily constrict inside his chest; tears sprang to his eyes and he blinked them away. Without saying another word, he downed his drink, placed the bottle down and strode towards her.

'Do you wanna get out of here?' he asked, bending down to speak privately in her ear.

He allowed himself to relax when Tina nodded in agreement. Petite and brunette, she may not have had Susan's blonde hair, figure, or class, but to a certain degree, she was still easy on the eye, just not his eye, he decided.

He marched out of the club with her tottering on dangerously high heels closely behind him. She may not be his type, but she could be exactly what he needed to let off a bit of steam – a welcome distraction – and a way to get Susan King out of his system, once and for all.

* * *

Six days later, Tina Fellowes grinned happily. She was getting herself dolled up for her date. Strewn across her bed was every outfit that she owned. She tilted her head to one side as she inspected a fitted black dress. She held the garment up against her petite figure and turned to look in the floor-length mirror.

'I've got nothing to wear,' she groaned to her best friend, Joanne.

'Nothing to wear?' Joanne laughed out loud as she cast her eyes across the pile of clothes flung across the floral bedspread. 'Where's he taking you anyway?'

'I don't know.' She spun around; a wide grin was etched across her face. 'Oh, he's so lovely, isn't he?' A dreamy expression replaced her smile. 'Fletch.' She said his name out loud, relishing the sound of it upon her lips. 'I think he could be the one,' she said, sinking down on to the bed and clutching the dress to her chest.

Joanne laughed even harder. 'You've known him less than a week. How could you possibly know he's the one?'

'Yeah, and so what?' Tina shrugged . 'When you know, you just know.'

Joanne rolled her eyes. This wasn't the first time her best friend had claimed her latest squeeze to be the one. 'So, where's he taking you then?'

'I've already told you, I don't know. He said it was a surprise.'

He hadn't actually said those words, but she wasn't about to tell her best friend that. The truth was, she had hardly heard from him all week, and she had a horrible, nagging feeling that he'd only agreed to this date to shut her up. She supposed it was her own fault, really. She'd opened her legs and given him what he wanted on the very first night.

'Oh, he's so nice.' She flounced off the bed, discarded the black dress and picked up a second outfit. 'What do you reckon?' She gave a little twirl whilst holding up a short emerald green and white polka dot dress that flared out at the waist.

'I think you're gonna knock his socks off.' Joanne beamed. 'He won't be able to keep his hands off you.'

'That's the general plan,' Tina giggled.

* * *

'So, have you had the low-down yet on where the next rave is gonna be? I don't want them little fuckers to try and get one over on us.'

'No.' Fletch scowled. He could barely look at his boss; the fact he was married to Suzy was enough to make him want to swing his fist back and wipe the smug grin off his face.

Billy narrowed his eyes. 'What the fuck is wrong with you? You've been a right miserable fucker lately.'

'Tell me about it,' Stevie mumbled. He felt Fletch punch him, and he rubbed at his arm. 'Well, Billy's right, you have been a miserable fucker.'

'It ain't none of your business, I keep telling you that.' He lit a cigarette and exhaled a plume of smoke above his head. The truth was, he was engulfed in misery and he just couldn't, for the life of him, shake it off. He didn't know how to.

'It's bound to be something to do with a bird,' Billy stated. 'Bound to be.' He heard Fletch give an annoyed sigh and he snapped his head towards him. 'Well, am I right, or am I right?'

At that moment, the dining room door opened, and as Spencer walked in, balancing a tray of drinks, Fletch could see Susan in the hallway.

'If you must know, I'm happy with Tina.' His voice was loud,

loud enough for Susan to be able to hear, and as she looked into the room, he locked eyes with her. 'Very happy actually. In fact, I've never been fucking happier.'

The door closed and he slumped backwards in his seat, feeling bereft once more. It wasn't true, and he'd only said the words for Susan's benefit. He wanted to hurt her, just like she'd hurt him.

'Well, if you're that fucking happy, smile for once. I'm sick to the back teeth of looking at your miserable boat race.'

He gave a mock smile and lowered his head. As for Tina, she was doing his nut in, constantly phoning him, constantly wanting to know where he was, checking up on him, checking that he wasn't talking to any other women. It wasn't as if she was even his bird. He'd only taken her out a couple of times, and even then, he'd done so begrudgingly. There and then, he knew what he had to do. For his own sanity, he had to get shot of her, and the quicker the better.

'Seeing as you're so happy,' Billy chuckled, 'you can bring this mystery woman to meet us tonight.'

'What?' Fletch's head sprang upwards. He wrinkled up his nose and sank lower into his chair. 'Nah, I don't think that's such a good idea.'

'Tonight,' Billy reaffirmed, 'and that's a fucking order.'

Inwardly, Fletch groaned. Introducing them to Tina was the last thing he wanted to do. He had zero intentions of making her a permanent fixture in his life. She was nothing but a stopgap until he found a way to get Susan out of his system, not that he could tell Billy that.

Left with no other choice, Fletch nodded. One drink and that would be it. After that, he would make his excuses and get the hell out of there, dragging Tina behind him, kicking and screaming, if need be.

* * *

Susan's heart was breaking; she flung herself on to the bed and slammed her hand over her mouth to stop the sobs that threatened to engulf her entire body, from escaping.

How could he have already moved on and met someone else? The very notion was alien to her; no man would ever come close to how she felt about him, never. He was her everything, and always would be.

Curling herself into a ball, she pushed her head into the pillow and sobbed her heart out, not for the first time wishing that she could take everything back and hold him in her arms again.

* * *

Closing the front door, Tina fluffed out her hair before making her way down the pathway towards Fletch's car. It was a brand-spanking-new black BMW with tinted windows and cream leather seats. She couldn't help but feel like a million dollars each and every time she climbed into it.

Instinctively, she knew he had money, not that she knew exactly how it was that he earned his living. He'd never divulged that little piece of information, despite her best efforts to try and get it out of him. Still, she guessed it must be something important. The fact that they had always been given the absolute best tables in restaurants was enough to tell her that.

He was obviously a man who commanded respect, and she loved that about him. A smile adorned her face. Little did he know that he was about to become her meal ticket, a means to a better life. She could just imagine it now – the big wedding, a beautiful house, holidays abroad, a life where money was no object. Oh yes, it was definitely the type of life she wanted for herself, and with a little bit of luck, his seed was already growing inside of her, cementing the deal.

'Hiya, babe.' She grinned, pulling open the car door and climbing inside.

He gave her a tight-lipped smile in return, and as she tore her eyes away from him to secure her seat belt, she noticed that he didn't wear his own.

'You should wear a seat belt,' she scolded.

'I'll be all right.'

'It's the law.'

She heard him sigh, and, as he started the ignition, there was a bored tone to his voice. 'Like I said, I'll be all right. We ain't going far anyway.'

'Okay.' She smiled once more. 'I called you earlier, but you didn't answer.' In fact, she had called him more than once – it must have been at least twenty times.

'I was in a meeting.'

'Oh.'

He watched as she rummaged around in her handbag and took out a tube of lip gloss, pulled down the sun visor and studied her reflection in the tiny mirror there. It was as though she owned the car, and it was her given right to manhandle it. The simple act grated on his nerves. She was far too comfortable around him. He gritted his teeth, flicked the indicator and pulled out on to the road.

'So, where are we going then?' As if on cue, he pulled the car back over to the kerb, and she craned her neck to look around her. They had barely reached the end of the street, and she knew for a fact there weren't any restaurants or bars this side of town. Her forehead furrowed. 'Where are you taking me then, babe?'

Fletch sighed. Fuck Billy and his orders. Enough was enough.

Hell would freeze over before he even contemplated taking her to meet the firm. 'Look, Tina...' He paused and gripped the steering wheel tightly.

'What's wrong?'

He stifled down the urge to not just come out with it and tell her to fuck off, to tell her that she wasn't wanted, and that her very presence was a threat to everything he held dear. How could Susan even consider taking him back with Tina clinging to him like a limpet, as though she owned him, as though he was nothing other than one of her many possessions?

He switched off the engine and took a deep breath. Without even looking at her, he spoke. His voice was low, steady and determined. He'd put off the inevitable for as long as he could and seeing Susan just that afternoon only reinforced his feelings. She was the only woman for him – the only woman he would ever want; no one else could ever come close. In fact, he'd already made up his mind he was going to tell Suzy that he loved her, and if it meant getting down on his hands and knees and begging for a second chance then he was prepared to do just that. He couldn't live without her; he didn't want to live without her.

'This isn't going to work, Teen.'

'What isn't going to work, babe?' A cold chill ran down Tina's spine and her breath caught in her throat. Her dreams, and her hopes for the future, were about to shatter in front of her eyes.

'Us.' He turned in his seat to face her. 'You're a nice girl, it's just that I'm not ready to have a girlfriend, not right now anyway. I've got a lot going on,' he said, in the way of an explanation. 'I've got a lot of shit that I need to work out before I even think about settling down with someone.'

'Are you finishing with me?' Her voice rose and tears sprang to her eyes.

Rubbing at his temple, Fletch nodded. What was there to finish? They hadn't even got started.

'You are, aren't you? You're finishing with me.'

'Like I said, you're a nice girl and all that.' He clasped her hand tightly in his. 'It's not you, honest...'

'Don't tell me,' she spat. 'It's not you, it's me?' Story of her life... she'd heard those same words hundreds of times before. Only this time, she'd thought things would be different; she'd thought he was different. She narrowed her eyes. 'You've met someone else, haven't you?'

'No.' And in a way, he hadn't. Susan had been there first; she would always be first.

'Yes, you have.' Her cheeks turned scarlet, and she snatched her hand away from his. 'You've met some little scrubber and now you're finishing with me.'

'She's not a scrubber.' His eyes flashed angrily. 'She ain't like that.' On hearing Tina audibly gasp, he leant his head back against the headrest and briefly closed his eyes. 'It's over between us anyway. She finished it.' He shrugged his shoulders. 'I don't expect you to understand, Teen. It's complicated.'

'Complicated? Fucking complicated?' she screamed, unclipping her seat belt and throwing it away from her. 'Am I supposed to feel sorry for you?' She climbed out of the car. 'You're a rotten bastard, Fletch,' she screeched. 'I got all dressed up for you for nothing.' She slammed the door shut and marched down the street with her arms folded across her chest.

'Tina.' Starting the ignition, Fletch wound down the passenger window, crawled the car beside her, and shouted across the passenger seat. 'Don't be like this. At least let me give you a lift back home.'

'Piss off,' she screamed back.

Shaking his head, Fletch put the car into first gear and sped away from the kerb. With a bit of luck, it would be the last he saw of her. Sadly, for him, it would turn out to be wishful thinking.

* * *

At that very moment, Joseph was pulling his car over to the kerb. Looking through the windscreen, his beady eyes darted around him. Beside where he had parked the car was a telephone box. He sat for a moment, contemplating his next move.

That fucking Fletch. His hatred of the younger man went beyond jealousy. It ate away at him like a cancer. Three hundred lousy quid, that was all he had been given from the rave turnover. He knew for a fact that Fletch had been given at least twenty times that amount. He'd seen the carrier bag filled to the brim with cash that Billy had handed over to him.

He stepped out of the car, dug deep into his pockets, and pulled out a scrap of paper with an address scrawled across it. He looked up and down the busy street, checking that the coast was clear, then made his way inside the telephone box.

An overwhelming scent of urine filled his nostrils, and he wrinkled his nose at the sour stench. The floor was littered with cigarette butts, and pinned to the board above the public telephone were advertising cards promoting the services of masseurs and call girls.

With one final glance around him, he snatched up the telephone receiver. He began to perspire, and, with his free hand, he pulled his shirt outwards to fan himself. The enormity of what he was about to do engulfed him, and for a moment, he questioned whether or not he could actually go through with it.

Yes, he could, he decided. Hatred spurred him on, and he pushed down on the metal, numbered buttons.

After a few beats, his call was answered.

'I've got some information,' he told the police dispatcher. 'Drugs are being stored at a premises.' He rattled off an address and a name for the culprit, then slammed down the receiver with such force that it almost broke in two.

His breath came in short bursts and he placed his hand on the back wall of the telephone box to steady himself. After an age, he straightened up and dragged his hand across his clammy forehead and neck.

How the mighty were going to fall, he smirked to himself, feeling happier than he had in a long time. He pushed open the door and stepped out on to the street with a spring in his step. Yes, how the mighty were going to fall.

* * *

The banging on the front door had all the hallmarks of the Old Bill turning up on the doorstep. Pulling on her dressing gown, Jenny Fletcher made her way wearily down the staircase.

'Who is it?' Yawning loudly, Fletch hung his head over the bannister rail.

'I don't know.' Glancing upwards, Jenny gave a shrug of her shoulders. Who the hell could it be at this time of the morning? She'd barely slid the chain across when the front door was smashed open, sending her flying backwards.

'Police!' The screams and shouts came from the rush of bodies storming into the house.

'What's going on?' Jenny cried. She watched helplessly as police officers raced up the wooden staircase. 'Will someone please tell me what's going on?'

A search warrant was pushed under her nose, and she blinked rapidly as she tried to focus on the words. 'I don't understand,' she cried. 'A search warrant, for what?'

'Drugs,' a booming voice shouted out.

'It's all right, Mum,' Fletch called out. 'Don't worry. They ain't gonna find anything.' And it was true. He knew for a fact that there was no incriminating evidence in the house.

'You heard my son; he's done nothing wrong.' She watched as the police officers dragged him bodily down the stairs and she rushed forward to intervene. 'Leave him alone, he's done nothing wrong. Drugs? My boy would never get himself involved in drugs.'

'Mum, it's all right,' Fletch reassured her.

'What's going on down there?' Wiping sleep from his eyes, Frank stood at the top of the stairs, wearing just his underpants and a singlet vest.

'It's nothing. Tell Billy to ring a brief for me...' The words caught in Fletch's throat as he was dragged down the remaining steps. 'All right, fucking hell, I'm coming,' he roared.

'Leave my son alone!' Jenny continued to cry. She wrung her hands in front of her body as tears filled her eyes. 'He ain't done nothing wrong. He's a good boy. He would never get involved with drugs.'

Her pleas were ignored and, in the pandemonium, she was pushed out of the way, causing her to crash heavily to the floor. It was just enough to make Fletch see red, and, clenching his fists, he lashed out at the police officer responsible.

'You bastard,' he screamed. 'You fucking mug. I'll have you for that. Who the fuck do you think you are?'

It took three officers to pin him to the floor, and with his face pushed into the threadbare hallway carpet, he screamed and hollered even louder.

'Assaulting a police officer.' A hint of amusement could be heard coming from the booming voice. 'You'll be going away for a very long time, sunshine... a very long time.'

'You dirty bastards,' Fletch screamed. 'You've fitted me up.'

Jenny pulled herself to her feet; tears streamed down her face. 'He didn't mean to do that,' she cried. 'Tell them, Frank! Tell them that he didn't mean to! It was an accident, that's all.'

For the first time in his life, Frank showed some compassion towards his stepsister and pulled her into his arms. Even he knew what this meant, and fair enough, they wouldn't find any drugs in the house. After all, he knew the boy wasn't that stupid to bring any home with him, but as for swinging for the copper, well, they would throw the bloody book at him for that. They were bound to, weren't they?

'I'll get on the blower to Billy,' he told her. 'Don't you worry, darlin', we'll have him back home before you know it.'

* * *

'Six fucking months. It's a crying shame.' Frank shook his head. They had just come out of court for Fletch's sentencing. 'Six fucking months,' he repeated.

Billy blew out his cheeks. In a way, it could have been a lot worse. The judge, a miserable looking old bastard, had looked set to lock him up for life and throw away the key.

'He'll be all right,' he said. 'It's only six months. It's not like he's been given proper bird, is it?' He paused as he took in Jenny's grief-stricken face and his voice softened. 'I've got a mate doing a ten stretch. I'll tip him the wink and tell him to make sure he has an easy time of it,' he said, to reassure her.

Wiping the tears from her eyes, Jenny nodded. She still couldn't believe it. Her boy, her eldest son, was being sent down. A fresh set of tears filled her eyes, and she began to cry once more.

'He'll be okay, Mum.' Spencer pulled her into his arms. 'Like

Billy said, Fletch will have an easy time of it, and you can even visit him, if he sends you one of those visiting orders.'

'I know, darling,' she said through her tears. 'But six months,' she cried. 'It's a bloody joke. He was only trying to be a good son by protecting me.'

'I don't think Fletch will find it very funny.'

Jenny sighed and linked her arm through her youngest son's. 'I didn't mean it like that, darling. Of course it isn't funny.' In a cloud of misery, she followed her stepbrother to where he had parked the car, and with one final glance at the court, she climbed inside.

8

Four weeks later, there was a knocking at the front door. Drying her damp hands on a tea towel, Jenny patted down her hair before making her way down the hallway. Opening the door, she stared at the girl before her.

'Hello, darling, can I help you?' she asked.

Tina Fellowes gave a shy smile. 'Mrs Fletcher?'

'Yes.'

'I'm Tina, Fletch's girlfriend.'

Jenny's face lit up. 'Come on in,' she cried, ushering the girl over the doorstep. 'Well, this is a lovely surprise. I didn't even know he had a girlfriend. Well, when I say I didn't know, what I mean is, I thought that maybe he did, but he never really confirmed it, if you know what I mean. He was keeping things close to his chest. He does that sometimes, has done ever since he was a little boy.'

Tears sprang to Tina's eyes. 'Oh, Mrs Fletcher,' she interrupted. 'I've been in such an awful state.'

'Course you have, my darling. That'd be the shock.' She led

the way into the lounge and indicated for Tina to take a seat on the chintz covered sofa.

'The shock? Wait a minute, but how? How could you possibly know?'

'Well, of course I know, darling. I am his mum,' Jenny laughed.

'But how? I mean, Fletch doesn't even know yet.'

Jenny narrowed her eyes. 'I thought you were talking about him being sent down.'

'No.' She shook her head and looked down at her lap. Taking a deep breath, she looked upwards and met Jenny's eyes. 'Mrs Fletcher, I'm pregnant with Fletch's child.'

Holding on to the arm of the chair, Jenny made the sign of the cross over her chest. Not that she was a religious woman by any means; it was just something you did when you received a shock, wasn't it?

'Oh, my Lord,' she cried. 'Pregnant? Are you sure? I mean, have you taken a test? Have you had it confirmed?'

Tina nodded, barely able to keep the sly grin from her face. 'I've taken several tests and they were all positive. My Fletch is going to be a daddy.' She smiled sweetly.

* * *

Turning over on his bunk, Fletch tried his best to ignore the loud rumbling snores that came from his cellmate, Chester Stopes. 'Fucking hell, Ches, I'm trying to get some kip here.'

'Sorry, mate.' Wiping away the saliva that had trickled down the side of his jaw and on to the pillow, Chester belched loudly. 'Was I snoring again?'

'Yeah, just a bit.'

'Sorry, mate,' Chester said again.

'Nah, you're all right.' Swinging his legs around, Fletch sat up. 'I couldn't really sleep anyway,' he said, leaning back on his elbows.

'You thinking about your girl again?'

Fletch sighed. 'Yeah, something like that.' Only she wasn't his girl. She was a grown woman and was also married to his boss. 'It's over between us anyway, so no point dwelling on it, I suppose.'

'That's defeatist talk, that is.' Chester reached out for a matchstick-thin roll-up and placed it between his lips. 'Twenty years ago, first time I was ever banged up, my old woman told me it was over between us. But look at us now, twenty years later, and we're still going strong.'

'That's because you've been locked up for the majority of that time.' Fletch rolled his eyes.

'No, it ain't.' Chester blew out a perfect smoke ring and lay back on his bunk. 'It's because I didn't give up. I knew, deep down, she still loved me, see.'

Following suit, Fletch lay back down and placed his hands behind his head. His thoughts turned back to Susan. Did she love him? he wondered. Had she ever loved him? He closed his eyes and drifted off to sleep, all the while, images of Susan King haunted his dreams.

'Are you any feeling better, darling?' Jenny tentatively knocked on the bathroom door. Having stayed up until the early hours of the morning talking, she'd invited Tina to sleep on the sofa, much to the chagrin of her stepbrother.

'Yes, thank you.' Tina pulled open the bathroom door. 'It's this morning sickness,' she complained. 'It's knocking me for six.'

Jenny smiled sympathetically. 'You do look a bit peaky. I was the same when I was carrying Fletch. I was as sick as a dog for the first four months.'

'Four months?' Tina groaned.

'It'll all be worth it. You just wait until you've got that baby in your arms and then you'll see,' Jenny chuckled. 'How about a cuppa before you have to go home?'

Crocodile tears sprang to Tina's eyes. 'I don't really have a home any more, Mrs Fletcher. My mum and dad went Garrity when they found out about the baby.' She lowered her voice. 'They demanded I get rid of it.'

'What? An abortion?' Jenny cried.

'Yep, my dad was all set to drag me off to the clinic.'

'Well, we can't have that, can we? That little bubba in there is my first grandchild. I'll tell you what, you can sleep in Fletch's room, and Spencer can kip on the sofa.'

'Oh no, I couldn't do that.' Tina flapped her hands as if embarrassed. 'I can't put you out like that.'

'Yes, you can, and you're not putting me out. Besides, it'll only be until Fletch comes home. I'm sure he'll want you to both have your own place before the baby is born.'

'Thank you, Mrs Fletcher. I can't thank you enough, really I can't.'

'No need to thank me, and it's Jenny. No need for formalities. You're family now.'

Tina smiled sweetly. 'How about I make that cup of tea? It's the least I can do.'

'That'd be lovely, darling.' She watched as her son's girlfriend set about filling the kettle and smiled to herself. Her boy had landed on his feet with this one, she was certain of it.

* * *

'Look lively, here he is.' Billy King grinned widely and jumped out of the car. It was five months later, and after his short stretch inside, Fletch was about to be released from prison.

Strolling through the iron gates, Fletch matched Billy's smile. 'Fucking hell, is that for me?' he asked, pointing towards the white stretch limousine parked outside Wormwood Scrubs.

'Nah, it's for that bloke behind yer.' Billy rolled his eyes. 'Course it's for you.' He opened the door to reveal Spencer, Stevie and Frank sprawled across the leather seats. Held aloft in their hands were bottles of the finest champagne, no cheap crap from the local supermarket.

'Bloody hell.' Fletch grinned. He slipped off his jacket, threw it across the seat, took the bottle of champagne that was handed to him and took a deep swig before getting in.

'Good to see you, Fletch,' Stevie said, shaking his hand.

'Same here. Anything happen while I've been away?'

'Nah, nothing.' He gave Spencer a sidelong glance, warning him to keep his mouth shut about Tina. He had a sneaky suspicion her little or not-so-little revelation, as the case happened to be, wasn't going to go down too well. In fact, it would be fair to say the shit was truly going to hit the fan. 'Here, a little sweetie for you.' He pulled out from his jacket pocket a small bag filled to the brim with tiny white pills and passed one across.

'Cheers, mate.' Fletch winked his appreciation and swallowed the pill down with a mouthful of champagne. 'And what about you, have you been behaving yourself?' he asked, turning his attention to his brother.

'Course I have, Fletch.' Spencer gave him a wide, beaming, lopsided grin. He'd missed his big brother.

'Good.' He clasped his brother's shoulder and gave it a reassuring squeeze. 'So, what's the plan then?' he asked, shuffling along the seat so Billy could climb into the limousine beside him.

'The plan is to get you shitfaced for a start.' Billy grinned. 'The guv'nor of the Robin Hood is gonna have a lock-in.'

Fletch nodded, impressed. He had a sneaky feeling the guv'nor wouldn't have had much of a choice on the matter. Billy could be persuasive when the mood took him, and if his charm didn't work, then the threat of a shotgun blast to the back of the head usually did the trick. 'I think I'll just nip home and see me mum first.'

'Nah, you don't wanna do that.' Stevie spoke fast, too fast.

'Why not?' Taking a swig of the champagne, Fletch's forehead furrowed.

'Because it's your first night out of clink, ain't it?' He gave a nervous laugh. 'You've got at least six months of boozing to catch up on.'

Fletch shrugged his shoulders and guzzled back the champagne. He supposed they were right. There was plenty of time to see his mum, and she would understand if he was a bit late coming home.

'Here, and this is for you. Your cut from the rave turnover.' Billy reached forward and picked up a carrier bag full of used banknotes. 'I kept it safe for you, mate.'

Peering inside the bag, Fletch laughed out loud. 'Cheers, Billy. I'm gonna need this to get back on me feet.'

'Yeah, you will an' all.' Frank belched loudly, ignoring the warning shots from the occupants of the car. 'This champagne is repeating on me,' he complained.

'What the fuck is going on?' Fletch looked around him. 'Why're you all acting so shifty?'

'Shifty? No we ain't. You're turning into a right paranoid twat.' Billy slapped him on the shoulder. 'It's good to see you back, that's all. I've even got a couple of jobs lined up for us.'

'Fucking hell, Billy. I've only just come out of nick. I don't wanna go back inside just yet.'

'Well, you're gonna need the money.' Frank continued to belch.

Narrowing his eyes, Fletch eyed his uncle over the rim of the bottle. 'Why am I gonna need the money, Frank? You chucking me out or something?'

'Course he ain't, are you, Frank?' Billy gave the older man a cold stare. 'Now, come on, get that booze down ya.' He grinned, changing the subject. 'There's plenty more where that came from.'

Amidst their laughter, Fletch couldn't help but think it sounded hollow to his ears. Something was going on, he knew that much. In fact, he'd bet his life on it that something was amiss.

* * *

The Robin Hood public house, in Dagenham, was crammed full of the usual punters. They let up a cheer as Fletch entered the bar, and he punched his fist in the air, giving them a wide grin.

'Drinks all around!' Billy shouted out, much to the joy of the regulars. 'And give us a dozen more bottles of your finest champagne for our exclusive party.' He paid for the drinks, then led Fletch over to a corner booth so they could speak in private. 'There's been some problems with the Bannermans,' he stated.

'What problems? Is it to do with the Es?' Fletch took a seat. He rested one of his forearms across the sticky tabletop; the other he draped casually around the top of the chair beside him.

'Nah.' Billy shook his head. 'That other business we took care of.'

Immediately, Fletch's eyes flickered across the bar. His brother was doubled over laughing at some joke he had been told. Even as Fletch watched him laugh, he highly doubted that Spencer even understood the punchline. Spencer was a people pleaser, always had been.

'They don't know, do they?' he asked, sitting forward and giving Billy his full attention.

'Of course they don't.'

'So.' He lifted his shoulders and leant back in the chair. 'What's the problem, then?'

Billy glanced behind him. 'I've heard through the grapevine that they've been asking around, wanting to know if anyone saw Albie the day he went missing.'

'But no one did, did they?'

'Not that I'm aware of.' He swallowed down a mouthful of champagne. 'They've got Mickey Shank terrorising people. The mad bastard is threatening to cut them up if they don't give him information.'

'Mickey Shank?' Fletch frowned. 'I didn't know he was involved with the Bannermans.'

'He's one of their relatives. A distant cousin or something like that.' Billy sighed. 'You can see now why it's causing a concern.'

'Yeah.' Fletch nodded, deep in thought. 'You're not worried though, are you?'

'About who, Shank? Nah, course I ain't. He's nothing but a fucking tool merchant. I'd muller the fucker with one arm tied behind my back.' He picked up a beer mat and rolled it between his fingers. There was a nervousness about him that Fletch had never seen before. 'Take away those fucking blades he carries around with him, and he's fuck all,' he added, full of bravado. 'No, what worries me is that those questions could end up one way or another leading back to me.' He nodded across the pub to where Spencer was standing. 'And of course to your brother, and let's face it, that's aggro we don't need.'

'So, who else knows about it?'

Billy paused. 'Well, obviously we had to dispose of the body, didn't we?'

'The breaker's yard down Crow Lane?'

'You've got it in one. Now, I trust this geezer in any normal circumstances, but faced with Mad Mickey Shank and a blade up to his throat, and, well, he may just start talking.'

'So, what do you want to do? Pay him a visit?'

'Yeah, I was thinking tomorrow morning, just you and me. We could take a trip down there and have a nice friendly little chat with him.'

'Yeah, okay.'

'Good lad.' With the business concluded, Billy made to stand up.

Remaining seated, Fletch glanced around the pub. 'Who was it that set me up?' he asked, tipping his chin in the air.

Billy sat back down. Like Fletch, his cold eyes glanced around the room. 'I don't know, mate.'

'Someone tipped the Old Bill the wink, you know that as well as I do.'

'Yeah, it looks that way,' Billy sighed.

'So, then.' Fletch shifted his weight. 'There is a snake in our camp, Billy.' His voice had a steely tone to it. 'And I wanna know who the fuck it is.'

'You're not the only one, mate.' Billy was thoughtful as he looked around the room. 'We'll sniff him out; he'll make a mistake. He can't stay hidden forever, can he?'

Fletch shrugged. Sniffing out the bastard was proving to be the hard part.

'Come on.' Billy grinned. 'Let's get back to celebrating your freedom.'

Fletch gave him a stilted smile. He looked down at his wristwatch. He would give it another hour or so, then slip out the back door and see his old mum. She would most probably be going out of her mind with worry, and the last thing he wanted, or needed, was to be stuck in the boozer for the lock-in. With a bit of luck, they wouldn't even notice he was missing.

* * *

'Mum, I'm home.'

An hour later, Fletch breezed into the house; a wide grin was spread across his face. In his fist was a bunch of carnations, and in his other hand, a box of her favourite milk chocolates. As he entered the lounge, his smile froze. Sitting on the sofa, beside his old mum was his ex, Tina.

'Surprise,' she gushed, spreading out her arms to reveal the large bump in front of her.

'What are you doing here?' Even as he said the words, he could hear the anger in his voice. The last person he wanted to see was his ex on returning home from his six months stretch inside.

'Fletch,' Jenny scolded. 'Where are your manners? Tina wanted to see you, been waiting six months, she has.' She nodded down to the bump. 'She's got something to tell you, son, something important.'

A feeling of dread swept over him. He looked to the bump, then to his ex's face. Tina's smug expression told him everything he needed to know.

'Is it mine?'

Tina gasped and crocodile tears filled her eyes. She snapped her head towards Jenny, her only ally. 'I knew he would be like this; I told you he would go off his head, didn't I?'

Jenny glared at her son. 'How could you be so insensitive? I've never been so bloody ashamed of you.'

'What?' He spread out his arms. 'I've got every right to ask. I've been banged up for the past six fucking months. How can that,' he said, pointing to the bump, 'possibly be mine?'

'I'm eight months gone.' Tina sniffed back her tears.

Her revelation struck a chill inside of him and, underneath the bright lightbulb, his face paled. 'Eight months?' he stammered. In his mind, he hastily calculated the dates.

'Didn't they tell you when they picked you up from prison?' Jenny asked.

'No, they fucking didn't,' Fletch snapped back. He'd known all along that they were acting shifty. Now he knew the reason why. He looked across to his mother, saw the beaming smile there at the thought of holding her first grandchild, and after throwing the presents he'd bought her on to the empty armchair, he began to back out of the room. 'I can't deal with this,' he yelled, retreating out of the house and running as fast and as far away as his legs would carry him.

* * *

Mickey Shank was grinning from ear to ear. Sitting on the back seat of George's car, he listened intently to what his cousin had to say. Clasped between his legs was his sword; he admired the intricate detailing of the hilt, appreciating the way in which the street lights streaming through the car windows bounced off the steel.

He could barely contain his excitement. After all, he'd waited patiently, biding his time, waiting for this moment to come.

'My grass has told me that that slippery little cunt King is gonna be in this boozer tonight,' George snarled. As he looked towards the Robin Hood public house, he could feel the familiar sense of anger begin to build inside of him once more. He could feel his pure hatred of the man seeping out of his pores.

The occupants of the car turned their heads to look across at the pub.

'Yeah, and what if he's wrong?' asked Jason Miller, one of George's firm members. 'It ain't like this snout of yours has given you much to go on in the past, is it? Ten months Albie has been missing for, and you've still had nothing concrete. No names, no nothing. He didn't just vanish into thin air, did he? Someone somewhere knows what happened to him.'

George shrugged. It was true. So far, Joseph Hatton had proved himself to be useless when it came to providing information. Still, the suspicion he had that King was involved in his brother's disappearance niggled at him.

'Yeah, well, I've got his cards marked.' He opened the car door and stepped out on to the pavement. As far as he was concerned, Joseph Hatton had served his purpose. His days were numbered.

'And you reckon King's definitely in there, then?'

'Only one way to find out, eh?' George raised his eyebrows as he answered.

They sauntered towards the pub and George put out his arm, bringing his firm to a halt, his fist clenched around a length of iron piping. 'Remember, that cunt King is mine,' he reminded them. Tonight, he would get his revenge on not only the theft of the Ecstasy pills, but also, more importantly, his brother's disappearance.

They nodded their heads, eager to get inside the pub, and even more eager to get stuck in and down to business.

* * *

There was only one place Fletch wanted to be, only one person he wanted to speak to, and that was his Suzy. Having raced to the nearest taxi rank, he'd jumped into the back of a black cab and told the cabbie to put his foot down.

Standing outside the house Billy owned, he dragged his damp hair away from his clammy forehead, desperately trying to make himself look more presentable. As an afterthought, he lifted his arms, gave his armpits a quick sniff, and then after wrinkling his nose, without hesitating, he banged his fist on the front door.

Through the glass windowpane, he watched her come into view; surprise was etched upon her face as she unlocked the door. Barefoot, and dressed in a pale pink cashmere sweater, dark denim fitted jeans, and with her hair tied up in a messy bun, as always, she looked beautiful.

'Fletch,' she cried. 'What are you doing here?'

'I had to see you.'

'Billy—' she began.

'He's still in the pub.'

She pulled the door open wider, and led the way into the lounge. 'When did you get out?'

'Today... this afternoon.'

At this, she turned around and smiled. 'It's good to see you. You look well.'

'No, I don't. I look like shit.' He resisted the urge to pull her into his arms. Instead, he sank down into the sofa and held his head in his hands. 'I'm in a right fucking mess, Suze, and I don't know what to do. I don't know if I'm coming or going.'

'It can't be that bad, surely?' She knelt on the Chinese silk rug before him, the rich tapestry a swirl of vibrant colours in the otherwise pale lemon room. He grasped hold of her hand tightly, his fingers curling around hers.

'It's Tina. She's...'

'Tina, the girl you're seeing?'

He shook his head. 'I'm not seeing her; I took her out a couple of times, that was it. She isn't my girlfriend. She's...'

'What is it?' Susan urged him.

'She's pregnant, and...'

Susan's heart lurched. She swallowed deeply and dropped his hand. He snatched hers back, holding on to it for dear life.

'I don't know what to do.' He looked down at her, holding her gaze, pleading with her. 'I don't know what to do, Suze. Tina and my mum, they've... they've just this minute sprung it on me. No warning, no nothing. Tell me what I should do.'

'I... I can't tell you what to do, Fletch. You have to do what's right.'

He rubbed his hand across his face. 'Please, Suzy, help me out here, please. I'm begging you.'

'I can't,' she repeated, her voice faltering. 'You know that I can't; how can I tell you what to do?'

'But I don't love her,' he cried. 'I'll never love her; you know that I won't. How can I when I—?'

'Maybe you don't right now,' she interrupted. 'But in time, you will.'

'No,' he shouted. 'No, I won't, Suze.' He wanted to shake her, to make her understand. 'Never.'

'Fletch.' She grasped his hand in hers even tighter. 'She's having your child, and you have to do what's right.'

'Yeah.' He gave a bitter laugh. 'She's having my kid, and I don't even know her surname. I barely even know her. I don't want to know her. I thought that I'd come out of nick and that we'd...'

'What?' She tilted her head. 'You thought that we'd what?'

'I thought that me and you...' He squeezed her hand. 'I thought that we'd, I don't know.' He watched her reaction closely, hoping more than anything that she still felt the same way. 'Be together, I suppose.'

'We can't.' She spoke softly, her heart and mind conflicting. How did this man, sixteen years her junior, have so much of an effect on her? All these months on and he still had the ability to make her heart quicken.

'But why not? The way I feel about you...' His shoulders slumped downwards in defeat, and despair flooded through him. If only she could see just how sincere he was. No other woman would ever compare to her; it was impossible. 'The way I feel about you, that's never going to change, Suze, and you know it isn't.'

'We've already been through all of this; we've already discussed it. It's over.'

'No,' Fletch spat. 'We haven't discussed shit.'

'Yes, we have.' Two pink spots appeared on Susan's cheeks. Her back was up, and she had no intention of backing down. 'And what about Billy, eh? My husband? What we did was wrong, Fletch, not to mention dangerous. You know he would have killed us both if he'd ever found out; we were walking a tight line and it was only a matter of time before he caught us. You work for him. You, of all people, should know what he is capable of.' She tilted her head to the side, watching him. 'You know what I'm saying is true.'

'You're scared of him.' Fletch's mouth tightened. 'You're scared of your own husband.'

As she nodded, Susan's cheeks flushed. 'And so should you be,' she answered, through gritted teeth.

'I could've handled Billy; I would have done that for you.'

'Done what exactly?' She snatched her hand away from his, sat back on her haunches, and threw her arms up in the air. 'What could you have possibly done, Fletch? This is Billy we are talking about; he kills people for fun, so what do you think he would have done to us?'

'I would have made him disappear.' Fletch stuck his chin out, thoroughly believing the words he spoke. He would have done just about anything to keep her by his side, even if that meant committing murder.

'And what about Tina? Would you have made her disappear, too? She's carrying your child, Fletch.'

'I already know that,' he snapped. 'It's all I've thought about since she told me.'

'You should have been more careful.'

A hot flush crept up his neck, and he looked away. Susan was the last person he wanted to discuss his sex life with. Even though he knew he was being irrational, he couldn't help but feel as though he'd betrayed her somehow.

'She told me she was on the pill,' he answered, his voice low.

Susan lifted her eyebrows; her expression said it all.

'I know,' he sighed. 'Oldest trick in the fucking book, and me, like a stupid prize prick, fell for it.' He caught hold of her hand. 'Forget about Tina. I just want us to be together, Suze. Just you and me. We could leave right now.' He clasped her hand tightly and began to stand up. Warming to his idea, he became more animated. 'I don't have much money, but it'd be enough for us to get away. We could go somewhere that Billy would never find us. We could...'

His enthusiasm was infectious, and a bubble of hope spread

throughout Susan's body. Coming to her senses, she shook her head. There was nothing more she wanted other than to be with him, every day and for the rest of her life, but she knew it never would happen. Billy would hunt them down, and more than likely murder them in the process. It was a risk she wasn't willing to take.

'But I...' He squeezed his eyes shut tight. 'You know how I feel about you.' His cheeks flamed a deeper shade of red. 'You know what I'm trying to say, Suze? What I'm trying to tell you. I love you, I always have, and I always will do; there will never be anyone else but you.'

'I know.' Susan gave him a sad smile; her heart broke all over again. 'But Billy—' She was interrupted by the shrill ring of his mobile phone. She watched as he fished the device from his jacket pocket.

'It's him...' he growled, looking down at the caller ID. He switched off the call and pulled his fingers through his hair. Within seconds, the phone rang for a second time.

'Maybe you should answer that.' Susan's voice was low. 'He could be on his way home.'

He gave her a pained expression, inhaled deeply, then pressed answer. Not taking his eyes away from her, he rubbed his palm across his jaw. 'Okay.' His voice rose as he spoke into the phone, the colour draining from his face. 'I'm coming.' Reluctantly, he stood up. 'I have to go; it's my uncle... he's just been stabbed at the boozer.'

'Is he okay?' Pressing her hand to her open mouth, she gasped out loud.

'I don't know.' Every fibre inside of him screamed at him not to leave this woman, yet he knew he had no other choice. He pulled her close and kissed the top of her head. 'I love you.'

'I love you too.' Tears rolled down her cheeks and, using her fingertips, she wiped them away.

'I'm gonna sort this out.' He swallowed down the hard lump in his throat that was choking him and pulled her into his chest. Even as he said the words, he knew this was one situation he wouldn't be able to magic away. No amount of wishing would make Tina, Billy or the baby disappear. 'I will sort it out, I promise.' With those parting words, he raced out of the house, leaving Susan to stare helplessly at his retreating back.

9

Amidst a sea of flashing blue lights, Fletch ran down the street towards the Robin Hood public house. Ambulances and police cars were parked haphazardly across the road. He glanced inside the back of an ambulance as he sped past and did a double take.

'Fletch.' Stevie pushed his way through the crowd of onlookers.

'What the fuck happened?' His breath coming in short bursts, Fletch tore his eyes away from the ambulance.

'Bannerman and his firm turned up,' Stevie answered as he came to stand beside his best mate. He nodded towards the paramedics as they worked on Frank. 'Before we even knew what was happening, Shank, the mad bastard, went for your uncle, sliced open his gut.'

'What?' Fletch brought his hands up to his head and made to move forward. As he inched closer, he could see his brother towards the back of the ambulance. He knelt beside the stretcher, his head hanging down low. Leaning inside the open back doors, Billy was speaking to a police officer, his arms moving around animatedly as he spoke.

'It ain't looking good, mate. There was claret everywhere.' Stevie cleared his throat, still feeling shocked. 'His fucking guts, Fletch... they were hanging out of him.'

Fletch had heard just about enough. His stomach churned, and he pushed his way past the police cordon. 'That's my uncle in there,' he yelled at the officer trying to block his way.

'Fletch.' Billy turned his head. 'Get over here, mate.'

'Is he gonna be okay?' His eyes were wide as he looked past Billy, into the ambulance.

'I don't know, mate.'

'Spence.' As he stepped up into the ambulance and over piles of discarded blood-stained gauze and empty sterile packaging, he tore his eyes away from the stretcher to look at his brother. 'How is he doing?'

Spencer's face was ashen. 'I don't know,' he cried. 'He's bleeding bad, and it won't stop. Why won't it stop, Fletch?'

Laid out on the stretcher, Frank's skin was grey and clammy, his eyes closed. Strapped across his face was an oxygen mask. Just like the discarded gauze on the floor, the white shirt he was wearing was soaked in deep red blood.

Fletch's stomach churned even harder, and he pressed his fist into his mouth as a wave of nausea swept over him. He could see the concern etched across the paramedics' faces. 'Come on, Frank,' he urged. 'Stay with us.'

'We need to blue light him to hospital.'

There was an urgency to their voices, and, still unable to believe his eyes, Fletch turned to speak quickly to Billy. 'Tell Stevie to go and get my mum and meet us at the hospital.'

As the rear doors were hastily closed on him, Billy solemnly nodded.

* * *

Tina was still feeling tearful when a loud banging on the front door caused her to widen her eyes in alarm.

'See, I told you he would be back soon.' Jenny grinned. 'You have to understand it was all a bit of a shock for him. I knew he would come around in the end, though.'

'But doesn't he have a key?' Tina wiped away her tears and looked to the living room door expectantly.

'Yes, he does.' Jenny frowned. She pushed herself out of the armchair, hoping and praying that it wasn't the police on her doorstep again. That was the last thing they all needed. Warily, she made her way out to the hallway and inched open the front door. 'Who is it?' she asked, peering outside into the darkness.

'It's Stevie, Fletch's mate.'

Relief flooded through her. She opened the door wider and beckoned him across the threshold. 'So, where is he then?' She crossed her arms over her chest and her tone became stern. 'I suppose he sent you to do his dirty work for him, did he? Well, you can go back to wherever he is and tell him, from me, to get his backside home and talk to that young girl in there. Going out of her bloody mind with worry, she is.'

'No.' Stevie shook his head. 'He did send me, Mrs Fletcher, but not for that reason. It's Frank. He's been in an accident.'

The colour drained from Jenny's face. 'Frank? In an accident, you say. Well, what kind of an accident?'

Stevie swallowed deeply and his breath caught in his throat. 'We were in the boozer and he was slashed. He's in a bad way. Fletch sent me to take you up the hospital.' He looked over his shoulder. 'Billy's waiting outside in a taxi. He's gonna take us there right now.'

'What?' She clutched at her chest, feeling slightly dizzy, and peered around the open door to see the taxicab waiting outside.

'Well, is he going to be okay?' she asked, leaning against the hallway wall to steady herself as she slipped her shoes on.

'I dunno, but it doesn't look good.' He hopped from one foot to the other. 'We have to get a move on, Mrs Fletcher. Fletch and Spence are waiting for us up the hospital.'

She put her coat on. 'Tina, darling, I have to go to the hospital,' she called out.

'Is it Fletch?' Tina asked as she came to stand in the hallway.

Jenny shook her head. 'It's Frank, he's been in an accident.' Without a backward glance, she left the house with Stevie leading the way down the path. They may have had their problems in the past, but Frank was still family. *Dear God*, she prayed, *please let him be okay*.

* * *

'Mum,' Spencer called out to his mother.

The scent of disinfectant filled Jenny's nostrils as she charged down the hospital corridor. Coming to a halt in front of her youngest son, she pulled him into her arms.

'Are you okay?' she asked, giving him a critical once-over.

'Yeah, it's Uncle Frank, he was bleeding a lot, Mum. It wouldn't stop.'

'I know, my darling.' She turned her head to look at her eldest boy. 'How is he?' Any animosity she may have felt was gone as she crushed Fletch to her chest and wrapped her arms around him.

'I don't know, Mum.' He glanced across to where the operating theatres were situated. 'They took him straight into theatre.' He rubbed at his forehead. Every time he closed his eyes, he could see not only the vast amount of blood Frank had lost, but also the wide slash across his abdomen. 'It's not looking good, Mum,' he said quietly, out of Spencer's earshot.

At this, Jenny nodded. She placed her arms around both of her sons' waists. 'All we can do is let the doctors do what they do best and make him better.' She gave them a warm smile and bit down on her bottom lip to stop the tears from flowing from her eyes. Now, more than ever, she had to be strong for the sake of her two sons.

* * *

As soon as he had exited the Rotherhithe Tunnel, George slammed his foot on the brake and brought the car to a screeching halt. With a face like thunder, he threw open the car door, jumped out, and pulled Mickey across the back seat.

'What did I tell you?' He threw his cousin up against the car door. 'What did I specifically fucking say?'

'What?' Barely able to catch his breath, shock was etched across Mickey's face. 'What... what have I done wrong?'

'I told you I wanted King. But oh no, not you, you mad bastard, you couldn't wait, could you? I don't recall telling you to slice that cunt wide open.'

'What?'

'Did I tell you to slice him open?' George roared.

'No, but...' He averted his eyes. 'He was asking for it. He looked at me funny.'

'Of course he looked at you! You would look as well if some mad bastard was swinging a sword around.' He pulled Mickey closer to him. Their faces were so close that George could smell Shank's rancid breath. 'I told you to fucking wait.'

'I'm sorry, George.'

George clenched his fist into a tight ball, his eyes becoming dark and murderous. 'Yeah, you fucking will be.'

Two fast jabs hit Mickey square on the jaw. As he stumbled

backwards, his cousin's heavy fists rained blows down upon him. Finally, and with as much strength as he could muster, George executed a sickening kick to the side of his head.

The occupants of the vehicle watched on warily as George proceeded to pull out a small handgun from the inside of his jacket.

'Don't, George, not here,' a voice yelled out.

The words instantly brought George to his senses. Exhaling loudly, he slumped backwards against the side of the car. As he dropped his arm to his side, his breath streamed out in front of him, and he dragged his free hand across his face. He had been so close to King, so close to finding out the truth.

'Chuck this piece of shit into the boot,' he ordered his men.

As he watched them scramble out of the car, he allowed himself to take deep breaths to steady the anger that rippled through him. He still couldn't believe it. He felt as though his head was all over the place. Not only had he been nearer to finding out what had happened to Albie, but a familiar face, a blast from the past, had sent his mind reeling.

'What are we gonna do with him now, Boss?'

George turned his head in time to watch the men bundle his unconscious cousin into the boot of the car. What he'd like to do was shoot the man in the head and then tip him into the Thames, but family was family, after all.

'Dump the mad bastard outside his front door,' he growled.

* * *

On seeing her husband's car pull on to the driveway, Susan jumped up from the sofa and made her way out to the grand hallway.

'How is he? How is Frank?'

Billy entered the house and narrowed his eyes. 'How do you know about Frank?'

'I...' Realising her mistake, Susan began to stutter. 'I-I heard about it on the news. I recognised the name,' she lied. As she spoke, she could hear the fear in her voice. She was terrified that her husband would see right through her lies and she took deep breaths to steady herself. Of course, she shouldn't have known about the incident. It had never been on the news. It was Fletch who'd told her.

'It's touch and go.' He threw his car keys on to the hallway table and kicked off his shoes. 'He'd just come out of theatre when I left them at the hospital.'

'But he will be okay, won't he?'

Billy shrugged. 'Like I said, it's touch and go.'

'Poor Fletch.'

'Frank, you mean?' Billy narrowed his eyes for the second time in less than five minutes. 'It was Frank who was sliced up, not Fletch.'

'Of course.' Susan gave her husband a light smile. 'I meant to say Frank. You know what I'm like. I heard the name and just panicked, thinking that you could have been hurt, too.' She kissed him lightly on the cheek, held her breath, and then turned to walk away.

Staring after his wife, Billy's mind began to race. Where exactly was it that Fletch had disappeared to when Bannerman and his firm had turned up at the boozer? It was a question that was to go on to plague him for the rest of the night.

* * *

Early the next morning, Billy pressed his foot on the brake and brought the car to a shuddering halt outside the breaker's yard in

Crow Lane, Romford. What with Mad Mickey Shank and George Bannerman's escapades the previous evening, it was even more of a pressing issue that they spoke to Trevor Wright, the owner of the yard where the car containing Albie Bannerman's body had been disposed of. He switched off the engine and glanced across to Fletch.

'You look fucked, mate. Did you manage to get any kip last night?'

Fletch shook his head. Thanks to Stevie and his little white pills, he'd been awake the entire night. If truth were told, he didn't think he could sleep, even if he wanted to.

'You need to lay off those pills,' Billy stated. 'I keep telling you that.'

'Yeah, well, I needed something to get me through the night. Me mum needs me.'

'Well, you ain't gonna be much use to her if you're buzzing off your fucking nut, are you?'

'I'm all right,' Fletch groaned. He flung open the car door and jumped out. 'I'll sort myself out.'

'Make sure that you do.' Following suit, Billy climbed out of the car. 'I don't want you becoming a liability,' he said, stabbing his finger towards Fletch, across the roof of the car.

'I won't.' Fletch rolled his eyes and looked across to the breaker's yard. He'd met Trevor once or twice in the past. He was a nice bloke, albeit a bit eccentric. Despite a large four bedroomed house at the front of the property, the man lived in a small, rusting, dingy caravan at the back of the yard, with his dogs. As a result, the yard was covered in puddles of dog urine and piles of excrement. 'Puts people off from robbing the place,' he'd once told Fletch with a cackle.

'Come on, then.' Billy made his way forward.

'The mutts are loose.'

'And?' Billy looked over his shoulder. 'They're always fucking loose.'

Swallowing down his fear, Fletch followed his boss towards the yard. 'Shouldn't we wait until he's put them away first?'

'What the fuck is wrong with you? They're dogs, not fucking lions.' Billy shook his head. 'Sometimes you worry the fucking life out of me.'

'All right, I was only saying.' His body tense, Fletch held his breath as he gingerly moved through the open gate. The Dobermanns ran towards them and he tensed his body up even further.

'Clever things, they are,' Billy stated, as he stooped down to tickle one of them behind the ear.

'I suppose so,' Fletch answered. He looked to the decrepit Portakabin where Trevor ran his business. He was just a few steps away from safety.

'Did you know that they can actually sense fear?' Billy crept up behind Fletch, grabbed hold of his leg, and burst out laughing as the younger man jumped up in the air. 'Fucking hell,' he roared. 'You should see your fucking face! You're a nervous fucking wreck.'

'All right, bloody hell,' Fletch cried. 'What did you do that for? You know that I don't like them.'

Barely able to catch his breath, Billy snorted with laughter. 'Don't like dogs?' he wheezed. 'Be honest with me, you're shit fucking scared of them.'

'Yeah, and? Haven't I got enough to deal with, without you pulling stunts like that?'

'I was only trying to cheer you up a bit,' Billy sniggered.

'I need your idea of a joke like I need a fucking hole in the head.' Fletch stormed across the yard to the Portakabin, leaving Billy to continue laughing in his wake. Banging his fist on the door, he gave his boss a scowl as it opened.

'Come on in.' Trevor was all smiles. Dressed in tattered, grease-stained overalls that were turned up at the ankles, and a red and black check shirt that was in good need of a boil wash, he held out his calloused hand.

Shaking the outstretched hand, Fletch resisted the urge to then wipe his down his jeans to rid himself of Trevor's grime. He wrinkled his nose at the sour stench that came from inside the cabin and looked around him.

In the corner sat an old paraffin heater; the cloying fumes it chugged out were enough to bring on the start of a headache. Every available surface was littered with grubby dog-eared paperwork, mouldy tea mugs, and what looked like engine parts.

'So, to what do I owe this pleasure? What is it I can I do for you?' Moving paperwork away from the threadbare chairs, he straightened up and gave them a wide, toothless grin.

Billy returned the smile. 'That business we took care of?'

'Yer?' Trevor was all ears. 'What about it?'

'I just want to remind you to keep it between us.' He perched on the edge of a frayed and dirty chair. 'I need to know that you're going to continue keeping schtum about it.'

'Course I will.' He took a seat behind his desk and spread out his arms. 'You know me; I won't say a dicky bird.' He gave a little wink. 'It never happened, that's what I'll say to anyone who comes near, asking questions.'

'So, someone has been asking questions?' Glancing towards Billy, Fletch's ears pricked up. He took a step closer to the old man. 'Someone has been here, then?'

'No.' Trevor flapped his hand dismissively. 'No one's been here, son.'

'Are you sure about that?' He took a step even closer, his fist clenched at his side. 'Who was it?' he growled. 'Bannerman or Mad Mickey Shank?'

'What? No.' Trevor looked helplessly towards Billy. 'Like I said, no one has been here, son.'

'He's fucking lying.' Fletch's eyes had a steely glint to them as he looked over his shoulder.

'For fuck's sake, Fletch, leave it out.' Billy leapt out of his seat and pulled him roughly away from the old man. 'What the fuck is wrong with you?' he snapped. 'He's just told you that no one has been here. What the fuck is wrong with you?' Billy repeated. 'You need to lay off them fucking pills. Look at the state of you. They're making you paranoid.'

Shaking his head, Fletch rubbed his hand across his jaw, the layer of dark stubble rough against his palm. 'I'm telling you, Billy, he knows something.'

Trevor spread out his arms. 'Come on, Billy, you know me from old, and you know at the first sign of trouble, I would've been on the blower to you.'

'Yeah, I know you would have, and I'm sorry, mate.' He pushed Fletch out of the Portakabin, shaking his head at him as he did so. 'What the fuck is with you lately? You're becoming a fucking liability,' he roared, his cheeks turning a deep shade of red. 'Nice friendly chat we were meant to be having. Not once did I tell you to go in all guns blazing.'

Striding angrily towards the gates, Fletch could practically feel the steam coming out of his ears. He brought his hands up towards his forehead and massaged his temples. He could barely get his head around what had taken place in the last twenty-four hours. Not only was it bad enough having to deal with Tina, but to top it all off, his uncle had been sliced wide open like a pig.

'Well?' Billy shouted after him. 'What the fuck is going on with you, eh?'

'This,' Fletch shouted, pointing to his temple. He spun around, retraced his steps, and came to an abrupt halt in front of his boss. 'All of this up here,' he said, pointing to his head a second time. 'I can't deal with it. I don't know how to fucking deal with it.' He took deep breaths to steady himself. 'That fucking bitch, Tina,' he growled. 'I finished things with her, and now she's walking around the gaff like I owe her something.'

'Well, she is up the spout, mate.'

'Yeah, and don't I know it.' He gave a bitter laugh. 'And then there's me uncle. Over a hundred fucking stitches, all thanks to that mad bastard, Shank. You know as well as I do that he's lucky to still be alive. Then there's Spence. I'm shit-scared that his name is gonna come out, and then there's...' His voice tapered off.

'What?' Billy narrowed his eyes.

'Nothing, it doesn't matter.' Realising he'd already said too much, he averted his eyes and ran his fingers through his dark hair, making it stand up on end. 'All of this is doing my nut in. I ain't even been out of clink for more than a day yet and look at the amount of shit I've had to deal with.'

Billy glanced behind him. He raised a hand apologetically to Trevor, who was still standing cautiously in the Portakabin doorway.

'You know what you need, don't you?' he asked, slinging his arm around Fletch's shoulders.

'What?' Fletch answered with an exasperated sigh.

'You need a good fucking drink.' He sensed the younger man begin to protest and he shook his head. 'I'm not taking no for an answer. Jump in the motor. I know just the place.'

* * *

Lying on his back, his head thumping, Mickey cautiously opened his bruised and swollen eyes, quickly shielding them from the blinding sunlight. How had he got here? He turned over on to his front, put out his hand and clawed at the grass, still dewy from the early morning frost. How the hell had he ended up on his front lawn?

He tried to think back. He could recall being in the boozer with George and his firm; he could recall the car journey as they headed back to South London; he could recall the car hurtling through the Rotherhithe Tunnel.

He opened his eyes wider; a panic filled him. Where was his sword? He pulled himself up on to all fours. His heart began to beat faster, as he looked anxiously around him. Where was it? He knew for a fact that he'd had the blade in the car. He could recall taking the sleeve of his coat and wiping away the streaks of blood smeared across the steel. He turned his head and looked upwards. 'Oi, that's mine.'

'Is it?' came the reply.

'Yeah,' Mickey growled. He began to pull himself to his feet; a snarl creasing his face. 'It's mine.' The figure took a step backwards and Mickey put out his hand. 'Give me my fucking sword.'

The figure remained silent, as if thinking it over.

Mickey was confused. What the hell was going on; who the fuck was this prick? 'Give me back my sword, you fucking cunt.'

Without saying another word, the figure lunged forward, the sword pointing straight ahead.

Mickey's mouth dropped open in shock as the steel blade sliced through his flesh and intestines. He fell towards his assailant, and as he fumbled to keep his balance, his fingers grasped the man's shoulders.

'You hurt my uncle,' the voice said into his ear before pushing him backwards.

Crashing heavily to the floor, Mickey cried out in terror. Blood oozed out of him, and as he pushed his hands down on the wound, he began to whimper. He wasn't ready to die, not yet. He began to scramble backwards, already feeling weak.

'Take the sword,' he choked out. 'Keep it; it's yours.'

'Nah, I don't want it.' The figure looked down at the weapon. 'It's dirty; it's got your blood all over it now.'

His eyes wide open, Mickey pushed himself back even farther, desperate to get away from the man. 'I... I said you can keep it.'

Spencer didn't speak. He didn't need to. He lifted the sword above his head. A white-hot fury spurred him on, and, using his considerable strength, he plunged the sword repeatedly downwards. Only when he was spent and out of breath did he allow himself to smile. Bannerman and his firm would be sorry for what they had done to his uncle. He was going to make sure of it.

* * *

A spieler tucked away in the back streets of Canning Town, East London, was where Billy drove to. 'This place,' he said, pulling the car over to the kerb and climbing out, 'has been like a godsend to me over the years.'

Taking in the dingy exterior, Fletch raised his eyebrows, causing Billy to laugh out loud.

'I have to have somewhere on the quiet I can take the birds, eh? Somewhere I know my Susan will never step inside.'

Billy's disregard of Susan made Fletch clench his fists. He would give his right arm to be married to Susan, and certainly wouldn't need some dark and dingy East End gambling den to take other women to.

'Come on, this way.' He grinned, slinging his arm around Fletch's shoulders.

The inside of the building was as grubby as the exterior. Fletch looked around him. Several tables were littered around the room, and a small bar was set towards the rear of the property. The carpet was sticky underneath their feet and a dense, heavy fog of cigarette smoke filled the air.

Greeted like a celebrity, Billy guided Fletch towards the bar area. He ordered brandies, paid for them, and then passed a glass across. Taking a sip, he eyed Fletch with suspicion. 'So, what happened to you last night?'

'When?' Swallowing down a mouthful of the dark liquid, Fletch stalled for time. He knew exactly what Billy was referring to.

'When Bannerman turned up, you were nowhere to be seen.'

'I just needed some air.' Even as he said the words, he knew how weak his alibi was. 'I went to see my mum, and then just walked for a bit.'

'You walked?' Billy narrowed his eyes. 'Walked where?'

Fletch shrugged. 'The streets. I needed time to think, what with Tina and everything.'

'Yeah, bit of a shocker that, eh?'

'Yeah, you could say that.' Immediately, his thoughts went to Susan and his heart constricted inside his chest.

'So, what will you do now? Marry her?'

Fletch's eyes widened. 'Like fuck I will,' he spat.

Signalling for a second round of drinks, Billy laughed out loud. 'The first rule when it comes to the enemy is to give them what they want. Makes life a lot easier in the long run. Look at my Susan, treated like a fucking queen, she is.' He gulped down his drink and, using the back of his hand to wipe across his lips, he studied Fletch. 'And do you know what I get in return?'

'I dunno.' Fletch shrugged, desperate to get away from the conversation of Billy's marriage.

'I know that I can trust her not to play the field. She wouldn't even dare look at another man.' He spread open his arms. 'And if she did, I'd break her fucking neck, and his,' he added as an afterthought. 'I'd muller the bastard if he so much as looked at what was mine.'

Fletch nodded and sipped at his drink. That was a bit rich coming from Billy. Talk about double standards. The man had no idea how to stay faithful and was the male equivalent of a slag. He studied his boss over the rim of the glass and wondered why he was bringing all of this up now.

As he watched Billy signal for a third round of drinks, a trickle of worry edged its way down his spine. He couldn't help but think that maybe Susan had been right, and that her husband was suspicious of them after all.

'Oi, over here.' Turning his head, Billy raised his arm in the air.

Fletch spun around. He took in the young woman walking towards them and lifted his eyebrows. Although not previously introduced, he recognised her from one of Billy's parties, 'I thought it was all over between you and Keith's missus?'

'What?' Billy laughed. He grabbed at his crotch. 'It ain't my fault if she can't keep away from the goods, is it? Besides, she's got an arse that could crack a fucking walnut, mate.'

Shaking his head, Fletch gulped at his brandy. Typical of Billy. So much for looking out for him. He'd only brought him along because he'd already arranged to meet his bit on the side here.

'Hiya, babe.' Melody Lewis was all smiles as she approached them. Dressed in an impossibly short, black dress that left little to the imagination, she tossed her dark curls over her shoulder and draped her arm around Billy's neck, staking her claim.

'Fletch, Melody.' Billy quickly did the introductions. 'And keep your fucking eyes off him,' Billy warned, stabbing his finger in her face. 'You're here with me. Remember that,' he said, leaning in to cop a quick feel of her backside.

'Leave it out, Bill.' Shaking his head, Fletch could feel his cheeks flush pink. The older man was always the same once he'd had a drink, not that Billy needed much of an excuse to kick off.

Billy's face was deadpan. No one, and he meant no one, touched what belonged to him. 'I mean it,' he warned.

'Yeah, if you say so.' Melody wriggled out of his arms and gave a coy grin. 'It's all right for some, ain't it? At the end of the night, he gets to go home to the little wife.' She threw Fletch a wink. 'What's good for the goose and all that, what do you reckon, babe?'

'What did you just fucking say?'

Inwardly, Fletch groaned. Melody obviously knew nothing of what her latest squeeze was capable of. 'She didn't mean anything by it, Bill.' He laughed off her words in a desperate bid to keep the peace. 'It was just a joke, that's all. Forget about it, mate.'

'Forget about it? Who are you, her fucking keeper?' Billy snarled. He slammed his glass down on the counter, and, shoving Melody up against the bar, his hand gripped tightly around her neck. 'So, do you wanna rephrase what you just said? And think carefully before you fucking answer me.'

The action was so fast that Melody was barely able to breathe. Panic set in and her face turned bright red as she desperately tried to free herself.

'Bill,' Fletch warned.

Billy released his grip, and, grasping hold of her jaw, he threw her away from him.

'You could have just killed me,' Melody choked out. Terror filled her as she rubbed at the red indentations that Billy's fingers had left around her slender neck.

'No "could have" about it.' Billy stalked forward until she was backed up against the wooden bar once more, his eyes two mere slits and his voice a low growl as he spoke. 'If I wanted you dead, I would have choked the fucking life out of you.'

Melody's eyes widened and as she held up her hands, her body shook. Looking up at the crazed man before her, she didn't doubt his words in the slightest. How on earth was she going to explain this away to Keith? It had taken weeks for her husband to even be able to stand in the same room as her, after he'd come home early from work and caught them in the act. There and then, she wished that she'd stayed at home, bored out of her mind, pretending to be the good little wife.

'The fact that I didn't is to remind you that you're nothing but the shit beneath my shoe. I own you. In future, you surrender to every one of my whims, without question.' His hand shot out and grasped around her jaw for a second time. 'Even if I tell you to strip butt naked and dance, you do just that. Do you understand me?'

Tears sprang to Melody's eyes and she glanced towards Fletch for help.

'So, what are you waiting for?' Billy sneered. 'If you want to act like a dirty whore, then that's exactly how I'm gonna treat you. Now, fucking strip.'

A hush fell across the room.

'Leave it out, Bill.' Aware that all eyes were on them, Fletch took a step forward. 'She gets the picture, mate.'

'I told you to fucking strip,' Billy roared, batting his protégé away from him.

Humiliation burnt through Melody and tears stung her eyes, blinding her vision. Not once had she believed that he would turn on her. It had only been a joke, a bit of banter. She'd fully expected him to laugh it off, just like her previous lovers would have done.

Fletch shoved out his hand. 'Bill, this ain't fucking right.'

'You've got a lot to learn,' Billy sneered as he stabbed his finger in Fletch's direction.

Ignoring the comment, Fletch put himself in between the two of them and nodded towards the exit. 'Just get the fuck out of here,' he ordered her. Much to his relief, Melody did just that, and without a backward glance, she ran for the safety of the exit as fast as her high-heeled shoes would allow her to.

'Yeah, you've got a lot to fucking learn,' Billy repeated as, this time, he shoved Fletch forcibly in the chest.

Running his tongue over his teeth, Fletch stood his ground. 'You were bang out of order.' He narrowed his eyes and shook his head. 'What the fuck is wrong with you, eh? Why do you always have to act like a prick? It was only a joke, and you go and attack her like that.'

With his hands placed on the bar, Billy took deep breaths in a bid to calm himself down. He chugged back his brandy and swallowed the dark liquid down.

Wiping his mouth on the cuff of his shirt, he turned his head in the direction of the doors that Melody had escaped through and gave a nonchalant shrug. 'Plenty more where she came from... two-bit slags, that's all they fucking are.'

Fletch shook his head. His chest muscles were taut as he picked up the brandy glass and took a sip. 'Well, that escalated quickly,' he grumbled.

Billy shot him a warning glare and, clicking his fingers towards the barman for a further round of drinks, he ignored Fletch's protests that he should get back to the hospital and check up on Frank.

As if he didn't have enough on his plate already, Fletch

inwardly groaned, as his boss placed a fresh glass in front of him. If Billy's mood was anything to go by, then it was going to be a long, long day.

* * *

Two days later, Tina eyed Fletch from across the living room. 'It's not going to go away, you know that, don't you?' She heaved herself up from the sofa and waddled towards the kitchen. 'This baby. Our baby,' she corrected, 'is going to come, whether you like it not.'

Fletch gave her a cold stare. A familiar sense of irritation spread through him. He couldn't bear to be in the same room as his ex, let alone share a bed with her, so intense was his dislike of her.

'So, Daddy,' she said, looking over her shoulder, 'you'd best get used to the idea, and the quicker the better.'

Watching her leave the room, Fletch scowled. A baby was the last thing he wanted. Actually, that was wrong. A baby with Tina was the last thing he wanted.

Despite the situation, if it had been his Suzy who was pregnant, he would have been over the bloody moon.

Jenny walked into the room. 'You okay, darling?' She eyed her son cautiously.

'What do you think?'

'I think that you're scared. Having a baby can be daunting at the best of times.'

Fletch screwed up his face. 'I'm not scared, Mum. I just don't want one with her.' He stabbed his finger towards the kitchen.

'Don't say that, Fletch. She's the mother of your child.' Jenny put her hand on his arm. 'Once the baby is born, things will be different. After you both get your own place to live, things will settle down, you just wait and see.'

'Our own place?' Fletch's mouth dropped open. 'I don't wanna live with her! It's bad enough that you let her move in here.'

'Well, you can't all stay here forever, darling. We're going to need all the space we can get when Frank comes out of the hospital.' She looked up towards the ceiling whilst thinking it over. 'I don't think he'll even be able to get up the stairs for a while. And as for your brother, well, you can't expect him to sleep on the sofa forever, can you? No, once the baby is born, you and Tina will need your own space. You need to make a go of it – be a proper family.'

Fletch shook his head. He could barely get his head around what she was saying. Why was his mum even taking Tina's side? 'I don't want to make a go of it, Mum. I don't love her. I will never ever love her.'

'In time, you will do.' Jenny smiled gently. 'When the baby is born, you will do.'

'No, Mum, I won't, and I wish people would stop saying that.'

She smiled once more. 'You just wait and see, my darling, everything will turn out just right.'

10

'I don't like it.' Tina was sulking. She placed her hands protectively across her bump and turned her face away from the car window.

'You ain't even looked inside yet.' Fletch gritted his teeth. Begrudgingly, and against his better judgement, he had driven them to view a two bedroomed apartment in Romford that had just come on to the market for rental.

'I don't need to see it.' She continued to sulk. 'Look at it. This place is a dump.'

'It ain't that bad.' He leant forward over the steering wheel and craned his neck to look up at the grey block of flats. Admittedly, it wasn't exactly what he'd been looking for either, but being in the centre of Romford, it was handy for him to get to and from work, and not to mention it was affordable. He opened the car door and climbed out. 'Just have a look at the place. You never know, you might even like it.'

'I doubt it.' Unclipping her seat belt, Tina followed suit, and, with great difficulty, eased herself out of the car. She looked up at the dreary façade and gave a long sigh. 'It'll be a waste of time,' she groaned.

Fletch rolled his eyes and gave an agitated sigh. 'Can we just take a look at this place without arguing for once, eh?' He walked towards the entrance door with Tina waddling behind him and pressed the intercom. Moments later, the door was buzzed open, and they were able to enter the building. He strode across the foyer, his footsteps loud upon the terracotta tiled floor, and pressed for the lift. In silence, they travelled up to the fourth floor, all the while Tina scowling.

The flat, in Fletch's opinion, was perfect for them. With two good-sized bedrooms, a sitting room, small kitchenette area and a bathroom, it had everything they needed. They followed the estate agent around the flat, peering in to the empty rooms and cupboards.

'It's perfect.' Fletch nodded as he stood in front of a set of patio doors that led out to a large wrap-around balcony.

Tina's head snapped towards him. 'No, it isn't,' she complained. 'I want a garden.'

'You can have a balcony instead,' he said, gesturing towards the patio doors.

'I don't want a bloody balcony. I want a garden. In fact, I want to live in a house, not this dump.' Tina's face had turned bright red, her nose was turned upwards and she resisted the urge to stamp her feet like a child having a temper tantrum. 'All of my mates are buying houses. I'm gonna be the only one living in a poxy flat.'

'We'll take it, mate.' Fletch cut off her words, uninterested in where her silly little mates lived.

Nigel Stubbs looked at the young couple in front of him. You could cut the atmosphere with a knife, and he cleared his throat, feeling more than a little bit uncomfortable. 'Are you sure that you don't want more time to think it over?' He gathered up his briefcase and adjusted his tie to hide his blushes.

'No need to think it over. We'll take it.'

'No, we will not take it,' Tina snapped. 'I've already told you, I want a house.'

'I said, we'll take it.' Fletch gave her a cold stare. 'And seeing as I'm the one stumping up the cash, I'll have the final word on the matter.' He turned away from her. It may have been a small victory, but the quicker she learnt that he wasn't about to treat her like some spoiled princess, the better. He indicated for the estate agent to take out the paperwork. 'Right mate. Show me where I need to sign.'

Nigel raised his eyebrows and opened his briefcase. Taking out a series of documents, he hastily signed on the dotted line, before handing the sheets of paper over. His eyes flickered across to Tina as Fletch added his signature, taking note of her pursed lips. She could be a pretty girl if she allowed herself to smile, he thought to himself.

'I can't believe you just did that.' On hearing the front door close after the estate agent, Tina's eyes flashed with anger. Every inch of her bristled. 'The very least you could have done is get us a house. I'm having your baby, and—'

Interrupting her, Fletch poked himself in the chest. 'Listen here. I didn't sign up for this. You wanted to saddle yourself with me, and I've given you no promises, have I? I didn't want this to happen. I told you from the start that I didn't want a relationship with you. I don't think I'm even ready to be a dad, and if I'm being totally honest, I don't know if I ever will be.'

'It takes two to tango,' Tina snapped back. 'And I don't remember you complaining at the time. In fact, the complete opposite.'

'Nah,' Fletch growled. 'You knew exactly what you were

doing.' He stabbed his finger forward. His eyes were cold and menacing as he recalled the look on Susan's face, the expression of heartache etched across her beautiful features, when he'd told her he was about to become a father. 'You set out to trap me, right from the very start.'

Tina's cheeks flushed pink at the accusation. It was true, she had set out to trap him. 'You bastard... you rotten, arrogant, self-centred piece of shit. You don't care about me or... or about this baby... our baby,' she spat.

'That's right, Teen. I am a bastard, and you're right on that one. I couldn't give a shit about you,' Fletch roared back. He knew he was going too far, but he couldn't stop the words from spewing out of his mouth. 'In fact, you can call me every name under the fucking sun, and I'll tell you why, shall I? Because it's true. I'm all those things, and more. And no matter what name you want to call me, it's not going to change anything, is it? It's not going to change the facts. I can't change who I am. I'm not suddenly going to care about you. I hardly even know you, and I know for a fact that you don't know me. You don't even know my real name for a start, do you?'

It wasn't a question; it was more of a statement. He had never told her his birth name. The only woman he had ever told was Susan. He stepped away from her and took deep, steady breaths to calm himself down. From across the room, he could see that his words had upset her, and, rolling his eyes, he came to stand in front of her, the anger leaving him as abruptly as it had arrived. He placed his hands on her quivering shoulders.

'I'm sorry,' he sighed. 'I didn't mean to yell at you like that. I'm just being honest, that's all.' He swallowed deeply. 'I'm really trying to do my best by you.' He glanced around the empty room. 'And this,' he said, lifting up his shoulders, 'is as good as it's ever going to get.'

Stunned, Tina's mouth fell open. 'You don't mean that,' she cried.

'Yes, I do. I'm not the man you think I am.' He took in her shocked expression and shook his head. 'I'm not right for you. We're not right for each other, and you know that as well as I do, don't you?' He gave her a sad smile, thankful that they had had this chance to talk, thankful that he had finally got his true feelings off his chest, and that he was able to let her know the score.

His words were like a knife to her heart, and she screwed up her face at the pain that flowed through her. He was right, and deep down she did know that they weren't right for one another, but she couldn't help herself. He was everything she had ever wanted in a man.

'You must know by now that I don't love you, right?' As if reading her thoughts, Fletch cocked his head to one side as he looked down at her.

Blinded by her tears, she nodded.

He took note of the tears that sprang to her eyes. She looked so small and so vulnerable as she stood beside him that his tone softened. 'I know this isn't what you want to hear, and I don't want to upset you, I really don't, but I don't know what else you want or expect me to say. You're fighting a losing battle, darling. Me and you are never gonna happen.'

He closed his eyes, briefly allowing his words to sink in. 'So, why don't we just try to make good of a bad situation, eh? I'll provide for that baby. I'll even help you out from time to time, but that's as far as it's ever going to go. I don't want to be with you, not in the same way that you want to be with me.'

Tears rolled down Tina's cheeks. She'd known all along that he didn't love her. Still, she'd hoped, prayed even, that since she was carrying his child, he would feel something towards her, however small that might be. In her eyes, anything would have been better than nothing.

'I'm sorry, okay?'

Swallowing down the hard lump in her throat, she finally spoke. Her voice took on a pleading tone. 'But maybe when the baby is born...'

'No, Teen.' He threw his arms up in the air and stepped away from her, his eyes becoming hard once more. Was she not listening to a word he said? 'Me and you, we're never going to work out, no matter how much you might want us to. I don't love you. I'm not ever going to love you.'

'Because of her, that woman?' Despite feeling as though her whole world had crashed down around her, she spat out the words.

At the mention of Susan, Fletch's heart constricted inside his chest. He gave a carefree shrug, hiding his true feelings.

'It is, isn't it? You want to be with her instead?'

'I've already told you, it's complicated,' he mumbled, by way of an answer. 'And I'm really not worth you crying over.'

Tina's lips curled down at the corners. How could he say that? He meant everything to her, and she had a horrible, nagging feeling that he always would.

George could barely take in the news he had just been given. With no known next of kin, it had taken just over a week for Mickey's death to become common knowledge. As he thought this through, a thousand possibilities rattled around inside his brain. He was certain that his cousin had still been alive when they had dumped him on his doorstep. He could recall being angry with the man, but surely he hadn't been so angry that he'd killed him.

'Rumour has it that the sword was still sticking out of him when the Old Bill turned up,' Pete said. He raised his eyebrows. 'I heard it was embedded into the fucking ground.'

'Sword?' Pete's words broke his thoughts and he sat back in his seat, contemplating what this could mean. He knew for a fact that neither he, nor any members of his firm, had used the weapon. 'So you're saying that someone did him in, then?'

'Looks that way. And I'm not being funny, George. I know he was your cousin and all that, but it was only a matter of time until someone topped him. I mean, let's face it, Shank has been raising hell and getting away with murder for years.' He raised his eyebrows to emphasise his point. 'And I mean that literally.'

'Yeah, I know.' Sinking back in his chair, George steepled his fingers in front of him. It shouldn't have come as a surprise that Mickey had been topped. It was common knowledge that he was a lunatic, a psychopath even. In a way, it was ironic. Some may even say it was poetic justice. The weapon that had made him feel safe was the very same instrument that took his life. 'So who did it? Has anyone claimed responsibility?'

'Nope, not as of yet,' Pete answered, with a shrug. 'No one's come forward, and the rumour mill is quiet, too fucking quiet. But if there's one thing that I do know, it's that the majority of people around here will be glad to see the back of him.'

George leant his forearms across the desk and sighed. 'We both know for a fact that Shank did a lot of damage over the years. It stands to reason that someone, somewhere, will boast about how they brought him down. They're bound to, and if they don't...' He left the unfinished sentence to hang heavy in the air.

'If they don't, then it could be the same person who was responsible for Albie going missing?'

Silently, George nodded. Was it just a coincidence that two members of his firm, one being his brother, were now either missing or dead?

'So, what do we do now, then, Boss?'

'Dig around for answers,' George said, his voice coming across a lot more confident than he felt. 'Someone out there knows what happened.' His thoughts wandered to his sister-in-law, and his three nephews. He was due to pay them a visit. The very thought of not being able to give June and the boys an update as to where her husband and their father had disappeared to, depressed him. 'Just keep looking,' he sighed.

An hour later, he was sitting in his brother's back garden, silently brooding as he watched his nephews play on the lawn. Their subdued little faces broke his heart. The disappearance of their father had hit them a lot harder than he'd anticipated.

Deep down, he knew that Albie was dead. He could feel it in his bones, and the thought of not seeing his brother again made his breath catch in his throat.

He pushed the dark thoughts away, pulled out his mobile phone, tapped in a number and spoke with a low growl. 'Enough is enough. I want it sorted out now. I want Albie found and brought home.'

By the time he had switched off the call, his heart already felt lighter. Leaping out of the garden chair, he forced a smile, scooped up a leather football, and moved towards the boys.

'I'll be goalie,' he shouted out as he threw the ball up into the air and watched it land in front of his eldest nephew's feet. He owed it to his brother to see that his sons were all right, to make sure that they didn't forget their father. As he watched the boys kicking the ball around the garden for a short while, everything was okay with the world.

* * *

'Oh, it is lovely.' Jenny smiled as she wandered around her son's new home. 'You'll both be happy here; I've got a good feeling about the place.'

Tina gave her a sad smile. Somehow, she couldn't see herself being happy, not now. Not now that she knew how Fletch really felt about her.

'It's all right, ain't it, Mum.' Fletch grinned as he followed his mother around the flat. 'And out here is the balcony.' He unlocked the patio doors and stepped outside.

'It's smashing, darling, it really is,' Jenny answered as she admired the view across Romford.

'What do you reckon, Spence?'

'It's nice... I suppose.' He stuck out his bottom lip, sulking. 'But I still don't get why you have to move out. It won't be the same without you at home, Fletch.'

Jenny rolled her eyes. 'We've already discussed this, Spence. And don't forget, you can have your own bedroom now, can't you?' she added brightly. 'That will be something to look forward to, won't it?'

'I don't care about my own bedroom.' Spencer continued to sulk. For as far back as he could remember, he had only ever shared a room with his brother. When they had been small boys, they had even shared the same bed. More often than not, after a troubling nightmare, he would crawl into Fletch's bed during the night, until, that was, they had grown too big to share and Fletch had begun to kick him out, wanting his own space.

'Come on, Spence, it won't be that bad. You'll see me every day at work, and I'll still come over to the house, I promise.' Fletch gave his brother a wide grin.

'She's ruined everything.' Turning his head, Spencer glared across to Tina. 'Why did you have to get with her? I don't like her.'

'That's enough,' Fletch chastised. He gave his brother a reassuring smile, slung his arm across his shoulders, and kept his voice light. 'It is what it is, Spence. You can't blame Tina for everything. It was me who made the mistake. I should have been more careful, and now I have to step up and pay the price.'

'Yeah, but...'

'No "yeah but"s. Everything will turn out okay, you just wait and see.' His grin widened, hiding the feeling of despair that flooded through him. Despite the words he spoke, he was as devastated as his brother. More than anything, he wished that he'd never met Tina that fateful night. 'Come on,' he said, gesturing to go back indoors. 'It's time to go and pick Frank up from the hospital.'

Frank Smith's head was bowed. Slumped in a high-backed chair beside the metal framed hospital bed, he shifted his weight, trying to make himself more comfortable. No matter which position he got himself in to, he was in a great deal of pain. He gripped the arms of the chair. As he moved, his fingertips turned a deathly shade of white, and he gasped out loud at the searing agony that ripped through his abdomen. He held his breath, waiting for the feeling to subside, and sank lower into the chair. The very thought of having to stand up and actually walk was enough to bring him out in a cold sweat.

'You all right, Frank?'

He gave a nod of his head, not trusting himself to speak, for fear of causing the wound to pull again.

'Are you ready to come home?' Jenny gave a forced smile as she fussed around him.

'Stop that.' He gritted his teeth as he spoke in a whisper. 'I can manage.'

Jenny's cheeks flushed crimson. Nothing ever changed with him.

He closed his eyes, knowing full well that he would soon need to move out of the chair. His fingertips gripped on to the wooden arms once more. He couldn't put the inevitable off for much longer because it was time to go. Sweat poured out of him as he slowly wriggled towards the edge of the seat.

'Do you need help?' Fletch made to move forward.

'I said, I can manage,' he growled. He gritted his teeth as he made to stand up. He'd barely lifted his backside three inches off the chair before collapsing in a heap. 'That fucking Shank,' he roared. 'He's ruined me.'

'You don't need to worry about Shank.' Spencer gave a lopsided grin. 'He's finished an' all.'

Fletch snapped his head towards his brother, his eyes narrowed. 'What do you mean by that?'

Spencer continued to grin. 'He got done in.'

'Done in?' Fletch looked from his brother to his mother and uncle. 'What do you mean, he got done in?' A cold shiver ran through Fletch. They had been here before when Albie Bannerman had been murdered. He moved closer and kept his voice low. 'What do you know about Shank, Spence?'

'Just that he's been done in.' Spencer shrugged his shoulders and continued to gather up Frank's belongings.

'And? Where did you hear that?'

'I dunno.' Spencer made to walk away, and his brother pulled him back towards him. 'What?'

'Who told you about Shank, Spence?'

'I already told you.' Spencer grinned. 'I don't remember.'

Watching his brother walk from the ward, Fletch had a sinking feeling that he just couldn't, for the life of him, shake off. The mere thought that his brother could have killed for a second time was not only disturbing, but downright terrifying.

After dropping his mum, uncle and brother back home to Dagenham, Fletch drove to the dingy spieler in East London, where he had arranged to collect Billy. He took a sip from his takeaway coffee, switched off the engine and stepped out of the car. Once he'd drained the contents of his drink, he tipped the dregs out into the gutter, crumpled the polystyrene cup in his fist, and then tossed it into a nearby waste bin.

He'd been about to cross the street, when out of the corner of his eye, he spotted two heavily set men approaching him from his right-hand side. Making a split-second decision, he moved off to his left, glancing over his shoulder repeatedly as he walked in the direction of the High Street. At a distance, the men followed.

He could feel his heartbeat quicken and as he looked around him for an escape route, he wanted to curse himself. He wasn't some pussy, and knew for a fact that he could hold his own, so why hadn't he just squared up to them or entered the spieler as he'd originally planned, instead of skulking away like a mouse, like a coward? Now he would have no other choice but to face the men, whoever they were, alone and without any likely backup, should he even need it.

On the busy High Street, he weaved in and out of the passers-by, hoping more than anything to shrug the two men off. Still they followed.

'Fuck,' he muttered. With one final glance over his shoulder, he ducked in to an alleyway, out of sight, and leant his back against the brickwork, whilst waiting for his racing heart to once again return to its familiar, steady rhythm.

Before he could stop himself, laughter coupled with relief pushed its way up through his chest and out of his mouth, and, with a shake of his head, he ran his hand across his clammy forehead. What the fuck was wrong with him? Billy was right, the pills were making him paranoid.

He shook his head for a second time. He needed to sort himself out, and in double-quick time, before the pills Stevie acquired for them left him acting and feeling like a quivering wreck. Using his foot, he propelled himself away from the wall. At that exact moment, two large, looming figures stepped forward, blocking his exit, bringing him to an immediate halt.

The tiny hairs on the back of Fletch's neck stood up on end. His instincts had been right after all. They had been following him. 'Oi,' he called out to them. 'What's your fucking problem?'

In silence, the men took a menacing step forward.

Looking over his shoulder, Fletch realised his mistake. All thanks to his stupidity, he was completely blocked in. He moved back even farther, another mistake. He was now out of view from anyone walking past the alleyway.

'I asked you a fucking question. What do you want?' Despite the concern that spread through him, his voice remained loud and confident, totally at odds to how he really felt.

A third man entered the alleyway – a man Fletch instantly recognised. George Bannerman.

'What do we want?' George spread out his arms in a theatrical gesture. Behind him stood his henchmen, and they cracked their knuckles ready for action. 'Unless you're stupid, you should already know the answer to that question.'

A flurry of different emotions swept over Fletch. Every day, he woke up wondering if this would be the day that they finally came face to face. After all, it was only sheer luck that had kept them apart for so long. A defiant gleam was in his eyes as he looked up at the man he had hated for the majority of his life.

'Hello, Dad, long time no see.'

11

Taken aback, George held up his hand and signalled for his henchmen to back off. Staring at the young man in front of him, he rolled his bottom lip between his teeth and searched his face, desperate to find something there that he recognised, something familiar. He cocked his eyebrows upwards.

'Harry?' he enquired.

Shaking his head, Fletch swallowed deeply. 'I haven't been called that for a very long time.'

George laughed out loud. 'Right there.' He vehemently stabbed his finger forward and narrowed his eyes. 'Right there is the reason I could never find you. The bitch actually went through with her threat and changed your name.'

'She did what she had to do to keep us safe,' Fletch answered defensively. 'And let's face it, even if Mum had put us in the middle of a war zone, it would have been a lot safer than living with you.'

'And there he is, my fucking son, the one with the big mouth.' Clapping his hands together, George gave a menacing chuckle. 'I wondered how long it would take for that smart mouth of yours to start working. I always said that you had a lot of front. Even as a nipper, you were a cocky little bastard. Always had just a bit too much to say for yourself, always watching me, always antagonising me, always ready and waiting to open that big fucking trap of yours and give me some lip.'

'Is that why you beat us black and blue? Is that why my brother nearly died? Is that why a court granted us a protection order from you?'

George's eyes darkened. 'I owned you.'

Leaning forward, Fletch screwed up his face. 'You owned jack shit; we couldn't wait to get away from you. In fact, I begged Mum day and night to take us away from you.'

'She really got into that head of yours, didn't she? So, what exactly did she do, eh, spin you a few tall stories, tell you some half-truths, tell you I'm the devil himself?'

'It's all true,' Fletch spat. 'I was there. I remember everything; I remember what you did to us.'

'I did fuck all,' George roared back.

'Tell that to Spencer.' Taking a step backwards, Fletch stuck his chin in the air. 'He's doing okay, before you ask.' It was a lie, but he wasn't about to give their father the satisfaction of knowing otherwise.

'I'm glad to hear of it.' George gave a wide smile that didn't quite reach his eyes.

'You know...' Maintaining a considerable distance between them, Fletch crossed his arms over his chest and stood with his legs spread apart. 'I always wondered how I'd react if I ever saw you face to face, what I'd actually say or do.'

'Is that so?' They continued to stare at each other, sizing one another up. 'Well, I'm not stopping you. If you think you can take a shot at your old man, then go for it, take the fucking shot.' Towering over his son, George took a step closer and closed the gap between them. 'Well, come on, I'm waiting. I'll tell you what,' he said, lowering his fists to his sides, 'I'll even let you have the first shot for free, but once you're done, don't be surprised if I go to town on that pretty little face of yours.'

Glaring across at the henchmen, Fletch took deep steady breaths. Nothing could have prepared him for the hatred he felt for this man, his own father.

'I still can't get my head around it.' George looked over his shoulder to address his heavies. 'My son, my own flesh and blood, running around after King.' He narrowed his eyes and turned back to face him. 'Let me guess, you're one of his many fucking gofers.' He tilted his head to one side, and a smirk spread across his face. 'Or maybe that honour falls upon your brother. Out of the two of you, he was always weaker. He takes after your mother in that respect.'

'You don't know anything about my brother,' Fletch spat.

'I know enough.'

Fletch took note of the snarl across his father's face. The famous temper that he remembered so well from his childhood was ready and waiting to erupt. He recognised the warning signs and took a cautious step backwards.

George's face twisted in anger, and, backing Fletch up against the brick wall, he clenched his meaty fists, ready to attack. 'Pity really, your mother,' he snarled. 'She ruined you. I would have made sure that my sons turned out to be real men, not gofers, and certainly not fucking pussies.'

Fletch gritted his teeth. 'Fuck you.'

George snorted with laughter and his tone became mocking, 'So, you do actually have a backbone in there?' He stabbed his finger forcibly into his son's chest. 'Maybe I underestimated you, pretty boy. I mean, after all, you are my son.'

'I'm no son of yours.'

'Son or no son, I'm done playing games,' George spat back. 'Where the fuck is my brother?'

'I dunno—' Before Fletch could even finish the sentence, George's fist slammed into his gut, causing him to double over and involuntarily clutch at his stomach.

'I asked you a question,' George roared.

Still bent over and with his eyes downcast, Fletch grappled for an answer. He'd always known his father was a monster, that he didn't care about his children, that he'd used violence to control them. 'I…' He looked up and shook his head. He would rather die at his own father's hands than divulge his brother's part in Albie's murder. 'I already told you, I don't know,' he choked out.

'Don't lie to me.' Yanking his son upright, George clasped the front of Fletch's shirt in his fist and, pushing his head forward, he bellowed in his face. 'Where is he?'

'Dad.' The word caught in Fletch's throat. They may have been father and son, but even more than that, they were strangers. 'I don't know; I swear to you.' The tone in which George spoke sickened him. All he wanted to do was lash out, to pummel his fists into this man's face. Instead, he pretended to cower backwards. He had to play the game; after all, Spencer's life was in his hands.

Throwing his son away from him, George ran his hand through his hair. 'What do you know about Shank?'

Once again, Fletch feigned ignorance, and in a way, he was telling the truth. He didn't know what had happened. 'I don't know anything about him.'

A snarl spread across George's face as he stalked forward. He revelled in his son's apparent discomfort and, indicating for his henchmen to drag Fletch in front of him, he balled his fists.

'Well, maybe, son,' he said, emphasising the word, 'this will help jog your memory.' With that, he pummelled his fists forward, taking great pleasure in the obvious damage he was causing to his own flesh and blood.

Stepping out on to the busy street, Billy looked around him. Parked across from the spieler was Fletch's black BMW. He pulled out his mobile phone. Still there were no missed calls or text messages. The fact that Fletch had never let him down before, coupled with the fact that his car was here, didn't sit right with him. He wandered back inside the building, double checking that they hadn't somehow bypassed one another.

'Back already?' the barman called out.

Billy shook his head. 'I'm looking for my pal. Did he come in here?'

'No one has been in here, mate; place is as dead as a dodo,' he complained.

A frown creased Billy's forehead. So where the fuck was Fletch, then?

He pushed his way back outside, and, dipping his hand into his jacket pocket, he pulled out his mobile phone. Without even hesitating, he hastily scrolled through his contact list, and, finding Fletch's contact number, he pressed dial. It rang out. His forehead furrowed, and, making his way across the street, he inspected the car.

Leaning his palm on the windowpane, he peered through the passenger side window. Just as he'd suspected, nothing was amiss. He straightened up and glanced up and down the street for a second time. A scowl etched its way across his face. He'd bet his life on the fact that the younger man was in the bookie's, oblivious to the time. He had to be. Where else could he have disappeared off to?

Ten minutes later, Billy emerged from the bookmaker's alone. None of this made any sense to him. The shrill ring of his mobile phone broke his thoughts, and, shoving his hand into his pocket, he pulled out the device. Fletch's name flashed up on the screen. A sneer weaved its way across his face. He pressed answer and growled into the mouthpiece.

'Fletch, where the fuck are you?'

* * *

A wolfish grin spread across George's face, and, holding Fletch's phone to his ear, he let out a low chuckle. 'Guess again, King.'

Before Billy could answer, he crouched down and held the phone close to his son's face. After a few beats, he stood up and moved a few paces forward. 'Do you hear that?' he asked, referring to the muffled groans. 'That's your boy having the shit kicked out of him.'

He held the device away from his ear as Billy screamed and hollered blue murder down the line.

'I'm done playing games. I want answers,' he spat into the phone. 'Where is my brother? And think hard before you fucking answer me, because this is only a taster of what is to come.'

He glanced down at his son and felt nothing. Why should he? He didn't even know the kid, he didn't want to know him, and that was the truth of the matter. As far as he was concerned, the boy was tainted.

'Tick, tock, King. You'd best find your boy. Time's running out fast, and his life is hanging by a fine thread. And when I say fine, I mean really fucking fine. I'm giving you twenty-four hours before I come looking for answers.'

With those parting words, he switched off the call, threw the phone down on top of Fletch's broken body and indicated for his henchmen to follow him out of the alleyway. He'd done what he'd set out to do. Now, all he needed to do was sit back and wait for King to deliver his brother back home, where he belonged, safe and sound.

* * *

'Tick, tock.' Bannerman's words rang loudly inside Billy's mind. How the fuck was he meant to find Fletch? He didn't even know where to start looking. He walked aimlessly up and down the High Street, his phone glued to his ear.

Once again, Fletch's mobile phone rang off. Each time the call ended, he pressed redial. Still he didn't pick up. Fuck it. Worry edged its way down his spine. What if he didn't find him in time? He pushed the terrifying thought to the back of his mind and continued pacing the pavement.

* * *

Pain flooded every inch of Fletch's body. After regaining consciousness, he pulled his knees up to his chest, in a bid to relieve the burning ache in the pit of his stomach. Counting to ten, he exhaled slowly and braced himself, before dragging his weary body into a sitting position. Just that small insignificant movement caused him to take a sharp intake of breath as indescribable pain shot through him, leaving him no other choice but to groan out loud.

Thankful to find that he was now alone, he felt around the floor for his mobile phone, and, grasping the device between his fingers, he pulled it in towards his chest, hugging it to him as though his life depended on it.

It didn't take a genius to tell him that his ribs were broken.

He could feel a sharp pain in his chest with each ragged breath that he took. He reached up to touch his eyebrow, and, taking his hand away, he stared down at the blood smeared across his fingertips. His father had really gone to town on him, and he rightly guessed that each punch, each sickening kick, had intensified in power as he took years of pent-up rage out on his son.

His hand shook as held his phone, and with great difficulty, he brought it away from his body. Screwing up his face, he scrolled through his contact list, and then pressed dial.

'Bill,' he croaked into the phone. 'Bannerman has done me over.'

* * *

Yanking aside the hospital cubicle curtain, Spencer bounded forward. 'Who did this to you, Fletch?' He cracked his neck and clenched his fists into tight balls. 'Who attacked you?'

'I don't know.' With his eyes fixated on a spot of dried blood splattered across the Aztec-patterned curtain, Fletch shook his head, pretending not to remember. 'It's all a bit of a blur.'

'But you must have seen him?' Spencer screwed up his face. He didn't understand. He knew his brother was no fool. He would have fought back. How could he have not seen his attacker?

'I said, I don't fucking know. Just drop it.'

For the first time since he'd arrived at the hospital, his brother turned to face him. Just as quickly, he looked away, but not before Spencer had seen the flash of anger in his eyes.

'Go home, Spence.'

'But...'

'I said, go home,' Fletch roared.

Spencer swallowed deeply. He didn't understand. He'd always

followed his big brother around, and not once had he ever told him to go away. 'Are you mad at me? Did I do something wrong?'

Fletch gritted his teeth. How could he even begin to tell his brother that he wasn't safe, that just being in his presence was enough to put his life at risk.

'I told you to fuck off.' Despite the pain that flooded through him, he kicked away the flimsy hospital blanket tangled around his legs and pushed himself up to a sitting position, his face a mask of anger and something else, fear. 'Go home, Spence,' he growled. 'I don't want you here.'

'Fletch,' Stevie warned. Never had he imagined the day that his best friend would turn on his younger brother. He turned to look at Billy, who shrugged his shoulders in return. 'What's going on?' he demanded.

Flopping back against the thin pillow, Fletch pinched the bridge of his nose and exhaled loudly. 'Just get him out of here.'

'What's your problem, Fletch?' Stevie chewed on the inside of his cheek as he studied his friend. 'This ain't like you, man.'

What was his problem, he wanted to roar back, what was his fucking problem? How about the fact that their father now knew exactly who he was? That he would know how to find them? That he could easily hunt them down and finish off what he'd started all those years before and kill them both if he so wished? After all, the man was more than a monster, he was the epitome of evil.

As his brother and best friend filed past him, Fletch put out his hand and brought Stevie to a halt beside him. He grasped the front of his jacket in his fist and pulled him close. 'Make sure that you see him to the front door,' he whispered in his ear. 'Make sure that he actually goes inside the house.'

Narrowing his eyes, Stevie nodded. He glanced up at Billy. The same confusion he felt was etched across their boss's face.

'Promise me.' Fletch spoke in a low growl.

'Of course, mate.' He took a step away, gave Billy one final glance and left the cubicle.

'What the fuck was that all about?' Sucking his teeth, Billy pushed himself away from the wall and came to stand at the end of the hospital trolley. 'You know exactly who it fucking was, you told me it was Bannerman.'

'I just want to get out of here.' Pressing the call bell, Fletch skipped over the question, and with his eyes remaining firmly closed, he blocked out Billy's quizzical stare whilst he kept his finger on the button and waited for the nurse to arrive.

Despite the protests from the hospital staff that he could be suffering from concussion, Fletch discharged himself. He hated hospitals at the best of times, and, ignoring their pitying glances, he walked out of the accident and emergency department as fast as he could, or at least as fast as his aching body would allow him to.

'What the fuck has got into you?' Billy growled as they walked across the hospital car park.

Avoiding eye contact, Fletch answered the question with one of his own. 'What are we going to do about Bannerman?'

Billy shrugged. 'Fuck all.'

'What do you mean, fuck all?' Fletch's eyes widened, and his voice began to rise. 'He gave you twenty-four hours to give his brother back.'

'And?'

'Bill...' He stopped walking, forcing Billy to come to a stand beside him. 'Twenty-four hours.'

'What do you want me to fucking do?' Billy glanced around him, checking that they weren't within earshot of any passers-by.

'I can't bring him back, can I? Fuck me, I know he might have looked like Frankenstein, but trust me, there ain't no way that fucker is coming back to life any time soon.' He shrugged his shoulders. 'The no-good cunt is exactly where he deserves to be, and that's brown bread in the boot of a fucking car.'

In a round about way, Fletch could see Billy's point. What's done was done. They couldn't change the facts, even if they wanted to. They continued walking across the car park.

'And what about Shank? Did you know that he's dead?'

'Yeah, I heard, not that I'm surprised.' Billy gave Fletch a sideways glance. 'The geezer was a lunatic and that's putting it mildly.'

'So, it wasn't you, then?'

'Fuck me, what is this?' He took one look at Fletch's face, saw the seriousness there, and shook his head. 'As much as I would have liked to end the mad bastard, no, it wasn't me,' he growled. 'Why the fuck would you think that I had a hand in it?'

Fletch shrugged, as they came to a halt in front of his car. 'It's nothing,' he said, clutching his arm across his broken ribs.

'No, come on, out with it,' Billy urged him. 'You can't just accuse me of shit and then not explain yourself.'

'It's Spence.' He flopped against his car and gingerly touched his stitched eyebrow. A part of him didn't want to say the words out loud; an even bigger part of him didn't want to believe that his brother could be capable of murder, not once, but twice. 'I dunno, it's just... I thought that maybe...'

'What?' Not one to have much patience, Billy came to stand beside him. He leant backwards against the car door and lit a cigarette. 'For fuck's sake, spit it out, will you. What about Spence?'

'He knew all about it.' Fletch's shoulders sagged. What with his aching head, he couldn't help but feel as though he had the weight of the world piled on top of him. 'He knew that Shank was dead. How did he find out something like that? Who told him?' he asked with narrowed eyes.

Exhaling a cloud of cigarette smoke, Billy lifted his eyebrows. 'It's hardly a secret, is it?' He offered across a cigarette and flicked the ignition on his gold lighter. 'Anyone could have told him that the mad bastard was brown bread.'

'I know, it's just...' Fletch took a long drag on his cigarette, waited for Billy to open the passenger door, and exhaled loudly before climbing inside. Just the slightest movement made him feel as though his stomach muscles were on fire. 'I just thought...' Stalling for time, he stretched out his long legs as far as he could, making his sore body feel more comfortable. 'Maybe I'm being out of line here, I don't know. It's just, I thought that after what happened with Albie Bannerman, you might have roped Spencer in to killing Shank as well?' He turned to look at Billy, studying his reaction, on the lookout for any tell-tale signs that he could be lying.

Billy screwed up his face and shook his head. 'I don't know what you're talking about. Until tonight, I hadn't even seen Spencer.' He was thoughtful for a moment. 'Is that what Bannerman wanted with you?'

Fletch nodded. 'Amongst other things...' he grumbled. Still, shame flooded through him.

He should have smashed his father in the face, and not stopped until the man was a bloodied and broken mess on the floor. Even though Billy hadn't said as much, he took a wild guess that the older man suspected something wasn't right – that a lot more had gone down than what he had told him. The fact that he hadn't even thrown a single punch was enough to tell him that.

He flicked the cigarette butt out of the open window, groaning in pain as he did so. 'If it wasn't you, then who told him?'

'Like I said, I ain't got a Scooby. It could have been anyone,' Billy answered as he climbed behind the wheel.

'Yeah, I suppose so.' He closed his eyes and waited for Billy to turn the key in the ignition. As the car purred to life, guilt ran through his veins. Maybe, just maybe, he had been wrong about his brother after all.

12

Twenty-four hours, that was the deadline George had given King. He sneaked a glance at his wristwatch. Time was running out, and fast. Sitting behind his desk, he glared around the room. 'King, the no-good bastard, is taking the fucking piss out of me.'

'Do you want him brought in?' Sitting forward in his seat, Pete rested his forearms on his knees. 'Just say the word, Boss, and it's as good as done.'

'No.' George shook his head, and as he adjusted the solid gold cufflinks at his wrists, an evil smile spread across his face. 'Let's just say, I've got a better idea.' He gave a menacing chuckle. 'There's a certain someone I know of who will make King's boys not only talk, but sing like fucking canaries.'

Abruptly, he stood up from his seat and hooked his car keys over his index finger. 'King will be expecting a backlash; I know how his mind works. He'll be ready and waiting for me to dish out my own form of retribution.' He looked down at his firm, crowded around the small room. 'But this he won't expect; not in his wildest fucking dreams would it even cross his mind.'

The men looked up. To say they were intrigued was an understatement. Bannerman was cunning and as sly as a fox. Right from the off, they should have known that he would have a plan in place.

Without saying another word, George flicked his head towards the office door, dismissing them. 'This, I do alone,' he spat, as they duly filed out of the house.

* * *

The fishing lake at Mayesbrook Park, known locally as Matchstick Island, was where Fletch found his brother. As kids, the lake had been their salvation, the place they headed to when they wanted to get away from Frank for a bit or just bunk off school for the day.

With his hands shoved into his denim pockets, Fletch made his way across the grass. He saw his brother turn his head as he approached, and he gave him a wide, apologetic smile.

'I thought that I might find you here.' He stood still for a moment, looking out across the lake. 'I just wanted to say that I'm sorry about what happened at the hospital. I didn't mean to yell at you or tell you to go away. I was just in a bad mood and I took it out on the wrong person.'

Attaching a piece of luncheon meat on to the fishing hook, Spencer shrugged his shoulders.

'You caught anything yet?' Fletch took his hands out of his pockets, held his arm across his broken ribs, then sat down beside his brother and dangled his legs over the side of the muddy bank.

'Nah, not yet.' Poking his tongue out slightly, Spencer concentrated on the task in front of him.

Fletch continued watching as his brother pulled back the rod and then cast the line out across the lake. For a short moment, the water rippled as the neon orange float bobbed up and down.

'Spot on.' He nodded, impressed. 'You always were better than me at casting out.'

'Course it's spot on.' Spencer puffed his chest out at the praise he was given. 'I had a good teacher, didn't I?'

'Yeah, I taught you well.' It was said tongue-in-cheek, and he ducked out of the way before his brother could punch him on the arm.

'Oi,' Spencer laughed. 'You didn't teach me how to fish.'

'Nah, I know I didn't.' The smile slid from Fletch's face. Fishing had been the only thing their father had ever done with them.

Come rain or shine, every Sunday morning, George Bannerman would have them up and out of bed at the crack of dawn. The car would then be loaded up with all the fishing gear, and with a large Tupperware box full of sandwiches, a flask of coffee for George and a can of pop each for the two boys. Then they would set off for the day.

'One day' – Spencer smiled – 'when Dad comes back, I'll bring him over here. He'd like that, wouldn't he?'

'Yeah.' Fletch gave his brother a sad smile. He bit down on his bottom lip and cursed himself for the lie he was about to tell. 'I think he'd really like that, Spence.'

Looking out across the lake, they sat in a comfortable silence.

'Hey.' Fletch glanced down at his wristwatch. He had an hour or so to kill before he needed to head back home, and he nudged his brother in his ribs. 'Until then, you can impress me with how good you are instead.'

Not taking his eyes away from the float in the middle of the lake, Spencer gave a beaming smile.

* * *

Jenny Fletcher was having the time of her life. Walking out of Mothercare, she was laden down with shopping bags. Excitement at the prospect of becoming a grandmother rippled through her, and she couldn't resist taking another peek inside the plastic bag. She grinned widely as she looked down at the tiny outfits she had bought. This baby, her first grandchild, would want for nothing. She was determined of that.

Unlocking the car door, she climbed inside, placed the shopping bags on the passenger seat beside her, and started the ignition, blissfully unaware that she was being intently watched.

George could barely keep the snarl from his face. It had been almost eighteen years since he had last seen the mother of his children – eighteen long years since she had had the audacity to run out on him, taking his sons with her.

Not that he had even wanted the boys in the first place. As far as he was concerned, they were nothing more than an inconvenience. Their very conception was a colossal mistake of the highest order. All they had ever been to him was an albatross hanging around his neck, always whining, always crying, always wanting attention, always disobedient.

Flicking the indicator, he pulled out on to the road, and, maintaining a safe distance between them, he continued to follow her dark blue Mini Metro. Briefly, he wondered what had brought her shopping for infant items. She was just as slim and petite as he remembered her all those years before, and certainly didn't look pregnant, not that he'd been able to take a very good look at her. Her tiny frame had been mostly hidden beneath the large shopping bags she'd been carrying.

He followed her towards Dagenham, and as she pulled in to a

side street and parked the car, he swiftly followed suit. From where he sat hidden out of sight, he was able to study her. She looked happy. There and then, he wanted to wipe the smug grin from her face.

* * *

As she locked the car door, Jenny smiled to herself. She couldn't wait to show Tina everything she had bought for the baby. Oblivious to everything and everyone around her, she absentmindedly hooked the carrier bags over her wrist, and, using her free hand, she rummaged around in her handbag, hunting for the house keys.

Her fingers grasped a faded, red, heart-shaped plastic keyring, and, giving it a tug, she pulled out a bunch of keys. The keyring had been a gift from Spencer, who'd bought it for her when he'd visited the seaside on a school trip as a young child, and all these years on, she still cherished it.

A looming shadow coming from behind caused her to smile. Typical Spencer; as per usual, he was playing silly buggers. One of his favourite pastimes was to creep up from behind and try to scare the living daylights out of her. She chuckled out loud.

'I know it's you, Spence. You didn't scare me this time,' she said, spinning around.

The vision in front of her caused her breath to catch in her throat and the hairs on the back of neck to stand up on end. There was no mistaking who he was. Other than his dark blond hair that had begun to turn grey at the temples, he hadn't changed at all. He towered over her and she felt her blood turn cold. Just being in close proximity to her ex-husband was enough to cause a knot of fear to twist in her stomach and a wave of nausea to sweep over her.

'No,' she cried out.

He stalked forward, and the steely glint in his blue eyes that she remembered so well from her past had her gasping in terror. In her haste to get away from the monster she had been married to, she dropped the bags on the pavement and darted down the pathway towards the front door. How had he even found her? As always, her first thought went to her two sons. Above all else, she had to keep them safe.

She fumbled with the key in her hand, and her body shook so violently, she was unable to slip it into the lock.

'Please,' she silently pleaded, 'please open.'

His hot breath on the back of her neck had her quaking with fear. 'Please, just leave us alone.' Her voice quivered as she spoke. 'We don't want you here.'

'Tough fucking luck.'

Finally, she was able to turn the key in the lock and the front door was flung open. She stumbled across the threshold and crashed heavily to her knees. Her brain didn't even register the pain. Only pure terror flooded through her body, and, crying out in fear, she managed to crawl a few feet down the hallway before his rough hands pulled her backwards and dragged her to her feet.

Twisting her body this way and that, she pulled herself free and was able to briefly escape from his clutches. Within the blink of an eye, he yanked on her arm so hard and fast that she thought it would come out of its socket.

'What do you want?' she screamed out the words, ignoring the pain in her shoulder as he flung her up against the wall and pinned her into place.

'What do I want?' He put his finger to her lips, instantly silencing her, and twirled a strand of her hair around his finger. He was so close that he could smell the peppermint on her breath. She always did smell nice – clean, like Pears soap and apple shampoo – not the usual stale tobacco and cheap perfume preferred by the slags who frequented the estate where they had grown up.

'Well, it ain't fucking you, darling. That ship sailed a long time ago.' He looked down the hallway. 'I've come to take back what's mine. Where are my sons?'

Before she could answer, Frank's booming voice called out from the lounge. 'What's going on out there?'

With his finger still wrapped around a strand of Jenny's hair, George's back stiffened, and he turned his head to look in the direction of Frank's voice. 'Get rid of him.'

'I can't.' Her heart pounded inside her chest. 'He was injured. He can't get out of the chair.'

'Jenny,' Frank repeated. 'What's all the noise about?'

'Unless you want me to go in there and finish the job off, tell him it's nothing.' George tightened his grip on her hair.

Jenny took a deep breath; she didn't doubt him in the slightest. 'It's nothing, Frank.' As she blinked up at her ex-husband, tears filled her eyes. 'I dropped the shopping bags, that's all.'

'You woke me up,' Frank grumbled. 'Make me a cuppa, will ya? Nice and strong, just how I like it, with three sugars.'

'Will do,' she called back, desperately trying to keep her voice from shaking.

George gave her a wicked grin. 'So, back to my question.' He looked back down the hallway towards the staircase. 'Where are they? Where are my sons?'

Jenny followed his eyeline, thankful that Spencer was obviously out. The last thing she wanted was for her ex-husband to see her youngest son, her baby.

'They're not here,' she stated. 'I don't know where they are.'

'Well, now, ain't that a shame.' He grinned down at her. 'Just you and me then, eh? Just like old times.' He pushed his weight against her, and, ignoring her cry of fear, he grasped her heart-shaped face in one hand. 'Now, you're going to deliver a message to those precious little bastards you call kids. You are going to tell them that I want to know where my brother is.'

'Albie?' There was confusion in Jenny's voice. Why would the boys even know of her former brother-in-law's whereabouts?

Ignoring the question, George tightened his grip. 'Do you understand me?'

Jenny paused.

'Do you fucking understand me?' he growled.

'Y... yes,' she cried.

'Good.' He dropped his hand to the side, and whispered in her ear. 'If I don't get answers, then I will come back here and pick you off, one by fucking one, starting with Spencer.'

Tears rolled down Jenny's cheeks. Despite the fear she felt, she pushed him roughly away from her. Sickness washed over her body and she could taste acrid bile rise up the back of her throat, before hastily swallowing it down.

In response, George raised his fist in the air. 'Don't make me angry,' he snarled. 'Have you forgotten what I'm capable of? Have you forgotten how angry you would make me? What your disobedience pushed me to do?'

She cowered backwards. She would never forget what he was, nor would she ever forget what he was capable of. She'd experienced first-hand the damage he could do to both her and the boys.

He stabbed his finger forward in a final warning. 'I'll be waiting.' Without saying another word, he then left the house as quietly as he'd arrived.

Sinking to the floor, tears rolled down Jenny's cheeks, and, placing her head into her hands, she began to weep.

'Jenny, where's my fucking tea?'

Her head snapped upwards, and, swiping at her tear-stricken eyes, she got to her feet. 'Piss off, Frank. You'll get your tea when I'm good and fucking ready.'

First things first – she needed to speak to her eldest son, so, grabbing her handbag, she cautiously opened the front door, before fleeing out of the house to the safety of her car.

Fifteen minutes later, Jenny's heart was still pounding. She pushed her foot on the brake and looked around her. Noting that the coast was clear, and that George was nowhere to be seen, she hastily switched off the engine, jumped out of the car, and pulled her woollen coat protectively around her slight frame, before rushing towards the tower block where her elder son lived. Ever so slightly, her fingers shook as she tapped in the digits on the keypad entry system. The heavy entrance door sprang ajar, and, flinging it open, she hurried across the foyer to the lift.

Moments later, the lift came to a shuddering halt on the fourth floor, and as she stepped out into the corridor, a strong odour of bleach hit her nostrils. She resisted the urge to wrinkle her nose, took a deep breath to steady herself, then walked across the communal landing towards her son's home.

'Mum, what are you doing here?' Standing at the front door, Fletch clutched his hand across his broken ribs and cocked his eyebrows. A shiver of worry edged its way down his spine. It was so unlike his mum to turn up unexpectedly.

'What am I doing here?' she shrieked. For the briefest moment her ex-husband was gone from her mind. 'What on earth happened to you?' She took his bruised face in her hands and tilted it from side to side, inspecting the damage. Across his left eyebrow, a slit had been stitched closed; the wound still dotted with dried blood looked angry and red. 'Who did this to you?'

'I don't know; I was jumped,' he muttered by way of an explanation. 'I'm all right, Mum, it's nothing, honest, it doesn't even hurt,' he lied.

'Well, you don't bloody well look all right.' She released him and folded her arms across her chest. 'And when were you going to tell me, your mum, about this, eh?'

Fletch shrugged. He'd hoped that he wouldn't need to tell her and had already decided to wait for the bruising to go down before paying a visit to the house.

'Tomorrow.' He gave her a cheeky grin, pulled the door open wider, and gestured for her to come in to the flat. 'I was going to pop over tomorrow. Honest, Mum, it's nothing for you to worry about. Tina should never have called you.'

'Tina?!' Jenny exclaimed. 'Tina didn't call me, darling.'

'What are you doing here then?' He paused abruptly, and, spinning back around, Fletch studied her.

Jenny's face fell. 'It's your...'

'What is it? What's wrong?' He searched her face, and his voice began to rise. 'Is it Spence? Has something happened to him?' He knew he'd only just left his brother at the fishing lake, but with his father's threat still hanging heavy in the air, he held his breath, waiting for her to answer.

'No.' She could hear the fear in his voice and vigorously shook her head to reassure him. 'Spencer is fine.'

'What is it then?'

'Your...' Jenny paused. She could barely believe this was happening. Just when she was finally happy and looking forward to the arrival of her first grandchild, George had to turn up and ruin everything. 'It's your dad, darling.'

'What?' He reeled backwards and brought his hand up to his head. He knew it. His worst fears were about to come true. 'What about the bastard?'

'He turned up at the house.' Her voice was a mere whisper as she answered. How had George even found them, and more importantly, why now, after all these years, had he shown his face at the front door? What did he want from them?

Fletch could feel the blood drain from his face. Almost immediately, the shock he felt was replaced with anger, and, indicating for his mum to step back out into the corridor, he pulled the front door firmly closed behind them. The last thing he needed was for Tina to hear what was being said. This was family business, and if there was one thing he knew for certain, it was the fact that Tina wasn't family. She never would be.

'He didn't hurt you, did he?' He stood back slightly, clenched his fists into tight balls, and swept his gaze over her face. 'He didn't threaten you or anything?'

Jenny hesitated. She reached up to touch her sore shoulder blade and grimaced. 'No, of course not.'

'Mum.' Fletch's voice rose even further. He, better than anyone, knew what his father was capable of. His broken ribs and stitched eyebrow were proof of that. 'Please, don't lie to me or try to make excuses for him. He would have done something; I know he would have. What did the bastard do to you?'

'He didn't do anything.' She placed her hand on her son's arm to placate him. 'But he said he had a message, a message for you and Spencer. He said that he wants to know where his brother is, and that if he doesn't get answers, he'll...' She swallowed deeply, not wanting to continue.

'He'll what?'

Jenny squeezed her lips together and shook her head, too afraid to say the words out loud.

'Mum, he'll what?'

She searched her son's face, and, seeing the fear in his eyes, she wanted to curse her ex-husband. 'Why would he even think that you and Spencer know where Albie is?'

'I don't know.' The lie rolled easily off his tongue. 'Don't change the subject. What exactly did that bastard say to you?'

Jenny sighed. She took her son's hand into her own and gently rubbed the fleshy area underneath his thumb. 'He said he will come back, come back and hurt us, starting with Spencer.'

'The fucking bastard.' Snatching his hand away, Fletch kicked out at the door frame, his face a mask of anger. 'The no-good bastard,' he roared. 'I knew this would happen; I fucking knew it.'

'What's going on out here?' Opening the front door, Tina looked from Jenny to Fletch.

'Nothing,' Fletch snapped.

'But...' She turned her attention back to Jenny. 'I thought I heard shouting.'

'I said, it was nothing.' Pushing past her, he grabbed his jacket from the coat stand in the hallway. 'It's family business, nothing to do with you.'

'That's charming, that is.' She rolled her eyes and placed her hand across her bump. 'I'm carrying—'

'Yeah, you're carrying my kid,' Fletch interrupted her. 'That doesn't make you family, Teen, and despite what you might think, not everything revolves around you.' He slipped his jacket on, then strode across the landing. 'Mum, come on, let's go.'

'What? You're going out already? You've only just got home,' Tina called after him.

Ignoring the question, Fletch pressed for the lift. 'Come on, Mum.'

Jenny shook her head apologetically and hurried after her son. Once she'd sorted out this business with George, she would need to have a serious word with her boy. The way he was treating the mother of his child just wasn't good enough in her eyes.

* * *

'Why didn't you stop him?' Charging into his uncle's house, Fletch's face contorted with rage as he confronted the older man.

'Me?' Slumped in the chintz-covered armchair, Frank poked himself in the chest. 'I didn't know he'd been here. And even if I did know, what could I do? I can't even get out of this poxy chair without help.'

Rubbing his hand across his face, Fletch's shoulders slumped downwards. He could see Frank's point. His uncle was half the man he used to be, all thanks to Mad Mickey Shank and his sword.

'How does he even know where we live?'

'I don't know, Mum.' Jenny broke his thoughts, and he traced his heavy boot across the brown shagpile carpet as he thought it over. He must have followed Stevie and Spencer home from the hospital. There was no other explanation for it. How else could George have known where they lived?

'What's going on?' Standing in the lounge doorway, Spencer narrowed his eyes.

'Nothing.' Fletch averted his eyes and walked across the room. Coming to stand in front of the three-bar electric fire, he placed his palms on the wooden shelf above it and swept his eyes across the framed portraits that were proudly displayed there. Most of them were of Spencer and himself as children. Wearing their school uniforms, they showed off gap-toothed grins and wonky haircuts as they beamed innocently into the camera. Where had it all gone wrong? How had they ended up surrounded by violence and murder?

'Tell him.'

'No.' Fletch swung his head towards his mother and raised his eyebrows, silently begging her not to say anything.

'Tell me what?'

'I said, no.'

'Why do you always do this?' Stepping into the room, Spencer carelessly flung his jacket across the arm of the sofa. 'Why do you always treat me like I'm a baby, like I'm stupid?'

Fletch sighed. 'That's not what I'm doing, Spence,' he mumbled.

'Yes, it is.' His brother's apology at the fishing lake was gone from his mind.

Stepping forward, Jenny rested her hand on her son's arm. Her voice was gentle as she spoke. 'I know that you're trying to protect him, my darling, but he deserves to know the truth.'

Three pairs of eyes stared at back at him, and, dragging his hand through his hair, making it stand up on end, Fletch gave an irritated sigh. 'It's Dad.'

'Our dad?' Spencer's eyes lit up and he gave a wide lopsided grin. 'Did he come looking for us? When can I see him? Can I take him fishing?'

Fletch put up his hand in a bid to stop the barrage of questions. 'You're getting ahead of yourself, Spence. It's not as easy as that. You're not going to see him.' He glanced towards Jenny, then slumped heavily in the armchair beside the fire. Up until now, they had kept the extent of George's abuse towards them to the bare minimum, and with barely any recollection of their father, Spencer had only ever been given the edited version of George's wrongdoings.

'Why not?'

'Because.' Fletch looked up, blew out his cheeks, and locked eyes with his brother. 'Because I said so, that's why.'

Spencer charged across the lounge. 'You don't get to decide,' he bellowed. 'I want to see my dad. I want to show him the lake.'

Leaping up out of the chair, Fletch stood toe-to-toe with his brother. His eyes flashed dangerously, his cheeks flushed pink and his nostrils flared. 'When it comes to you, I do get to decide, all right?'

'No.' Spencer puffed out his chest and pushed his face forward, his eyes two mere slits, as spittle gathered at the corners of his lips. 'No, you don't.'

'Yes, I do,' Fletch roared back. He clenched his fists into tight balls, even though he knew he wouldn't physically lash out at his brother. He wasn't so sure he could say the same about Spencer. 'When it comes to you, I do. I look out for you, Spence; I make sure that you're okay, and I intend to keep it that way. You're not seeing him, and that's that, end of the conversation.'

'Enough.' Tears filled Jenny's eyes as she stepped between her two sons. 'Enough of this, please. Don't you see that this is what he wants, what he's always wanted? He wants to control us. He wants the two of you at one another's throats. He wants to tear our family apart.'

'Yeah, well, he's finally succeeded.' Fletch clapped his hands together, the action both loud and sarcastic in the otherwise quiet room. 'Well done, Dad, you got exactly what you wanted.' As he said the words, his shoulders sagged. Of course it wasn't true. Nothing could ever tear them apart. They were a family, and he was determined it would always stay that way.

'You're becoming a right arsehole, Fletch. Nah, actually, you're more than that.' Spencer's body shook with rage. 'You're a first-class fucking cunt, and I'll tell you something else, shall I? Ever since you got with her, that Tina, you've changed.'

Taken aback, the words twisted in Fletch's gut. 'What?' He

looked between his mother and brother, the fight suddenly leaving him. 'No, I haven't.'

'Yes, you have.' Spencer screwed up his face. 'Even Stevie said the same. You're pussy-whipped, Fletch.' He pretended to look at his watch. 'About time you went home to her, ain't it? We don't even want you here. Tell him to get out, Mum.'

'Fuck you.'

'Nah, fuck you.' Spencer lifted his fist in the air, ready to strike out.

'Do it, Spence, and I'll put you on your fucking arse,' Fletch warned.

'Enough, the pair of you. Will you give it a rest?' Frank shifted his weight in the chair and stabbed his finger forward. 'You're giving me a poxy headache. If you wanna kill each other, then do us all a favour and take it outside.'

The two brothers glared at each other, and Jenny held her breath, hoping, praying even, that at least one of her sons would have the sense to back down.

'I've had enough of this. Bollocks to you, Spence, and bollocks to that bastard of a man we have the misfortune to call Dad,' Fletch spat out as he stormed towards the lounge door.

'Where are you going?' Panic-stricken, Jenny called after her eldest son. Her eyes pleaded with him. 'Don't leave, darling, not yet. We can sort this out. We all just need to calm down and talk the situation through.'

Pausing in the lounge doorway, Fletch's fingers gripped either side of the door frame, his back ramrod straight, the muscles in his forearms straining.

'That's what I plan to do,' he snarled. 'I'm gonna sort this out, once and for all.'

* * *

'So, how do you know where he lives?' Stevie eyed his best friend suspiciously.

Flicking the indicator, Fletch remained tight-lipped. A huge part of him regretted bringing his best friend along for backup.

'Well?' Stevie turned his body in the passenger seat. 'It ain't exactly common knowledge, is it? C'mon, spill the beans. How the fuck did you find out where Bannerman lives?'

'I just know, okay?' Fletch gritted his teeth.

He'd known from the off that he should have come alone. If he wasn't careful, his true parentage would be revealed, and that was the last thing he wanted or needed. He turned in to a tree-lined avenue. The houses on this side of Blackheath were large and as grand as mansions. Boasting top-of-the-range cars parked up on the driveways, and Olympic-sized swimming pools in the back gardens, the affluent area was a far cry from the Dagenham council estate that he and Spencer had been forced to grow up on.

Stevie whistled through his teeth. Despite himself, he was clearly impressed. 'Looks like Bannerman, the no-good cunt, is doing well for himself, eh?'

Pulling over to the kerb and switching off the engine, Fletch shrugged. From his position behind the wheel, he eyed his childhood home, somewhat surprised to see that despite there being at least five large bedrooms, the mock Tudor double-fronted house didn't seem as big as he'd remembered it.

'So, what's the plan?'

Fletch turned his head. There was no plan, and, remaining silent, he shrugged his shoulders for a second time. He was more than aware that this was a suicide mission. If he made it back out of the lion's den in one piece, then it would be nothing short of a miracle.

'You've gotta have a plan.' Stevie's mouth dropped open.

'Nope.' Fletch curled his fingers around the door handle, ready to fling the car door open and jump out. 'I'm just gonna talk to him, see if we can come to an understanding.'

'Fletch,' Stevie warned. 'You can't just bowl up to the front door and expect to have a cosy little chat with him. As soon as he finds out who you are, that you're one of Billy's boys, he's gonna tear you apart, limb from fucking limb.'

'Yeah, probably,' Fletch agreed. As far as he was concerned, it was too late for that. George already knew of his identity. He tore his eyes away from the house. 'Do me a favour, mate. If it looks like shit is going down, don't try to be a hero.' He shoved the car keys into Stevie's hand. 'Get the fuck out of here and don't stop until you're back on our manor.'

'Are you crazy?' There was disbelief in Stevie's voice. 'I can't just drive off and leave you in there.'

'Yeah, you can, and you will.' Fletch gave a small smile, trying to make light of the precarious situation they were in. 'No point in us both ending up battered, is there?' He took a ragged breath, eased open the door and stepped out of the car.

'Fletch.'

Resting his palms on the car roof, Fletch paused, bowed his head and looked through the open window. 'If it all goes tits up' – he glanced over his shoulder to look at the house – 'look after my mum and Spence for me. Promise me you'll do that.'

Swallowing deeply, Stevie nodded.

'Promise me,' Fletch urged his best friend.

'Yeah, of course I will.' Following Fletch's eyeline, Stevie studied the house. 'You don't have to do this, mate, not single-handed anyway. I know that you've got beef with him, what with Frank and everything that went down, but you'd be better off getting on the blower to Billy, get him down here, and arrange for backup.'

'No.' Fletch shook his head. 'I need to do this alone.' He stepped away from the car and made to move forward. 'Don't forget, at the first sign of trouble, put your foot down and don't stop until you're back on the manor.'

Shifting his weight, Stevie grimaced. He didn't like this, didn't like what he was agreeing to, one little bit.

Flashing a wide smile that didn't quite reach his eyes, Fletch tapped the car roof, then hastily jogged across the street.

He stood in front of his former home and took in his surroundings, familiarising himself with the layout of the house. Noting that his hands ever so slightly shook, he shoved them deep into his denim pockets. Taking shallow breaths, he ignored the pain from his ribs and turned his focus on the hatred he felt for his father. In that instant, his eyes became hard, and his body tense, as muscles he didn't even know he had strained against the thin fabric of his shirt. He could do this. He had to do it, he corrected himself.

Before he could change his mind, he forced himself to move forward, more than aware that each step he took brought him closer, not only to his father, but also to a certain fate, possibly even death.

At the front door, he hesitated, glanced back over his shoulder, then took another deep breath. It was now or never. No time to back out, at least not without losing face.

Just as he remembered the elaborate cast iron door knocker was in the shape of a lion's head, he lifted it, and then in quick succession slammed it back down three times. From the hallway, he could hear footsteps approaching. He took his fists out from his pockets and hastily wiped his clammy palms down his denim jeans. Nerves were beginning to get the better of him. Stevie was right, his dad was going to tear him limb from limb.

'Yeah, what do you want?'

Fletch cleared his throat. His mouth felt dry, and he ran his tongue over his teeth. 'I want to speak to George.' He peered past the man into the wood panelled hallway. 'Your boss, George Bannerman,' he clarified.

'Get the fuck outta here.' Bannerman's henchman was a heavy-set man. Dressed in a dark suit that strained against his bulging gut, he proceeded to push the door closed.

'I said, I want to speak to George.' Fletch shoved his heavy boot in the door, preventing it from being slammed in his face.

'And I told you to fuck off. If you wanna see the boss, then make a fucking appointment, like everyone else does.'

Behind them came a loud chuckle, and, leaning against the door frame to his study, George shook his head. 'You never seem to learn you, do you?' He took in the sneer spread across his son's face, and his tone became serious. 'Let the little fucker in.'

Stepping across the threshold, Fletch gritted his teeth as he was slammed up against the wall. His clothing was then patted down to check he was not carrying any concealed weapons.

'He's clean.'

'Of course he is.' George made his way into the study. His movements were that of a man used to being in control. He exuded authority and confidence; some may even say he had a certain charisma about him. He took a seat behind the desk and leant back on the dark green Italian leather office chair, all the while a smirk played across his lips.

Straightening out his clothes, Fletch made his way forward. At the doorway to the office, he hesitated. He could still recall the good hiding he'd received as a child, all because he'd had the audacity to enter this room, his father's office, his sole domain, uninvited.

'Leave us.' In one swift movement, George flapped his hand, dismissing the henchman. His actions were both fluid and precise as he lounged back even farther on the chair and slowly picked up a balloon glass, freshly filled with brandy. He took a long sip, all the while observing his son over the rim of the glass. 'What the fuck do you want?'

A bead of cold sweat trickled down the back of Fletch's neck. He snaked his tongue over his bottom lip and sucked it inwards.

'Well?' George snapped. He downed the brandy and placed the empty glass on the desk, then steepled his fingers in front of his chest. 'I'm waiting.'

Fletch glanced over his shoulder at the now empty hallway. From his position, he could see the door that led to the kitchen, the very same room where Spencer had almost lost his life. He turned back to face his father.

'You went to my uncle's house,' he spat.

'And?' Not taking his eyes away from his eldest son, George sneered.

'And you threatened my mum.'

George laughed out loud. 'You've got some bottle coming here, I'll give you that. Must have balls made of fucking steel.'

Fletch screwed up his face, dismissing the comment. 'You threatened my mum,' he repeated. 'And no one gets away with that.'

'Is that so?' George heaved himself to his feet, walked around the desk, leant casually against it, and spread out his arms. 'I'm still waiting for the punchline,' he barked. 'Why the fuck are you in my house?'

Swallowing deeply, a flurry of emotions rippled through Fletch – anger, hatred, unease, fear. It was anger that got the better of him. 'I should have smashed your face in while I had the chance.'

'And like I've already told you...' George tensed his body,

waiting for the oncoming assault. 'If you think you can take a shot at your old man, then take the fucking shot.'

Without giving the matter a second thought, Fletch clenched his fists and charged forward.

Sidestepping his son, George threw a wolfish grin as Fletch's fist grazed past the side of his jaw.

Unconcerned by his son's attempt to lash out at him, George balled his own fists. 'I'm warning you now, this is not going to end well for you,' he growled.

Steam was practically coming out of Fletch's ears. He swung his fist a second time, and felt nothing but satisfaction as, this time, he successfully hit his target. His victory was short-lived.

A series of expertly executed jabs rained down upon him. George may have been tall and lean, but he was also strong – a lot stronger than he looked. Fletch guessed correctly that it was one of the many traits from their father that he and Spencer had inherited.

A stinging blow reopened Fletch's stitched eyebrow, and, using his fingertips, he smeared the blood away. 'I fucking despise you.'

George had barely broken out in a sweat. 'You had enough yet?'

Without answering, Fletch charged forward once more, and, grasping hold of George's shirt, he attempted to slam his knee into his father's stomach. George was too fast for him, and, after swinging him around like a rag doll, within seconds Fletch found himself lying on his back with George above him. His meaty fist was clenched into a tight ball, poised to attack.

'I'll ask you again, have you had enough yet?' He stabbed his finger, none too gently, into the side of his son's head. 'I'm giving you the chance to walk away, and, trust me, that's me being fucking generous.'

'Fuck you.' Rolling away from his father, Fletch breathed heavily as he got to his feet. He took the cuff of his shirt and wiped away the blood that trickled down from his eyebrow.

Shaking his head, George grinned as he returned to his seat behind the desk. As he'd known from the start, his son was of no threat to him. He leant back in the chair and lit a cigarette.

'I'll tell you what your problem is.' He mockingly stabbed the cigarette towards his son. A stream of bluish grey smoke curled its way upwards, away from the burning red embers. 'You've been following that cunt King around for too long. You've got no fight in you. If I didn't know better, I'd even question the fact that you are really my son. I mean, perhaps your mother...' He kissed his teeth, pretending to think it over. 'Maybe she spread her legs for someone else, and you' – he looked Fletch up and down – 'are the fucking outcome.'

The words his father spoke hurt, much more than Fletch had ever expected them to. 'Nah, I'm not that lucky,' he snapped back.

George sniggered. 'I guess that makes two of us.'

'I want you to leave my family alone—'

'Can't do that,' George interrupted. With one eye remaining on Fletch, he stubbed out the cigarette in a glass ashtray. 'I want to know where my brother is, and you,' he said, pointing his finger forward, 'are going to tell me exactly where he is.'

Fletch's heart sank. He should have expected this question.

'The fact that you're even here, running scared, tells me everything I need to know.' George leant backwards in the chair and studied his son. 'I'm close, I know I am.' He held his thumb and forefinger an inch apart to emphasise his point. 'And I know for a fact that you know where he is.' He cocked one eyebrow upwards as a sudden thought sprang to his mind. 'Or is it that brother of yours? Is he the culprit? Is he the one responsible, and you're covering up for him?'

'Spence?' Fletch kept his voice light, hiding the panic that spread through him. 'Spence knows nothing. He doesn't even know who you are.'

'Now I am insulted.' George shook his head and glanced down at his wristwatch. 'As lovely as this little family reunion is, you're boring the fuck out of me now.' He gestured towards the door. 'You can fuck off back the way you came in. Oh, and Harry,' he said, using his son's birth name, 'my threat still stands.' He made the shape of a pistol with his two fingers. 'I want answers, and you'd best give them to me before someone gets hurt. After all, I'm pretty certain your mother won't want to bury both of her precious sons.'

With his tail between his legs, Fletch retreated out of the house. His cheeks burnt with shame. His father was right. He was weak; he had no fight in him. He reached the car and kicked out at the tyre.

'Bastard,' he screamed out.

He'd fallen for the trap all right. George had been expecting him, that much was obvious, and he, like the stupid prize prick he was, had fallen for it yet again. He glanced back at the house, and he leant his forearms over the car roof. George was on to them. He was close to learning the truth. The very thought made him shudder, and, closing his eyes tight, he breathed heavily through his nostrils.

'You all right, mate?' There was trepidation in Stevie's voice.

'No.' Fletch exhaled loudly. 'No, I'm not fucking all right,' he muttered.

13

Five days later, tears glistened in Fletch's eyes as he held his newborn son for the first time. He looked down at the bundle in his arms and felt nothing but love and pride for this tiny being who he had helped to create.

The fact that he could very well have missed out on this moment and ended up dead in a ditch with his head caved in, if his father had had his way, was at the forefront of his mind.

'He's a smasher, Teen. He really is perfect.'

Lying back against the pillows, Tina's whole body ached, and as for her nether regions, well, she didn't even want to think about down there. All she knew was that it stung like hell. She shifted her weight, making herself more comfortable, and watched him as he cradled their son in his arms.

A tiny part of her couldn't help but feel smug. Despite his earlier speech about not loving her, she knew now that there was absolutely no way he would ever walk out on their son. Not now, not ever.

'He is perfect.' She beamed. She closed her eyes briefly. After a twelve-hour, gruelling, excruciating labour, as far as she was concerned, he owed her, owed her big time. 'I was thinking that we could call him Austin?'

'Austin?' Fletch was about to screw up his face, but after seeing what she had been through to bring their son into the world, he didn't have the heart to tell her that he didn't like the name. 'Austin it is then.' He tilted his head to one side, pretending to study his son's face. 'I think it actually suits him,' he lied.

Tina smiled even wider. She held out her arms and he carefully passed across their baby. She unwrapped the towel covering him and began to count his tiny fingers and toes.

'All present and correct,' Fletch laughed. 'I've already checked.'

She laughed in return. 'He's worth all of that pain that I went through. I would do it all over again, without even hesitating.'

Fletch gave her a cautious smile. Not with him, she wouldn't. He'd been caught out once, and never again would he make the same mistake. 'You don't want to be thinking about more babies. He's gonna be running rings around us before we even know it.'

'But I don't want him to be an only child,' she protested. 'I don't want him to grow up lonely like I did. I mean, look at you. At least you had a brother to grow up with, someone to play with.'

'Yeah, I suppose so,' Fletch answered, not that he and Spencer had ever had much time to play when they had been kids. All thanks to their dad, and his heavy fists, they'd had to grow up a lot faster than their peers. He gave her a gentle smile. 'I'll think about it, okay?' he answered, knowing full well that he would do no such thing.

Satisfied, Tina kissed her son's button nose. Yes, she knew for a fact that he would never leave them. This little boy in her arms was going to be her guarantee of that.

* * *

On returning home from hospital the next afternoon, Tina basked in the attention the family gave her.

'Oh, he is a handsome little boy.' Jenny cradled her grandson in her arms. Ever since her son had telephoned her the previous evening to inform her of his safe arrival, she'd been practically chomping at the bit to have a cuddle. 'I'm so bloody proud of you, my darling.' Turning to look at Tina, she gave her a beaming smile.

Tina smiled her thanks. Despite the soreness between her legs, she eagerly unwrapped a pile of gifts stacked up beside the sofa. In all her life she had never seen so many presents, and, ripping open the brightly coloured wrapping paper, she took great pleasure in discovering the items well-wishers had bought for her baby.

'Of course he's bloody handsome. He takes after me.' Fletch grinned.

Giving Tina a knowing smile, Jenny pulled the baby towards her and breathed in his special scent. 'Frank?' She looked up. 'Would you like to hold your great-nephew?'

'No.' An expression of horror spread across Frank's face.

'Go on, Frank.' Taking the baby from his mother, Fletch walked across the room.

'I said, no.' Frank flapped his hand in the air. 'He's too small; I might drop him.'

'Don't be daft.' Kissing his son's button nose, Fletch carefully positioned the tiny bundle into his uncle's arms. 'See, he likes you.'

Gazing down at his great-nephew, Frank nodded. 'You're right; I think he does like me.'

'Course he does.' Unscrewing a bottle of Babycham, Fletch indicated towards the bottle. 'Mum, would you like a top-up?'

'Oh, go on then, seeing as it's a celebration.' She held out her glass. Not one to drink alcohol very often, already, the bubbles had gone straight to her head, making her feel tipsy.

'What about you, Frank?' Holding up an empty glass, Fletch gestured to his uncle.

'No, not for me.' Frank shook his head. 'I'm off the drink; I'll have a cup of tea instead.'

'So, why did you never get married and have kids, Frank?' Throwing Fletch a knowing wink, Stevie drank deeply from his can of lager, before cocking his head to one side to look at the older man.

'No one would bloody have him.' Fletch grinned.

'Oi.' Frank stabbed his finger forward. 'I had many a woman interested in me, I'll have you know.'

'Then how come you never brought any girlfriends home?' Fletch raised his eyebrows. 'How come we never met them?'

'What, and introduce them to you two scallywags?' Frank looked between his two nephews. 'The two of you, out causing havoc, day and night, would have scared them right bleedin' off.'

'We weren't that bad, were we?' Fletch gave his brother a beaming smile, thankful that they were once again on speaking terms. Their mum was right. They were brothers and no one could come between them, especially not George.

'Nah.' Frank's features softened, and he gave his nephew an affectionate wink. 'From what I can remember, you weren't so bad, son.'

* * *

An hour later, Fletch, Spencer, Stevie, Billy and the rest of his firm were in the Westbury Arms public house, in Barking, wetting the baby's head.

'Austin, what kind of a fucking name is that?' Billy laughed.

'Tell me about it,' Fletch groaned. He gulped at his glass of champagne. 'She's mad about some actor, Austin something-or-other, and wanted to name the baby after him.' He swallowed down a second mouthful of alcohol. 'I dunno though, I think it's got a bit of a ring to it. Austin Fletcher.' He grinned.

'Yeah, I suppose so,' Billy agreed. He pulled a wad of cash out from his trousers pocket and ordered two further bottles of champagne. 'Oh, I nearly forgot...' He dug deeper into his pocket and took out a solid gold infant's bangle. 'That's from me and my Susan. The missus wanted to give the baby a present.'

Taking the bangle, Fletch turned it over in his hand. 'Cheers, mate.' His thoughts immediately turned to Susan, and he swallowed deeply at the mess he had got himself into. As much as he loved his newborn son, he would still give his right arm to be with her. He dropped the bangle into his jacket pocket. 'I'll see that Tina gets it.'

'Good man.' Billy grinned. 'Oi, Joe?' He held aloft the wad of notes, looked across the bar, and caught Joseph's attention. 'Another drink, mate?'

Joseph held up his empty glass and nodded.

Fletch studied the man. For most of the evening, Joseph had stood away from their group, barely even bothering to make conversation. He narrowed his eyes. He had always had a feeling that the older man didn't like him. He'd never said as much, though it was an unspoken assumption – the way he looked at him, the way he spoke to him with disregard, as though he were still fourteen years old, as though he were still a kid. Fuck, he even addressed him as 'the kid'. The term was used in a derogatory manner.

'Joe, why don't you come and join us?' Fletch called out to him, testing the waters.

As he shook his head, a fleeting smear of hatred crossed

Joseph's face. 'Nah, you're all right, kid.' He gritted his teeth as he emphasised the word. 'I'm good where I am.'

It was a lightbulb moment. In that instant, Fletch knew. He knew it was Joseph who'd tipped off the Old Bill. It had to be him. A cold shiver ran down his spine, and despite the shock that rippled through him, all he felt was anger – an anger that began to grow in his belly, until it had pushed its way up through his chest, engulfing him.

'Here you go.' Billy topped up his glass.

Without tearing his eyes away from Joseph, he took the glass and gulped the champagne down in one go. Why? He wanted to scream. Why would Joseph have tipped off the Old Bill? What had he ever done that was so bad for the bloke to even contemplate doing that to him?

Unable to stop himself from staring across the bar, he continued to seethe. As if tipping off the Old Bill wasn't bad enough, what else could he be capable of? The realisation that Joseph, Billy's number two, could well be the snake in the grass, hit him full-on in the face.

Surely not! Surely to God it wasn't Joseph! Billy had always trusted him, tenfold. As he asked himself the question, a snarl slid across his face. Of course it fucking was. There was no one else it could have been. There was no one else within Billy's firm who would have wanted him taken down.

'What's up with you?' Taking in his protégé's expression, Billy frowned.

'Not here, outside. I need to speak to you in private.'

'What, now?' Billy looked around him, unsure of what was going on.

'Yes, now,' Fletch snapped. He slammed his glass down on the bar, gave Joseph one last seething stare, and stormed out of the pub.

'Well?' Following Fletch out of the pub, Billy lit a cigarette, whilst waiting for the younger man to explain what the problem was.

'Joseph,' Fletch spat.

Billy exhaled a plume of cigarette smoke above his head. 'What about him?' he asked, with a shrug.

Fletch began to pace.

'Well?' Billy demanded.

Stopping abruptly, he came to stand just inches away from his boss. 'It was him.'

'Him?' Still unsure of what was meant, Billy tilted his head to one side, his forehead furrowed. 'What the fuck are you going on about? Are those pills messing with your nut again?'

Fletch shook his head. 'It was him, Billy. It was him who tipped off the Old Bill.'

'Don't be ridiculous.' Snorting with laughter, Billy began to make his way back inside the pub.

'I'm telling you, it was him.'

Billy's laughter tapered off. Aware that Fletch was being serious, he came to a halt and swallowed deeply before answering. 'Nah.' He waved his hand, dismissing the notion. 'No way, no fucking way. You've made a mistake; you've misread the situation. Those fucking pills that you shove down your neck are clouding your judgement. We go back years; he wouldn't do something like that.' He stabbed his finger forward, rattled by Fletch's accusation. 'Joseph, of all people, would never betray me. He's like a brother; he's like family.'

With his eyebrows raised, Fletch argued his point. 'Think about it, Bill. We both know that he doesn't like me...'

'And?' Billy's loud voice became menacing. 'That's hardly a fucking crime, is it?'

'Who else would have gained from me being sent down?' Fletch persevered. 'Think about it, Bill.'

'Nah.' Having heard just about enough, Billy continued to walk back in to the pub. His back was up, his mind reeling.

'Billy.' Fletch called out after him. 'Deep down, you know it makes sense.'

Billy placed his hands on either side of the door frame, his head bowed. Straightening up, he stared inside the pub, before turning back around. As much as he didn't want to acknowledge the obvious, he could see that Fletch had a point, and as much as he hated to admit it, it was a valid point at that. Whoever the grass was, they had to know him well; they knew of his movements and knew what went on within the firm.

'Well?' Fletch took a step closer. There was an urgency in his tone. 'Do you see my point?'

'Yeah.' Dragging his hand across his jaw, Billy turned once more to look inside the bar. He could recall the snide comments that had come from Joseph, and his expression of contempt each time Fletch's name had come up in conversation. Why had it taken him until now to see what was right underneath his nose? To know that it could be Joseph who was responsible was like a punch in the gut – the ultimate kick in the teeth. After a moment of silence, he spoke. His voice was a low growl, his expression hard. 'Keep schtum about this. Don't breathe a word of it to anyone, right?'

Fletch nodded in agreement. Like Billy, he glanced inside the building. 'But he needs to be sorted out, Bill, and fast. We need to deal with this.'

Without saying another word, Billy walked back in to the pub. Outwardly, nothing appeared to be amiss. Only a pulsating vein at the side of his temple gave away his true thoughts. He reached the bar and lifted the champagne flute to his lips.

His eyes were hard as he studied his number two. If what Fletch said was true, then Joseph would have to go. Deep down he knew that, and as much as it would pain him, he knew, without a shadow of a doubt, that the man, his best friend, would need to be disposed of. There was simply no other alternative.

* * *

Six weeks later, Tina lay staring up at the ceiling. In the bedroom next to hers, Fletch was sleeping. An idea formed in her mind and, as she threw the duvet away from her, she gave a crafty smile. Tiptoeing in to his room, she watched Fletch's chest rise and fall as he slept. Ever so slowly, she eased herself in to his bed and shuffled forward until she was snuggled up against his side.

The last thing she wanted to do was wake him up, at least not yet anyway. She held her breath as she slipped her arm underneath the bed sheet. When he didn't stir, she snaked her hand down inside his boxer shorts. One way or another, she was determined that he would give her another child, even if it meant using dirty tactics to get what she wanted.

Fletch's eyes flickered open, and for a moment, he froze. 'What the fuck do you think you are doing?' he finally growled as he ripped her hand away from him and threw it across the bed.

'What?' she answered, her voice full of mock innocence. In the darkened bedroom, she gave a coy grin. 'I thought it was what you wanted.' She licked at her lips and nodded to the hard bulge between his legs.

'Leave it out, Teen.' He used his hands to cover himself. 'It ain't gonna happen, I'm telling you that now. What the fuck is wrong with you, eh?' He jumped out of the bed and moved across the room, adjusting his boxer shorts as he did so.

Thumping her fists down on the bed, the smile slipped from

Tina's face. Frustration coursed through her veins. She slumped back against the plump pillows with a long, exasperated sigh. 'How am I meant to get pregnant if you don't come near me, if you won't even touch me?'

'Pregnant?' Fletch choked on the word. 'What are you going on about? You've only just had a baby,' he spat.

'Yeah, but that was six weeks ago.' She flapped her hand and leant up on one elbow to look at him. 'The midwife said that it's safe now.'

'Safe?' Fletch's eyes creased together. 'Safe for what?'

'To start trying for baby number two.'

'Have you lost your fucking mind?' He pulled a T-shirt over his head and headed for the bathroom. 'It's not going to happen, Tina,' he said over his shoulder. 'You caught me out once, and like fuck am I going to let you do it to me a second time.'

Tina pursed her lips, and, scrambling off the bed, she followed him through to the bathroom. 'You promised me, though.' She curled herself around the door frame, positioning herself so her short nightie rose to flash a generous amount of bare thigh. 'You agreed that you didn't want Austin to grow up as an only child.' She batted her eyelashes and pouted her lips, her voice sounding almost childlike. 'You don't want him to grow up lonely, do you?'

'I...' He tore his eyes away from her shapely legs. 'Just get out, Teen.' He pushed her forcibly out of the bathroom, slammed the door closed and snapped the lock across.

Silently, he counted to ten, then as quickly as he could, he undressed and proceeded to jump into the shower. He switched on the tap and allowed the cold water to wash over him, dulling his senses, before his body had the chance to betray him – before he ran back out of the bathroom, threw Tina down on to the bed that they shared, and pounded into her. After all, he was a red-hot-blooded male, and it had been months since he'd been with a woman. In fact, it had been so long that his balls felt like they were the size of watermelons.

Thirty minutes later, he emerged from the bathroom. Wearing dark denim jeans and a black hoodie, he was barefoot as he padded through to the lounge. He glanced in Tina's direction and was more than thankful to see that she'd had the sense to put some clothes on.

Lounging back on the sofa, Tina looked up at him expectantly. 'I need some money.'

'For what?' Slipping his socks and trainers on, Fletch didn't bother to look up. She was always after something. If it wasn't his body, it was his money, and even worse than that, his time.

She let out a long sigh. When it came to getting money out of her son's father, it was like getting blood from a stone. 'I need to buy nappies, some baby formula, oh, and I've seen the cutest outfit that he just has to have.'

At this, Fletch's head snapped upwards. 'I thought you were breast feeding?'

'I am.'

He shook his head, confused. 'Then why do you need formula?'

Tina glared. She pointed down at her breasts as though he were stupid. 'Just in case he needs more milk.'

'Oh.' He pushed his hand into his denim pocket, pulled out a roll of cash, and passed it across.

Still holding out her hand, Tina looked up at him, her eyebrows raised.

'More?' he groaned, delving his hand into his pocket for a second time. 'Fuck me, Teen, money doesn't grow on trees, you know, and despite what you might think, I'm not your personal bank.'

At this, Tina began to laugh. She knew he was good for it. She'd seen how he paid for everything in cash, even the wine-coloured chesterfield leather sofa that had come to the grand sum of almost two thousand pounds.

She stuck out her bottom lip. 'You don't want Austin to go without, do you?'

He shook his head. Of course he didn't want his son to go without, but even he had to question why Austin needed designer outfits. The boy was barely six weeks old, and within a matter of weeks, he would outgrow them. 'Just go easy, yeah?' He passed across a second bundle of notes.

'I will do.' Tina smiled sweetly. Already, the money was burning a hole in her pocket.

Littered around the lounge were unopened parcels; items that their son needed, she protested each time Fletch came to question her shopping sprees.

'I mean it, Teen,' he scolded. 'Enough is enough now, this has to stop.'

Tina rolled her eyes. 'Okay,' she answered dismissively. She had no intention of stopping – not now, not ever. Her shopping sprees filled a void in her life that only he could fill. She watched him as he peered inside a cardboard box containing a pile of still unopened packages, shaking his head at her as he did so. 'What?' She lifted her chin in the air defensively. 'I said I'm going to stop.'

He straightened up, slung on his jacket and fished around for his car keys. He had a big day ahead of him. The fact that today was going to be Joseph Hatton's last day on earth lay heavy on his mind. He hastily planted a kiss on his sleeping son's forehead, and after barely even giving Tina a second glance, he slipped out of the flat without so much as a goodbye.

Exiting the lift, he pushed through the heavy entrance door and lifted his arm up in the air in a greeting. Stevie sat on the bonnet of his BMW, his head buried in his mobile phone, while Spencer lounged casually against the driver's door, smoking a cigarette as they waited for him.

'You took your fucking time,' Stevie growled as Fletch approached them.

Fletch rolled his eyes. 'Try living with Tina,' he answered, by way of an explanation.

'I told you she was bad news. I don't like her,' Spencer grumbled. 'Why can't you just get shot of her, Fletch? Tell her to go away.'

Clouting his brother around the back of his head, Fletch sighed. If only it was that simple. 'Just get in the motor, Spence.'

He used his key fob to unlock the car doors and watched as his brother climbed in.

'Are you gonna get in?' He narrowed his eyes at his best friend, who'd, so far, made no attempt to move off the bonnet.

'Not yet.' Stevie shook his head, hopped down from the bonnet, closed the passenger door, and leant back against the car. 'Talk to me, man.'

'About what?'

'You and her.' He flicked his chin towards the block of flats.

'There ain't nothing to tell.' Fletch averted his eyes.

'I know you, Fletch, just remember that, and I haven't ever seen you look this miserable.'

With a long sigh, Fletch crossed his arms over his chest. 'What?' He gave a small shrug of his shoulders.

'Spence is right; you need to get shot of her.'

'It ain't that easy, is it?' He glanced upwards. 'She's got me by the fucking bollocks, mate. She's got my kid. How can I just walk out on him?' He rubbed his hand over his face. 'I grew up without a dad. I know how it feels to always wonder if he cared about me.

I can't do that to my own son. What kind of a fucking hypocrite would that make me?'

Stevie thought this through. 'I get that, mate. I get that you want to do the honourable thing, but you can't live like this either, can you? She's destroying you, but you just can't see it yet.' He clapped Fletch on the back, opened the car door and climbed inside.

Taking a deep breath before he got into the car and positioned himself behind the wheel, Fletch looked up towards the balcony. Tina was outside looking down. Her eyes burnt into him, watching his every movement. He shook his head and inwardly groaned. Stevie was right. No matter what he said to her, she never seemed to take the hint.

Preoccupied with his own thoughts, he failed to notice the excited glint in his brother's eyes of what was to come.

* * *

Joseph didn't have a care in the world as he followed Billy and the rest of his firm into one of the safe houses. On the pretext that they were distributing profits from the latest rave, he eagerly descended the cellar steps with more than just a spring in his step. The sight that met him caused his breath to catch in his throat and his heart to beat faster. The entire cellar had been covered over in plastic sheeting.

'What's this?' he asked, spinning around. It wasn't the first time that he'd seen the cellar covered over, but it was the first time he hadn't been privy to what was about to go down. As a result, the hairs on the back of his neck stood up on end and his forehead furrowed. 'What the fuck is going on, Bill?'

With his firm behind him, Billy took a step forward. Still a part of him refused to believe that Joseph was the spy in his camp

– that the man he had known since childhood, the man he considered to be more like a brother than a friend, could be the very same person ratting him out.

Panic began to set in, and Joseph pushed his way forward. How had Billy even found out it was him? 'Get out of my way,' he growled.

Billy shoved out his hand, sending his one-time number two flying backwards. 'It was you,' he spat. 'It was you who betrayed me.'

In a blind panic, Joseph pulled himself to his feet and rushed forward. Once again, they pushed him back into the centre of the cellar, their large frames crowding around him.

'Nah.' He gave a nervous laugh. If he wanted to survive the ambush, then he had to play smart. He had to play the game, play dumb, and deny everything. 'You've got it wrong, Bill. I haven't done anything. It's not me. I'd never betray you; you know that. We go back years, don't we? We're more like brothers than pals. Come on, mate, you know we are.' He was talking fast, too fast, and as beads of cold sweat broke out across his forehead and upper lip, he resisted the urge to swipe the droplets away.

For a moment, Billy faltered. Just maybe, Joseph was telling the truth and Fletch was mistaken. He would give his right arm for Fletch to be wrong.

'Don't listen to him, Bill. You know he's the rat. Everything points to him. He's a fucking grass.' Fletch's face was murderous, and he stabbed his finger forward. 'You, you cunt,' he growled. 'You ratted me out to the Old Bill. I went down because of you.'

Joseph smirked, and the mask he wore in Billy's company slipped away. As quick as a flash, he composed himself, his expression once again neutral, but it was too late; Billy had already seen the interaction.

There and then, Billy's stomach dropped. Everything Fletch had said was true.

'I don't know what you're talking about.' Joseph gave a carefree shake of his head. 'Bill, come on, mate.' He turned to face Billy and spread out his arms. 'You don't believe all of this old bollocks, do you? The kid is talking shit.' He kept his arms out, throwing Fletch a sly grin. 'As per fucking usual.'

Fletch lunged forward, his knuckles connecting just underneath Joseph's jaw. The loud crack echoed around the cellar. 'It was you,' he roared, 'I know it was.'

Joseph rubbed at the side of his face. The punch had been hard, a lot harder than he'd expected. He had to keep face. He could handle himself; he knew that. After all, he hadn't been Billy's number two for no reason. A low chuckle escaped from his lips, the cackle growing louder, until he was doubled over laughing.

'Is that the best you can do?' he taunted. He dragged the tears of laughter from his eyes. 'Seriously, Bill, I'm starting to worry about your judgement, mate. If this is the future of your firm, then fuck me, your reputation is gonna end up in tatters. All that hard work in the gutter, and for what, eh? For this little prick?'

Fletch swung his fist for a second time, sending Joseph hurtling to the floor. 'Admit it was you,' he shouted. When he received no reply, he pulled back his heavy boot, ready and poised to kick out. 'Go on, just fucking admit it.'

Joseph laughed even harder.

'Do him again, Fletch.' Spencer hopped from one foot to the other; excitement creased his face. 'Fuck him up, finish him off.'

Ignoring his brother's words, Fletch breathed heavily. Blood rushed to his head, filling his ears with white noise, while adrenaline coursed through his veins. 'Fucking admit it,' he roared.

Blood trickled down from one of Joseph's nostrils. He wiped

the blood away with the back of his hand, leaving a red smear across his cheek. 'Seriously, Bill,' he began again. More than a hint of laughter was in his voice, mocking. 'If this little shit is the future of your firm...'

Billy had heard just about enough. He charged forward, shoving Fletch out of his way, and using every ounce of strength that he possessed, he pummelled his fists down upon his one-time best friend. Right from the beginning, when they had been kids, it had been just the two of them taking on the world together, getting into scrapes, building their empire. *Why?* he wanted to scream, *Why did you do this to me; why did you betray me?* Behind him, his firm egged him on, baying for blood.

Joseph struggled to breathe. His nose was splattered across his cheek and bent up at an awkward angle. He grasped on to Billy's shirt, pulling him close, his fingertips clenching and unclenching as he struggled to keep his grip.

Having hardly broken out a sweat, Billy pulled back his bloodied fist, ready to finish off the job in hand.

'Betrayal? You should have looked closer to home,' Joseph rasped. His head was a bloodied mess, his swollen eyes barely able to open, let alone focus.

Billy narrowed his eyes. He allowed Joseph to drag him down closer to him. Clearly, the words he was about to speak were for his ears only.

'You should have taken more interest.' He gasped for breath, his voice coming out as a gurgle as he choked on the blood filling his mouth and lungs. 'You should have kept a closer eye.' His breath began to rasp.

'On what?' Billy growled. He grasped Joseph's shirt in his fist, keeping the man from falling to the floor. 'On what?' he demanded to know.

'On the kid and your wife.' Joseph's eyes rolled back into his head. It took a few beats for him to refocus. 'On what they get up to when you're not around. I've seen them.'

Billy's blood ran cold. Not for a single second had he expected this. His wife and Fletch, together? An image of them cavorting sprang to his mind, and he swallowed down a trickle of bile, the acrid liquid burning the back of his throat.

'I've seen him,' Joseph croaked, 'seen him creeping out of your house.'

As Joseph slumped forward on to his chest, Billy slammed him to the floor and began to kick out. A white-hot anger surged through him. Each blow, each devastating kick, intensified in viciousness, as he imagined it to be Fletch's head on the floor, bloodied, bruised and beaten to a pulp. Finally, Joseph took his last ragged breath and his body lay still.

An eerie quietness fell upon the cellar. It was over. Joseph Hatton was dead.

Billy unclenched his fists. His hard knuckles, scarred from previous tear-ups, were grazed and bloodied. Large, shiny globs of claret-coloured blood and traces of pink brain matter slid to the floor from the front of his steel-toe-capped boots. He inhaled sharply and his breath, as it fought its way back out of his mouth and nostrils, streamed out ahead of him.

The exertion, coupled with the anger he felt, made his heart pump so hard and fast that he thought it would fly out of his chest. Never had he felt so angry, so livid, so incensed. Slowly, he turned his large frame around and, with his eyes resembling two dark pits that were both lethal and murderous, scanned the crowd.

With an expression the epitome of pure evil, he zoned in on Fletch. He didn't speak; he couldn't speak. At the side of his temple, a nerve convulsed, all the while Joseph Hatton's last words rang loud in his ears.

* * *

'You know what to do?' George paused, before passing across a black leather holdall containing fifty thousand pounds in cash. His eyes were hard as he studied his newly appointed number two, and his free hand formed a fist at his side. It was imperative that he understood the task ahead of him. He wouldn't, couldn't, allow another fuck-up.

Pete nodded his dark head. 'Course I do, Boss.' More than anything, he wanted to impress. Having already lost a small fortune, all thanks to the stolen Ecstasy pills, he knew just how much George was counting on this deal to go ahead. 'I won't let you down.'

'You'd better not,' George growled. He watched Pete leave the room, then slumped down in his office chair. The hard leather creaked underneath his weight as he shifted his body, making himself more comfortable.

A thick layer of stubble covered his jaw, and he rubbed his hand across it, his mind preoccupied with thoughts of his brother, sons and, ultimately, Billy King. There was a link between the latter and Albie's disappearance, he knew there was. He could feel it in his gut and his instincts had never let him down before.

He scooped his mobile phone out of his trousers pocket, scrolled through his contact list, and hit dial when he reached Joseph Hatton's number. It went straight to voicemail. He dialled a further three times before slamming the phone down on to the desk. Where the fuck was the little rat?

There and then, he decided to have a serious word with his grass. When he made contact, he expected Hatton to jump to attention, regardless of where or who he was with.

* * *

Three miles off the coast of Southend, Joseph's mobile phone lay on the seabed. A quarter of a mile away, his swollen body swayed along with the current. Separated from his belongings, fish nibbled and tore at his bloated, rotting flesh.

Around his neck, a heavy steel chain had been double looped, preventing him from resurfacing. Enveloped within his watery grave for all of eternity, for all intents and purposes, Joseph had simply vanished into thin air.

* * *

From her vantage point in the lounge, Susan had watched Fletch's black BMW roll its way down the long, winding driveway before coming to a grinding halt yards from the front door. There and then, she'd had to resist the urge not to run out of the house and jump into his arms.

It had been months since they had last seen each other, and although they'd had more than their fair share of closeted telephone conversations, this was the first time she had laid her eyes upon him since the birth of his son.

'He's early.'

Susan snapped her head around. 'Is he?' She gave a carefree shrug of her shoulders. 'I hadn't noticed.'

She averted her eyes, looking anywhere other than at her husband. Of course she had noticed that he was early and knew for a fact that he was as eager to see her as she was him. He told her so, every opportunity he could.

'Yeah, he is,' Billy growled back.

Striding out of the lounge and in to the hallway, Billy flung open the front door. He leant against the door frame in a bid to stop his body from physically shaking, so intense was the white-hot fury inside of him.

'You okay, mate?' he forced himself to call out.

Fletch nodded; a wide grin was plastered across his face. 'Yeah, all good.'

Billy allowed a stilted smile to pass his lips. He moved aside so the younger man could step across the threshold, all the while he had to stop himself from pulling back his fist and smashing him to the ground. He pretended to look at his watch.

'Bit eager, ain't you?'

'What?' Preoccupied with his own thoughts, Fletch turned his head.

'I said that you're eager.' He glanced at his watch for a second time. 'You're early.'

'Am I?'

'Yeah, you are.' He narrowed his eyes. It hadn't escaped his notice that both his wife and so-called protégé used the exact same tone when they spoke to him, like he was a mug, like he was a fucking muppet.

'Well, I wouldn't want to be late, would I?' Fletch clapped him on the back. 'Is Mrs King ready to go shopping?' he asked as he wandered across the marble floored hallway towards the lounge.

Staring after him, a low, guttural growl escaped from Billy's lips. 'Yeah, she's ready for you, all right,' he spat out.

* * *

Spencer cocked his head to one side, listening. Fifteen minutes earlier, he had followed one of George Bannerman's henchmen to this low-rise, privately owned block of flats, in Bermondsey. In the past, the flats had belonged to the council, until, that was, they had been sold off, developed, and then resold for thousands of pounds more than they were actually worth. No amount of sprucing the dwelling up could mask the fact that it had once been a council slum.

From his hiding place, he'd watched Pete bound up the steps, and, remaining hidden, he had followed just far enough to see which flat on the top floor he had entered.

Anger bubbled inside of him, and he clenched and unclenched his fists. Each time he thought of his uncle, how Frank suffered, how all these weeks later, he still struggled to get out of bed, or walk around the house unaided, those dark thoughts in his mind intensified.

He wanted revenge. He wanted Bannerman and his firm to suffer for what they had done. He wanted to have their blood on his hands. He wanted them dead, and above all else, he wanted to destroy everything that George Bannerman held dear, starting with his firm.

* * *

'I thought he would never leave.' Watching Billy's car drive away, Fletch spun around. 'Come here.' Cocking his head to one side, he gave Susan a wide smile, his first genuine smile in weeks, and pulled her into his solid arms. He kissed her deeply and ran his fingers through her blonde hair, breathing in her scent. It was intoxicating and he couldn't get enough of her.

'I've fucking missed you.'

'I've missed you, too.' She shuddered at the feel of his hard body against hers and glanced out of the window. 'I wish that he would just go away and never come back.'

'One day, babe.' Fletch scooped her up in his arms and made his way towards the oak staircase. 'One fucking day, I promise.'

* * *

As soon as he'd pulled out of the driveway, Billy swerved the car over to the grass verge and parked up. Shaded by overhanging trees on either side of the lane, he was able to stay hidden, out of sight from the house, whilst waiting for the Mercedes to follow suit and join him on the road.

Thirty minutes later, the Mercedes still hadn't emerged. That was the moment when he knew everything Joseph had said was true. It was blatantly obvious that his wife and protégé were up to no good, and that they had taken him for a fool, a mug. Seething with anger, the muscles in his forearms were rigid as he gripped the steering wheel.

He shoved his fist into his trousers pocket and pulled out a fresh pack of cigarettes. Lighting up, he exhaled the smoke noisily, barely taking a breath in between each short, sharp puff, as he began to chain smoke.

The minutes ticked by and the anger inside of him intensified. His lips were set in a thin, hard line, and the vein at his temple pulsated. Jealousy and hatred surged through him. No one touched what belonged to him, no one. Susan was his. He owned her lock, stock and barrel, and had done so from the very first moment he had clapped his eyes on her.

In his mind's eye, images of the two of them frolicking on his king-sized solid oak bed became more and more graphic, until he snapped his eyes shut tight in a bid to block out the sickening scenes, and pressed his fist to his mouth to stop the tidal waves of nausea from consuming him. His body shook with rage and he slammed his fist down on the steering wheel. They wouldn't get away with this, of that he was certain.

He checked the time on his watch. Consumed by his thoughts, more than ninety minutes had passed by since he had left the house, and, after taking one long, last drag on the cigarette, he flicked the butt out of the open window, twisted the key in the ignition and started the engine.

Executing a three-point turn, he made his way back. Already a plan had formed in his mind, and a wicked snarl creased his face. No, they wouldn't get away with this. He would make sure of that, even if it was the last thing he ever did.

As soon as he exited the flat, Pete made his way along the upper corridor and rounded the stone staircase. Pete was on red alert. More aware of his surroundings than usual, he'd noticed the looming shadow of a figure loitering on the ground floor.

His boss's threat to not fuck this deal up hung heavy in the air, and with fifty thousand pounds worth of Ecstasy pills in the black leather holdall slung over his shoulder, it was his duty to make sure that there were no cock-ups.

In his back pocket was a flick knife. He took it out, flicked it open, and grasped his fist around the aluminium handle. Taking a further two steps down, he paused slightly, before jogging down the remainder. On the ground floor, he looked around him, fully expecting someone to jump out of the shadows at any moment. The lobby was, for all intents and purposes, empty.

He grasped the knife tighter. There had been someone. He'd clearly seen the figure lurking in the shadows. Taking a tentative step forward, the muscles in his forearm were taut as he turned his head to look at the darkened storage area underneath the stone staircase.

A figure rushed towards him, almost knocking him off balance. Convinced it was a set-up and that the man wanted the contents of the holdall, he slung the leather strap over his head and across his body, then swung into action. Over his dead body would he allow the haul to be taken from him willingly. No, if the man wanted the merchandise, then he would have to kill him first.

A struggle ensued, and as he poised his fist in front of him, he was able to get a good look at his assailant. Tall, dark-haired, aged early to mid-twenties, and of a heavy build: he burnt the man's face in to his memory.

'You've picked on the wrong fucking man,' Pete warned.

Spencer cocked his head to one side and smirked.

There and then, Pete decided his instincts were right. It was a set-up; it had to be. What else could the nutcase want from him? He clenched his meaty fist around the blade handle and snarled.

Spencer continued to smirk.

Without giving the matter another thought, Pete lunged forward. He had to attack first. Pulling back the fist that held the knife, he slammed it into the man's side. A whoosh of air escaped from his opponent's lips and he watched him stagger backwards. Right then, Pete knew that he'd hit his target, that he'd hurt the man badly enough to make him rethink and back off.

Spencer's eyes widened at the pain. He'd been punched many times before, but never had it hurt like this. Involuntarily, his body leant to the side, and as the henchman lifted his fist a second time, he backed away.

A cold numbness took hold. He narrowed his eyes, unsure of what had just taken place, and then it hit him. A dull throbbing soon took the form of a pulsating pain, the likes of which he'd never experienced before.

He hesitated, unsure of what to do next, when the henchman lunged forward once more. He turned on his heel, and ran as if his life depended on it.

* * *

Switching off the ignition, Billy's mood was both murderous and calculating. He leant his head against the headrest and closed his eyes tight. He needed to get a grip of himself and fast, before the white-hot fury that flooded through his veins gave the game away, and more importantly, before the two of them came to realise that he had cottoned on to their deceit, their treachery. His movements were easy, and his expression was cloaked as he exited his car and pocketed the keys.

Up ahead of him on the driveway, Fletch was sitting inside his BMW, exactly where, under any normal circumstances, he would have expected to find him. Silently, he counted to ten before striding towards his so-called protégé. As he approached, his expression remained neutral, masking the hatred that seeped out of his pores.

'You all right, mate?' There was a calmness to his voice, and that fact alone both shocked and impressed him.

'Yeah.' Fletch gave him a wide smile.

Billy nodded. He placed his hands behind his back and balled his fists. 'Did you take my missus shopping?'

'Yeah, just this minute got back.' Fletch leant back in his seat and grinned up at his boss, as though he didn't have a care in the world. 'I have to warn you, though, I think that Mrs King went to town on your credit card.'

Billy returned the smile, all the while his blue eyes remained cold. *Lying cunt*, he thought to himself. He resisted the urge to sarcastically applaud him. The traitorous bastard was wasted in their world. He should have been up on a stage someplace, surrounded by bright lights, quoting Shakespeare.

'You might as well get yourself off home.' He glanced across to the house and narrowed his eyes. 'Go and see that boy of yours while you can.' Without another word, he abruptly turned and headed for the front door.

There and then, he decided that he was going to decimate them, but not before he'd taken his rage out on his so-called wife first.

* * *

Adrenaline spurred Spencer on, and, sprinting as fast as he was able to, he made his getaway from the run-down council estate. From his open mouth, his breath tore out of him in short, sharp, ragged bursts. His heart pumped hard and fast, and in his side, the pain that had started as a dull ache had begun to intensify beyond anything he had ever known before. He grimaced as the sickening, twisting, burning sensation took hold, engulfing him.

Discarded takeaway containers, crumpled cola cans and sweet wrappers littered a deserted alleyway, and he slowed his pace down. More than anything, he needed to catch his breath.

With one hand curled around a six foot iron railing, he twisted his head this way and that, checking that he was alone. Then he pressed his hand to his side, in a bid to stop the searing pain. His body was hunched over, and he could barely breathe as his lungs fought against the exertion to inhale the air that his body needed. He breathed in and out, inhaling and exhaling large gulps of air. Why was the pain in his side getting worse?

He straightened up, brought his hand away from his body, and looked down at the bright red blood smeared there. Panic rose within him, and a low guttural groan that resembled a wounded animal's spilt from his lips. He'd thought that Bannerman's henchman had punched him in the gut, not stabbed him. Where had the blade even come from?

Gingerly, he touched the wound for a second time and looked

down. His fingers were wet, sticky, and coated in red. He was bleeding out, just like his Uncle Frank had done when Shank slashed him. Pressing down on the wound even farther, his eyes were wide, scared. He didn't want to die.

He continued walking, and as he approached the busy High Street, he picked up his pace. He wasn't being followed, he was certain of that. Up ahead of him, he spotted a taxi rank. The pain was becoming so much worse, and he was beginning to feel dizzy.

He needed to get home, and fast. Breaking out into a jog, he kept one hand pressed to the wound. As he barged his way through the throng of passers-by, they turned to look as he ambled on his way, muttering out obscenities that he should look where he was going.

At the taxi rank, he stumbled in to the back seat of a waiting car, and, yanking the door closed behind him, he gritted his teeth, leant back slightly, then reached into his denim pocket and pulled out a wad of cash. Throwing the money on to the passenger seat, he briefly closed his eyes. 'Take me to Dagenham,' he groaned. 'And put your foot down.'

* * *

'Just wait here for me, yeah?' Fletch glanced across to his boss's front door. He and Stevie had been on their way to get some food, and just as he'd pulled up outside a Turkish restaurant in Green Lane, Dagenham, his mouth already watering at the prospect of filling his belly with chicken kofte, Susan had telephoned him and told him to come back to the house, as a matter of urgency.

Just hearing her husky voice was enough to make him instantly hard. He couldn't get enough of her. As far as he was concerned, it was a no-brainer. The food could wait, much to Stevie's annoyance.

'I won't be long,' he told his best mate.

Pulling open the glove box, Stevie began sorting through a selection of compact discs. 'Hurry up then,' he said, looking upwards. 'I'm starving.'

'All right, just give me a minute.' Fletch rolled his eyes and climbed out of the car. His mobile phone began to buzz, and he looked down at the screen. It was Spencer. He didn't have time for this right now. The call rang off. He glanced back at the house, then tossed the phone across. 'It's Spence. If he rings again, answer it for me, mate.'

He walked towards the front door and, noting that Billy's car was absent from the driveway, he briefly wondered if he had time to drag Susan upstairs for a quick session before Stevie came looking for him. *Probably not*, he groaned to himself.

As he lifted his hand to rap the brass knocker, the front door edged open. Taking a quick glance back at his car, he cautiously took a step across the threshold.

'Suzy?' he tentatively called out.

When he received no reply, he entered the hallway. His body was on full alert as he moved forward. What the fuck was going on? Why was the front door open? He paused in front of the door leading to the dining room.

'Suze?' he called out for a second time. Still no reply.

Even though he knew it was a long shot, he opened the dining room door anyway. The room that Billy used for business meetings was just as he'd expected it to be, empty. He edged his way towards the lounge, and as he pushed open the heavy oak door, he braced himself.

'For fuck's sake, Suze.' He physically relaxed when he saw her sitting on one of the high-backed chairs facing him. 'You worried the fucking life out of me, babe. Didn't you hear me calling you?'

With her eyes remaining downcast, Susan lifted her head.

Terror was etched across her beautiful face. Her left eyelid had swelled to three times its usual size, and a trickle of blood snaked its way down from one nostril, towards the edge of her full, pink lips, the same lips he had kissed, over and over again, just that afternoon. Across her high cheekbones, already he could see bruises beginning to form, and her body shook so violently that his blood ran cold, just thinking about the horror she must have been through before he arrived.

'What the fuck, Suze, who did this to you?' He raced into the room and gently took her face in his hands, forcing her to look up at him. 'Tell me, babe,' he urged her. 'I swear, before God, I'm going to fucking kill them with my bare hands.'

'Hello, Fletch. Fancy seeing you back here so soon.'

The booming voice caught Fletch off guard, and as he swung his head to the right, the hairs on the back of his neck stood up on end. Shards of ice-cold fear slammed down his spine, and his throat became suddenly dry.

'Bill,' he spluttered.

'From the look on your face, I think it's safe to say that I'm the last person you were expecting to see.' Billy grinned.

Fletch swallowed deeply, and, coming to his senses, he sprang away from Susan, in the hope of creating what he prayed looked like a reasonable distance between them. A pink flush crept up his neck, and he shoved his hands deep into his denim pockets, trying to make himself look less suspicious, as if their interaction were a lot more innocent than it actually looked.

Without needing to be told, he already knew they had been caught red-handed, and he let out an annoyed groan. There was absolutely no way on earth that an eagle-eyed Billy would have misread what had just taken place.

As he stared down at the floor, a thousand thoughts raced through his mind. What the fuck was going on? What was Billy doing here? Why wasn't his car on the drive? Who was it that had attacked Susan? Was it Billy himself, and his heavy fists?

'Cat got your tongue, kid?'

Jerking his head towards Billy for a second time, the breath caught in Fletch's throat. 'Kid' had been a word Joseph would use to address him. It had been his way of putting him in his place.

'That's right, our mutual friend, Joseph.' Billy stabbed his finger forward. 'The one you told me was the snake, the one I topped because you told me he was a fucking grass.' He shook his head. 'When, all along, it was you. You who I should have been watching out for.'

'Nah, Bill.' Finding his voice, Fletch gave a nervous laugh. Maybe this wasn't about him and Susan after all. Perhaps Billy had found out who his father was? Out of the two, it was the better scenario. He looked his boss in the eyes and swallowed down the urge to look back at Susan for confirmation. 'You know it's not me, mate. I haven't been giving Bannerman information.'

'You're not my fucking mate.' Billy's eyes darkened. 'But I can tell you what you are, and that's a cunt.'

Fletch opened his mouth to speak, and then, just as quickly, snapped it closed again. His stomach dropped and he dragged his hand across his jaw.

'Is there something you need to tell me?' He looked between his wife and protégé. 'Well, come on, I'm waiting. Fill me in on all the gory details. What have I missed, eh? What have the two of you been getting up to behind my back?'

This was it; the moment Fletch had been waiting for. All he needed to do was admit to the truth, let Billy throw his toys out of the pram, maybe even smash the place up a bit – or a lot – grab Susan, and then fuck off someplace where he would never find them again. Only he wasn't stupid. He knew it wouldn't be that easy. Nothing with Billy ever was.

'Well, answer me.' Billy lifted his arms in the air and his voice began to rise. 'I'm still waiting for you to deny the fact that you've been shagging my fucking wife.'

Fletch took this as his chance, and hastily threw a glance in Susan's direction. He could feel the fear she felt seeping out of her pores and his first instinct, his only instinct, was to fight tooth and nail. She was his life, and he would do everything in his power to protect her. At that same moment, she lifted her eyes to meet his, and with a slight nod of her head, gestured towards the left of where he was standing. The sight that met him made him instantly reel backwards.

'Whoa, Bill,' he yelled, 'there's no fucking need for that.'

'How did you think this would end?' There was amusement in Billy's voice. 'Did you really think I was just going to let the two of you sail off into the sunset, hand-in-hand, with my approval?'

Fletch's heart began to pump faster. He could barely drag his eyes away from the plastic sheeting that had been rolled out across the wooden floorboards. 'You don't have to do this, Bill.' His voice was high. 'Not fucking this.'

'Then explain to me what I should do?' Billy cracked his blood-stained knuckles and took a menacing step closer to his wife. 'Come on, Fletch, I'm all ears – how exactly should this,' he said, sweeping his hand between them, 'go fucking down?'

Fletch shook his head. How was he supposed to answer? For the first time in his life, he was at a loss for words.

'Maybe I should just kill her, take her out of the equation?' Lunging forward, Billy grasped his thick fingers around Susan's slender neck.

The attack was more than enough to make Fletch see red. He charged after his boss, flung his arms around Billy's waist, and forcibly hauled him away from her. He could hear Susan gasping for air, alerting him to the fact that she was okay – shocked and hurt maybe – but still conscious, and more importantly, still alive.

They tumbled to the floor, and with one hand still clamped around Billy's waist, he used his free hand to jab punches into his boss's face and ribs. It wasn't enough, he knew that, and panic began to rise within him. He had to take Billy out. He had to somehow stop him.

Punches continued to fly, and despite each one hitting his target, Fletch could feel his grip on Billy's waist loosening. He kicked out his feet as his fingers struggled to reclaim the hold he'd had on him. His efforts were fruitless. With ease, Billy was able to twist his body around, and much to Fletch's despair, the older man now had the upper hand. Effortlessly, Billy pulled back his meaty fist and began to pummel it forward. Thick and fast, the punches came crashing down, catching Fletch wherever they landed.

Even though stars danced in front of his eyes, as each sickening punch now connected with the side of his head, Fletch tried to hold Billy off. He rammed his thumbs into Billy's eye sockets, hoping for a reprieve. It did the complete opposite, and as Billy howled with pain, it only enraged him further.

Fletch wasn't going to walk away from this, he knew that now. He'd been a fool to even think he could take Billy on and succeed. Images of his son entered his mind. He would grow up fatherless, just like he himself had done. In that instant, he knew that he couldn't give up, not now, not like this. He owed it to Austin to try and survive.

He thrashed his body around. If only he could get Billy off him, he stood a chance of fighting back. In front of him, a tiny window of opportunity appeared, and, using his elbow, he slammed it hard into Billy's face.

A loud grunt escaped Billy's lips, his eyes clouded over and he slumped forward.

Briefly closing his eyes, Fletch threw his head back and exhaled loudly. A thin layer of sweat covered his forehead, and his chest heaved with each breath he took.

'Have I...'

He snapped his eyes open and looked upwards. Susan was standing over them. In her hand, she held a heavy crystal ashtray. The look across her face was one of pure panic.

'Have I killed him?'

* * *

Pete's face was ashen as he barged his way into George's study and slung the holdall on to the desk.

'It was a fucking set-up.' He breathed heavily. 'Someone was waiting for me as I came out of the flat.'

Tearing his eyes away from his number two, George jumped to his feet, raced around the desk, yanked the zip across and peered inside the bag. As he eyed up several large zip bags containing the Ecstasy pills, relief surged through him.

'Who was it?' he demanded to know.

'Dunno.' Pete rolled his eyes. 'Funnily enough, I was a bit too busy to catch his name.' Pete scratched at his jaw as he thought it over. 'I got a good look at him, though – big bloke, young, probably in his early twenties. I jibbed the fucker up and he had it away on his toes.'

'Good.' Satisfied, George nodded. He took out one of the polythene bags and turned it over in his hand.

Pete came to stand beside his boss. 'The more I think about it, I can't help thinking it all seemed a bit personal. He didn't even attempt to snatch the bag. If he'd wanted the goods, then surely he would have made a beeline for the holdall.'

'Big bloke, you said?' George snapped his head upwards.

'Massive bastard, had a mean right hook on him an' all.' He touched the side of his face, recalling the jab that had landed on his jaw.

At this, George chewed the inside of his cheek. If it had been King, then Pete would have instantly recognised him. He looked into the distance. From what he had seen of Fletch and knowing for a fact that he was roughly the same height as Pete, it was safe to say he could rule him out. Besides, if he knew him as well as he thought he did, then he was certain the little fucker wouldn't dare try to cross him.

'He didn't say a single word, just grinned at me manically.' He tapped the side of his head. 'I don't think he was the full ticket.'

Spencer? As of yet, George hadn't encountered his youngest son, and he narrowed his eyes at the possibility of his involvement. 'How big are we talking?'

Pete eyed George's six-foot-three frame up and down. 'I'd say your height, give or take an inch.'

Snarling, George tossed the bag of pills inside the holdall. It was about time he made it his business to have a meeting with his youngest boy.

* * *

Fletch's eyes were wide as he rolled Billy off him and scrambled to his feet.

'He is, isn't he?' Susan's voice began to rise. 'I've killed him.'

As he edged towards her, Fletch held out his arms. 'Don't look at him, darling.'

Susan backed away, her face deathly pale. 'Tell me,' she pleaded. 'Is he dead?'

Glancing behind him, Fletch shook his head; he couldn't tell. 'Don't look, Suze.' He steered her back. 'Don't do this to yourself.'

Behind them, as he lay slumped out on the floor, Billy groaned.

A startled scream escaped from Susan's lips, and without hesitating, Fletch snatched the crystal ashtray out of her hands and pounced forward. Repeatedly, he slammed the object down over his boss's head, oblivious to the spray of blood that covered him, the ceiling, and walls. He couldn't stop; he had to keep going. He had to finish what he'd started, and above all else, he had to keep Susan safe.

Finally, and out of breath, he sat back on his haunches. It was clear to see that Billy was dead. One side of his face and skull had been caved in. Blood, bone and brain matter seeped into the Chinese silk rug. Across the rich, swirling tapestry formed a scarlet puddle that spread out across the polished floorboards beneath.

'What have you done?' Susan began to scream even louder.

Fletch got to his feet. He walked towards her, and she backed away.

'You've killed him.' Her eyes were wide and her hair in disarray. 'You've killed him,' she repeated.

'I did what I had to do,' Fletch answered. He jerked a bloodstained hand behind him. 'It was him or us, and I've got a son to think about.'

'No.' Susan glared as she shook her head so vigorously that her hair flew out in all directions.

'It was him or us, Suze,' Fletch reaffirmed. 'I had to do it. He was gonna kill us.' He glanced behind him, and his voice began to rise. 'I did this for us. It was what you wanted. You said you wanted him to go away and never come back.'

Susan's eyes sprang wide open, and her voice was high. 'No,' she screamed. 'I said that I wanted him to disappear, that I wanted him to go away, not this, not murder. I didn't want him to die.' She looked around her for an escape route. 'Dear God,' she cried. 'What have you done?'

'Do you think I actually wanted to do this? That I wanted to kill him? We had no other choice, darling.'

'We could have talked to him,' she cried. 'We could have made him see sense.'

'And what exactly did you think was going to happen after we'd had this talk?' Fletch growled. 'That I'd be able to send him away on a holiday, and tell him not to come back until me and you had fucked off some place?'

She shook her head and began to cry.

'Look, we can be together now.' His voice became gentle once more. 'Just you and me, Suze. We can start over. We can be a proper couple.' He attempted to pull her into his arms. She roughly pushed him away from her and slid past him.

'Don't touch me,' she warned.

He reached out a second time. 'C'mon, babe, this is what we wanted.'

'I told you not to fucking touch me,' she screamed. Her hands flew out to attack him, and her fingernails raked down his face and chest.

'Enough.' Fletch's heart plummeted. He caught hold of her wrists and pulled her towards him. 'I did this for us,' he gently reminded her.

'No,' she spat. 'You did it for you.' She wriggled out of his arms and turned her face away. She couldn't look at him; she didn't want to look at him. Walking across the lounge, she stood with her back to him, and took deep breaths in an attempt to quash the panic that was building inside of her. Billy was dead.

'Suze, don't.' There was desperation in Fletch's voice. 'Please don't, babe,' he pleaded with her.

'Don't what?' Susan spun around. 'You can't make this right, Fletch.' She looked down at her husband's broken body and her voice cracked. 'You can't make this go away.'

'I can.' Fletch leapt forward and hope filled him. 'I can take care of this, I can.' He glanced behind him. 'I can dispose of him. I've had to do it before. No one will ever find him. They won't even realise that he's dead. We could say he left you, and that he went to live at the villa in Marbella.'

'Dispose of him? What, like he's a piece of trash?' Susan's eyes hardened, sickened by his words. 'He was my husband!'

Fletch swallowed deeply. He should have known better than to use those words. He looked around him, at a loss. Of course she was right. He didn't know how to make this better. He couldn't make it right. Nothing he said or did was going to help matters. 'Please, Suze.'

His pleas fell on deaf ears, and with her back ramrod straight, she refused to look at him. In that moment, he knew that he'd lost her. Even in death, Billy had won.

'Fletch.' Waving the mobile phone in front of his face, Stevie bounded through the lounge door. He took in the scene in front of him, and instantly recoiled backwards. 'What the fuck happened in here?' he gasped.

Fletch briefly closed his eyes. 'It was him or us.' He saw Susan's back stiffen and carried on regardless. 'He was going to kill us, and I did what I had to do.'

His eyes wide, Stevie could barely take it all in. He looked down at the phone in his hand and, recalling the reason why he had entered the house in the first place, he waved the device in the air. 'Mate, your day is about to get so much worse.'

Looking up, Fletch groaned. How could his day possibly get any worse than this?

'It's Spence,' Stevie quickly explained. 'He just called back. He's in a right fucking state. He's been stabbed.'

Fletch didn't know whether to laugh or cry. He massaged his temples. Stevie was right, his day was about to get so much worse.

14

Between them, Fletch and Stevie heaved Billy's body out of the house and towards the car. Out of Susan's earshot, Stevie rounded on his best friend. 'I told you this would fucking happen.'

'No, you didn't,' Fletch groaned. 'You said that Billy would kill me.'

'Details, Fletch, fucking details.' Stevie rolled his eyes. All along, he'd said it was a bad idea and that Fletch needed to end the affair before someone got hurt.

Stripped of his clothing, Billy's corpse had then been wrapped in the plastic sheeting and placed inside the boot of Fletch's car. They looked down at their handiwork, turning their heads this way and that as they inspected the body. It was a tight squeeze, but in the circumstances, it was their only option.

'We'll dump him in the same place that he dumped Joseph.'

'We?' Stevie gave a hollow laugh. 'Since when did this become "we"? This is your fucking mess.'

'Don't you think I already know that?' Fletch looked along the driveway, hoping more than anything they couldn't be seen by any passing traffic on the lane. 'You have to help me out, mate.'

'I don't have to do fuck all.' Even as he said the words, Stevie knew he wouldn't abandon his mate, not like this, not when he needed him more than he'd ever needed him before. He let out a long sigh, and as he slammed down the boot, he stabbed his finger in Fletch's direction. 'If I go down for this, I'll make sure you never know a day's peace again.'

'If we do exactly what we did with Hatton, then everything will be okay.' He said the words more to reassure himself than anything else.

'It'd better be.'

'It will.' Tipping his head up, there was a determined glint in Fletch's eyes. He glanced back towards the house. He needed to speak to Susan. He needed to make things right between them. 'Just give me a minute, yeah?'

'Yeah, I've heard that before, and look what fucking happened the last time you said you were only gonna be a minute. You ain't planning to kill her an' all, are you?'

Fletch narrowed his eyes. Just the mere thought of hurting Susan made him feel physically sick. 'Of course I'm fucking not, I wouldn't harm a hair on her head.'

'Just checking. Right, well, hurry up then.' He gestured towards the car. 'We've got more pressing issues other than the state of your love life, in case it's slipped your notice.'

In the lounge, he found Susan on her hands and knees, scrubbing at the polished floorboards. She dipped the wire brush into a bucket of hot soapy water, tapped the bristles against the side, then resumed the task of cleaning up the blood.

'Suzy?'

Her back stiffened, the only sign she gave to let him know that she'd heard him.

'I'm leaving now to dis...' He stopped himself just in time and began again. 'I'm leaving now to take care of everything.'

Susan continued scrubbing.

'Do you want me to come back after, I mean, after it's done?' He shifted his weight from one foot to the other.

She remained silent, and as he watched her back arch, and saw the muscles in her arms tighten, he took a step forward. 'I could come back and make sure that there is no evidence left behind.'

She shook her head and sat back on her haunches, refusing to look at him. 'I want you to leave this house and never come back. I don't want to know where you take him, how you...' A strangled sob escaped from her lips and she resumed scrubbing.

Chewing on the inside of his cheek, Fletch turned to look at the front door. He knew he had to get a move on and fast, but he couldn't leave without knowing what would become of them. 'What about us?'

At this, Susan turned her head. Her eyes were devoid of any emotion. It had to be the shock, he told himself, but it was her words that shocked him instead.

'There is no us. There will never be an us, ever again.'

'But...'

Susan snarled. 'The mere thought of being near you repulses me.' She screwed up her face in disgust. 'Just thinking about you putting your hands on me, touching me, or even being in your presence, turns my stomach.' She nodded towards the front door. 'Now, get out, before I call the police and tell them that you're an intruder, that you attacked me, and that you killed my husband.'

Fletch's eyes widened. He could barely take in what she'd just said. And with as much dignity as he could muster, he walked from the room, gently pulled the lounge door closed, and then walked out of the house. Striding across the driveway, he kept his head down low. He still had some pride in him. He couldn't allow Stevie to see him like this, and, taking the cuff of his shirt sleeve, he hastily wiped it across his eyes. Without giving the house so much as a backward glance, he climbed into the car.

'All sorted?' Stevie asked.

'Yeah.' Fletch's voice became instantly hard. He started the ignition and drove the car forward. Susan had more than made her feelings clear. He was beginning to think it had all been a sick game on her part, after all. 'It's sorted out all right.'

* * *

After disposing of Billy's body off the coast of Southend, Fletch had driven them at breakneck speed, straight to Stevie's flat. It was early evening by the time he'd showered and changed into the jeans and sweater that Stevie hastily passed across. Thoughts of what had taken place just that afternoon rattled around inside his mind. Billy was gone. Susan wanted nothing more to do with him. And now Spencer had been stabbed. How the hell had all of this happened in the space of just twenty-four hours?

'Here, put this on.' Stevie passed him one of his freshly cleaned trainers, and he slipped it on. As he took the second trainer, he paused. 'Thanks, mate, for everything you did for me today.'

Stevie waved him away.

'I mean it,' Fletch told him. 'I couldn't have done it without your help. I owe you one.'

'Yeah, you do an' all.' Stevie watched as Fletch slipped on the second trainer and blew out his cheeks. 'You know the worst part in all of this?'

Fletch looked up.

'The day ain't even over yet.'

Fletch nodded. Wasn't that the truth.

Thirty minutes later, they pulled up outside Newham General

Hospital, raced inside, and found Jenny on the first floor, in the relatives' room adjacent to the operating theatre.

'Mum, any news yet?' Fletch was still out of breath as she pulled him into her arms.

Her face was pale, and underneath the bright lights, the wrinkles around her eyes seemed more prominent. 'A nurse just this minute came in. She said the surgeon is going to come and talk to us.' Tears glistened her eyes. 'That can't be a good sign, can it?'

'I dunno.' Fletch had no idea if it was good or bad. Maybe it was protocol, at least that was what he hoped it was. Tearing his eyes away from her, he looked towards the door, expectantly, as a man whom he guessed correctly was the surgeon walked in.

Wearing blue cotton theatre scrubs, he gestured for them to take a seat.

'How is he?' Before he had even sat down, the words were out of Fletch's mouth.

'The surgery was successful, and I'm hopeful that he will recover well.'

Jenny gasped with relief. She clutched her hand across her heart. Her free hand found Fletch's, and she gave it a reassuring squeeze. 'So he's going to be okay?' she tentatively asked. 'Can we see him?'

They were taken into the recovery area, and at the far end of the ward, Spencer began to stir as they approached.

'Oh, you did worry us.' Jenny smiled down at her youngest son.

'I'm sorry, Mum.'

'No need to apologise, my darling, I'm just pleased that you're okay now, and the doctor said you should be able to come home in a few days, if all goes well.'

'Fletch.' Spencer turned his head.

'Yeah, I'm here, mate. How are you feeling?'

Fletch gave his brother a wide smile, all the while a thousand thoughts ran through his mind. How the hell had Spencer managed to get himself stabbed? Where had it taken place? Who was responsible? He narrowed his eyes, waiting for his mum to move away so he could grill his brother. He knew the Old Bill were bound to turn up at any moment, and wanted to get to the truth before Spencer had the chance to make up some cock-and-bull version of events.

'Mum, why don't you go and get us all a cup of tea?'

Jenny looked between her two sons and sighed. 'I'll go and ask if Spence is allowed to have anything to drink yet.' She patted her youngest son's arm, then wandered off towards the nurses' station.

Once she was out of earshot, Fletch got down to business. 'What the fuck happened, Spence?'

Spencer averted his eyes.

The hairs on the back of Fletch's neck stood up on end. *Please, not again*, he said to himself. 'Spence.'

'I dunno.'

'Yeah, you do.' Fletch lowered his voice. 'What did you do, Spence? Why did someone stab you?'

'It wasn't meant to happen like that.'

'What wasn't?' Walking closer to the bed, Fletch was all ears. 'What wasn't supposed to happen?'

'Bannerman's man. He got to me before I got to him.'

Fletch reared back. 'Bannerman? Why the fuck would you be anywhere near one of Bannerman's men?'

Spencer balled the blanket in his fist and screwed up his face. 'I want them to pay for what they did.'

'Pay?' There was disbelief in Fletch's voice. He looked up to see where their mum was and, seeing that she was still talking to the nurses, he gave his brother his full attention. 'What are you talking about, Spence? Pay for what?'

'Uncle Frank.'

To say that Fletch was shocked was an understatement. He stood open-mouthed, staring at his brother.

'I thought that if I could make him pay, then it would make everything better for Frank.'

Mickey Shank. The name popped into Fletch's mind, and he recalled the sinking feeling he'd had at the time when he'd found out the man had been topped. 'Was it you, Spence? Did you kill Shank?'

Spencer looked away. 'I was angry, Fletch.'

Fletch's breath caught in the back of his throat and he shook his head vigorously. 'No, Spence, please, tell me you didn't.'

'I'm sorry, Fletch.' He lowered his eyes. 'Are you mad at me?'

How was he supposed to answer? He felt like punching something, anything would do, as long as he could take his anger out on it.

'You are, aren't you? You're mad at me.'

Fletch closed his eyes. He really couldn't take much more of this today. 'I'm not mad, Spence,' he finally answered, 'but this has to stop, do you understand me? You can't go off on fucking rampages.'

Spencer gave a slight nod of his head, leaving Fletch unconvinced that his words had sunk in.

'Here we are.' Jenny placed two Styrofoam cups filled with tea on top of the portable table. 'Only water for you, Spence.' She lifted the jug and poured out a glass of water. 'Just little sips,' she said, as she lifted the glass to her son's lips.

'Mum, I've got to go.' Fletch rubbed wearily at his temples. All he wanted to do was sit in a darkened room to think through the day's events.

'What about your tea?'

'You have it.' He began backing away.

'Okay, darling.' She reached forward, pulled him back towards her, and kissed his cheek. 'I'll stay here for a bit, just until Spence has been settled on to a ward, and then shoot off home and bring him back some bits.'

Barely even listening, Fletch had already turned and walked away. Outside in the corridor, Stevie joined him.

'Well, what happened?'

Striding towards the exit, Fletch ignored the question.

'Oi.' Pulling back on his mate's arm, Stevie raised his eyebrows. 'What the fuck happened?'

'Nothing.' Pulling his arm free, Fletch continued walking. 'I fucking hate hospitals,' he stated.

'Don't we all,' Stevie agreed, wrinkling his nose. As they continued on their way to the car, he threw Fletch a sideways glance. 'Talk to me, man.'

'I can't.' Fletch shook his head. 'There's too much to tell, and you wouldn't understand.' He climbed behind the wheel, purposely looking everywhere other than at his best friend.

'Try me.'

Fletch ignored the comment. He started the ignition and inched out of the car park. After a few minutes, he spoke. 'You know how much I love my brother, right? That I look out for him?'

'Yeah.' Stevie turned his head. Of course he knew, everyone knew.

'It's just, sometimes...' Fletch paused. 'Sometimes I don't understand what goes on inside that head of his.'

Stevie sighed. He didn't know how to answer and wasn't entirely sure that Fletch expected one from him. Finally, they turned in to his road and he cleared his throat. 'I think me and you need to have a proper chat, mate. Maybe we can work this problem, whatever it is, out between us.'

'Yeah, maybe.' He watched Stevie climb out of the car. 'I'll give you a bell tomorrow.'

Tapping the roof of the car, Stevie made his way towards the flats. Fletch watched him go. There was a heaviness in his heart, a heaviness that he was unable to shrug off.

The truth was, he didn't know what to do with himself. He didn't want to go home and didn't want to go to his uncle's house either; as for going back to see Susan, well, that was out of the question. Starting the ignition, he put his foot down and just drove.

15

Three hours later, darkness had descended. He'd put off the inevitable long enough. He had to go home, and as much as he didn't want to have to face Tina, there was nowhere else he could go. Having parked the car, he took the lift to the fourth floor and let himself in to the flat.

Thankful that the place was in darkness, he made his way through to the lounge, sank down on the sofa, and brought his hands up to his face.

'Fletch.' Tina switched on the table lamp.

Inwardly, he groaned. He couldn't deal with Tina on top of everything else. He looked up in time to watch her as she walked back across the lounge and positioned herself on the arm of the chair opposite from where he sat.

He noted that she pulled down the hem of her short nightie. It should have made him happy to see that she'd finally taken the hint and realised that he wasn't interested. It did the opposite, and only depressed him even further.

'What's wrong?'

'What makes you think anything is wrong?' He shook his head at her, annoyed that she would even ask him the question.

She gave him a gentle smile in return, a lot gentler than he deserved, and he held his head in his hands once more, feeling thoroughly ashamed of himself. Susan, Billy, Spence – images of the three of them plagued his mind, and he slammed his eyes closed in a bid to block them out.

'Because I know you, and I know when something is wrong.' She walked across the room and knelt beside him.

He wanted to shake his head at that. She didn't know him at all. If she did, she would run a mile in the opposite direction and take Austin with her. 'Where's the baby?'

'In his crib, fast asleep.' She smiled up at him.

'You should run away from me.' He dragged his hand through his hair, not looking at her.

Tina cocked her head to one side, puzzled. It was the most civil he had been to her in weeks. 'Why would I do that?'

'Because I'm not good for you, Teen, either of you,' he sighed.

She reached out to touch his arm, and he snatched hold of her hand. Any other day, he would have thrown it away from him and warned her not to touch him. Tonight, he did no such thing. He needed to feel her, someone, anyone, and so pulled her hand closer towards him, as though it were a lifeline.

The action startled her, and a gasp escaped from her lips. She stared down at his hand covering hers.

'Fletch...' she began.

He shook his head silently, begging her not to speak, and, lifting her to her feet, he placed her down on his lap and buried his face in her hair. The first start of tears welled up in his eyes, and in an attempt to hide the despair that raged through him, he pushed his head in to her long dark hair even farther.

Tina held on to him, and slowly, his stiff body moulded with her own. She had no idea what had caused him to react like this, and she bit down on her bottom lip. As much as it was what she had always wanted, she couldn't help but feel scared. If she was being totally honest with herself, it was downright unnerving. She tilted her head back and studied him. Her voice wobbled as she spoke.

'Has something bad happened?'

Had something bad happened? Fletch almost laughed out loud. Even if he wanted to tell her, which he didn't, he would have no idea where to even begin.

'Spence was stabbed.' He saw her eyes widen and quickly added, 'He's gonna be okay; they stitched him up.'

Tina nodded. He continued to hold her in his arms, and she held her breath, not wanting the moment to end. Using her fingertips, she wiped strands of dark hair away from his forehead.

'That's a good thing, right?'

'Yeah.' He nuzzled his face in to her hair once more. For a moment, he considered tipping her from his lap and telling her to go to bed. Before today, he would have done just that, but now, right now, he couldn't. He needed this.

His hand reached out and snaked the length of her bare thigh, and she wriggled in closer. In the back of his mind, he knew it was wrong of him, and that when the morning light shone through the windows, he would feel differently, that he wouldn't want her, that he was only using her for a second time to try and get over the loss of Susan.

He tipped her back on to the sofa, and her short nightie rose. He noticed that, this time, she didn't attempt to pull it down and cover herself. Even with the knowledge that she wanted another baby, and not to mention that she had tricked him in getting her pregnant with the first one, it wasn't enough to stop him. He eagerly kicked off his trainers and jeans. He didn't bother to ask her if it was what she wanted; he already knew it was. He could see the want, the lust, the need, in her eyes.

'You went on the pill, right?' As he lowered himself down, he took a moment to pause.

'Of course I did.' Tina chewed on her bottom lip. She hadn't but wasn't about to tell the truth and put an end to what was about to take place.

'Good,' he muttered in return.

* * *

A pounding at the front door roused Fletch from his sleep. With one eye still closed, he reached out his hand to feel for Tina's side of the bed. The sheets were cold to his touch.

Slamming his eyes closed, he groaned out loud as the memory of the previous night's events came back to haunt him. He turned over and lay on his back, staring up at the ceiling. He couldn't believe he'd been so careless, so stupid, and had gone back to Tina for a second time. The worst part of it all was that he couldn't even blame it on alcohol. He'd been as sober as a judge.

'Babe.' Fully clothed, Tina poked her head around the bedroom door. 'Stevie's here to see you.'

He rubbed at his jaw, swung his legs over the side of the bed, and hastily pulled on a clean pair of boxer shorts and T-shirt, before making his way through to the lounge.

'I'm taking Austin to the health centre for his weekly check-up.' Placing their son in to his pushchair, Tina looked up and gave him a wide smile.

He gave her a small smile in return and watched as she left the flat.

'She seems happy, for once.' Stevie raised his eyebrows and

jerked his thumb in Tina's direction. 'I even managed to get a "hello" out of her this morning.'

Shrugging his shoulders, Fletch dragged on his jeans, then slumped down on the sofa. 'She's probably after money.' He averted his eyes away from his best mate's quizzical stare. There was no way on earth he was going to tell the truth, and admit that the only reason she was happy was because she now believed everything was okay between them, that they were together, a couple.

'So?'

'What?' Fletch looked up.

Stevie narrowed his eyes. 'You know what.'

'No, I don't. What?' Fletch repeated.

'We're gonna be here all fucking day if we keep on like this.' Stevie chuckled out loud, only it sounded hollow to Fletch's ears. 'What's going on with Spence?'

'What about him?'

'For fuck's sake, Fletch.' Losing patience, Stevie's face turned red. 'Don't you know how to give a straight answer to a question any more?'

Fletch swallowed. 'It's not that. It's just, there isn't anything to tell.'

'Jesus fucking Christ.' Walking across to the patio doors, Stevie leant his palms on the glass. As he looked out at the view across Romford town centre, the muscles in his back strained against the thin fabric of his shirt. 'I ain't leaving here today without an explanation,' he warned. 'So' – he turned back around – 'you'd best start talking, and fast.'

Fletch paused. He didn't understand any of it himself, and Spencer was his own brother, so how the hell did Stevie expect to be able to get his head around everything that had gone on? 'Spence, he...'

'What?' Stevie bounded across the room and came to stand inches away from the sofa. 'C'mon, spit it out.'

Pulling in his knees, Fletch sat forward. He really didn't know where to start. Finally, he spoke. 'My name, Fletch... it's a nickname, and comes from my surname Fletcher, right?'

'Yeah, I already know this,' Stevie spat.

'But the truth is, my surname isn't Fletcher.' He looked up at Stevie. 'It never was.'

'What are you talking about? Of course it is.' Stevie thought back. He'd known his best mate for most of his life. They'd even gone to school together.

'It's not.' He paused and rubbed at his temples, not sure how to continue. 'My real name is Harry. Harry... Bannerman.'

Stevie's face paled and he took a step backwards. 'Bannerman? As in, George Bannerman?' He tilted his head to one side. 'That's just a coincidence, right?'

Fletch shook his head. Shame flooded through him, and he could barely look his best mate in the eyes.

'Okay, so somewhere down the line, he's a relative, like a distant cousin or something.'

'No, and believe me, I wish that was the case.' He took a deep breath. 'He's... he's mine and Spence's dad.' There, he'd finally said it, and in a way, it felt good to have finally got it off his chest, to have come clean. He'd already lost the one person he cared about and so if his best mate turned against him too, what did it matter?

'Are you kidding me?' Stevie placed his hands on the arm of the leather chesterfield sofa. The shock across his pale face was quickly replaced with anger, and he backed away. 'And what, all this time you've been in cahoots with Bannerman, playing us?'

'No.' Fletch leapt off the sofa and spread open his arms. 'It wasn't like that, mate.'

'Don't call me "mate",' Stevie sneered. 'It was you all along. All this time, you've been running back to Bannerman, telling him what was going down. You're the fucking grass.'

'No.' Fletch inched closer and there was a desperation in his voice. 'That wasn't me. It really was Joseph; you have to believe me on that.'

'Believe you?' Stevie puffed out his cheeks. How was he supposed to believe anything that came out of his so-called best mate's mouth ever again? He didn't even know who he was any more.

'My mum, she took us away from him when we were kids. Up until recently, I hadn't seen George in years. I didn't even want to see him. I still don't want to see him.'

'I don't understand this.' Stevie sank down on the leather chair and dragged his hand across his face. 'Is this true? Bannerman's really your old man?' He looked up at Fletch through hooded eyes.

Fletch nodded. 'I'm hardly gonna make that up, am I?' He paused for a moment, allowing his words to sink in. 'The thing is, what happened to Albie—'

'Your uncle?' Stevie interrupted him.

'Yeah, I suppose so.' Fletch looked into the distance. He'd never really thought of it like that. 'Well, it was Billy. Billy and Spence who topped him.'

'No, hold up a minute.' Stevie held his hand up in the air. 'Let me get this straight. You're telling me that Spencer killed his own uncle?'

'Yeah, but he didn't know.' Fletch hastily defended his brother. 'Spence has no idea of who our dad even is.'

Shaking his head, Stevie looked down at the floor. 'I can't get my head around any of this.'

'How do you think I feel, then? The thing is, Spence has got it into his nut that he needs to avenge Frank. It's like he's on some fucking crusade. It was him who killed Mickey Shank, and then last night, he went for one of Bannerman's henchmen, only they got to him first. That's how he ended up getting stabbed.'

Stevie's mouth dropped open, and he slammed his fist down on the arm of the chair. 'Then put a stop to it and tell him the fucking truth.'

'I can't.'

'Can't or won't?' Stevie growled.

Fletch shrugged. 'Spence must never know the truth. He can't ever find out who our dad is, or what he put us through as kids.'

'Jesus Christ, Fletch. Have you heard yourself?' Stevie stood up and began to pace the floor. 'You need to end this now, before this causes a fucking war.'

'I can't. I've already told you that.'

Stevie stopped pacing. He stabbed his finger in Fletch's direction. 'Then you need to do all of us a favour, and take Spencer out of the picture, before this spirals out of control, before we end up getting killed in the crossfire.'

'What?' Air whooshed out of Fletch's mouth. He felt as though he'd been kicked in the gut. The very notion of even harming his brother was alien to him. All his life, he'd only ever looked out for him. He slumped down heavily on the sofa. 'He's my brother. I can't do that, you know I can't.'

'There it is again, that word "can't".' Stevie screwed up his face. 'He's a fucking liability, that's what he is, and the worst part of all this is that he's doing it in our name. Have you, even for one second, asked yourself what's gonna happen to Spence when Bannerman gets his hands on him? When he learns the truth?'

'It won't come to that.' Fletch shook his head.

'It's already come to it,' Stevie roared back. He jabbed his finger towards the patio doors. 'He's out there on a fucking rampage, trying to kill all and sundry, and you're just sitting there like it's nothing. How long have you even known about all of this, eh?'

Fletch looked down at the floor. 'Since the first one... Albie.'

Stevie's mouth dropped open, and he shook his head. 'And you're allowing him to get away with it? You're actually condoning what he's doing?'

'Of course I'm fucking not.' He jerked his head up.

'Then what are you doing to stop him, eh?' Stevie breathed heavily through his flared nostrils. 'When Bannerman finds out, he's gonna hurt him, you know that as well as I do. Do you even understand what I'm saying to you, Fletch? He is really going to fucking hurt him, and that'll be on your head. Is that what you want?'

'Of course it ain't.' Fletch swallowed and looked away. 'He won't find out. I'll speak to Spence again. If I have to, I'll even speak to Bannerman. I'll clear everything up.'

Stevie shook his head sadly. 'It's your funeral, Fletch, and you know that as well as I do.'

Lost in his own thoughts, Fletch didn't answer. He didn't know how to.

Taking in the scene before him, George sneered. From his position behind the wheel, he studied the terraced house in Dagenham where his wife and sons lived. Just a few moments earlier, a taxicab had pulled up outside the house and he'd watched Jenny hop out. He continued watching as she fussed over a young man, who gingerly climbed out behind her.

He narrowed his eyes as he watched the man straighten up. He was tall, roughly the same height as himself, but with a mop of dark brown hair, and similar features to his eldest son. George guessed correctly that this was Spencer. It had to be.

Fury rippled through him. He wasn't stupid, and as each second passed, it became more and more evident to him that it was his youngest son who had been responsible for trying to steal the merchandise from Pete. Right then, he wanted to smash his fist into his boy's face, to teach him a lesson that he wouldn't forget in a hurry.

His hand curled around the door handle, ready to leap out of the car and have it out with him. Spencer. He repeated his son's name, over and over, in his mind. What was it that Pete had said – that he believed the attack had been personal, rather than an attempted robbery?

He looked across in time to see them disappearing inside the house, and he narrowed his eyes once more at the possibility of his son's involvement in his brother's disappearance, and the murder of his cousin, Mickey.

The notion niggled at him. It wasn't the first time he had wondered if this was what his eldest son had been trying to cover up, and, dropping his hand away from the door handle, he turned the key in the ignition and drove forward.

As he passed the house, he began to dissect everything he knew to be fact. Albie was missing, presumed dead. Mickey had been topped, and now on top of everything else, Pete had been marked. It was only through sheer luck that he'd been able to walk away from the scene of the attack unscathed.

With a sudden clarity, he knew it had to be a vendetta against himself, and let's face it, his own sons had more than enough ammunition. He wasn't exactly father of the year, not that he'd ever pretended to be anything different. If anyone personally wanted to see him maimed, then it would be his two boys. He'd even heard it from the horse's mouth, so to speak. Hadn't his eldest son said as much?

In the rear-view mirror, he glanced back at the house. There was only one way of knowing for certain if his youngest son was involved, and that was to have Pete identify him as the culprit. Driving back towards South London, George's lips were set into a hard line. More than ever, he rued the day the boys had been conceived. Not for the first time did he wish that he'd successfully beaten them out of his wife's belly, and God only knows, at the time, he'd tried.

* * *

Despite the pain in his side, Spencer grinned at his brother before taking a seat on the sofa.

'Now, these are your painkillers.' Jenny set the little brown bottle down on the nest of tables beside her son. 'You need to take one after your lunch, and then one more before bed. Just the one though, Spence, no more than that.'

Spencer nodded. He could feel his tummy growl with hunger. 'Can I have something to eat now, Mum? I'm really hungry.'

Jenny glanced at her wristwatch. 'Course you can, my darling. How about you, Fletch, do you fancy a sandwich? I've got your favourite ham in the fridge.'

'No thanks, Mum.' Fletch shook his head from side to side. Food was the last thing he wanted or needed. He waited for her to leave the room, then took a seat on the edge of the armchair.

From across the room, Spencer continued to grin at his brother. 'You should have seen the nurses who were looking after me, Fletch. Some of them were proper stunners, looked just like supermodels, they did.'

'I'm sure they did.' Fletch leant forward in the chair, uninterested in what the nurses looked like. 'Spence, what we talked about at the hospital, what you said about Albie Bannerman, and Mickey Shank.'

Spencer turned his head away. 'Have a go at me, you mean?' he grumbled.

'No, I mean talk. What you said about Bannerman. You know this needs to stop, right? That you have to get these thoughts of revenge out of your head.'

'I suppose so.' Spencer shrugged.

Gritting his teeth, Fletch shook his head. 'No "suppose" about it, Spence. It needs to stop, right now.'

'Here we are.' Jenny returned to the room, putting an end to the conversation.

As she set a bowl of steaming chicken soup and four slices of thick buttered bread in front of his brother, Fletch studied him as he ate. There was no getting through to Spencer, he knew that as well as he knew his own name. No matter how much his brother may try to, he was unable to comprehend the severity of his actions. The bottom line was, he just didn't get it.

Silently brooding, Fletch wiped his hand over his jaw and briefly closed his eyes, wishing more than anything that he could go back in time. He couldn't help but blame himself for everything that had taken place. He should have listened to his gut instincts and questioned Billy at the time, when he'd picked out Spencer to do a lone job for him.

He could have put a stop to the murder of Albie, and now this was the upshot. His brother had a taste for blood. Killing meant nothing to him. It didn't even register in his brain that he was doing wrong. As he continued to watch Jenny fuss around, he couldn't help but feel depressed. When was it all going to end? And even more importantly, how was it going to end?

16

Pete was impressed – talk about a fast worker. In just twenty-four hours, George had come up with the name of a suspect.

'How did you find him so quickly?' Pete asked.

'That isn't important.' George dismissed the question. He leant back in his office chair and steepled his fingers in front of his chest. 'What is important is that you give me the nod if it's the same geezer who was waiting for you.'

'Yeah, I can do that.' Pete tapped the side of his head. 'I got a good look at the bastard, and believe me, I won't forget him in a hurry.'

'Good.' George thought it over then stood up from behind his desk. 'Well then, no time like the present.'

'What, now?' Pete raised his eyebrows. He knew that his boss had taken the attempted attack on him seriously but hadn't realised just how much.

'Yes, now.' George was out the door before Pete had even stood up.

Chasing after his boss, Pete's chest swelled with pride. He was obviously a lot more important to George Bannerman than he'd realised.

* * *

Thirty minutes later, George pulled the car over to the kerb. 'That's the house over there.' He pointed towards the house where Frank, Jenny and Spencer lived. 'See the one with the green front door. Go knock there and ask for Spencer.'

'Spencer?' Pete reaffirmed.

George chewed on the side of his cheek. 'Just ask for Spencer. Take a good look at him and then come straight back to the car.'

'Yeah, all right.' Staring towards the house, Pete nodded. He'd like to do a bit more than walk away, not that he would go against an order. George obviously wanted to play this out his own way, and a ripple of excitement filled him at the prospect of seeing the prick who'd attacked him pay for what he'd done.

He opened the car door, stepped outside and flung back his shoulders. With a purposeful swagger, he crossed the street, opened the gate, and then walked down the pathway. At the front door, he rapped his knuckles on the small windowpane.

'Yes, can I help you?'

He gave the woman who opened the door his best smile, instantly putting her at ease. 'I'm looking for Spencer, darling. Is he in?'

'Yes.' Jenny returned his smile. 'Let me just get him. I think he's having a little doze in the armchair.'

The door was closed on him and he heard her footsteps retreating down the hallway.

Moments later, the door reopened, and instead of the woman, a man stood there. Pete took a good look at him and eyed up his six-foot-three frame. His dark hair and face were exactly as he remembered. It was the same man who'd attacked him. He'd recognise him anywhere.

'Sorry, mate, wrong house.' He released his clenched fist, then turned and walked away.

From his position in the car, George watched as Pete crossed back over the street and walked towards him. As he neared, he stuck his thumb up in the air. Bingo. As he'd already known, his suspicions were correct. They had their man.

* * *

'So, what are you gonna do, Fletch?' Stevie eyed his best friend over the rim of the pint glass.

'I dunno,' Fletch sighed. It was lunchtime, and he glanced around the pub before gulping at his beer. Swallowing a mouthful down, he wiped the back of his hand across his lips and shrugged. 'I suppose I'm gonna have to go and have a chat with Bannerman, ain't I?'

'You know he's not going to take it lying down, though, don't you?'

'Yeah, I know.'

'Look.' Stevie moved in closer and lowered his voice. 'At the end of the day, Spence is his son. Is he really gonna do him that much damage?'

Fletch raised his eyebrows, and without answering, downed the remainder of his drink.

'I mean, I know I said that Bannerman would hurt him, but you don't do that to family, do you, especially not to your own son?'

'And how do you think I ended up with broken ribs, or how I got this?' Fletch asked, pointing to the pink scar above his eyebrow. 'Why do you think my mum left him in the first place, or how Spence ended up the way he is? He won't care that Spencer is his son. He's never cared about us, end of.'

Stevie's eyes widened. 'Fucking hell, Fletch, what did he do to him?'

'It doesn't matter.' Fletch shook his head. 'But yeah, you were right. In fact, everything you said was right. He's gonna really hurt Spence if he finds out the truth, son or no son. It'll make no difference to him.'

Stevie thought this over. 'So, how do we stop him from finding out?'

Turning to look at his mate, Fletch gave him a small smile. He couldn't help but notice that his problem had now become their problem. 'I'm going to have to take the bull by the horns, aren't I? I'll talk to him. Maybe, with a bit of luck on my side, I'll be able to steer him in a different direction, one that's far away from Spence.'

'And if you can't?'

'If I can't' – Fletch looked around the pub for a second time – 'then I'll be left with no other choice. I'll have to take matters into my own hands, won't I?'

* * *

With Austin's pram loaded up with shopping bags, Tina struggled to push her way through the entrance door of the flats. Not for the first time did she want to curse her son's father. If only he had rented them a house instead of the flat, then it would have made her life so much easier.

'Here, let me help you.'

Tina looked up at the man standing behind her, and smiled her thanks as he leant across her and pushed open the door.

George Bannerman returned her smile. 'These buildings are not really suitable for young families, are they?'

'You can say that again,' Tina laughed. She set about rearranging the shopping bags. 'That's exactly what I said to my baby's father, but he wanted to live here, and so here we are.' She gave a bitter shrug of her shoulders and made to walk forward.

Glancing at little Austin as he lay wrapped up in the pram, George studied the child's face. There was no mistaking who his father was. The baby was a mirror image of his eldest son. He followed Tina through the lobby towards the lift.

'I've come to visit my son,' he said casually.

Pressing for the lift, Tina glanced over her shoulder and gave him a wide smile. 'That's nice.'

'Yeah.' George nodded. 'My eldest son, Harry. He lives here. Maybe you know him?' He watched her reaction closely, and when he saw no recognition flicker across her face, he quickly added, 'He often goes by the nickname Fletch.'

'Fletch?' Tina's eyes widened. 'Of course I know him! I live with him.' She gestured down at the pram. 'He's my son's father.'

'Get out of here.' George feigned surprise. 'So you must be...'

'Tina,' she volunteered.

'Of course, you're Tina.' He stood back slightly, as if to take a better look at her. 'He said you were pretty, and I can see now that he wasn't exaggerating.'

Fluffing out her hair, Tina couldn't stop the smile that spread across her face. 'He didn't say that about me,' she giggled.

'Course he did.' George guided her inside the open lift. 'He couldn't stop talking about you when we last met up.'

Still basking in the compliments Fletch's father was giving her, Tina pressed the button for the fourth floor. 'I think that Fletch is out, but... would you like to come up for a while, maybe have a cup of tea and wait for him?' She chewed on her bottom lip, feeling suddenly shy around her son's grandfather. 'I'm not too sure what time he will be home, though,' she warned.

George glanced once more at his grandson. Taking a step closer, he bent over the pram and rubbed the baby's tiny hand. 'I'd like that.' He straightened up and flashed a wolfish grin. In fact, he could think of nothing he would like better than to gain access to his eldest son's home.

* * *

Sipping at a cup of tea, Jenny was in a world of her own.

'You all right, girl?' Frank joined her at the kitchen table.

'You know how it is.' She rubbed at her eyes wearily, smudging mascara across her eyelid.

'Something on your mind?' Taking out a cigarette, he lit up and noisily exhaled a plume of smoke above his head.

It wasn't often that they sat down for a chat. In fact, Jenny could count on one hand the amount of times they had. The bottom line was, even though they had been brought up together, they had never really been particularly close. They may have shared the same roof over the years, but that was as far as it had ever really gone. If truth were told, she'd always felt as though she and the boys had been a burden to him, and somehow held him back.

'Well, come on, I know something's up.'

'I was just reminiscing is all.' She placed the mug on the table in front of her and gave him a small smile. 'I was thinking back to when me and the boys first came here to live. Do you remember?'

Frank nodded. 'I can remember picking you up from over the other side of the water. You looked half scared to death.'

'That's because I was,' Jenny laughed. She looked down at the table. It wasn't funny, not really. She could still recall the terror she'd felt as they stood in a freezing cold telephone box, waiting for Frank to collect them. Her arms had been wrapped around her two sons, while they clung to her legs, petrified that George would find them. 'I think he would have ended up killing us if we'd stayed.'

She leant her face on her hand, with her elbow on the table. 'What if the things they witnessed when they were little, damaged them?' She pointed to her temple. 'I mean up here.'

'Where's all this coming from?'

She shook her head to rid herself of the familiar sense of foreboding that shuddered through her. 'I see and hear things that they don't want me to, but I'm not stupid. I know what's going on, and sometimes, the things I hear frighten me. It's almost like listening to George all over again.'

'Nah, they are nothing like him,' Frank spat out. 'They're good lads.' He looked down at the table, clearly embarrassed. 'I wanted to kill him, you know.'

'Who?' Jenny raised her eyebrows.

'George, for what he did to you and the boys.'

Reaching across the table, Jenny clasped his hand in hers. She didn't answer him; she didn't need to. Just knowing that, all along, he had cared about her and her sons, was enough.

* * *

'Would you like to hold your grandson?' Tina unclipped the straps that secured her son in the pram and looked up at George.

'Thought you were never going to ask.' George laughed lightly as he took a seat on the sofa and held out his arms.

'His name is Austin, but I expect you already know that.'

Taking the infant, George pretended to gaze down adoringly at his first grandchild. 'He's a smasher. Looks just like his dad.'

'He does,' Tina giggled. Walking through to the kitchen, she flicked the switch for the kettle to boil. 'It's strange, though,' she said, coming to lean against the kitchen door. 'Fletch never mentions you.'

'Well, he wouldn't, would he? If there is one thing I can say about my son, it's the fact that he's loyal. His mum, well, let me put it this way, we parted on bad terms, and, well, Harry, he doesn't want to upset her any further than necessary.'

'Ah, I see.' His explanation made sense, and she wandered back through to the kitchen to make the tea.

'Bet he's a great dad though, eh?' George called out. Uninterested in his grandson, he held Austin at arm's length and looked around the small room.

'He is.' Walking through to the lounge, Tina placed two steaming mugs of tea on the coffee table, then took a seat on the edge of the armchair.

George returned his attention back to the sleeping infant. 'My first grandchild,' he remarked. 'I still can't believe that I'm a grandad.'

Tina rolled her lips together. She was dying to tell someone her secret, and so she gave the older man a coy grin.

Cocking his head to one side, George raised his eyebrows.

'Oh, I have to tell someone before I burst!' Flinging herself back against the plump cushions, Tina grinned wildly. 'No.' Still grinning from ear to ear, she used her hands to cover her face, as though she were embarrassed. 'I really shouldn't say anything at all.'

'No, come on, out with it.' George held out his free arm. 'I mean' – he nodded down at Austin – 'I'm this little lad's grandad. That practically makes us family now, doesn't it?'

She let out a giggle. 'I'm pregnant. It's still early days, though.' She gave a cautious smile. 'And I haven't even told Fletch yet.' She bit down on her bottom lip. 'I don't think he will be very happy when I tell him.'

George's eyes widened. He leant forward and gently patted her hand, all the while his mind was scheming. 'Of course he'll be happy, and don't you worry, sweetheart, your secret is safe with me.' He took a sip of his tea. 'And what about Spencer?' he casually asked. 'Where does he like to hang out? I'd really like to surprise him by turning up unannounced.'

Tina chewed on the side of her cheek as she thought the question over. She wasn't particularly close to Fletch's brother and had a feeling he didn't like her too much. 'Well, they like to go fishing sometimes.' She shrugged her shoulders. 'If he isn't out with Fletch, I suppose that's where you'll more than likely find him.'

George continued to sip at his tea. Storing the information away, he allowed her to carry on chatting, telling him everything he wanted to know.

* * *

After leaving the pub and dropping Stevie back home, Fletch found himself driving along a series of familiar country lanes. Call him a fool, but he had to see Susan one last time.

Pulling on to the drive, he parked the car, and for a few moments, he just sat there staring at the house. Finally, he climbed out and made his way towards the front door.

Before he had even lifted his hand to press the bell, nerves got the better of him, and, cursing himself, he spun back around. He should never have come. It was a stupid idea. She didn't want him and had more than made her feelings clear.

He was almost at his car when he heard the front door open.

'Fletch?'

The breath caught in his throat and he slowly turned back around. 'I'm sorry,' he said, backing away. 'I shouldn't have come.'

'No, it's okay.' Susan stepped outside of the house.

'It's just...' Fletch walked back across the driveway towards her. 'I was worried about you and needed to see for myself that you're doing okay.'

Susan shrugged her shoulders and sighed. 'I'm getting there.'

They stood in silence for a moment.

'I feel I should apologise.' Susan broke the silence. 'The things I said, they were hurtful.' She curled her fingers around his forearm. 'I didn't mean it, well, not all of it.'

Fletch smiled. 'So, you meant just some of it then?'

Susan returned the smile. 'You could never repulse me. I'm so sorry. I should never have said that. I love you, I always will.'

Fletch's heart soared. 'What part did you actually mean?'

Walking back towards the front door, Susan glanced down at the suitcases lined up in the hallway. 'The part where I said there will never be an "us" again.'

Fletch swallowed deeply. Deep down, he'd already known what she would say, yet hearing her confirm his worst fears didn't make the situation any easier. He looked down at the suitcases in an attempt to hide the pain that shot through him.

'Are you going somewhere?'

'I'm going to the villa. I can't stay here.' She shuddered. 'Too many memories. I leave tonight.'

'Will you be okay?'

'I will, in time. And how about you? Will you be okay?'

'Have to be, don't I?' He gave her a smile to show there were no hard feelings. 'I have to do something, though.' He stared into the distance and an image of his father sprang to his mind. 'I don't know how it's going to pan out, or if I'll even be able to walk away from it this time.'

'But you'll try.' She slipped the leather strap of her handbag over her shoulder. 'Promise me that you'll try to walk away from whatever it is.'

'Yeah, I will do.' He pushed his hands into his pockets and looked over his shoulder as a taxicab approached the house. 'Do you need help?' He nodded down at the suitcases.

'No, I think I can manage.'

Standing back slightly, Fletch watched as she passed the luggage to the driver. When the car was loaded up, she pulled the front door closed, looked at the key in her hand, sighed, then posted it through the letter box.

'So, this is it then? You're really not coming back?'

Susan shook her head and opened the rear passenger door. 'I don't plan to,' she answered, looking up at the house. She gave him a sad smile. 'Well, goodbye, Fletch.' She stepped forward, kissed his cheek, and whispered in his ear. 'Thank you. Thank you for making me feel alive again.'

With bated breath, Fletch watched as she climbed into the car and closed the door behind her. As the car drove forward, a hard lump formed in his throat, and he chewed on his bottom lip, hoping more than anything that she would change her mind and come back to him. A huge part of him still couldn't believe that he'd lost her.

Feeling helpless, he stood rooted to the spot, silently willing her to turn back around and look at him one last time. She didn't. Only when the car had turned out of the driveway and on to the lane did he exhale the breath he'd been holding, and slowly made his way towards his own car.

Climbing inside, he rested his forehead on the cool steering wheel; silent tears slipped down his cheeks. *Enough*, he told himself. Straightening up, he turned the key in the ignition, ran his hand over his face, wiping away the tears, and then gave the house one final glance, before driving away for the last time.

'Fletch, is that you?'

Closing the front door behind him, Fletch rolled his eyes. 'Who else has a key to the flat?' he growled.

'You'll never guess what.'

Fletch shrugged off his jacket and hung it up on the hook in the hallway. 'What?' he asked in a bored tone.

Joining him in the small hallway, Tina leant against the wall and gave him a wide grin.

'Well?' Losing patience, Fletch gave her a cold stare. He wasn't in the mood for playing games.

'Someone came to see you today.' She hugged her arms around her petite frame. Her eyes were sparkling, and her grin grew even wider as excitement began to ripple through her. She couldn't wait to see his face when she told him that she'd met his dad.

'Who?' Fletch's eyebrows shot up and he cocked his head to one side. As far as he was aware, no one, other than his immediate family and Stevie, knew where he lived.

'Your dad. He came to see you, oh, and he just loved Austin.' She held open her hand, revealing the fifty pound note there. 'Look what he gave us to buy the baby a present.'

'What?' Staring at the red note in her hand, the tiny hairs on the back of Fletch's neck stood up on end, and he narrowed his eyes. 'What did you just say?'

'Y-your d-dad...' Tina stuttered on the words, and gooseflesh covered her arms, making her involuntarily shiver. Not for a single second had she expected this reaction from him. She'd thought he would be pleased. 'He came here...'

Charging down the hallway, Fletch's heart was in his mouth. He glanced around the living room. Nothing looked out of place. 'Where is my son?' he barked out. If George had harmed one hair on his son's head, he swore before God that he would kill him stone dead.

'In the bedroom.' She fell back against the wall as he barged past her.

Standing over his son's crib, Fletch cast his eyes over the sleeping baby, and let out a huge sigh of relief to see that he had come to no harm.

'Fletch, you're scaring me.'

He spun around and stabbed his finger forward. He was so angry, he had to physically stop himself from lashing out. 'I do not want that man anywhere near my son. Do you understand me, Teen? I do not want him in this flat.'

Tina's mouth fell open as she recalled the lovely afternoon she had spent with George. 'But...'

'No buts.' Fletch pounced forward, and, pulling back his fist, he punched the wall above her head, making her physically cower away from him. 'If he ever turns up here again, you do not answer the door.' He studied her with dark eyes and roughly pulled her face forward, forcing her to look up at him. 'Are you listening to me, Teen?' he growled. 'He's evil, and more than capable of...' He nodded his head towards the bedroom, where little Austin lay sound asleep. 'He'll do anything to get back at me, and I mean anything.' He left the sentence to hang heavy in the air, in the hope that his words were sinking into her brain.

Tears filled Tina's eyes. She couldn't get her head around what he was saying. It couldn't be true, surely not. George had seemed so nice, so caring and understanding, when she'd told him about her pregnancy. Averting her eyes, she decided not to mention the fact that she had already promised to meet up with George the next afternoon.

* * *

Despite Fletch's warning not to have any contact with George, Tina had driven to the local park, Matchstick Island, to meet him. She pulled into a parking space and switched off the engine. For months, she'd begged Fletch to buy her the vehicle. Only now, she found that her joy of owning the brand new Ford Fiesta was beginning to wear thin. She should have upped her game and chosen something a lot flashier, something that would have made her the envy of her friends.

She was early for the meeting with George, and so took her time climbing out of the car and assembling Austin's pram. Lifting her son out of his car seat, she laid him down, buckled him in, and then set about covering him over with a thick woollen blanket.

Locking the car, she slipped the keys into her handbag and set off towards the fishing lake. Briefly, she wondered if George would dip his hand in his pocket again and hand over some cash. She hoped so. She looked down at her white, pasty skin and wrinkled her nose. She could do with a couple of sun bed sessions, something her son's father had flat out refused to give her the money for.

Up ahead, she spotted George as he lounged back on a wooden bench facing the lake. His tall, lean frame looked far too large for the seat, and she stifled the urge to giggle. It almost felt as though, in meeting the man, she was doing something naughty. But how could she be? She rationalised to herself that he was Austin's grandfather, not some stranger she'd never met before.

As she neared, he turned his head, gave a beaming smile, and stood up. She came to a halt in front of him and put on a theatrical sigh, one that she'd rehearsed on the drive over. 'I can't let Fletch know that I came here today.' She pretended to look around her, checking that he hadn't followed her. 'He'd go mental if he found out.'

George gave her a wide smile, and, holding out his hand, he signalled for her to take a seat. 'We'll keep it between us.' He grinned.

Tina gave a smile in return. He was so easy to talk to, unlike Fletch. She began chattering away, telling him how Fletch and Spencer often came here to fish, and every time his hand wandered towards his coat pocket, her eyes followed in the hope that he would take out his wallet.

After an age, George cleared his throat. He glanced towards Austin. 'Why don't you leave him with me for an hour or so? It'd do you the world of good to have a break.' He had no actual interest in spending time with his grandson. If nothing else, the infant would make a great bargaining tool.

Tina hesitated and bit down on her lip. Fletch's warning sprang to her mind. 'I shouldn't. Fletch would go really mental if he found out.'

'And I suppose you do everything that my son tells you to?' George lightly chuckled.

'No, not everything.' Tina shook her head, defiant.

Glancing once more at his grandson, George dipped his hand into his pocket and pulled out a roll of cash. Just a few hours in her presence, and already he had her sussed out. He knew the girl would do just about anything to have a bit of cash in her purse.

'Come on now, why don't you go and treat yourself? Spend

the afternoon doing some shopping, while I look after the nipper.'

Tina eyed the cash, then turned to look at her son. The weather had begun to turn bitter cold, and she suddenly wondered if the woollen blanket was enough to keep him warm. She stood up and fussed over him as he lay in the pram, thinking it over. Where was the harm in George looking after the baby for a few hours, she reasoned. After all, he was little Austin's grandfather.

'I don't know,' she said, still in two minds. 'Maybe I should get him home.' She looked up at the grey sky. 'It's starting to get cold.'

'I can bring him home later. Here...' George held out the money. 'Go on, treat yourself.'

Tina bit down on her bottom lip. She was in half a mind to take the money. After all, wasn't that the only reason she had agreed to meet the man?

'Take the money.' Losing patience, there was a harshness to George's voice and his tone became menacing. 'Come on, be a good girl and take the fucking money.'

Tina looked around her. The area was deserted, and with Fletch's words echoing in her mind, she suddenly didn't feel as safe as she should have done. Shaking her head, she made to walk away. 'I... I think that I should get him home now.'

'What's the rush, eh?' George pulled back on her arm.

Looking down at the older man's long fingers clenched around her forearm in a vice-like grip, Tina shuddered, and gooseflesh covered her arms again.

'I'm sorry, but I have to go.' She wrenched her arm free, and walked as fast as she could away from him.

She couldn't put her finger on what it was exactly, but there was something dark in George's cold eyes and wolfish grin that she hadn't noticed before. Whatever it was, it frightened her. Her heart in her mouth, she began to run towards the car park. Every now and then, she glanced over her shoulder, in the hope that her son's grandfather wasn't following.

Panic set in as she fumbled with the straps securing her son in the pram. Finally, she lifted Austin out and settled him into his car seat, then set about dismantling the pram.

'Last chance... go on, take the money.' Approaching her, George held out the roll of cash.

Startled by his presence, Tina screamed. 'I... I can't. I really need to go. Fletch will be wondering where we are.' It wasn't entirely true. Fletch had no idea she had even left the flat. She heaved the pram into the car, slammed the boot closed, and then, maintaining a safe distance between them, she edged her way around to the driver's door.

Grappling with the key in her hand, she quickly unlocked it, climbed behind the wheel, then locked the doors behind her, before starting the ignition. It was greediness that had brought her here today, and there and then she decided she needed to change her ways. All the sun bed sessions in the world were not worth putting little Austin at risk for.

'Don't be stupid, girl,' George shouted. 'I only want to spend some time with my grandson.' With one hand placed on the driver's side window, he used his free hand to try and prise open the locked door.

Narrowly missing the car parked directly behind her, the tyres squelched across the gravel as she reversed out of the parking spot. 'Leave us alone,' she cried.

In the rear-view mirror, she saw the snarl upon George's face, and for the first time since meeting him, she was able to see him for who and what he really was.

How could she have been so stupid as to believe George's lies? How could she have been so blind as to put her son at risk, and for what? Some easy cash? Just the very thought of what could have happened was enough to make her want to weep.

Later that evening, when Fletch returned home, Tina flung herself into his arms. She felt his body stiffen and she held on even tighter, praying that he would return the hug and comfort her. It was on the tip of her tongue to tell him about the meeting with his father earlier on that afternoon, and as she followed him through to the lounge, she bit down on her lip.

'Fletch.'

'What?' Barely even looking at her, Fletch flopped down on to the sofa, kicked off his boots, and, picking up the remote control, he pointed it towards the television.

'I...'

'What?' Fletch turned his head. 'Spit it out, Teen.' His voice took on a bored tone. 'Don't tell me, I can already guess. You want money out of me, as per fucking usual.'

'It's not that.' Tina shook her head.

Turning his attention back to the television, Fletch sighed. 'What do you want then?' When she didn't answer, he turned his head once more and shrugged his shoulders. 'Well?'

Tina began backing away. 'Don't get angry, but... it's your dad.'

Fletch felt his body involuntarily stiffen and threw the remote control down beside him. He clenched his jaw tight and braced himself for what was about to come out of her mouth next.

'You were right.' She grimaced. 'He's bad news.'

'What have you done?' Fletch jumped up from the sofa and advanced towards her.

'Nothing.' Tina's heart began to pound inside her chest. She'd known that he would be angry but seeing him stalk towards her with his fists clenched at his sides didn't just frighten her, it absolutely terrified her. In that instant, she made a dash for it and ran towards the safety of the bedroom.

'What did you do, Teen?' Fletch chased after her. As she ran around to the far side of the divan bed, putting distance between them, he thumped his fists down on the duvet cover.

Tina put out her hand. 'Okay, okay. I met him at the park.' She swallowed deeply, barely able to catch her breath, so acute was her fear. 'He scared me, Fletch. He wanted to take Austin away from me, from us.'

'What?' Fletch snapped his head towards his sleeping son. He could barely take in what she was saying. Was his dad prepared to go that far to break him?

'But I didn't let him near the baby. He didn't even touch him. I swear on Austin's life, I made a run for it.'

'You met up with my dad, even when I told you not to?' Fletch straightened up. 'You put our son at risk?' he snarled. 'For what, Teen? What were you going to get out of it?'

'It wasn't like that.' Tina had the grace to look away. The shame she felt flooded through her. 'I'm sorry,' she choked out.

'You're sorry, fucking sorry?' He shook his head, disgusted at her. 'Answer me, Teen, what were you going to get out of it?'

'Nothing.' She looked away a second time.

He raced around to the other side of the bed and grasped her elbow, yanking her towards him. 'Answer me, for fuck's sake.'

Tears slipped down Tina's cheeks. 'Nothing,' she cried, shaking her head from side to side. 'Nothing, I swear.'

'Tina.'

'Money.' Her body sagged. 'I thought he would give me money.'

In the cot, Austin stirred, and they both snapped their heads towards where he lay.

'Money?' Fletch growled. He shoved her away from him and watched as she fell across the bed. 'You put our boy at risk for a few lousy quid?' As he looked down at her, his lip curled up in disgust. 'Me and you,' he spat, 'we're done.'

'No,' Tina cried. 'No, don't say that, please,' she begged of him.

'We're done,' he reaffirmed.

With those parting words, he walked out of the bedroom and slammed the door behind him so hard that the vibrations shook the hallway wall. Behind the closed bedroom door, he could hear Tina comforting their now screaming son. The very thought of what could have happened made his body shake.

He massaged his temples, wishing more than ever that he could strangle her with his bare hands, and get her out of his life, once and for all. The fact that she had put Austin at risk for money, for greed, sickened him to the core.

He made his way into the lounge and sat down on the edge of the sofa, wiped his hand across his face, and closed his eyes.

'I'm sorry.'

Fletch snapped his head upwards. Standing beside the lounge door was Tina, and in her arms, she held their son. He looked at his boy's face, so like his own, and shook his head.

Silent tears slipped down Tina's face, and as the front door slammed closed, she physically jumped.

'I'm sorry,' she screamed, before slumping down on the armchair and sobbing her heart out.

17

'Are you sure you want to do this?' Stevie asked.

All thanks to Tina and her antics, for most of the night Fletch had lain awake, staring up at the ceiling, as he pondered over his next move.

'I haven't got any other choice. No matter what, I need to keep my family safe.' Switching off the ignition, he followed Stevie's eyeline, and gestured towards his father's mock Tudor mansion. Of course he didn't want to do it. In fact, short of poking out his own eyeballs with a rusty spoon, he could think of nothing worse than stepping inside the lion's den and having a chat with his father. 'I can tell you now, though, this is the last fucking time I come here. The bastard has got me running around after him like a headless chicken.'

Stevie nodded. 'Do you want me to come in with you? Because I will, if that's what you want.'

'What, and put yourself on his radar? Trust me, mate, you're better off out of it.'

'I dunno, Fletch.' Stevie turned to look back at the house. 'I've got a really bad feeling about this.'

'I'll be all right,' Fletch answered, full of bravado. He pulled on the door handle, swung open the door, and climbed out of the car. 'Just remember what I said the last time. If it looks like shit is going down, get the fuck out of here, and don't stop until you're back on our manor.'

'Yeah, I will,' Stevie promised him, knowing full well he would do no such thing.

'Right then, here goes.' He slammed the car door shut and made his way across the street. As he stood in front of the house, he looked over his shoulder and gave Stevie a wide reassuring smile, then walked towards the front door. Pausing for just a second, he hastily lifted the cast iron door knocker before he could change his mind.

As soon as the front door was opened, Fletch was hauled across the threshold, slammed up against the wall and patted down.

'I'm clean.' Gritting his teeth, Fletch spat out the words.

'Shut your mouth,' the henchman growled. He turned to look at his boss, and nodded, confirming the fact that Fletch was carrying no weapons.

'Bring him in.' Walking into his study, George's face was a mask of anger as his eldest son was frogmarched behind him into the room.

'We need to talk.' Fletch winced as he was slammed down into a leather bucket chair opposite the desk.

'What you need to do is tell me where your brother is.'

Screwing up his face, Fletch's throat felt suddenly dry. 'Why?'

'Why, he asks.' George gave a menacing chuckle and tipped his head towards the group of henchmen gathered in the hallway.

Ice-cold fear ran down the length of Fletch's spine as he turned and watched the men leave the house. 'Where are they going?'

'Where do you think?' George growled. 'If the mountain won't come to Mohammed, then...' He left the sentence unsaid.

Even from his position, Fletch could see that the men were armed, and he began to push himself up out of the chair, only for the two remaining henchmen to push him back down. 'If they touch one hair on my brother's head, I'll kill 'em,' he roared.

'Your brother.' George pondered over the word. 'Now, your brother, he's in a lot of fucking shit.' He clenched his fists into tight balls and stepped towards his son. 'And when I get him here, when I get my hands on him, he's going to know what pain really feels like.'

'Don't, Dad.' Fletch's voice cracked, and he hated himself for addressing his father in such a manner. 'Don't touch him. He hasn't done anything wrong. He didn't do anything to Albie or Mickey, I swear he didn't.'

'Who said anything about Albie or Mickey?' George gave him a wolfish grin. 'But while we're on the subject of my brother' – he took a menacing step closer – 'you'd best start fucking talking, and tell me everything you know.'

Immediately, Fletch realised his mistake and inwardly groaned. 'What I meant was...'

'What?' Leaning forward slightly, George spread open his arms. 'Well, come on... I'm all ears.'

'I meant...' Fletch briefly closed his eyes. How the hell was he going to get out of this one? He looked up at his father. 'I dunno. I just thought that's what you meant, that's why you wanted to see Spence.'

George chuckled. 'You're good, I'll give you that, but you're not quick enough to pull the wool over my eyes.' He resumed his position and leant casually against the desk. 'Now, I've put everything together. You could say that I've connected the dots, and each time I look at the situation, only one person jumps out at me. There's only one culprit who could be responsible for all of this fucking aggro, and that's your brother.'

'Nah, you've got it wrong.' Fletch's voice was high as he answered.

'I'm not wrong. Pete, here' – he waved his hand towards his number two – 'Pete got a good look at him and identified him as the cunt who attacked him.'

Turning his head, Fletch looked up at the henchman behind him. He squirmed in his seat as Pete's large fingers dug into his shoulders and kept him in place. 'He's got it wrong. Spence didn't do anything.'

'Do you hear that, Pete?' There was amusement in George's voice. 'He reckons you've made a mistake.'

'Nah.' Pete dug his fingers in even harder. 'There's no mistake. I know who I saw.'

'So, that leaves us with a bit of a dilemma, doesn't it? Who exactly should I believe, one of my own men, or one of King's?'

'I'm your son.'

'Thought we'd already had this conversation.' George grinned. 'Your mother…'

'And I've already told you,' Fletch spat out, 'I'm not that fucking lucky.'

'No, I suppose you're not.' With slow, fluid movements, he took a cigarette out of its packet, tapped it on the box, then placed it between his lips. 'So, is Spencer still hiding out at home?'

'I don't know what you mean.' Fletch clenched his jaw tight as he answered.

Lifting his head to blow out a stream of cigarette smoke, George studied his son.

'From what I can tell, he either hasn't left the house in weeks or he's elsewhere. If I didn't know better, I'd think he was avoiding me. But make no mistake, he can't stay hidden away forever, and when I do get my hands on him, I'm going to do more than tear him apart. I'm going to destroy him.'

It took all of Fletch's strength to not shudder at his father's words. There and then, he knew what he had to do. As always, Stevie was right. Someone needed to die, and he knew that he wouldn't be able to get to his father easily. The fact that he was surrounded by henchmen, day and night, was enough to tell him that.

'So, where do we go from here?' George pretended to think the question over. 'I could always get your mother in here, or how about your uncle?' He gave an evil grin. 'I could wipe out your entire family.'

'You don't need to do that. I'll find him and bring him to you.' Fletch's shoulders slumped downwards in mock defeat.

'That's exactly what I thought you might say.' Looking to the henchmen, he indicated for them to step back, and as his son got to his feet and turned to leave, he called after him. 'Harry.'

Fletch turned his head.

'Do you see this here?' Between his fingers, George held a cigar. He ran the length of it underneath his nose and inhaled the aroma, before tucking it into his shirt pocket. 'I'll keep hold of this.' He took note of the expression across his son's face and laughed. 'The perfect way to celebrate your brother's demise, don't you think?'

'Fuck you.'

George laughed even harder. 'Oh, and Harry, one more thing. Don't even think about crossing me. I'm not the kind of man who likes to be messed around. If you don't believe me, just ask your mother.'

Without answering, Fletch smoothed down his shirt, slung back his shoulders, and walked out of the house.

* * *

'Well?' Stevie's eyes were wide open as Fletch climbed back into the car.

Gripping the steering wheel, Fletch's knuckles had turned white as he stared ahead of him. 'We do it today, right now.'

'Do what?' Whipping his head around to look over at the house, Stevie's forehead furrowed. 'What do we do?'

Still not turning his head, Fletch's voice was hard. 'We take Spence out of the equation.'

'Woah, hold on a minute. I didn't mean what I said. I was only trying to make you see how serious the situation was. You can't kill him, he's your brother.'

Fletch turned his head. 'I'm not going to kill him, fuck me, what do you take me for?' He shook his head, astounded that Stevie would even suggest such a thing. Hell would freeze over before he would even contemplate the idea of hurting his brother.

'Sorry, mate.' Stevie put up his hands. 'I just thought... I dunno... I thought that maybe, you know...'

Leaning forward in his seat, Fletch stretched his forearms over the steering wheel, thinking the question over. 'We need to hide him away for a bit.' He turned his head a second time. 'Can he stay at your place for a while, just until I've sorted this mess out?'

Stevie held open his arms. 'You should already know the answer to that question, mate.'

It was exactly what Fletch had expected him to say, and starting the ignition, he screeched away from the kerb. The sooner he got his brother to safety, the better.

* * *

'Don't you bloody dare.' Stepping inside the kitchen, Jenny wagged her finger towards her youngest son.

'What?' With a Tupperware box held in his hand, Spencer froze.

'Don't you dare put those filthy things on my kitchen table.' Eyeing the box, Jenny shuddered. 'I still have nightmares from the last time you dropped the whole bloody lot all over my floor.'

'That wasn't me, it was Fletch.' Spencer gave a lopsided grin. 'They're not maggots anyway. Look.' He prised open the lid and held out the box for Jenny to inspect. 'It's only luncheon meat.'

'Well, that's all right then.' She gave him a playful wink and moved across the kitchen. Filling the kettle, she eyed him warily. 'Are you sure that you're up to going fishing today? The doctor said you should rest.'

'Course I am, Mum.' Spencer flexed his biceps. 'I'm as strong as an ox, me.'

'Well, just be careful, darling. I don't want you overdoing things.'

'I won't.' Turning his back on her, Spencer began to pack his fishing bag.

'Here. I've made you your lunch.' She passed across a second Tupperware box filled with cheese sandwiches, and watched as her son placed it into his bag. 'And make sure that you take these with you.' She handed him the painkillers he'd been prescribed by the hospital. 'Remember to take one after you've had your lunch, and only one, Spence, no more than that.'

'I know.' Rolling his eyes, Spencer slipped the little brown bottle of painkillers into his jacket pocket. 'You worry too much,' he complained.

'That's what mums do.' She gave him a warm smile and watched him gather up his belongings. 'Don't stay out too late, sweetheart.'

'I won't.' Kissing her cheek, Spencer bounded out of the kitchen and made his way towards the front door. 'See you later, Mum,' he called out.

'Bye, my darling.' She gave a soft smile, and, looking out of the kitchen window, she shook her head in wonder. Still, to this day, she was unable to see the attraction in fishing. She'd much rather be curled up in the armchair, in front of the box, with a nice glass of wine.

* * *

An hour later, Spencer was in a world of his own. Pulling back his arm, he cast the fishing line into the lake, and, standing back slightly, he watched as the neon float bobbed up and down, causing large circular ripples to fan out across the water. Satisfied that the hook was exactly where he intended it to land, he sat down on the grass and leant back on his elbows.

Feeling that his tummy had begun to rumble, he suddenly realised just how hungry he was. Beside him in a plastic carrier bag was the packed lunch his mum had made him. He delved his hand inside and pulled out the Tupperware box. Prising open the lid, he lifted out a cheese sandwich and sank his teeth into the thick slices of buttered bread.

Aware of activity behind him, Spencer lazily turned his head. The smile across his face turned to a frown when he saw two men approaching. Smartly dressed, they looked out of place, and without a fishing rod between them, even he could see that they weren't there for the fish. He swallowed down the last mouthful of his sandwich, then pushed himself to his feet.

'Are you Spencer?' one of them called out.

Unsure of exactly what was going on, Spencer took a step

backwards, causing him to lose his footing and slip down the muddy bank.

'Who wants to know?' He threw out his arms in a bid to regain his balance, and, ankle deep in water, he glared at the men. All thanks to them, his brand new trainers were now ruined.

'Mr Bannerman wants a word with you.'

Bannerman. Hearing the name was the equivalent of a red rag to a bull, and, puffing out his chest, Spencer squared his broad shoulders and clenched his fists. If they wanted him, then they would have to come and get him.

* * *

Pulling into a parking space, Fletch looked across the park. 'He'd better be here,' he said to Stevie.

'He's gotta be.' Flinging open the door, Stevie stepped out of the car. 'Your mum said he'd gone fishing.'

Fletch bit down on his lip. All he wanted to do was find Spencer and get him back to Stevie's flat as quickly as he could, and with the minimum of fuss. He pocketed the car keys, and together they set off across the park.

'So, what are you going to tell your mum? I mean, won't she want to know where Spence is? It's gonna seem a bit fucking weird if he just disappears off the face of the earth, ain't it?'

Fletch shrugged. If truth were told, he hadn't thought that far ahead. 'I dunno, I'll think of something though, mate.'

They continued walking, each lost in their own thoughts.

'Fletch.'

The urgency in Stevie's voice was enough to cause the blood to drain from Fletch's face, and as he looked up, an ice-cold chill shot down the length of his spine.

'Is that a...' Leaving the sentence unsaid, Stevie thumped his best friend on the back and broke out into a run.

Up ahead of them, floating face down in the middle of the lake was what appeared to be a body.

'It's not him.' Fletch's voice was high as he matched Stevie's long strides. 'It's not fucking him,' he screamed.

In unison, they jumped into the lake and swam forward. Oblivious to the icy cold water that saturated their clothes and stung their skin, they reached out for the lifeless form.

A sense of panic filled the air, and for just a few short moments, no words were spoken. Before they had even turned the body over, they knew who it was. There could be no mistaking Spencer's lifeless frame.

'No!' Fletch roared, breaking the silence. The hairs on the back of his neck stood up on end, and his heart began to hammer wildly inside his chest. 'Wake up, Spence,' he cried. 'Come on, wake up.'

With great difficulty, they pulled the body from the lake, and, taking one look at the gaping bullet wounds peppered across Spencer's chest, Stevie promptly spun around and heaved.

Collapsing over his brother's body, Fletch's eyes were wide, and he tugged at his dark hair, almost pulling it out by the roots, so intense was his pain. 'Help him,' he begged Stevie. 'Phone for an ambulance. Do something.'

With his fist pressed to his mouth, Stevie shook his head. 'He's gone, Fletch.'

'No!' Fletch looked down at his brother. Spencer was still, too still. 'Come on, Spence, wake up.'

'He's gone, mate.' Wrapping his arms around himself, Stevie shivered.

Tears slipped down Fletch's cheeks. 'Come on, Spence,' he cried, shaking him harder. 'You've gotta wake up now.'

Looking around him, Stevie's eyes were wide. 'Mate, we need to get out of here. If the Old Bill turns up...'

'No, I'm not leaving him.' His shoulders heaving, Fletch leant across his brother's body.

'Fletch.' Stevie tugged at his arm.

'I said, I'm not leaving him.' Batting Stevie away from him, Fletch's face was a mask of pain. 'Get the fuck outta here. Go on, get the fuck away from us.'

'I'll get help.' As he raced back towards the car park, the heartbreaking sobs that came from his best friend spurred Stevie on.

18

Jenny had been given a sedative, and still she screamed the house down. 'Not my baby,' she cried, 'not my baby.'

Slumped in the armchair, Fletch covered his ears. He couldn't bear to hear the raw grief in her voice, believing all along it was him who had caused her heartache. If only he had found his brother in time, then Spencer would still have been alive and well. His heart was broken in two, and the pain in his chest intensified.

'Mum.' Getting up from his seat, Fletch sat down beside her on the sofa and took her cold hand in his. 'You don't need to go and identify the body. I'll do it,' he volunteered.

'No.' Jenny shook her head. 'I want to see my baby.' She glared around the room. 'And if anyone so much as dares to try and stop me, then so God help you.'

He grasped her hand even tighter and gave it a reassuring squeeze. 'Mum, no one is going to try and stop you.'

Jenny tugged her hand free and shakily stood up. 'I'm ready to see him now.'

'What, now? You don't need to do it today.' Fletch's eyes were wide. 'We could go tomorrow morning.'

'I warned you,' Jenny growled. 'Don't try and stop me.' She pulled her coat on and turned to look at the police officer standing beside the living room door. 'I want to see my son, now.'

Fletch watched her go, and, turning to look at Stevie, he shook his head. This was all his fault, and the guilt he felt ate away at him like a cancer. His mum was never going to get over Spence's death, and he knew for a certainty that he wouldn't either.

* * *

George was grinning like a Cheshire cat. Clamped between his teeth was a large cigar, and as he puffed on it, he listened intently to what was being said.

'The bastard got what he deserved.' The henchman touched the side of his battered face, before turning to look at his equally bruised colleague standing beside him.

Both were big men with bull necks and broad shoulders. They could handle themselves, but begrudgingly, even they had to admit that Spencer had given back twice as much as they had dished out.

'We had no other choice but to end him. The bastard took enough digs to sink a ship, and still he wouldn't go down.'

As he lounged back in his chair and sucked on his cigar, a thick cloying fog filled the room. Elation coursed through George's veins, and he chuckled loudly, as though he had just been told an amusing tale or joke. 'You did well, boys.'

The fact that he had just been told that his youngest son had been brutally murdered meant absolutely nothing to him. As far as he was concerned, it was a case of one down, one to go. Using the crook of his finger, he beckoned Pete towards him and spoke privately in his ear.

'See to the other one,' he hissed.

Straightening up, Pete paused for a moment before nodding his head. All along, he had known that George Bannerman was ruthless, and that just like his cousin Mickey, he had psychopathic tendencies. He walked towards the doorway, and, turning to look over his shoulder, he couldn't help but feel his blood run cold.

Sitting back in his office chair as though he was sat holding court, George rested his elbows on the leather arms. His long fingers were curled around a balloon glass filled with brandy, and across his face was the hint of a dark smirk.

Looking Pete dead in the eyes, he lifted his chin in the air. 'And make it soon,' he growled.

Pete swallowed deeply. The fact that George had just ordered the death of his remaining son troubled him, and, pausing beside the front door, he took out his wallet, lifted out a photograph of his own two young sons, and felt his heart sink.

Without saying another word, he walked out of the mock Tudor mansion. At the end of the day, an order was an order, and unless he wanted to end up supporting a flyover, he knew he would see the task through to the bitter end. He had no other choice on the matter.

* * *

Three weeks later, it was the day of Spencer's funeral. All through the service, Fletch had kept the tears at bay. Each time he felt a hard lump form in his throat, he swallowed it down, afraid that if he allowed the tears to fall, they would never stop.

They filed out of the church and walked behind the coffin as

Spencer was carried towards his final resting place. It was a nice plot with a large blossoming tree and a wooden bench directly behind the graveside. Jenny had already told him that they could spend their afternoons there and chat with Spencer, to tell him their news, just as though he was still alive. He already knew that after today, he wouldn't return. He just couldn't bear the thought of his brother being underneath his feet, in the cold ground.

The coffin was lowered down, and as the pall-bearers stood back, Jenny and Fletch stepped forward. They crouched down, grabbed a handful of earth, and threw it on top of the coffin.

Wiping the dirt from his hands, Fletch moved away from the graveside.

'Mum.' He clasped his hand around Jenny's elbow. 'I can't do this; I'm going home.'

'Home?' Jenny's mouth dropped open. 'You can't go home yet. What about the wake?'

'I'm not going.' Fletch shook his head.

'What are you talking about?' Jenny gestured to the crowd of mourners gathered at the graveside. Most of them were business associates of Billy's. 'All these people, all of Spencer's friends, they've come to pay their respects, to say goodbye. You can't just leave them all here and go home.'

'Say goodbye?' Fletch hissed. 'They didn't even know Spence. They're only here so it looks good for them, so they can brag that they were at Spencer Fletcher's funeral. Ask any one of them to name something Spence liked, and they won't be able to answer you. Go on, ask them. They didn't give a shit about him when he was alive, and they still don't give a shit now that he's dead.'

'Fletch,' Jenny gasped.

'No, Mum, it's the truth.' He turned to walk away, and, stopping abruptly, he retraced his steps. 'All of this' – he swept his arm around him – 'it's a fucking farce. Is that how you want your son to be remembered?'

'I want my son to have a good send-off.' Jenny bristled at his words. 'My poor baby is dead, and I don't want him to be forgotten, to be just another statistic, another mugging gone wrong. I want people to remember him, to remember this day, to remember that he was someone, that he was loved.'

'Mugging?' Fletch snapped his head towards her. 'He was found, face down, in the middle of the lake. Are you that stupid that you actually believe he was mugged?'

Jenny's mouth fell open again, and her mind began to reel.

'You know, I blame you for this.' Two pink spots appeared on Fletch's cheeks and his eyes flashed dangerously.

Taken aback, Jenny gawped at her eldest son. 'What do you mean, you blame me?'

'This is all your fault. You knew what George was like, and you still stayed with him, still had kids with him. You should have aborted us the minute you found out you were pregnant. You should never have even allowed yourself to get pregnant in the first place. All because of you, the life you dragged us into, me and Spence have had to pay the price.' He knew he was going too far but couldn't stop the words from spewing out of his mouth. 'So yeah, now you know, Mum. I blame you for everything that's happened.'

Tears filled Jenny's eyes as Fletch turned and walked away, and, stomping over the grass, he reached the roadside. Bypassing the funeral cars, he made his way towards the exit.

'Hey, Fletch,' Stevie called after him.

He carried on walking.

'Fletch.' Stevie caught up with him and pulled back on his arm, bringing him to a halt. 'Where are you going, mate?'

'Away from here,' Fletch growled. 'I can't stand this. The

whole fucking thing is fucking bollocks. None of that lot gave a fuck about Spence when he was alive. All he ever was to them was a fucking joke – someone they could take the piss out of.'

Stevie looked across to the mourners. 'Yeah, I know, mate. Just keeping up appearances, ain't they? At the end of the day, they're only here for the free booze.'

'Yeah, well, I can't stomach it,' Fletch spat. He tapped the side of his head. 'You know as well as I do that it was no fucking mugging.' Slipping his hand into his jacket pocket, he took out a tiny white pill, popped it into his mouth, and swallowed it dry.

'Yeah, I know.' Stevie looked around him, checking that Jenny wasn't within earshot. 'You need to lay off the pills for a bit, mate. They ain't gonna help, are they?'

'And you need to keep your nose out of my business,' Fletch barked back. 'What am I, the Pied fucking Piper? Every time I turn around, you're there, creeping up on me.' He screwed up his face. 'What the fuck do you even want, eh? What do you want from me?'

'Look, I'm just worried about you, man. We're all cut up about Spence...'

'Cut up?' Fletch growled back. 'You ain't got a fucking clue. My brother's dead!' He could feel a tightness in his chest, and, closing his eyes, he massaged his temples, taking several deep breaths to steady the anger building inside him. 'In here' – he poked himself in the chest – 'in here, it never goes away, and fucking Bannerman is walking around like he ain't got a care in the world.'

Stevie watched Fletch walk away from him and threw up his arms. 'Where are you going?' he called out.

'Home,' Fletch shouted back.

* * *

Twisting the key in the lock, Fletch let himself into the flat. He walked straight to the bedroom, took down the box of photographs from on top of the wardrobe, and began sorting through them.

'Fletch, what are you doing back so early?' Standing in the bedroom doorway with Austin in her arms, Tina tilted her head to one side to look at him.

'I have to go somewhere, Teen.' He paused, and then took a deep breath, knowing that the words he was about to speak would more than upset her. 'And I don't know if I'm going to be coming back.'

Tina's mouth fell open and her blood ran cold. 'What about us?'

'There is no us,' he sighed. 'I've told you that, over and over again.'

'Then what about your son?' she pleaded.

With a heavy heart, Fletch glanced towards his son; as much as he loved him it wasn't enough to deter him from leaving. He shook his head. 'I have to do this.'

'You're going to her, aren't you?' Tina spat. 'I always knew this would happen. You're leaving your own son to be with another woman.'

Picking up one of the photographs, Fletch studied it. It was of him and Spencer and had been taken on Spencer's twenty-first birthday. Beaming into the camera, they had their arms wrapped around one another's shoulders. 'I'm not going to another woman, I promise you.'

'And what about me, eh? What am I supposed to do without you?'

'You, Teen...' He gave her a gentle smile. 'You're going to be the best mum to our boy that you can be. You're going to bring him up, away from this bastard of a life that I've been living, and you're going to teach him right from wrong.' He turned his back on her and stuffed the photograph into his jacket pocket.

'I'm pregnant.'

Pausing, Fletch closed his eyes, rubbed his palm over his face and groaned. The timing couldn't have been any worse if she'd tried. 'It's not going to change matters, darling. I need to do this, and for once in my life, I'm going to do what's right.'

'And what about your children?' Tina screamed back. She could feel the hysteria growing inside of her and pulled their now screaming son to her chest even tighter. 'What about what's right for them?'

Fletch looked up; his eyes were devoid of any emotion. 'I killed my brother.' He watched her back away from him, just like he'd known she would. Fear filled her eyes. 'They are better off without me.'

'No,' she gasped. 'You wouldn't do that, you... you loved your brother.'

'I did. It was me.' He poked himself in the chest. 'I could have saved him; I should have fucking saved him, but I didn't.' He turned his head away, feeling thoroughly ashamed of himself. 'So, now you know why I need to do this.'

He shoved past her, out of the bedroom. Nearing the front door, he stopped and turned his head. 'If I don't make it back, at my uncle's house, underneath the floorboards in Spencer's room, are five bin bags filled with cash. I can't get out of this life – it's ingrained in me, it's all I know – but you can, you can still get away. Take the money, spend it on the kids, make sure they have a good life away from all of this, give them everything we never had.'

With those parting words, he slammed out of the flat, leaving Tina to stare at the empty space his departure had created.

* * *

It wasn't until he'd been sitting in the church, that Fletch had known exactly what he needed to do. As the vicar had spoken about his brother, he realised that every memory he had, involved Spencer. As far back as he could remember, all he'd ever done was look out for his little brother.

On autopilot, he had driven to his uncle's house. He knew he would find his mum there, and after the cruel things he'd said to her, he knew that she, too, would have abandoned the wake.

He dipped his hand in his jacket pocket and took out a small polythene bag filled to the brim with Ecstasy tablets. He tipped one out into the palm of his hand, and then tipped out a second one. Swallowing them down dry, he grimaced, then climbed out of the car.

He needed to make amends, and now that he'd had the time to calm down, he wanted to apologise for his outburst. The words he'd said were untrue, and he should never have blamed his mother for Spencer's death.

It was Stevie who opened the front door, and, after tipping his head in a greeting, Fletch walked into the house.

'What the fuck did you say to your mum? She's in bits.' Stevie's voice was harsh as he cornered his friend in the hallway.

'I know.' He gave Stevie's shoulder a reassuring squeeze and moved forward.

'You should be bloody ashamed of yourself.' Coming to stand in the doorway to the lounge, Frank shook his head from side to side. 'Of all the days to go and have a pop at your mum, you pick today? The day of your own brother's funeral?'

Barely able to look his uncle in the eye, Fletch paused. Shame flooded through him, and he bowed his head.

'That's why I'm here,' he answered softly. Moving off to the kitchen, he leant his body against the kitchen door frame. 'Mum.'

Jenny's body stiffened and she closed her eyes tight and tried to sniff away her tears. It was fruitless. Her shoulders heaved and she began to sob.

Stepping forward, Fletch wrapped his arms around her. 'I'm sorry, Mum. I should never have said those things. I was bang out of order and lashed out at the wrong person. I didn't mean what I said. None of this was your fault.'

'I know, my darling. I know it was the grief talking.' She turned around and looked up at him. 'But I will never, ever be sorry for giving you and Spencer life.' She rested her palm upon his cheek. 'You were my boys, my babies, my life.'

'I know, Mum.' Pulling her closer, Fletch allowed her to cry against his chest. 'I'm sorry, I really am.'

She gave him a sad smile, and, after wiping the tears from her eyes, she stepped out of his arms. 'How about a cup of tea?' she asked, with a deep sigh, desperate to do something mundane, something normal, something that for just a few short moments would make her forget that her baby was gone and never coming back.

'Yeah, go on then. Stick the kettle on.' He gave her a reassuring smile, and then walked out of the kitchen.

'Everything sorted out?' Stevie raised his eyebrows as Fletch joined him in the hallway.

'Yeah.' Looking over his shoulder back towards the kitchen, Fletch nodded his head. 'Do me a favour, mate, and keep my mum talking for a couple of minutes.'

'Why?' Stevie narrowed his eyes. 'Where are you going now?'

As he bounded up the stairs, Fletch gave him a smile that didn't quite reach his eyes. 'Nowhere. I'm just collecting something. Something that belongs to me.'

* * *

Fletch hesitated as he walked in to the bedroom he and Spencer had once shared. The room was exactly as his brother had left it the morning he had been murdered. Typical of Spencer, the curtains were still drawn, and the bed was unmade. The duvet remained pushed towards the foot of the bed, trailing on to the floor, and the bottom sheet was wrinkled.

Moving forward, he yanked open the heavy curtains, and blinked his eyes at the sudden daylight that shone through the window. A hard lump formed inside his throat. Hastily, he swallowed it down and dismissed the familiar shard of pain that stabbed at his heart.

Reaching out his hand, his fingers glided across the cotton pillowcase. He snatched his hand back and brought it up to his chest, wishing more than ever that his brother would burst into the room and give him one of his lopsided grins.

He closed his eyes tight, and took a deep breath, before walking across the room and pulling out his brother's divan bed. At first glance, nothing would appear to be amiss, until you looked closely at the edge of the navy blue carpet. The frayed threads were a dead giveaway that the carpet had been pulled up more than once over the years.

Getting down on his hands and knees, he pulled back the carpet, revealing the dusty wooden floorboards underneath. With relative ease, he was able to dislodge a board nearest the skirting. He slipped his hand in to the gap and felt around. He knew that what he was looking for was there somewhere, because it had been him who'd hidden it.

Finally, his fingertips skimmed across something hard and cold. 'Gotcha.' He pulled the item closer, until he could curl his fingers around it, and with a smile across his face, he sat back on his haunches and looked down at the firearm resting in the palm of his hand.

* * *

'Did you find what you were looking for?'

Coming back down the stairs, Fletch nodded, and, glancing towards the kitchen, he called out, 'Mum, I'm off. I'll see you later.'

'What about your tea?' Jenny made her way down the hallway and gestured towards the kitchen. 'I've just made it for you.'

'Stevie can have it.' He patted his friend's arm and headed for the front door.

'Where are you going, Fletch?' Stevie narrowed his eyes.

'Out.' He looked between his mother and best friend and lowered his voice. 'Just out.'

'I'll come with you.'

'Nah, you're all right.' Fletch put up his hand and he kept his voice light. 'Do me a favour and keep Mum company for a bit.'

Squaring his shoulders, Stevie shook his head. 'I said, I'll come with you.'

Fletch gritted his teeth. The last thing he needed was his best friend along for the ride. 'Like I said—'

'And like I said,' Stevie interrupted, 'I'm coming with you.'

Running his tongue over his teeth, Fletch stared his friend down, and, shaking his head, he slammed out of the house with Stevie hot on his heels.

* * *

'So, where are we going then?' Stevie forced his voice to sound a lot chirpier than he felt.

'Where do you think?' Fletch growled.

As the car sped down the A13, Stevie gripped on to the door handle for dear life. 'For fuck's sake, Fletch, will you slow down? Are you trying to get us both killed?'

Fletch eased his foot off the gas.

Thankful that the car was now moving at a relatively normal pace, Stevie took his hand away from the door handle. 'I thought you said you would never run after Bannerman again?'

'I'm not.' Flicking the indicator, Fletch raised his eyebrows. 'He's gonna come out to me.'

Wincing as the car weaved in and out of the traffic, Stevie's voice was high. 'Come out to you? Are you off your fucking head? How many pills have you had today, eh? Because you sound like you're buzzing off your nut.'

Fletch ignored the comment and, shrugging his shoulders, continued to hurtle down the motorway. 'Besides,' he added with a grin, 'I'd never get past the front door, at least not in one piece anyway.'

Narrowing his eyes, Stevie thought this over. 'Why not?'

'Let's just say, Bannerman's too protected. I'd never get in the house.'

'Are you carrying?' There was a hint of shock in Stevie's voice.

'I'm just gonna talk to him.' Fletch turned his head. 'Don't worry about it, okay?'

'Fletch, are you carrying? Answer the question!' He looked him up and down. From where he was sitting, he couldn't see the outline of a weapon, but that didn't mean he hadn't stashed it elsewhere. He pulled open the glovebox and rifled through the contents.

'You won't find anything.' Fletch smirked.

'Where is it?' Slamming the glovebox closed, Stevie turned in his seat. 'Where is it, Fletch?'

'Look, I told you not to come. I didn't want you here, just remember that.' Turning in to a tree-lined avenue, Fletch looked up at the rear-view mirror. 'We've got company, anyway. That car behind us has been trailing us for the last fifteen minutes.'

Stevie turned to look back at the car. 'Tell me something, Fletch,' he said, giving his friend a sidelong glance, 'and be honest with me. Is this a suicide mission?'

Feeling for the photograph in his jacket pocket, Fletch shrugged his shoulders. He knew that his chances of walking away from what was about to go down were slim, but maybe, in a way, it was what he deserved – it was his atonement for not saving his brother.

'I've got a really bad feeling about this,' Stevie stated.

As he pushed his foot down on the brake, bringing the car to a grinding halt, Fletch gave a wide grin, then without missing a beat, he banged his fist down on the car horn.

* * *

Sipping at his brandy, George looked up. 'What the fuck is that noise?' he bellowed.

'Dunno, Boss.' Heaving his large frame up off the sofa, Damon Wheeler made his way down the hallway towards the front door.

'Tell them to fuck off,' George instructed.

Damon nodded, and, opening the front door, he stepped outside the house.

* * *

Sitting hunched over the steering wheel, Fletch watched the front door open and a heavy-set man walk out of the house. He turned his head to look at Stevie.

'Showtime,' he said, before punching his fist on the car horn once more for good measure.

'Oi,' Fletch shouted as he climbed out of the car. 'Go tell your boss that I'm here, and if he wants to know what happened to his brother, then he'd better come out and face me.'

Following suit, Stevie climbed out of the car. 'I hope you know what you're fucking doing,' he groaned.

'I always do.' Fletch grinned back.

* * *

Damon lifted his hand to his eyes in a bid to shield the sun from his vision. He recognised the driver of the car and heaved his heavy frame back towards the house as fast as he could.

'Boss.' His breath streamed out ahead of him. 'You need to come and see this.'

'What is it?' Leaning back in his chair, there was a bored tone to George's voice.

'It's your kid.' Damon jerked his thumb behind him. 'He's out there, reckons he knows what happened to Albie.'

A slow smile crept across George's face. Hadn't he already stated once before that his son never seemed to learn? He sucked his teeth, placed the brandy glass down beside him, then lounged back in his chair for a few moments. Aware that all eyes were on him, he rubbed his hands together, then slowly pushed himself to his feet. It was about time he taught his son a lesson or two.

* * *

Seeing his father exit the house, Fletch tensed his muscles. 'You killed my brother,' he shouted out.

George shrugged. The hint of a dark smirk played across his lips.

Fletch could feel his heartbeat quicken. He skimmed his palm down the side of his jacket, and his fingertips brushed against the hard outline of the firearm. 'I'm gonna kill you for that,' he growled.

'Fletch,' Stevie warned. 'What the fuck are you doing?'

'That's right,' Fletch continued. 'I'm gonna kill you and love every fucking second of it while I do it.'

George chuckled out loud and spread open his arms. 'You killed my brother and then I killed yours. That makes us even in my book.'

'Nah.' Fletch sprang forward. 'You owe me a lot more than that, and I won't be happy until you're fucking dead.' He pulled the handgun out from the waistband of his jeans and aimed it towards his father.

'Jesus fucking Christ, Fletch, what are you trying to do, start World War Three?' Not taking his eyes away from his best friend, Stevie ducked down behind the car.

'Come on now, you don't want to do that.' George's eyes flickered towards his number two, as he quietly climbed out of his car. Noting the firearm in Pete's hand, his shoulders visibly relaxed.

Spinning to his side, Fletch re-aimed the gun. 'Don't come any closer,' he roared at Pete.

'Put the gun down.'

Fletch spun back around. 'Not until I've blown your brains all over this fucking street,' he growled, taking a step closer to his father.

Even though outwardly he appeared calm, beads of cold sweat broke out across George's forehead. He glanced once more towards his number two. What was taking him so long to shoot the little fucker down? He narrowed his steely eyes, urging him to take aim and fire.

Seeing the interaction, Fletch spun to the side; his finger hovered over the trigger. 'I told you not to come any closer,' he told Pete.

The gunshot that rang out was deafening. Throwing himself to the floor, Stevie's heart was in his mouth, and with his ears still ringing, he gingerly lifted his head. A huge sigh escaped from his lips, and he bowed his head for a few moments, before staggering to his feet. Fletch, much to his relief, was still standing. It had been a warning shot.

'End him,' George roared. 'Shoot the fucking bastard.'

Pete looked towards his boss. Reminded of the photograph of his children in his wallet, he shook his head, threw the gun to the kerb and lifted both hands into the air.

George swallowed deeply.

In the distance, the wail of a police siren broke the silence.

'Fletch,' Stevie called out, 'don't do this, mate.'

Fletch shook his head. 'I won't stop until this no-good bastard is dead.' He re-aimed the gun at his father's head.

'Fletch, come on, man. Don't do this.' There was more than a hint of desperation in Stevie's voice.

'Listen to your friend, son.'

Fletch's face contorted with rage. 'Don't call me that,' he spat. 'You lost the right to call me "son" a long time ago.'

The sirens became louder, indicating that the police were close by. Cocking his head to one side, George smirked. There was no way his son would be stupid enough to shoot him in front of the Old Bill. In the distance, a series of flashing blue lights could be seen.

'Then take the fucking shot.' George's cocky tone was goading. 'If you think you're man enough, do it.'

Fletch snarled. His finger toyed with the trigger. All he had to do was pull it and the nightmare that had become his life would be over.

'Do it,' George sneered.

As the flashing blue lights got closer, Fletch took aim.

'Do it!' George roared a second time.

The second gunshot was just as deafening as the first, and as his father fell to the ground, Fletch threw his head back and exhaled loudly. Flinging the gun to the kerb and holding his arms up in the air in surrender, he looked across to his best friend. He could see the shock etched across Stevie's face, and felt a moment of pity for him. He should never have allowed him to come along for the ride, should never have allowed him to witness the murder.

'I'm sorry,' he mouthed.

* * *

Within moments of the police officers exiting their vehicles, Fletch was slammed across the bonnet of a car, and his arms were twisted up behind his back. He took this time to turn his head. The sight of his father's body sprawled out across the pavement brought a smile to his face, and despite the situation he now found himself in, his heart felt lighter in the knowledge that not only did Bannerman no longer exist, but that he'd also avenged his brother's murder. He was dragged away from the scene, and with his wrists encased in handcuffs, he passed Stevie by as he was led towards the waiting police van.

'Look after my mum and my kids for me,' he told him.

'Kids?' Stevie's eyebrows shot up. 'Don't you mean "kid"?' He didn't receive an answer, not that he'd even expected one. That was Fletch all over. He'd always kept matters close to his chest.

EPILOGUE

ONE YEAR LATER

Sitting at a table in the visiting room, Fletch bowed his head. Wearing prison issued grey tracksuit bottoms and a T-shirt, he heard a series of familiar clip-clops walking across the hard floor and looked up. Dressed to kill, Tina sauntered towards him. He watched other inmates turn their heads as she passed them by and couldn't help but smile.

From the designer sunglasses perched on top of her head, to the high-heeled shoes that cost more than most families lived on per week, she looked stunning. It was a shame, really, that he could never find it in himself to love her.

In a cloud of expensive floral perfume, she sat down opposite him and gave a beaming smile.

'You look well,' he said, and it was true. She'd lost her baby weight, and it was clear to see from her freshly cut hair and polished fingernails that she was looking after herself. He wondered briefly if she'd found herself a new man, and hastily pushed the thought of another man bringing up his children to the back of his mind.

'Thank you,' she breathed huskily. 'And so do you.'

Fletch raised his eyebrows and chuckled. He highly doubted that, although he had recently been taking advantage of the gym. 'Did you move into the house okay?'

As she nodded her head, Tina's face lit up. 'The kids will love growing up there. It has everything they could ever need – great area, fantastic back garden for them to run around in, and as soon as they are old enough, I'll teach them to swim. Gotta make use of that pool, eh?'

Fletch smiled, pleased that Tina had spent the money he'd left her on something useful, something that would benefit his children in the long run. After all, it wasn't as though he was ever going to be much use to them. After being handed down a life sentence, without the possibility of parole, it meant that he was more than likely going to stay behind bars for the remainder of his life.

'How are the kids?'

'Oh, great! Austin looks more and more like you with each passing day.'

'And Kitty?' he asked of his daughter.

'She's doing great. Your mum is looking after them. She and Frank both said to say hello, and that she will try to visit you next month.'

His heart sank at the mention of his mum. He could still remember seeing the disappointment across her face as he'd been sentenced. He allowed her to carry on chatting, and all too quickly, the visit was over.

She reached out to touch his hand, before quickly snatching it back. 'I wish you would change your mind about us.'

Fletch shook his head and gestured around him. 'There's no future for us.' He gave a smile to take the edge off his words. 'How can there be? I'm stuck in here, and you're out there in the real world.'

'I know,' Tina whispered back. It was exactly how she had expected him to answer, but still, she'd needed to ask. It was almost a compulsion inside of her. She stood up slowly and a false smile spread across her face. 'Well, take care of yourself, Fletch. I'll see you next month.'

Fletch nodded and watched her walk out of the visiting room. All Tina had ever wanted was the big house, the flashy car, pots of money, and above all else, to know where he was, day and night. And now, all thanks to him and his actions, to a certain degree, she'd finally got her wish.

As he watched her go, he couldn't help but laugh out loud. It may have come at a price, but in the end, at least one of them had finally got what they'd always wanted.

ACKNOWLEDGMENTS

A huge thank you to Deryl Easton, Sammee Hart and Sarah Warman: your encouragement has been invaluable. Thank you to Plan B, and ManLikeb.Dot, whose music kept me company through the many late nights while I was writing.

A huge thank you to the readers at NotRights book club: I really cannot thank you enough for your support.

Also, a huge thank you to LondonCrime for your continued support over the years.

Finally, a huge thank you to my family and friends who endured the endless scenarios and plot twists as the book took shape.

MORE FROM KERRY KAYA

We hope you enjoyed reading *The Price*. If you did, please leave a review.

If you'd like to gift a copy, this book is also available as an ebook, digital audio download and audiobook CD.

Sign up to Kerry Kaya's mailing list for news, competitions and updates on future books.

http://bit.ly/KerryKayaNewsletter

ABOUT THE AUTHOR

Kerry Kaya is the hugely popular author of Essex based gritty gangland thrillers with strong family dynamics. She grew up on one of the largest council estates in the UK, where she sets her novels. She also works full-time in a busy maternity department for the NHS.

Follow Kerry on social media:

 twitter.com/KerryKayaWriter

 instagram.com/kerry_kaya_writer

 facebook.com/kerry.bryant.58

ABOUT BOLDWOOD BOOKS

Boldwood Books is a fiction publishing company seeking out the best stories from around the world.

Find out more at www.boldwoodbooks.com

Sign up to the Book and Tonic newsletter for news, offers and competitions from Boldwood Books!

http://www.bit.ly/bookandtonic

We'd love to hear from you, follow us on social media:

 facebook.com/BookandTonic

 twitter.com/BoldwoodBooks

 instagram.com/BookandTonic

Printed in Great Britain
by Amazon

81629303R00200